# The Fib

*The Swap, The Trick*
*and Other Stories*

# GEORGE LAYTON

# The Fib

## The Swap, The Trick
## and Other Stories

### MACMILLAN CHILDREN'S BOOKS

The stories in *The Fib* first published in two volumes as *The Balaclava Story and Other Stories* (1975) and *The Fib and Other Stories* (1978) by the Longman Group. This edition is published by arrangement with Addison Wesley Longman Limited. *The Fib* first published as one volume 1997 by Macmillan Children's Books

*The Swap* first published 1997 by Macmillan Children's Books

'The Promise' in *The Trick* first published in *War* 2004 by Macmillan Children's Books
*The Trick* first published 2006 by Macmillan Children's Books

This edition published 2015 by Macmillan Children's Books
an imprint of Pan Macmillan
20 New Wharf Road, London N1 9RR
Associated companies throughout the world
www.panmacmillan.com

ISBN 978-1-4472-8673-8

The Acknowledgements on page 293 constitute an extension of this copyright page.

1 3 5 7 9 8 6 4 2

A CIP catalogue record for this book is available from the British Library.

Typeset by Intype Libra Ltd
Printed and bound by CPI Group (UK) Ltd, Croydon CR0 4YY

# Contents

# Introduction

In the early 1970s I was commissioned to write and read a short story for BBC radio that I had called *The Fib*, in which the unnamed narrator, a troubled boy from a single-parent family, who loathed football, told a lie that his uncle was Bobby Charlton. Understandably, the broadcast of *The Fib* was somewhat dependant on acquiring the great man's blessing.

As a matter of courtesy, I telephoned Mr Charlton (as he then was) at Preston North End Football Club, where he was the manager. After introducing myself and giving the reason for telephoning, the conversation went something like this:

George: . . . *Yes, it's called* The Fib *and it's going to be broadcast on the radio. On the BBC.*

Bobby Charlton: *Oh aye?*

George: *Yes, and honestly, Mr Charlton, you really do come out as quite a hero in it.*

Bobby Charlton: *Oh aye?*

George: *Yes, and I am really hoping that you will . . .*

Bobby Charlton: *Give my permission?*

George: *Erm . . .*

[Awkward pause. I had conveniently failed to mention that the story had already been recorded and would be listed in the forthcoming edition of *Radio Times*.]

George: . . . *Erm, yes, please.*

Bobby Charlton: *Away you go, son!*

Now, I wasn't sure if 'Away you go, son!' meant please go away, I'm a very busy man or away you go and write it. I chose it to mean the latter.

Happily it has been an enduring friendship, culminating when Sir Bobby was guest of honour at a concert at Cadogan Hall, London, in 2011, where, accompanied by the Royal Philharmonic Orchestra, I read *The Fib* to music especially composed by the eminent composer Debbie Wiseman MBE.

Although the earliest edition of my stories was published in 1975, *The Fib* was the last to be written. I wrote the first story, 'The Gang Hut', in 1960, during my first term at drama school in London. Returning home for the Christmas holidays I met a girl on the train also from Bradford and she kindly offered to type out my scribbled, handwritten copy. What I didn't know was that she worked for the producer of the popular BBC radio programme *Morning Story*.

With the kind of luck that I have been blessed with throughout my career, she gave the typed copy to her boss, Hazel Lewthwaite, who liked it, bought it and booked me to read it. After leaving drama school in 1962, I auditioned to be a reader on *Woman's Hour* and I used 'The Gang Hut' as my audition piece. The producer, Virginia Browne-Wilkinson, liked it enough to commission four further stories, which I read as a *Woman's Hour* serial under the title *A Northern Childhood*. These evocative period stories written for an adult audience proved so popular that five more *A Northern Childhood* stories were commissioned. *A Northern Childhood* was published as an educational book by Longman, now Pearson, and is still available today.

Whilst hugely grateful that my books have found this ongoing younger audience, not least helped by the fact that *The*

*Fib and Other Stories* has been on the national curriculum for over twenty-five years, I have to say that I am not a children's writer. I write about childhood: the pain of childhood, the traumas, the day-to-day worries, bullying, guilt, peer pressure – all voiced through the thoughts of a young, troubled narrator with limited vocabulary.

This narrator lives in a different age to the young reader of today. No internet, no computers, no mobile phones, no video games, no DVDs, no television. No central heating! So why do my stories resonate with today's young readers? Because the bullying, guilt, peer pressure and prejudice that my narrator has to deal with are for them just as relevant today. The issues I write about based on my own 1950s childhood are timeless. For example, I am writing this introduction on the first day of the 2015 general election campaign. In *The Swap and Other Stories*, my second collection, there is a story called 'The Pigeon', which deals with immigration and prejudice in 1954.

When I wrote these stories for radio, specifically for an adult audience, I never thought for one moment that any of them might ever be published. To be writing this introduction to the fortieth anniversary edition for Macmillan Children's Books is for me nothing less than astonishing.

Each book has a dedication, which was relevant at the time of publication and gave me much pleasure. I have not only been blessed with luck in my career, I have been blessed with the most wonderful family, not least my dear wife of nearly forty years.

Therefore I dedicate this fortieth anniversary edition to Moya, my four children, my brother and sister and their children, indeed all my extended family – and one in particular:

*For my dear grandson*
*THEO*

George Layton
March 2015

# The Fib

*For my children Tristan, Claudie,
Daniel and Hannah*

# Contents

# THE BALACLAVA STORY

Tony and Barry both had one. I reckon half the kids in our class had one. But I didn't. My mum wouldn't even listen to me.

'You're not having a balaclava! What do you want a balaclava for in the middle of summer?'

I must've told her about ten times why I wanted a balaclava.

'I want one so's I can join the Balaclava Boys . . .'

'Go and wash your hands for tea, and don't be so silly.'

She turned away from me to lay the table, so I put the curse of the middle finger on her. This was pointing both your middle fingers at somebody when they weren't looking. Tony had started it when Miss Taylor gave him a hundred lines for flicking paper pellets at Jennifer Greenwood. He had to write out a hundred times: 'I must not fire missiles because it is dangerous and liable to cause damage to someone's eye.'

Tony tried to tell Miss Taylor that he hadn't fired a missile, he'd just flicked a paper pellet, but she threw a piece of chalk at him and told him to shut up.

'Don't just stand there – wash your hands.'

1

'Eh?'

'Don't say "eh", say "pardon".'

'What?'

'Just hurry up, and make sure the dirt comes off in the water, and not on the towel, do you hear?'

Ooh, my mum. She didn't half go on sometimes.

'I don't know what you get up to at school. How do you get so dirty?'

I knew exactly the kind of balaclava I wanted. One just like Tony's, a sort of yellowy-brown. His dad had given it to him because of his earache. Mind you, he didn't like wearing it at first. At school he'd given it to Barry to wear and got it back before home-time. But all the other lads started asking if they could have a wear of it, so Tony took it back and said from then on nobody but him could wear it, not even Barry. Barry told him he wasn't bothered because he was going to get a balaclava of his own, and so did some of the other lads. And that's how it started – the Balaclava Boys.

It wasn't a gang really. I mean they didn't have meetings or anything like that. They just went around together wearing their balaclavas, and if you didn't have one you couldn't go around with them. Tony and Barry were my best friends, but because I didn't have a balaclava, they wouldn't let me go round with them. I tried.

'Aw, go on, Barry, let us walk round with you.'

'No, you can't. You're not a Balaclava Boy.'

'Aw, go on.'

'No.'

2

'Please.'

I don't know why I wanted to walk round with them anyway. All they did was wander up and down the playground dressed in their rotten balaclavas. It was daft.

'Go on, Barry, be a sport.'

'I've told you. You're not a Balaclava Boy. You've got to have a balaclava. If you get one, you can join.'

'But I can't, Barry. My mum won't let me have one.'

'Hard luck.'

'You're rotten.'

Then he went off with the others. I wasn't half fed up. All my friends were in the Balaclava Boys. All the lads in my class except me. Wasn't fair. The bell went for the next lesson – ooh heck, handicraft with the Miseryguts Garnett – then it was home-time. All the Balaclava Boys were going in and I followed them.

'Hey, Tony, do you want to go down the woods after school?'

'No, I'm going round with the Balaclava Boys.'

'Oh.'

Blooming Balaclava Boys. Why wouldn't *my mum* buy *me a balaclava*? Didn't she realize that I was losing all my friends, and just because she wouldn't buy me one?

'Eh, Tony, we can go goose-gogging – you know, by those great gooseberry bushes at the other end of the woods.'

'I've told you, I can't.'

'Yes, I know, but I thought you might want to go goose-gogging.'

'Well, I would, but I can't.'

I wondered if Barry would be going as well.

'Is Barry going round with the Balaclava Boys an' all?'

'Course he is.'

'Oh.'

Blooming balaclavas. I wish they'd never been invented.

'Why won't your mum get you one?'

'I don't know. She says it's daft wearing a balaclava in the middle of summer. She won't let me have one.'

'I found mine at home up in our attic.'

Tony unwrapped some chewing gum and asked me if I wanted a piece.

'No thanks.' I'd've only had to wrap it in my handkerchief once we got in the classroom. You couldn't get away with anything with Mr Garnett.

'Hey, maybe you could find one in your attic.'

For a minute I wasn't sure what he was talking about.

'Find what?'

'A balaclava.'

'No, we haven't even got an attic.'

I didn't half find handicraft class boring. All that mucking about with compasses and rulers. Or else it was weaving, and you got all tangled up with balls of wool. I was just no good at handicraft and Mr

Garnett agreed with me. Today was worse than ever. We were painting pictures and we had to call it 'My Favourite Story'. Tony was painting *Noddy in Toyland*. I told him he'd get into trouble.

'Garnett'll do you.'

'Why? It's my favourite story.'

'Yes, but I don't think he'll believe you.'

Tony looked ever so hurt.

'But honest. It's my favourite story. Anyway what are you doing?'

He leaned over to have a look at my favourite story.

'Have you read it, Tony?'

'I don't know. What is it?'

'It's *Robinson Crusoe*, what do you think it is?'

He just looked at my painting.

'Oh, I see it now. Oh yes, I get it now. I couldn't make it out for a minute. Oh yes, there's Man Friday behind him.'

'Get your finger off, it's still wet. And that isn't Man Friday, it's a coconut tree. And you've smudged it.'

We were using some stuff called poster paint, and I got covered in it. I was getting it everywhere, so I asked Mr Garnett if I could go for a wash. He gets annoyed when you ask to be excused, but he could see I'd got it all over my hands, so he said I could go, but told me to be quick.

The washbasins were in the boys' cloakroom just outside the main hall. I got most of the paint off and as I was drying my hands, that's when it happened. I don't know what came over me. As soon as I saw that balaclava lying there on the floor, I decided to pinch it. I couldn't help it. I just knew that this was my only chance. I've never pinched anything before – I don't think I have – but I didn't think of this as ... well ... I don't even like saying it, but ... well, stealing. I just did it.

I picked it up, went to my coat, and put it in the pocket. At least I tried to put it in the pocket but it bulged out, so I pushed it down the inside of the sleeve. My head was throbbing, and even though I'd just dried my hands, they were all wet from sweating. If only I'd thought a bit first. But it all happened so quickly. I went back to the classroom, and as I was going in I began to realize what I'd done. I'd *stolen* a balaclava. I didn't even know whose it was, but as I stood in the doorway I couldn't believe I'd done it. If only I could go back. In fact I thought I would but then Mr Garnett told me to hurry up and sit down. As I was going back to my desk I felt as if all the lads knew what I'd done. How could they? Maybe somebody had seen me. No! Yes! How *could* they? They could. Of course they couldn't. No, course not. What if they did though? Oh heck.

I thought home-time would never come but when the bell did ring I got out as quick as I could. I was going to put the balaclava back before anybody noticed; but as I got to the cloakroom I heard Norbert Lightowler shout out that someone had pinched his balaclava. Nobody took much notice, thank goodness, and I heard Tony say to him that he'd most likely lost it. Norbert said he hadn't but he went off to make sure it wasn't in the classroom.

I tried to be all casual and took my coat, but I didn't dare put it on in case the balaclava popped out of the sleeve. I said tarah to Tony.

'Tarah, Tony, see you tomorrow.'

'Yeh, tarah.'

Oh, it was good to get out in the open air. I couldn't wait to get home and get rid of that blooming balaclava. Why had I gone and done a stupid thing like that? Norbert Lightowler was sure to report it to the Headmaster, and there'd be an announcement about it at morning assembly and the culprit would be asked to own up. I was running home as fast as I could. I wanted to stop and take out the balaclava and chuck it away, but I didn't dare. The faster I ran, the faster my head was filled with thoughts. I could give it back to Norbert. You know, say I'd taken it by mistake. No, he'd never believe me. None of the lads would believe me. Everybody knew how much I wanted to be a Balaclava Boy. I'd have to get rid of the blooming thing as fast as I could.

My mum wasn't back from work when I got home, thank goodness, so as soon as I shut the front door, I put my hand down the sleeve of my coat for the balaclava. There was nothing there. That was funny, I was sure I'd put it down that sleeve. I tried down the other sleeve, and there was still nothing there. Maybe I'd got the wrong coat. No, it was my coat all right. Oh, blimey, I must've lost it while I

7

was running home. I was glad in a way. I was going to have to get rid of it, now it was gone. I only hoped nobody had seen it drop out, but, oh, I was glad to be rid of it. Mind you, I was dreading going to school next morning. Norbert'll probably have reported it by now. Well, I wasn't going to own up. I didn't mind the cane, it wasn't that, but if you owned up, you had to go up on the stage in front of the whole school. Well, I was going to forget about it now and nobody would ever know that I'd pinched that blooming lousy balaclava.

I started to do my homework, but I couldn't concentrate. I kept thinking about assembly next morning. What if I went all red and everybody else noticed? They'd know I'd pinched it then. I tried to think about other things, nice things. I thought about bed. I just wanted to go to sleep. To go to bed and sleep. Then I thought about my mum; what she'd say if she knew I'd been stealing. But I still couldn't forget about assembly next day. I went into the kitchen and peeled some potatoes for my mum. She was ever so pleased when she came in from work and said I must've known she'd brought me a present.

'Oh, thanks. What've you got me?'

She gave me a paper bag and when I opened it I couldn't believe my eyes – a blooming balaclava.

'There you are, now you won't be left out and you can stop making my life a misery.'

'Thanks, Mum.'

If only my mum knew she was making *my* life a misery. The balaclava she'd bought me was just like the one I'd pinched. I felt sick. I didn't want it. I couldn't wear it now. If I did, everybody would say it was Norbert Lightowler's. Even if they didn't, I just couldn't wear it. I wouldn't feel it was mine. I had to get rid of it. I went outside and put it down the lavatory. I had to pull the chain three times before it went away. It's a good job we've got an outside lavatory or else my mum would have wondered what was wrong with me.

I could hardly eat my tea.

'What's wrong with you? Aren't you hungry?'

'No, not much.'

'What've you been eating? You've been eating sweets, haven't you?'

'No, I don't feel hungry.'

'Don't you feel well?'

'I'm all right.'

I wasn't, I felt terrible. I told my mum I was going upstairs to work on my model aeroplane.

'Well, it's my bingo night, so make yourself some cocoa before you go to bed.'

I went upstairs to bed, and after a while I fell asleep. The last thing I remember was a big balaclava, with a smiling face, and it was the Headmaster's face.

I was scared stiff when I went to school next morning. In assembly it seemed different. All the boys were looking at me. Norbert Lightowler pushed past and didn't say anything. When prayers finished I just stood there waiting for the Headmaster to ask for the culprit to own up, but he was talking about the school fete. And then he said he had something very important to announce and I could feel myself going red. My ears were burning like anything and I was going hot and cold both at the same time.

'I'm very pleased to announce that the school football team has won the inter-league cup . . .'

And that was the end of assembly, except that we were told to go and play in the schoolyard until we were called in, because there was a teachers' meeting. I couldn't understand why I hadn't been found out yet, but I still didn't feel any better, I'd probably be called to the Headmaster's room later on.

I went out into the yard. Everybody was happy because we were having extra playtime. I could see all the Balaclava Boys going round together. Then I saw Norbert Lightowler was one of them. I couldn't be sure it was Norbert because he had a balaclava on, so I had to go up close to him. Yes, it was Norbert. He must have bought a new balaclava that morning.

'Have you bought a new one then, Norbert?'

'Y'what?'

'You've bought a new balaclava, have you?'

'What are you talking about?'

'Your balaclava. You've got a new balaclava, haven't you?'

'No, I never lost it at all. Some fool had shoved it down the sleeve of my raincoat.'

# THE CHRISTMAS PARTY

Our classroom looked smashing. Lots of silver tinsel and crepe paper and lanterns. *We'd* made the lanterns, but Miss Taylor had bought the rest herself, out of her own money. Oh, only today and tomorrow and then we break up. Mind you, if school was like this all the time, I wouldn't be bothered about breaking up. Putting up Christmas decorations and playing games – much better than doing writing and spelling any day. I watched the snow coming down outside. Smashing! More sliding tomorrow. I love Christmas. I wish it was more than once a year. Miss Taylor started tapping on the blackboard with a piece of chalk. Everybody was talking and she kept on tapping until the only person you could hear was Norbert Lightowler.

'Look, if I get a six and land on you, you get knocked off and I still get another go!'

The whole class was looking at him.

'Look, when Colin got a six, he landed on *me* and *he* got another . . .!'

Suddenly he realized that he was the only one talking and he started going red.

'Thank you, Norbert, I think we all know the rules of Ludo.'

Miss Taylor can be right sarcastic sometimes. Everybody laughed. Even Miss Taylor smiled.

'Now, since it is getting so noisy, we're going to stop these games and do some work.'

Everybody groaned and Tony and me booed – quietly so Miss Taylor couldn't hear. She hates people that boo. She says people who boo are cowards.

'Who is that booing?'

We must have been booing louder than we thought.

'Who is that booing?'

Miss Taylor looked at Tony. I looked at Tony. They both looked at me. I put my hand up.

'It was me, Miss.'

Tony put his hand up.

'It was me an' all, Miss.'

She looked at us.

'You both know what I think of booing, don't you?'

We nodded.

'Yes, Miss.'

'Yes, Miss.'

'Don't ever let me hear it again.'

We shook our heads.

'No, Miss.'

'No, Miss.'

She turned to the class.

'Now, the work I have in mind is discussion work.'

Everybody groaned again, except me and Tony.

'I thought we'd discuss tomorrow's Christmas party!'

We all cheered and Miss Taylor smiled. We have a Christmas party every year, the whole school together in the main hall. Each class has its own table and we all bring the food from home.

'Now, does everybody know what they're bringing from home for the party tomorrow?'

I knew. I was bringing a jelly. I put my hand up.

'I'm bringing a jelly, Miss!'

Everybody started shouting at once and Miss Taylor moved her hands about to calm us down.

'All right, all right, one at a time. Don't get excited. Jennifer Greenwood, what are you bringing?'

Jennifer Greenwood was sitting in the back row next to Valerie Burns. She wriggled her shoulders and rolled her head about and looked down. She always does that when she's asked a question. She's daft, is Jennifer Greenwood.

'C'mon, Jennifer, what are you bringing for tomorrow?'

She put her hand up.

'Please, Miss, I'm bringing a custard trifle, Miss.'

Norbert Lightowler pulled his mouth into a funny shape and pretended to be sick.

'Ugh, I hate custard. I'm not gonna have any of that!'

Everybody laughed, except Miss Taylor.

'Well, Norbert, if I was Jennifer I wouldn't dream of giving you any. Right, Jennifer?'

Jennifer just rolled her head about and giggled

13

with Valerie Burns. Norbert was looking down at his desk.

'And, Norbert, what are you bringing to-morrow?'

'Polony sandwiches, Miss, my mum's making 'em, and a bottle of mixed pickles, Miss, home-made!'

Miss Taylor said that would be lovely, and carried on asking right round the class. Tony said that he was bringing a Christmas cake. I was bringing the jelly that my mum was going to make, and Colin Wilkinson was bringing some currant buns. Valerie Burns said that she was bringing some lemon curd tarts, and Freda Holdsworth called her a spiteful cat because *she* was bringing the lemon curd tarts, and Valerie Burns *knew* she was bringing lemon curd tarts because she'd told her and she was a blooming copycat. Anyway Miss Taylor calmed her down by saying that it was a good job they were both bringing lemon curd tarts, because then there would be enough for everybody, and everybody would want one, wouldn't they? And she asked everybody who would want a lemon curd tart to put their hands up, and everybody put their hands up. Even I put my hand up and I hate lemon curd. Well, it *was* Christmas.

After everybody had told Miss Taylor what they were bringing, she said that there'd be enough for the whole school, never mind just our class, but we should remember that Christmas isn't just for eating and parties, and she asked Tony what the most important thing about Christmas is.

'Presents, Miss!'

'No, Tony, not presents. Christmas is when the baby Jesus was born, and that is the most important thing, and when you're all enjoying your presents and parties this year, you must all remember that. Will you all promise me?'

Everybody promised that they'd remember Jesus and then Miss Taylor started asking us all how we were going to spend Christmas. Freda Holdsworth said she was going to Bridlington on Christmas Eve to stay with her cousin, and on Christmas Eve they'd both put their stockings up for Father Christmas, but before they'd go to bed, they'd leave a glass of milk and some biscuits for him in case he was hungry. Norbert Lightowler said that that's daft because there's no such thing as Father Christmas. Some of the others agreed, but most of them said course there is. I just wasn't sure. What I can't understand is, that if there *is* a Father Christmas, how does he get round everybody in one night? I mean the presents must come from somewhere, but how can he do it all by himself? And Norbert said how can there be only *one* Father Christmas, when he'd seen *two* down in town in Baldwin Street and another outside the fish market, and Neville Bastowe said he'd seen one in Dickenson's. Well, what about the one my mum had taken me to see at the Co-op? He'd promised to bring me a racer.

'Please, Miss, there's one at the Co-op an' all. He's promised to bring me a racer.'

And then Miss Taylor explained that all these others are Father Christmas's brothers and relations who help out because he's so busy and Freda Holdsworth said Miss Taylor was right, and Norbert said he'd never thought of that, but that Paul Hopwood, he's in 2B, had told him that Father Christmas is just his dad dressed up, and I said that that's daft and it couldn't be because Father Christmas comes to our house every year and I haven't got a dad, and Miss Taylor said that if those who didn't believe in Father Christmas didn't get any presents, they'd only have themselves to blame, and I agreed! Then she asked me what I'd be doing on Christmas Day.

'Well, Miss, when I wake up in the morning, I'll look round and see what presents I've got, and I'll play with them and I'll empty my stocking, and usually there are some sweets so I'll eat them, and when I've played a bit more I'll go and wake my mum up and show her what I've got, and then I'll wake my Auntie Doreen – she always stays with us every Christmas; and then after breakfast I'll play a bit more, and then we'll have Christmas dinner, and then we'll go to my grandad's and I'll play a bit more there, and then I'll go home to bed, and that'll be the end!'

Miss Taylor said that all sounded very nice and she hoped everybody would have such a nice Christmas, but she was surprised I wasn't going to church. Well, I told her that there wouldn't really be time because my grandad likes us to be there early to hear Wilfred Pickles on the wireless visiting a hospital, and to listen to the Queen talking, and then the bell went for home-time and Miss Taylor said we could all go quietly and told us not to forget our stuff for the party.

I went with Tony to get our coats from the cloakroom. Everybody was talking about the party and Barry was there shouting out that their class was going to have the best table because their teacher had made them a Christmas pudding with money in it! I told him that was nothing because Miss Taylor had given everybody in our class sixpence, but he didn't believe me.

'Gerraway, you bloomin' fibber.'

'She did, didn't she, Tony?'

Tony shook his head.

'Did she heckers like – she wouldn't give 'owt away.'

Huh! You'd think Tony'd've helped me kid Barry along.

'Well, she bought all our Christmas decorations for the classroom . . .' and I went to get my coat. I took my gloves out of my pocket and they were still soaking wet from snowballing at playtime, so I thought I'd put them on the pipes to dry.

'Hey, Tony, my gloves are still sodden.'

'Well put 'em on the pipes.'

'Yeh, that's a good idea.'

While they dried I sat on the pipes. Ooh, it was lovely and warm. There's a window above the basins and I could see the snow was still coming down, really thickly now.

'Hey, it isn't half going to be deep tomorrow.'

Everybody had gone now except for Barry, Tony and me. Tony was standing on the basins looking out of the window and Barry was doing up his coat. It has a hood on it. I wish I had one like it. I could see through the door into the main hall where the Christmas tree was. It looked lovely. Ever so big. It was nearly up to the ceiling.

'Hey, isn't it a big Christmas tree?' Tony jumped down from the basin and came over to where I was sitting.

'Yeh. It's smashing. All them coloured balls. Isn't it lovely, eh, Barry?'

Barry came over.

'Not bad. C'mon you two, let's get going, eh?'

'Just a sec, let's see if my gloves are dry.'

They weren't really but I put them on. As I was fastening my coat, Barry said how about going carol singing to get a bit of money.

Tony was quite keen, but I didn't know. I mean, my mum'd be expecting me home round about now.

'I suppose *you* can't come because your mum'll be cross with you, as usual!'

Huh. It's all right for Barry. His mum and dad aren't bothered where he goes.

'Course I'll come. Where do you want to go?'

Barry said down near the woods where the posh live, but Tony said it was useless there because they never gave you nowt. So we decided to go round

Belgrave Road way, where it's only *quite* posh. It takes about ten minutes to get to Belgrave Road from our school and on the way we argued about which carols to sing. I wanted *Away in a Manger* but Barry wanted *O Come all Ye Faithful*.

'*Away in a Manger* isn't half as good as *O Come all Ye Faithful*, is it, Tony?'

Tony shrugged his shoulders.

'I quite like *Once in Royal David's City*.'

In the end we decided to take it in turns to choose. Belgrave Road's ever so long and we started at number three with *O Come all Ye Faithful*.

'O come all ye faithful, joyful and trium . . .'

That was as far as we got. A bloke opened the door, gave us three halfpence and told us to push off.

Tony was disgusted.

'That's a good start, halfpenny each.'

Barry told him to stop grumbling.

'It's better than nothing. C'mon.'

We went on to number five and Tony and Barry started quarrelling again because Tony said it was his turn to choose, but Barry wanted his go again because we'd only sung one line. So we did *O Come all Ye Faithful* again.

'O come all ye faithful, joyful and triumphant, O . . .'

We didn't get any further this time either. An old lady opened the door and said her mother was poorly so could we sing a bit quieter. We started once more but she stopped us again and said it was still just a little bit too loud and could we sing it quieter.

'O come all ye faithful, joyful and triumphant, O come ye, o come ye to Be-ethlehem . . .'

And we sang the whole thing like that, in whispers. We could hardly hear each other. I felt daft and started giggling and that set Tony and Barry off, but the old lady didn't seem to notice. She just stood there while we sang and when we finished she said thank you and gave us twopence each.

At the next house we sang *Once in Royal David's City* right through and then rang the doorbell, but nobody came. We missed number nine out because it was empty and up for sale, and at number eleven we sang *Away in a Manger*.

We went to the end of the road singing every carol we knew. We must've made about a pound between us by the time we got to the other end, and Barry said how about going back and doing the other side of the road. I was all for it, but I just happened to see St Chad's clock. Bloomin' heck! Twenty to nine! I couldn't believe it. I thought it'd be about half-past six, if that. Twenty to nine!

'Hey, I'd better get going. It's twenty to nine. My mum'll kill me!'

The other two said they were going to do a bit more carol singing, so they gave me my share of the money and I ran home as fast as I could. I took a short cut through the snicket behind the fish and chip shop and I got home in about five minutes. I could see my mum standing outside the front door talking to Mrs Theabould, our next door neighbour.

She saw me and walked towards me. I tried to act all calm as if it was only about half-past five or six o'clock.

'Hello, Mum, I've been carol singing.'

She gave me a clout. She nearly knocked me over. Right on my freezing cold ear an' all.

'Get inside, you! I've been going mad with worry. Do you know what time it is? Nine o'clock. Get inside!'

She pushed me inside and I heard her thank Mrs Theabould and come in after me. I thought she was going to give me another clout, but she just shouted at me, saying that I was lucky she didn't get the police out, and why didn't I tell her where I was? By this time I was crying my head off.

'But I was only bloomin' carol singing.'

'I'll give you carol singing. Get off to bed,' and she pushed me upstairs into my bedroom.

'But what about my jelly for tomorrow? Have you made it?'

I thought she was going to go mad.

'Jelly! I'll give you jelly. If you think I've nothing better to do than make jellies while you're out roaming the streets! Get to bed!'

'But I've told Miss Taylor I'm bringing a jelly. I've got to have one. Please, Mum.'

She just told me to wash my hands and face and get to bed.

'And if I hear another word out of you, you'll get such a good hiding, you'll wish you hadn't come home,' and she went downstairs.

I didn't dare say another word. What was I going to do about my jelly? I had to bring one. I'd promised. There was only one thing for it. I'd have to make one myself. So I decided to wait until my mum went to bed, and then I'd go downstairs and make one. I don't know how I kept awake. I'm sure I nodded off once or twice, but after a while I heard my mum switch her light out, and when I'd given her enough time to get to sleep, I crept downstairs.

I've seen my mum make jellies tons of times and I knew you had to have boiling water, so I put the kettle on. I looked in the cupboard for a jelly and at first I thought I'd had it, but I found one and emptied it into a glass bowl. It was a funny jelly. Not like the ones my mum usually has. It was sort of like a powder. Still, it said jelly on the packet, so it was all right. A new flavour most likely. I poured the hot water into a bowl, closed the cupboard door, switched off the light, and took the jelly upstairs and I put it under my bed. I could hear my mum snoring so I knew I was all right, and I went to sleep.

Next thing I heard was my mum shouting from downstairs.

'C'mon, get up or you'll be late for school.'

I got up and pulled the jelly from under the bed. It had set lovely. All wobbly. But it was a bit of a funny colour, sort of yellowy-white. Still, I'd got my jelly and that's what mattered. My mum didn't say much when I got downstairs. She just told me to eat my breakfast and get to school, so I did. When I'd finished I put my coat on and said tarah to my mum in the kitchen and went off. But first I sneaked upstairs and got my jelly and wrapped it in a piece of newspaper.

The first thing we had to do at school was to take what we'd brought for the party into the main hall and stick on a label with our name on it and leave it on our table. Norbert Lightowler was there with his polony sandwiches and mixed pickles. So was Neville Bastowe. Neville Bastowe said that my jelly was a bit funny looking, but Norbert said he loved jelly more than anything else and he could eat all the jellies in the world. Miss Taylor came along then and told us to take our coats off and go to our classroom. The party wasn't starting till twelve o'clock, so in the morning we played games and sang carols and Miss Taylor read us a story.

Then we had a long playtime and we had a snowball fight with 2B, and I went on the slides until old Wilkie, that's the caretaker, came and put ashes on the ice. Then the bell went and we all had to go to our tables in the main hall. At every place was a Christmas cracker, and everybody had a streamer, but Mr Dyson, the Headmaster, said that we couldn't throw any streamers until we'd finished eating. I pulled my cracker with Tony and got a red paper hat and a pencil sharpener. Tony got a blue hat and a small magnifying glass. When everybody had pulled their crackers we said grace and started eating. I started with a sausage roll that Neville Bastowe had brought, and a polony sandwich.

Miss Taylor had shared my jelly out in bowls and Jennifer Greenwood said it looked horrible and she wasn't going to have any. So did Freda Holdsworth. But Norbert was already on his jelly and said it was lovely and he'd eat anybody else's. Tony started his jelly and spat it out.

'Ugh, it's horrible.'

I tasted mine, and it *was* horrible, but I forced it down.

'It's not that bad.'

Just then Tony said he could see my mum.

'Isn't that your mum over there?'

He pointed to the door. She was talking to Miss Taylor and they both came over.

'Your mother says you forgot your jelly this morning, here it is.'

Miss Taylor put a lovely red jelly on the table. It had bananas and cream on it, and bits of orange. My mum asked me where I'd got my jelly from. I told her I'd made it. I thought she'd be cross, but she and Miss Taylor just laughed and told us to enjoy ourselves, and then my mum went off. Everybody put their hands up for a portion of my mum's jelly – except Norbert.

'I don't want any of that. This is lovely. What flavour is it?'

I told him it was a new flavour and I'd never heard of it before.

'Well, what's it called?'

'Aspic.'

'Y'what?'

'Aspic jelly – it's a new flavour!'

Norbert ate the whole thing and was sick afterwards, and everybody else had some of my mum's. It was a right good party.

# THE LONG WALK

I loved it when my grandad took me out – just me and him. I never knew when I was going out with him. It just happened every so often. My mum'd say to me, 'C'mon, get ready. Your grandad's coming to take you out. Get your clogs on.' That was the one thing that spoilt it – my clogs. Whenever my grandad took me out, I had to wear a pair of clogs that he'd given to me. Well, he'd made them you see, that was his job before he retired, clog-maker. I didn't half make a noise when I was wearing them an' all. Blimey, you could hear me a mile away. I hated those clogs.

'Aw, Mum, do I have to put my clogs on?'

'Now don't ask silly questions. Go and get ready.'

'Aw, please ask Grandad if I can go without my clogs.'

'Do you want to go or don't you?'

My mum knew that I wanted to go.

'Course I want to go.'

'Then go and put your clogs on.'

'Oh, heck.'

Honest, I'd never ever seen anybody else wearing clogs. I wondered where my grandad would take me today. Last time I'd gone to the zoo with him. It was great. I was just about ready when I heard him knock at the front door. I knew it was my grandad, because he always had his own special knock. Everybody else used the bell. I could hear him downstairs, he was wearing clogs himself.

'I'm nearly ready, Grandad.'

I put on my windcheater that I'd been given last Christmas. It was maroon-coloured. My friend Tony had got one as well only his was green, but I liked mine best. Then I went downstairs.

'Hello, Grandad.'

My mum told me to give him a kiss.

'He's getting too big to give his old grandad a kiss, aren't you, son?'

He always called me son.

'No, course not, Grandad.'

He bent down so I could kiss him on his cheek. He was all bristly and it made me laugh.

'Ooh, Grandad, you haven't shaved today, have you?'

He was laughing as well. We were both laughing, we didn't really know why, and my mum started laughing. There we were, all three of us laughing at nothing at all.

'No, son, I haven't shaved. But it doesn't matter today. It'll bother nobody else today. There's just the two of us.'

'Where are we going, Grandad? Where are you taking us?'

He looked at me. His eyes were watering a bit

and he wiped them with a dark blue hanky he always had in his top pocket.

'We're going on a walk, a special walk.'

He was almost whispering, as if he didn't want my mum to hear, bending down with his whiskery face next to mine.

'Where are we going, Grandad? Where are we going? Is it a secret?'

'You'll see, son, when we get there.'

He looked a bit sad for a minute, but then he smiled and put on his flat cap.

'C'mon, son, let's get going.'

My mum gave us each a pack of sandwiches, and off we went. We must have looked a funny sight walking down the road together, me and my grandad. Him dressed in his flat cap and thick overcoat and clogs. Me in my maroon windcheater and short grey trousers and clogs. But I was so happy. I didn't know where we were going and neither did anybody else. Only Grandad knew, and only I was going to find out.

'Are we walking all the way, Grandad?' He took such big strides that I was half walking and half running.

'No, son, we'll get a trackless first to get out a bit.'

By 'trackless' he meant a bus, and I'd heard him say it so often that I never wondered why he said trackless.

'I'll show you where I used to go when I was a lad.'

We didn't have to wait long before a bus came, and we went upstairs and sat right at the front. Grandad was out of breath when we sat down.

'Are you all right, Grandad?'

'Oh, aye, son. You get a better view up here.'

'Yes, Grandad, you do.'

Soon we were going through the 'posh part' where the snobs lived. This was on the other side of the park.

'At one time there were no roof on't top deck. That were before the trackless. Completely open it was – daft really.'

The conductor came round for our fares.

'One and t'lad to the basin.'

I'd never heard of the basin before. I asked my grandad what it was.

'What's the basin, Grandad?'

'That's where we start our walk.'

'What basin is it? Why is it called "basin"?'

'The canal basin, it's where the canal starts. You'll see.'

By now we were going through a brand new shopping centre.

'Hey, look, Grandad, that's where that new bowling alley is. My friends Tony and Barry have been. They say it's smashing.'

Grandad looked out of the window.

'That's where I used to play cricket a long time ago.'

'Where the bowling alley is?'

'That's right, son, when they were fields. It's all

changed now. Mind, where we're going for our walk, it's not changed there. No, it's just the same there.'

We heard the conductor shout 'basin'.

'C'mon, son, our stop, be careful now.'

While we were going down the stairs, I held tight on to my grandad. Not because I thought I might fall, but I was scared for him. He looked as though he was going to go straight from the top to the bottom.

'Are you all right, Grandad? Don't fall.'

He just told me not to be frightened and to hold on tight.

'That's right. You hold on to me, son, you'll be all right, don't be frightened.'

We both got off the bus, and I watched it drive away. I didn't know where we were, but it was very quiet.

'It's nice here, isn't it, Grandad?'

'This is where my dad was born, your great-grandad.'

It was a lovely place. There weren't many shops and there didn't seem to be many people either. By the bus stop was a big stone thing full of water.

'Hey, Grandad, is that where the horses used to drink?'

'That's right, son. I used to hold my grandad's horse there while it was drinking.'

I couldn't see anything like a basin.

I wondered where it was.

'Where's the basin, Grandad?'

'We've got to walk there. C'mon.'

We went away from the main street, into a side street, past all these little houses. I don't think any cars ever went down this street because there was washing strung out right across the road all the way down the street. Outside some of the houses were ladies washing down the front step and scraping that yellow stone on the edges. A lot of the houses had curtains over the front door, so that you could leave the door open and the wind didn't blow in. Mind you, it wasn't cold even though it was October. It was nice. The sun was shining, not hot, but just nice. When we got further down the street, I saw that it was a cul-de-sac.

'Hey, Grandad, it's a dead-end. We must've come the wrong way.'

Grandad just smiled.

'Do you think I'm that old, that I can't remember the way? Here, look.'

He took my hand and showed me the way. Just before the last house in the road was a tiny snicket. It was so narrow that we had to go through behind each other. I wouldn't even have noticed this snicket if my Grandad hadn't shown it to me.

'Go on, son, through there.'

It was very dark and all you could see was a little speck of light at the other end, so you can tell how long it was.

'You go first, Grandad.'

'No, after you, son.'

I didn't want to go first.

'No, you'd better go first, Grandad. You know the way, don't you?'

He laughed and put his hand in his pocket and brought out a few boiled sweets.

'Here you are. These are for the journey. Off we go for the last time.'

I was just going to ask him what he meant, but he carried on talking. 'I mean it'll soon be winter, won't it? Come on.'

And off we went through the dark passage. Grandad told me that when he was a kid they used to call it the Black Hole of Calcutta. Soon we reached the other end and it was quite strange because it was like going through a door into the country. We ended up at the top of some steps, high up above the canal basin, and you could see for miles. I could only see one barge though, in the basin. We went down the steps. There were a hundred and fifteen steps – I counted them. Grandad was going down slowly so I was at the bottom before him.

'Grandad, there are a hundred and fifteen steps there. C'mon, let's look at that barge.'

I ran over to have a look at it and Grandad followed me.

'It's like a house isn't it, Grandad?'

'It is a house. Someone lives there. C'mon, let's sit here and have our sandwiches.'

And we did.

The sun was very big and round, though it wasn't very hot, and the leaves on the trees were golden, and the reflection in the water made the canal look golden. There was nobody else about, and all the noises that you never notice usually suddenly sounded special, different. Like the siren that let the workers know it was dinner time. I've heard sirens lots of times since then but they never sound so sweet. The same with the train. It must have been miles away because I couldn't see any steam or anything, and you had to listen quite hard, but behind the hum of the country and town sounds mixed together you could hear this knockety-knock.

When we'd finished our sandwiches we walked along the canal. Grandad showed me how to open the lock-gates, and we were both puffed out afterwards because it was hard work. After a while we walked away from the canal, up a country lane. I don't suppose we were really that far away from home, but we seemed to be miles out in the country, and soon we came to a village. My grandad said we'd catch a bus home from there, but first he wanted to show me something, and he took hold of my hand. I didn't have a clue where he was taking me, but I got a shock when we ended up in the graveyard. It had gone cold now. I wanted to go home.

'C'mon, Grandad, let's go home now.'

But he didn't seem to be listening properly.

'In a minute, son, I just want to show you summat.'

And hand in hand we walked among the gravestones.

'There you are, son, there's my plot. That's where I'll be laid to rest.'

I didn't know what to say.

'When, Grandad?'

'Soon.'

He smiled and looked very happy and he bent down and pulled out a couple of weeds. It was a very neat plot.

'C'mon, son, we'd best get going now.'

When I told my mum that night that Grandad was going to die soon, she got very cross and told me not to talk like that.

'He's as fit as a fiddle is your grandad. Don't you talk like that.'

It happened three days later, at dinner time. It came as a great shock to everybody, except of course to me and Grandad.

# THE HOLIDAY

It wasn't fair. Tony and Barry were going. In fact, nearly all of them in Class Three and Four were going, except me. It wasn't fair. Why wouldn't my mum let me go?

'I've told you. You're not going camping. You're far too young.'

Huh! She said that last year.

'You said that last year!'

'You can go next year when you're a bit older.'

She'd said that last year, too.

'You said that last year an' all.'

'Do you want a clout?'

'Well you did, Mum, didn't you?'

'Go and wash your hands for tea.'

'Aw, Mum, everybody else is going to school camp. Why can't I?'

Because you're coming to Bridlington with me and your Auntie Doreen like you do every year.

'Because you're coming to Bridlington with me and your Auntie Doreen like you do every year!'

I told you. Oh, every year the same thing; my mum, me, and my Auntie Doreen at Mrs Sharkey's boarding house. I suppose we'll have that room next door to the lavatory: a double bed for my mum and

37

my Auntie Doreen, and me on a camp bed behind a screen.

'I suppose we'll have that rotten room again.'

'Don't be cheeky! Mrs Sharkey saves that room for me every year – last week in July and first week in August. It's the best room in the house, facing the sea like that, and nice and handy for the toilets. You know how important that is for your Auntie Doreen.'

'Aw, Mum, I never get any sleep – the sea splashing on one side and Auntie Doreen on the . . . aw!'

My mum gave me a great clout right across my head. She just caught my ear an' all.

'Aw, bloomin' heck. What was that for?'

'You know very well. Now stop being so cheeky and go and wash your hands.'

'Well, you've done it now. You've dislocated my jaw – that's it now. I'll report you to that RSPCC thing, and they'll sue you. You've really had it now . . . ow!'

She clouted me again, right in the same place.

'It's not fair. Tony's mum and dad are letting him go to school camp, and Barry's. Why won't you let me go?'

She suddenly bent down and put her face right next to mine, right close. She made me jump. Blimey, that moustache was getting longer. I wish she'd do something about it – it's embarrassing to have a mum with a moustache.

'Now, listen to me, my lad. What Tony's mum and dad do, and what Barry's mum and dad do, is their lookout. You will come with me and your Auntie Doreen to Bridlington and enjoy yourself like you do every year!'

Huh! Enjoy myself – that's a laugh for a start. How can you enjoy yourself walking round Bridlington town centre all day looking at shops? You can do that at home. Or else it was bingo. 'Key-of-the-door, old-age pension, legs-eleven, clickety-click' and all that rubbish. You could do that at home as well. And when we did get to the beach, I had to spend all day rubbing that oily sun stuff on my Auntie Doreen's back. It was horrible. Then the rain would come down and it was back to bingo. Honest, what's the point of going on holiday if you do everything that you can do at home? You want to do something different. Now camping, that's different. Tony's dad had bought him a special sleeping bag, just for going camping. Huh! I wish I had a dad.

'I bet if I had a dad, he'd let me go to school camp.'

I thought Mum was going to get her mad up when I said that, but she didn't at all.

'Go and wash your hands for tea, love. Your spam fritters will be ready in a minute.'

Ugh. Bloomin' spam fritters! Not worth washing your hands for!

'Yeh. All right.'

I started to go upstairs. Ooh, I was in a right mess now. I'd told all the other lads I was going. Our names had to be in by tomorrow. We had to give Mr Garnett our pound deposit. Well, I was going to go.

I didn't care what Mum said, I was going to go – somehow! When I got to the top of the stairs, I kicked a tin wastepaper bin on the landing. It fell right downstairs. It didn't half make a clatter.

'What on earth are you doing?'

She would have to hear, wouldn't she?

'Eh. It's all right, Mum. I just tripped over the wastepaper bin. It's all right.'

'Oh, stop playing the goat and come downstairs. Your tea's ready.'

What was she talking about, playing the goat? I couldn't help tripping over a wastepaper bin. Well, I couldn't have helped it if I had tripped over it, an' well, I might have done for all she knew. Well, I wasn't going to wash my hands just for spam fritters. Oh, bet we have macaroni cheese as well. I went straight downstairs.

'Are your hands clean?'

'Yeh.'

'Here we are then. I've made some macaroni cheese as well.'

'Lovely.'

'C'mon. Eat it up quickly, then we'll have a nice bit of telly.'

I didn't say anything else about the school camp that night. I knew it was no good. But I was going to go. I'd told Tony and Barry I was going, I'd told all the lads I was going. Somehow, I'd get my own way. When I got to school next morning, I saw Tony and Barry with Norbert Lightowler over by the Black Hole. That's a tiny snicket, only open at one end, where we shove all the new lads on the first day of term. There's room for about twenty kids. We usually get about a hundred in. It's supposed to be good fun, but the new kids don't enjoy it very much. They get to enjoy it the next year.

'Hello, Tony. Hello, Barry.'

Norbert Lightowler spat out some chewing gum. It just missed me.

'Oh, don't say "hello" to me then, will ya?'

'No. And watch where you're spitting your rotten chewing gum – or you'll get thumped.'

Barry asked us all if we'd brought our pound deposit for school camp. Tony and Norbert had got theirs, of course. Nobody was stopping them going. I made out I'd forgotten mine.

'Oh heck. I must have left mine on the kitchen table.'

'Oh, I see. Well, maybe Garnett'll let you bring it tomorrow.'

I didn't say anything, but Norbert did.

'Oh, no. He said yesterday today's the last day. He said anybody not bringing their deposit today wouldn't be able to go. He did, you know.'

'Aw, shurrup, or I'll do you.'

'I'm only telling you.'

'Well, don't bother.'

Tony asked me if I'd learnt that poem for Miss Taylor. I didn't know what he was talking about.

'What poem?'

Norbert knew, of course. He brought a book out of his pocket.

41

'*Drake's Drum*. Haven't you learnt it?'

Oh crikey! *Drake's Drum*. With all this worry about trying to get to school camp, I'd forgotten all about it. Miss Taylor had told us to learn it for this morning.

'We're supposed to know it this morning, you know.'

'I know, Norbert, I know.'

Honest, Norbert just loved to see you in a mess, I suppose because he's usually in trouble himself.

'*I* know it. I spent all last night learning it. Listen:

' "Drake he's in his hammock an' a
        thousand mile away.

Captain, art thou sleeping there below?

Slung a'tween the round shot in Nombres Dios
        bay . . ." '

I snatched the book out of his hands.

'Come 'ere. Let's have a look at it.'

'You'll never learn it in time. Bell'll be going in a minute.'

'You were reading it, anyway.'

'I was not. It took me all last night to learn that.'

Barry laughed at him.

'What, all last night to learn three lines?'

'No, clever clogs. I mean the whole poem.'

Just then, the bell started going for assembly. Norbert snatched his book back.

'C'mon, we'd better get into line. Garnett's on playground duty.'

Norbert went over to where our class was lining up. Barry's in Class Four, so he went over to their column.

'See you at playtime.'

'Yeh. Tarah.'

While we were lining up, we were all talking. Mr Garnett just stood there with his hands on his hips, staring at us, waiting for us to stop.

'Thank you.'

Some of us heard his voice and stopped talking. Those that didn't carried on.

'Thank you.'

A few more stopped, and then a few more, till the only voice you could hear was Norbert Lightowler's, and as soon as he realized nobody else was talking, he shut up quickly.

'Thank you. If I have to wait as long as that for silence at the end of this morning's break, then we shall spend the whole break this afternoon learning how to file up in silence. Do you understand?'

We all just stood there, hardly daring to breathe.

'Am I talking to myself? Do you understand?'

Everybody mumbled 'Yes, sir', except Norbert Lightowler. He had to turn round and start talking to me and Tony.

'Huh! If he thinks I'm going to spend my playtime filing up in silence, he's got another think coming.'

'Lightowler!'

Norbert nearly jumped out of his skin.

'Are you talking to those boys behind you?'

'No, sir. I was just telling 'em summat . . .'

'Really?'

'Yes, sir . . . er . . . I was just . . . er . . . telling them that we have to give our pound in today, sir, for school camp, sir.'

'I want a hundred lines by tomorrow morning: "I must not talk whilst waiting to go into assembly." '

'Aw, sir.'

'Two hundred.'

He nearly did it again, but stopped just in time, or he'd have got three hundred.

'Right. When I give the word, I want you to go quietly into assembly. And no talking. Right – wait for it. Walk!'

Everybody walked in not daring to say a word. When we got into the main hall, I asked Tony for the book with *Drake's Drum* in, and during assembly, I tried to snatch a look at the poem but, of course, it was a waste of time. Anyway, I was more worried about my pound deposit for Mr Garnett. After prayers, the Headmaster made an announcement about it.

'This concerns only the boys in Classes Three and Four. Today is the final day for handing in your school camp deposits. Those of you not in Three B must see Mr Garnett during morning break. Those of you in Three B will be able to hand in your money when Mr Garnett takes you after Miss Taylor's class. Right, School turn to the right. From the front, dismiss! No talking.'

44

I had another look at the poem while we were waiting for our turn to go.

' "Drake he's in his hammock an' a thousand
        mile away.

Captain, art thou sleeping there below?" '

Well, I knew the first two lines. Tony wasn't too bothered. He probably knew it.

'Don't worry. She can't ask everybody to recite it. Most likely she'll ask one of the girls. Anyway, what are you going to do about Garnett? Do you think he'll let you bring your pound deposit tomorrow?'

'Yeh, sure to.'

If only Tony knew that it'd be just as bad tomorrow. I had to get a pound from somewhere. Then I'd have about four weeks to get my mum to let me go. But I had to get my name down today or I'd . . . I'd had it. Miss Taylor was already waiting for us when we got into our classroom.

'Come along, children. Settle down.'

Miss Taylor took us for English and Religious Instruction.

'Now today, we're going to deal with some parts of the Old Testament.'

Tony and me looked at each other. She'd got mixed up. Today was English and tomorrow was Religious Instruction.

'Now you've all heard of the Ten Commandments . . .'

Bloomin' hummer. What a let-off. Tony was grinning at me.

'Do you know the first of these Ten Commandments?'

Jennifer Greenwood put her hand up. She was top of the class every year. Everyone reckoned she was Miss Taylor's favourite.

'Yes, Jennifer.'

Jennifer Greenwood wriggled about a bit in her seat and went red. She's always going red.

'Please, Miss, it's English this morning, Miss; it's Religious Instruction tomorrow, Miss.'

Honest, I could've thumped her. Then Norbert put his hand up.

'Yes, Miss. You told us to learn *Drake's Drum* for this morning, Miss.'

I leaned across to Tony.

'I'll do him at playtime.'

'Quite right, Norbert. Thank you for reminding me. Now, who will recite it for me?'

Everybody shoved their hands up shouting, 'Miss, Miss, me, Miss, Miss', so I thought I'd better look as keen as the rest of them.

'Miss! Miss! Miss!'

I stretched my hand up high. I got a bit carried away. I was sure she'd pick one of the girls.

'Me, Miss. Please, Miss. Me, Miss!'

She only went and pointed at me. I couldn't believe it.

'Me, Miss?'

'Yes. You seem very keen for once. Stand up and speak clearly.'

I stood up as slowly as I could. My chair scraped

on the floor and made a noise like chalk on the blackboard.

'Hurry up, and lift your chair up. Don't push it like that.'

Everybody was looking at me. Norbert, who sits in the front row, had turned round and was grinning.

'Er ... um *Drake's Drum* ... by Henry Newbolt ...'

Miss Taylor lifted up her finger.

'*Sir* Henry Newbolt!'

'Yes, Miss.'

I was glad she stopped me. Anything to give me more time.

'Carry on.'

I took a deep breath. I could feel Norbert still grinning at me.

'Ahem. *Drake's Drum* ... by Sir Henry Newbolt.'

I stopped: then I took another deep breath ....

' "Drake is in his cabin and a thousand mile away ..." '

I stopped again. I knew after the next line, I'd be in trouble.

' "Cap'n, art thou sleeping down below ..." '

The whole class was listening. I didn't know what I was going to say next. I took another breath and I was just about to tell Miss Taylor I couldn't remember any more, when Norbert burst out laughing. Miss Taylor went over to him:

'What are you laughing at, Norbert?'

'Nothing, Miss.'

'You think you can do better – is that it?'

'No, Miss.'

'Stand up!'

Norbert stood up. Miss Taylor looked at me. 'Well done. That was a very dramatic opening. Sit down, and we'll see if Norbert Lightowler can do as well.'

I couldn't believe it. Tony could hardly keep his face straight.

Norbert went right through the poem. Miss Taylor had to help him once or twice, but he just about got through. Miss Taylor told him he hadn't done badly, but not quite as well as me. After that a few of the others recited it, and then we went on to do some English grammar.

After Miss Taylor, we had Mr Garnett. He gave the girls some arithmetic to do, while he sorted out the deposits for school camp. He went through the register, and everybody that was going gave him their pound deposit – until he got to me.

'I've forgotten it, sir.'

'You know today is the last day, don't you?'

'Yes, sir.'

'And all the names have to be in this morning? I told you all that yesterday, didn't I?'

'Yes, sir. Yes, sir – I'll bring my pound tomorrow, sir.'

Mr Garnett tapped his pencil.

'I'll put the pound in for you, and I want you to repay me first thing tomorrow morning. All right?'

'Er . . . um . . . yes, sir. I think so, sir.'

'You do want to go to school camp?'

'Yes, sir.'

'Right then. Don't forget to give me your pound tomorrow.'

'No, sir.'

I didn't know what I was going to do now. I reckoned the best thing was to tell Mr Garnett the truth, so when the bell went for playtime, I stayed behind in the classroom, and I told him about my mum wanting me to go to Bridlington with her and my Auntie Doreen. He told me not to worry, and gave me a letter to give to my mum that night. I don't know what it said, but after my mum had read it, she put it in her pocket and said she'd give me a pound for Mr Garnett in the morning.

'Can I go to camp, then?'

'Yes, if that's what you want.'

'I don't mind coming to Bridlington with you and Auntie Doreen, if you'd rather . . .'

My mum just got hold of my face with both her hands.

'No, love, you go to school camp and enjoy yourself.'

So I did – go to school camp, that is – but I didn't enjoy myself. It was horrible. They put me in a tent with Gordon Barraclough: he's a right bully and he gets everybody on to his side because they're all scared of him. I wanted to go in Tony's and Barry's tent, but Mr Garnett said it would upset all his schedules, so I was stuck with Gordon Barraclough and his gang. They made me sleep right next to the opening, so when it rained, my sleeping bag got soaked. And they thought it was dead funny to pull my clothes out of my suitcase (my mum couldn't afford a rucksack) and throw them all over the place.

'Huh! Fancy going camping with a suitcase!'

'Mind your own business, Barraclough! My mum couldn't afford a proper rucksack. Anyway, I'm off to Bridlington on Sunday.'

And I meant it. Sunday was parents' visiting day, and my mum and Auntie Doreen were coming to see me on their way to Bridlington. So I was going to pack up all my stuff and go with them. Huh . . . I couldn't stand another week with Gordon Barraclough. I wished I'd never come.

So on Sunday morning, after breakfast in the big marquee, I packed everything into my suitcase and waited for my mum and my Auntie Doreen to come. They arrived at quarter to eleven.

'Hello, love. Well, isn't it grand here? You are having a nice time, aren't you?'

'Yeh, it's not bad, but I want to tell you summat.'

My mum wasn't listening. She was looking round the camp site.

'Well, it's all bigger than I thought. Is this your tent here?'

She poked her head through the flap. I could hear her talking to Gordon Barraclough and the others.

'No! No! No! Don't move, boys. Well, haven't you got a lot of room in here? It's quite deceiving from the outside.'

Her head came out again.

'Here, Doreen, you have a look in here. It's ever so roomy.'

She turned back to Gordon Barraclough.

'Well, bye-bye boys. Enjoy the rest of your holiday. And thank you for keeping an eye on my little lad.'

I could hear them all laughing inside the tent. I felt sick.

'Mum, I want to ask you something—'

'In a minute, love, in a minute. Let's just see round the camp, and then we'll have a little natter before your Auntie Doreen and I go. Oh, and I want to say hello to Mr Garnett while I'm here. You know, on the way here today, I kept saying wouldn't it be lovely if I could take you on to Bridlington with us. Wasn't I, Doreen? But now I'm here, I can see you're all having a real good time together. You were right, love, it's much better to be with your friends than with two fuddy-duddies like us, eh, Doreen? Well, c'mon, love, aren't you going to show us round? We've got to get our bus for Bridlington soon.'

I showed them both round the camp site, and they went off just before dinner. I didn't feel like anything to eat myself. I just went to the tent and unpacked my suitcase.

# THE GANG HUT

We used to have a gang hut, Barry, Tony, and me. It was smashing. It used to be in Tony's back garden, in fact I think it's still there. I remember one of the last meetings we ever had – it wasn't long after August Bank Holiday. I went to the gang hut straight after school. There was a short cut you could take over a broken wall. You got a bit mucky, but it was quicker. I got to the hut and knocked the secret knock, two quick knocks, a pause, then followed by three more.

'Give the password.'

That was Barry, our leader. I stared at the door which had 'The Silent Three' painted on it (I'd done that), and thought.

'What password?'

'What do you mean, what password?'

'What do *you* mean, what do I mean, what password?'

Barry's voice became deeper, and bossy!

'Well, if you'd attended the last gang meeting, you would know what password!'

Oh, of course, that's why I didn't know this blooming password that Barry was talking about. Of course, I didn't go to the last gang meeting. How can you go on Bank Holiday Monday? I'd gone with my mum and Auntie Doreen to Scarborough and it rained all blooming day. I'd felt a bit daft carrying my bucket and spade and ship on the sea front when it was pouring with rain. Yes, and when I'd cheeked my Auntie Doreen off my mum had hit me, and I'd cried – even though it didn't hurt.

'Come on, Barry, tell us what the password is.'

'Well, you haven't to tell anybody.'

'Course not.'

'All right then, it's "Ouvrez la porte".'

'Y'what?'

' "Ouvrez la porte".'

I didn't know what he was talking about.

'It's a blooming long password, isn't it?'

'It's three words, they're French. Not many people will know what it means.'

'What does it mean?'

'It means "open the door".'

'It's a bit ordinary, isn't it?'

'Not if you say it in French.'

'I suppose so. Anyway, open the door.'

'Say the password!'

'You know it's me, let us in!'

'Say the password!'

'Oh, all right, "Ouvrez la porte".'

At last I was in the den. It was only small, but at least it was ours, Barry's, Tony's and mine, that is, 'The Silent Three'. And now that we'd got a lock and key from Barry's dad, nobody else could get in. Come to think of it, neither could me and Tony, because Barry always kept the key, seeing as his dad had given us the lock. Tony had said that *he* should keep the key because the den was in his back garden. I'd agreed. Not that I wanted Tony to have the key either, but Barry always got things his way. He used to be like that a lot, Barry did, pushing his weight around and telling us how much better he did things than we did. Barry started going on about Tony being late.

'Where's Tony, isn't he coming?'

Tony was in the same class as me.

'Yes, but Miss Taylor kept him in for eating in class. Rotten thing. She's always keeping people in, y'know.'

'Yes, I know. She took us last year.'

Barry was in Class Four and was going in for his scholarship in December. Tony and me were only in Class Three. If I'd been taking my scholarship, I'd have been scared stiff, but Barry didn't seem to be.

'Eh, Barry, do you think you'll be scared when you take your scholarship?'

'Yeh, course, everybody gets scared. Wouldn't you?'

'Oh, yeh, I know everybody gets scared, but I just wondered if you did. Which school do you want to go to if you pass?'

'Oh, I don't know, same as my brother I suppose. I don't know.'

Just then, there were two knocks on the door, followed by three more.

'Hey, Barry, that might be Tony.'

'What do you mean, *might* be Tony? It must be Tony, he's the only other one who knows the secret knock, isn't he?'

'Oh, yeh. Ask him the password, go on!'

'I'm going to, don't you worry. Give the password!'

I heard Tony's voice stuttering, trying to think of the password. Oh, ho, he'd forgotten it. He didn't know it. I was right glad he didn't know it.

'Do you know it? Do you know it? You can't come in if you don't know it, can he, Barry?'

'Hang on, I'm thinking. I'll get it, don't tell me. Err . . . I know! "Ouv the report".'

'No, "Ouvrez la porte".'

'Well, near enough, wasn't it, let us in.'

'All right, come on.' Barry opened the door and let Tony in.

'Now we all know the password, don't we?'

I knew Barry would say something.

'You should have known it before. I shouldn't really have let you in.'

'Well, I nearly knew it, didn't I, Barry?'

Tony looked at Barry for some kind of praise. Although Tony and me didn't really like Barry being the leader of 'The Silent Three', we accepted him as such, and also accepted his decisions on certain gang matters. It was Barry, for instance, who had decided on the gang's policy, which was 'to rob the rich to help the poor', because that was what Robin Hood did, although it was Tony who had thought of the name 'The Silent Three'.

We had lots of things in the gang hut. There was a window, with a frame which opened and closed on proper hinges. You had to admire Barry because he'd made that and it was very clever. Of course, there was no real glass in it, but there was some sacking which kept nosey parkers out. There was also a picture on one of the stone walls of a lady, dressed in a long white robe, holding a little baby on her knee, and the baby had long curly hair and it didn't have any clothes on, but you couldn't tell if it was a boy or a girl. *Barry* didn't like it because he thought it looked soppy. Tony said his grandma had given it to him, and that they ought to be glad they had it because he bet there weren't many gangs that had a picture. I thought it looked nice.

There was also a table, which had two drawers, one for Barry, and one for me and Tony to share. We kept all sorts of things in it, from a rubber stamp which said 'Albert Holdsworth (Worsteds) Limited' to half a potato which, when you dipped it into some paint, and stamped it, said 'The Silent Three'. We had one chair, and we took it in turns to sit in it, and two orange boxes. Also, there was a small carpet which my mum was going to throw away. She'd said to me, 'Oh, you don't want that dirty old thing.' And I'd said yes, I did, and I'd muttered something about the fight against evil and 'The Curse of the Silent Three', but by then my mum wasn't listening. Anyway, the most important thing was that I'd got the carpet and proudly presented it to Barry and Tony at the next gang meeting, and what had really pleased me was that the other two were impressed as I'd hoped they'd be. Well, that was really all we had in the gang hut. Oh, except two candles which were kept for emergency.

'What shall we do then?'

Tony looked at Barry for an answer. This was usually the way gang meetings started, and most times the question was directed towards Barry, because his were usually the best ideas, and anyway, we always did what he suggested.

'Well, first I've got to give you the secret seal, the curse of "The Silent Three".'

I knew this was what Barry would say, and it was just what I didn't want.

'Oh, not again, Barry. I got into trouble with my mum last time. It took ages to get it off. My mum says I haven't to let you do it again.'

This didn't bother Barry.

'You've got to have the secret seal or else you're not a member of "The Silent Three". Isn't that right, Tony?'

Tony had to agree, although I knew by his face that *he* wasn't that keen to have the stamp *either*.

'Anyway, it won't go on so strong this time, because I won't put any more paint on.'

Barry took out the half potato from his drawer. It had dried blue paint on it from the last time we'd used it, and he spat on it to make it wet.

'Ooh, we'll all get diseases!'

'No, you won't. Hold out your hand.'

'No, I'm not having your spit all over me.'

'C'mon, you've got to have it or you'll be banned from "The Silent Three". You've got to have it, hasn't he, Tony?'

Tony nodded in agreement, but he was even more reluctant now than he was earlier on. Barry looked right at me.

'C'mon – are you going to have it or not?'

I just sat there.

'Well, you should have let us do our own spitting.'

'Well, it's too late now. Are you going to have it or not?'

'No, I'm not!'

Barry just lost his temper then and threw the potato on the floor.

'Well, I'm not bothered about the secret seal anyway, or the gang hut for that matter. I was only joining in to please you kids!'

Tony and me, he meant. I was really shocked, because I mean after all he was the leader of 'The Silent Three'. I didn't know what to say. I just sat there.

Tony picked up the potato, I held my hand out and he stamped it. Then he stamped his own. He tried to stamp Barry's hand, but Barry wouldn't let him. 'The Silent Three' sat in silence, me and Tony waiting for the secret seal to dry and Barry, well, just not interested.

When the secret seal had dried, I started to talk to Barry.

'Eh, Barry, you know that kid in your class with that big red patch on his face . . .'

'That's a birthmark!'

'Yes, that big red birthmark. He was crying his head off in the lavatory this morning.'

'Yeh, I know, his grandad died last night. He went home at dinner time.'

'I remember my grandad. We used to go for walks when I was little. He's dead now. I don't remember my grandma though. She died when I was two.'

'What about your other grandad and grandma?'

I didn't know what Barry was talking about. I looked at him.

'What other grandad and grandma?'

'Your other grandad and grandma. You know, your other grandad and grandma. You have two grandads and grandmas, you know. Or don't you even know that?'

Tony said that he had two as well.

'Yes, I've got two grandads and grandmas. I've got my grandad and my grandma Atkinson, and my grandad and my grandma Spencer.'

Barry seemed to be really enjoying this.

'Oh, don't you know you have two grandads and grandmas?'

'All I know is, I've never seen my grandma, because she died when I was two, and my grandad's dead as well.'

And as far as I was concerned, that was that, although really it surprised me to hear that Barry and Tony both had two sets of grandads and grandmas. Why hadn't I? I'd have to ask my mum.

Tony and Barry started talking about swimming.

'We start swimming lessons next year.'

Tony meant me and him. You didn't have swimming lessons until you got into Class Four. Barry had been having lessons for a while. He was quite good.

'I can do two lengths, and half a length on my back.'

Tony could float a bit.

'I'm right looking forward to having swimming lessons, aren't you?'

I wasn't really looking forward to having swimming lessons. To be quite honest, I was scared stiff.

'Yes, I suppose so. I might be a bit scared though.'

'What for?' Oh, it was all right for Barry to talk. 'What is there to be scared about? You scared you might drown?'

Yes, I was.

'Course I'm not.'

I'd only been to the swimming baths once in my life, and somebody had pushed me in then. It was very scaring. I thought I was going to drown that time. The pool attendant had pulled me out and thumped the lad who'd pushed me in. I'd never been to the baths again since then. Barry was still going on about being scared.

'There's nowt to be scared of, y'know. It's dead easy, swimming is. Isn't it, Tony?'

'Don't know, I can't swim. I can float a bit.'

61

'Ah, floating's easy, anyone can float.'

Huh, I couldn't! I was fed up with this talk about swimming. It reminded me too much of what was to come. So I started to talk about something else.

'Eh, it'll be bonfire night soon.'

This got us all quite excited and Barry said we'd have the biggest bonfire in the neighbourhood. Tony said we should start collecting wood because it was the end of August already.

'We'll have to go down the woods. We could go down on Sunday afternoon.'

Barry agreed, but I said I'd have to ask my mum.

'You're always having to ask her. Can't you do anything without asking her?'

'Course I can, but she doesn't like me going down those woods.'

I had to go then because my mum told me I had to be in by a quarter to six. Tony had to go too, because he was sleeping at our house that weekend, because his mum was going away to stay with his big sister for a few days, who was married and lived in Manchester.

'My mum says by the time she gets back from Manchester, I'll be an uncle.'

So the gang meeting ended. Tony and me had to go to town next day with my mum, but we said we'd see Barry at the gang hut at about four o'clock. Barry said all right, and that he was going home to see if he could find any empty bottles to take back to the shop so he'd have some money to buy toffees for the Saturday morning matinee.

Barry started locking up the hut.

'Eh, are you two going to the pictures tomorrow morning?'

'I don't know. We might do. See you tomorrow afternoon anyway. Tarah.'

I asked my mum that night why I didn't have two grandads and grandmas like Tony and Barry, but she just told me not to ask silly questions and to get on with my supper.

We didn't go to the matinee next day because my mum said that we both had to have our hair cut before going into town that afternoon. I tried to get out of it, but I couldn't, and Tony didn't help either because he agreed with my mum and said we did really need our hair cut.

Anyway, that was what happened, and at about quarter to four, we came back from town with lots of shopping. Tony and me changed out of our best clothes. Mine were brand new. I'd only got them just before the Bank Holiday. Then we went straight over to the gang hut. Well, we'd just got over the broken wall into Tony's back yard, and I knew something was wrong. When I realized what it was I just couldn't believe it; the whole gang hut was wrecked. Honest, I'll never forget it. The door was wide open and inside the place was in a real mess. The two orange boxes were broken, the table was knocked over and the picture (of the lady) was lying on the floor. The window frame was pulled away from the hinges.

It was awful. All I could feel was this great thumping in my head.

'Hey, Tony, I wonder who did it?'

'Barry did. Look!'

He pointed to the door, and instead of 'The Silent Three', it said 'The Silent Two'.

'Why did he do it?'

Tony shrugged his shoulders and said he'd probably felt like it.

Neither of us knew then why Barry had done it, but Tony somehow didn't seem too bothered either. I suppose he knew that he'd be the leader of the gang now. *I* just couldn't understand it at all. Why would Barry wreck the whole gang hut like this? Especially since he had built most of it himself, specially the window frame.

When Tony left the gang, I became leader, for a while. Tony didn't do anything like wrecking the hut, nor did I when I left. We just got tired of it and, well, lost interest.

Some other younger lads used the hut for their meetings after us, but Barry, Tony and me weren't bothered. We didn't care who had the gang hut now.

# THE FIB

Ooh, I wasn't half snug and warm in bed. I could hear my mum calling me to get up, but it was ever so cold. Every time I breathed, I could see a puff of air. The window was covered with frost. I just couldn't get myself out of bed.

'Are you up? I've called you three times already.'

'Yes, Mum, of course I am.'

I knew it was a lie, but I just wanted to have a few more minutes in bed. It was so cosy.

'You'd better be, because I'm not telling you again.'

That was another lie. She was always telling me again.

'Just you be quick, young man, and frame your-self, or you'll be late for school.'

Ooh, school! If only I didn't have to go. Thank goodness we were breaking up soon for Christmas. I don't mind school, I quite like it sometimes. But today was Monday, and Mondays was football, and I hate blooming football. It wouldn't be so bad if I had proper kit, but I had to play in these old-fashioned shorts and boots that my mum had got from my Uncle Kevin. They were huge. Miles too big for me. Gordon Barraclough's mum and dad had bought him a Bobby Charlton strip and Bobby Charlton boots. No wonder he's a better player than me. My mum said she couldn't see what was wrong with my kit. She couldn't understand that I felt silly, and all the other lads laughed at me, even Tony, and he's my best friend. She just said she wasn't going to waste good money on new boots and shorts, when I had a perfectly good set already.

'But Mum, they all laugh at me, especially Gordon Barraclough.'

'Well, laugh back at them. You're big enough aren't you? Don't be such a jessie.'

She just couldn't understand.

'You tell them your Uncle Kevin played in those boots when he was a lad, and he scored thousands of goals.'

Blimey, that shows you how old my kit is! My Uncle Kevin's twenty-nine! I snuggled down the bed a bit more, and pulled the pillow under the blankets with me.

'I'm coming upstairs and if I find you not up, there'll be trouble. I'm not telling you again.'

Oh heck! I forced myself out of bed on to the freezing lino and got into my underpants. Ooh, they were cold! Blooming daft this. Getting dressed, going to school, and getting undressed again to play rotten football. I looked out of the window and it didn't half look miserable. I *felt* miserable. I *was* miserable. Another ninety minutes standing between the posts, letting in goal after goal, with Gordon Barraclough shouting at me:

'Why didn't you dive for it, you lazy beggar?'

Why didn't *he* dive for it? Why didn't *he* go in goal? Why didn't he shut his rotten mouth? Oh no, *he* was always centre forward wasn't he, because *he* was Bobby Charlton.

As I stood looking out of the window, I started wondering how I could get out of going to football . . . I know, I'd tell my mum I wasn't feeling well. I'd tell her I'd got a cold. No, a sore throat. No, she'd look. Swollen glands. Yes, that's what I'd tell her, swollen glands. No, she'd feel. What could I say was wrong with me? Earache, yes, earache, and I'd ask her to write me a note. I'd ask her after breakfast. Well, it was only a fib, wasn't it?

'You're very quiet. Didn't you enjoy your breakfast?'

'Err . . . well . . . I don't feel very well, Mum. I think I've got earache.'

'You *think* you've got earache?'

'I mean I *have* got earache, definitely, in my ear.'

'Which ear?'

'What?'

'You going deaf as well? I said, which ear?'

'Err . . . my right ear. Perhaps you'd better write me a note to get me off football . . .'

'No, love, it'll be good for you to go to football, get some fresh air. I'll write to Mr Melrose and ask him to let you go in goal, so you don't have to run around too much.'

She'd write a note to *ask* if I could go in . . .! Melrose didn't need a note for me to go in goal. I was *always* shoved in goal. Me and Norbert Light-owler were always in goal, because we were the worst players.

Norbert didn't care. He was never bothered when people shouted at him. He just told them to get lost. He never even changed for football. He just stuffed his trousers into his socks and said it was a tracksuit. He nearly looked as daft as me in my Uncle Kevin's old kit.

'Mum, don't bother writing me a note. I'll be all right.'

'I'm only thinking of you. If you've got earache I don't want you to run around too much. I don't want you in bed for Christmas.'

'I'll be OK.'

Do you know, I don't think my mum believed I'd got earache. I know I was fibbing, but even if I had got earache, I don't think she'd have believed me. Mums are like that.

'Are you sure you're all right?'

'Yes, I'll be OK.'

How could my mum know that when I was in goal I ran around twice as much, anyway? Every time the other team scored, I had to belt halfway across the playing field to fetch the ball back.

'Well, finish your Rice Krispies. Tony'll be here in a minute.'

Tony called for me every morning. I was never ready. I was just finishing my toast when I heard my mum let him in. He came through to the kitchen.

'Aw, come on. You're never ready.'

'I won't be a minute.'

'We'll be late, we'll miss the football bus.'

We didn't have any playing fields at our school, so we had a special bus to Bankfield Top, about two miles away.

'If we miss the bus, I'll do you.'

'We won't miss the bus. Stop panicking . . .'

I wouldn't have minded missing it.

' . . . anyway we might not have football today. It's very frosty.'

'Course we will. You aren't half soft, you.'

It was all right for Tony, he wasn't bad at football. Nobody shouted at him.

'It's all right for you. Nobody shouts at you.'

'Well, who shouts at you?'

'Gordon Barraclough.'

'You don't want to take any notice. Now hurry up.'

My mum came in with my kit.

'Yes, hurry up or you'll miss your bus for football.'

'We won't miss our rotten bus for rotten football.'

She gave me a clout on the back of my head. Tony laughed.

'And you can stop laughing, Tony Wainwright,' and she gave him a clout, as well. 'Now go on, both of you.'

We ran to school and got there in plenty of time. I knew we would.

Everybody was getting on the bus. We didn't

have to go to assembly when it was football. Gordon
Barraclough was on the top deck with his head out
of the window. He saw me coming.

'Hey, Gordon Banks . . .'

He always called me that, because he thinks
Gordon Banks was the best goalie ever. He reckons
he was called Gordon after Gordon Banks.

'Hey, Gordon Banks, how many goals are you
going to let in today?'

Tony nudged me.

'Don't take any notice.'

'Come on, Gordon Banks, how many goals am
I going to get against you . . .?'

Tony nudged me again.

'Ignore him.'

' . . . or am I going to be lumbered with you on
my side, eh?'

'He's only egging you on. Ignore him.'

Yes, I'll ignore him. That's the best thing. I'll
ignore him.

'If you're on my side, Gordon Banks, you'd
better not let any goals in, or I'll do you.'

Just ignore him, that's the best thing.

'Get lost, Barraclough, you rotten big-head.'

I couldn't ignore him. Tony was shaking his
head.

'I told you to ignore him.'

'I couldn't.'

Gordon still had his head out of the window.

'I'm coming down to get you.'

And he would've done, too, if it hadn't been for

Norbert. Just as Gordon was going back into the bus, Norbert wound the window up, so Gordon's head was stuck. It must've hurt him, well, it could have choked him.

'You're a maniac, Lightowler. You could have choked me.'

Norbert just laughed, and Gordon thumped him, right in the neck, and they started fighting. Tony and me ran up the stairs to watch. They were rolling in the aisle. Norbert got on top of Gordon and put his knees on his shoulders. Everybody was watching now, and shouting:

'Fight! Fight! Fight! Fight!'

The bell hadn't gone for assembly yet, and other lads from the playground came out to watch.

'Fight! Fight! Fight! Fight!'

Gordon pushed Norbert off him, and they rolled under a seat. Then they rolled out into the aisle again, only this time Gordon was on top. He thumped Norbert right in the middle of his chest. Hard. It hurt him, and Norbert got his mad up. I really wanted him to do Gordon.

'Go on, Norbert, do him.'

Just then, somebody clouted me on the back of my head, right where my mum had hit me that morning. I turned round to belt whoever it was.

'Who do you think you're thumping . . .? Oh, morning, Mr Melrose.'

He pushed me away, and went over to where Norbert and Gordon were still fighting. He grabbed them both by their jackets, and pulled them apart. He used to be in the Commandos, did Mr Melrose.

'Animals! You're a pair of animals! What are you?'

Neither of them said anything. He was still holding them by their jackets. He shook them.

'What are you? Lightowler?'

'A pair of animals.'

'Gordon?'

'A pair of animals, sir. It wasn't my fault, sir. He started it, sir. He wound up that window, sir, and I got my head stuck. He could have choked me, sir.'

Ooh, he was a right tell-tale was Barraclough.

'Why was your head out of the window in the first place?'

'I was just telling someone to hurry up, sir.'

He's a liar as well, but he knew he was all right with Melrose, because he's his favourite.

'And then Lightowler wound up the window, for no reason, sir. He could've choked me.'

Melrose didn't say anything. He just looked at Norbert. Norbert looked back at him with a sort of smile on his face. I don't think he meant to be smiling. It was because he was nervous.

'I'm sick of you, Lightowler, do you know that? I'm sick and tired of you. You're nothing but a trouble-maker.'

Norbert didn't say anything. His face just twitched a bit. It was dead quiet on the bus. The bell went for assembly and we could hear the other classes filing into school.

'A trouble-maker and a hooligan. You're a disgrace to the school, do you know that, Lightowler?'

'Yes, sir.'

'I can't wait for the day you leave, Lightowler.'

'Neither can I, sir.'

Melrose's hand moved so fast that it made *everybody* jump, not just Norbert. It caught him right on the side of his face. His face started going red straight away. Poor old Norbert. I didn't half feel sorry for him. It wasn't fair. He was helping me.

'Sir, can I . . .?'

'Shut up!'

Melrose didn't even turn round, and I didn't need telling twice. I shut up. Norbert's cheek was getting redder. He didn't rub it though, and it must've been stinging like anything. He's tough, is Norbert.

'You're a lout, Lightowler. What are you?'

'A lout, sir.'

'You haven't even got the decency to wear a school blazer.'

Norbert was wearing a grey jacket that was miles too big for him. He didn't have a school blazer.

'Aren't you proud of the school blazer?'

'I suppose so.'

'Why don't you wear one, then?'

Norbert rubbed his cheek for the first time.

'I haven't got a school blazer, sir.'

He looked as though he was going to cry.

'My mum can't afford one.'

Nobody moved. Melrose stared at Norbert. It seemed ages before he spoke.

73

'Get out of my sight, Lightowler. Wait in the classroom until we come back from football. And get your hands out of your pockets. The rest of you sit down and be quiet.'

Melrose went downstairs and told the driver to set off. Tony and me sat on the back seat. As we turned right into Horton Road, I could see Norbert climbing on the school wall, and walking along it like a tightrope walker. Melrose must've seen him as well. He really asks for trouble, does Norbert.

It's about a ten-minute bus ride to Bankfield Top. You go into town, through the City Centre and up Bankfield Road. When we went past the Town Hall, everybody leaned over to look at the Lord Mayor's Christmas tree.

'Back in your seats. You've all seen a Christmas tree before.'

Honestly, Melrose was such a spoil-sport. Course we'd all seen a Christmas tree before, but not as big as that. It must have been about thirty feet tall. There were tons of lights on it as well, *and* there were lights and decorations all round the square and in the shops. Tony said they were being switched on at half past four that afternoon. He'd read it in the paper. So had know-it-all Gordon Barraclough.

'Yeah, I read that, too. They're being switched on by a mystery celebrity.' Ooh, a mystery celebrity. Who was it going to be?

'A mystery celebrity? Do you know who it is?'

Gordon looked at me as though I'd asked him what two and two came to.

'Course I don't know who it is. Nobody knows who it is, otherwise it wouldn't be a mystery, would it?'

He was right there.

'Well, somebody must know who it is, because somebody must've asked him in the first place, mustn't they?'

Gordon gave me another of his looks.

'The Lord Mayor knows. Of course he knows, but if *you* want to find out, you have to go and watch the lights being switched on, don't you?'

Tony said he fancied doing that. I did as well, as long as I wasn't too late home for my mum.

'Yeah, it'll be good, but I'll have to be home by half past five, before my mum gets back from work.'

When we got to Bankfield Top, Melrose told us we had three minutes to get changed. Everybody ran to the temporary changing room. It's always been called the 'temporary changing room' ever since anyone can remember. We're supposed to be getting a proper place some time with hot and cold showers and things, but I don't reckon we ever will.

The temporary changing room's just a shed. It's got one shower that just runs cold water, but even that doesn't work properly. I started getting into my football togs. I tried to make the shorts as short as I could by turning the waistband over a few times, but they still came down to my knees. And the boots were great big heavy things. Not like Gordon Barraclough's Bobby Charlton ones. I could've worn mine on either foot and it wouldn't have made any difference.

Gordon was changed first, and started jumping up and down and doing all sorts of exercises. He even had a Manchester United tracksuit top on.

'Come on, Gordon Banks, get out on to the park.'

Get out on to the park! Just because his dad took him over to see Manchester United every other Saturday, he thought he knew it all.

The next hour and a half was the same as usual – rotten. Gordon and Curly Emmott picked sides – as usual. I went in goal – as usual. I nearly froze to death – as usual, and I let in fifteen goals – as usual. Most of the time all you could hear was Melrose shouting: 'Well done, Gordon', 'Go round him, Gordon', 'Good deception, Gordon', 'Give it to Gordon', 'Shoot, Gordon', 'Hard luck, Gordon'.

Ugh! Mind you, he did play well, did Gordon. He's the best player in our year. At least today I wasn't on his side so I didn't have him shouting at me all the time, just scoring against me! I thought Melrose was never going to blow the final whistle. When he did, we all trudged back to the temporary changing room. Even on the way back Gordon was jumping up and down and doing all sorts of funny exercises. He was only showing off to Melrose.

'That's it, Gordon, keep warm. Keep the muscles supple. Well played, lad! We'll see you get a trial for United yet.'

Back in the changing room, Gordon started going on about my football kit. He egged everybody else on.

'Listen, Barraclough, this strip belonged to my uncle, and he scored thousands of goals.'

Gordon just laughed.

'Your uncle? Your auntie more like. You look like a big girl.'

'Listen, Barraclough, you don't know who my uncle is.'

I was sick of Gordon Barraclough. I was sick of his bullying and his shouting, and his crawling round Melrose. And I was sick of him being a good footballer.

'My uncle is Bobby Charlton!'

That was the fib.

For a split second I think Gordon believed me, then he burst out laughing. So did everyone else. Even Tony laughed.

'Bobby Charlton – your uncle? You don't expect us to believe that, do you?'

'Believe what you like, it's the truth.'

Of course they didn't believe me. That's why the fib became a lie.

'Cross my heart and hope to die.'

I spat on my left hand. They all went quiet. Gordon put his face close to mine.

'You're a liar.'

I was.

'I'm not. Cross my heart and hope to die.'

I spat on my hand again. If I'd dropped dead

on the spot, I wouldn't have been surprised. Thank goodness Melrose came in, and made us hurry on to the bus.

Gordon and me didn't talk to each other much for the rest of the day. All afternoon I could see him looking at me. He was so sure I was a liar, but he just couldn't be certain.

Why had I been so daft as to tell such a stupid lie? Well, it was only a fib really, and at least it shut Gordon Barraclough up for an afternoon.

After school, Tony and me went into town to watch the lights being switched on. Norbert tagged along as well. He'd forgotten all about his trouble with Melrose that morning. He's like that, Norbert. Me, I would've been upset for days.

There was a crowd at the bottom of the Town Hall steps, and we managed to get right to the front. Gordon was there already. Norbert was ready for another fight, but we stopped him. When the Lord Mayor came out we all clapped. He had his chain on, and he made a speech about the Christmas appeal.

Then it came to switching on the lights.

'. . . and as you know, ladies and gentlemen, boys and girls, we always try to get someone special to switch on our Chamber of Commerce Christmas lights, and this year is no exception. Let's give a warm welcome to Mr Bobby Charlton . . .'

I couldn't believe it. I nearly fainted. I couldn't move for a few minutes. Everybody was asking for his autograph. When it was Gordon's turn, I saw him pointing at me. I could feel myself going red. Then, I saw him waving me over. Not Gordon, Bobby Charlton!

I went. Tony and Norbert followed. Gordon was grinning at me.

'You've had it now. You're for it now. I told him you said he's your uncle.'

I looked up at Bobby Charlton. He looked down at me. I could feel my face going even redder. Then suddenly, he winked at me and smiled.

'Hello, son. Aren't you going to say hello to your Uncle Bobby, then?'

I couldn't believe it. Neither could Tony or Norbert. Or Gordon.

'Er . . . hello . . . Uncle . . . er . . . Bobby.'

He ruffled my hair.

'How's your mam?'

'All right.'

He looked at Tony, Norbert and Gordon.

'Are these your mates?'

'These two are.'

I pointed out Tony and Norbert.

'Well, why don't you bring them in for a cup of tea?'

I didn't understand.

'In where?'

'Into the Lord Mayor's Parlour. For tea. Don't you want to come?'

'Yeah, that'd be lovely . . . Uncle Bobby.'

Uncle Bobby! I nearly believed it myself! And

I'll never forget the look on Gordon Barraclough's face as Bobby Charlton led Tony, Norbert and me into the Town Hall.

It was ever so posh in the Lord Mayor's Parlour. We had sandwiches without crusts, malt loaf and butterfly cakes. It was smashing. So was Bobby Charlton. I just couldn't believe we were there. Suddenly, Tony kept trying to tell me something, but I didn't want to listen to him. I wanted to listen to Bobby.

'Shurrup, I'm trying to listen to my Uncle Bobby.'

'But do you know what time it is? Six o'clock!'

'Six o'clock! Blimey! I've got to get going. My mum'll kill me.'

I said goodbye to Bobby Charlton.

'Tarah, Uncle Bobby. I've got to go now. Thanks . . .'

He looked at me and smiled.

'Tarah, son. See you again some time.'

When we got outside, Tony and Norbert said it was the best tea they'd ever had.

I ran home as fast as I could. My mum was already in, of course. I was hoping she wouldn't be too worried. Still, I knew everything would be all right once I'd told her I was late because I'd been having tea in the Lord Mayor's Parlour with Bobby Charlton.

'Where've you been? It's gone quarter past six. I've been worried sick.'

'It's all right, Mum. I've been having tea in the Lord Mayor's Parlour with Bobby Charlton . . .'

She gave me such a clout, I thought my head was going to fall off. My mum never believes me, even when I'm telling the truth!

# THE FIREWORK DISPLAY

Norbert was hanging from this branch, swinging his legs about, and trying to break it off. If the Park Ranger had come by and seen him, we'd all have been in trouble. Barry got hold of him round the ankles.

'Norbert, I'll do you if you don't come down.'

Norbert pulled his legs free, and moved along the branch towards the trunk. Barry chased after him and tried to pull him down again, but Norbert had managed to hoist himself up on to his tummy and was kicking Barry away.

'Gerroff!'

Barry punched him on the back of his leg.

'Well, get down then, or you'll get us all into trouble. Park Ranger said we could only take dead stuff.'

We were collecting for Bonfire Night. We were going to have the biggest bonfire in the district. It was already about twelve feet high, and it was only Saturday, so there were still two days to go. Three if you counted Monday itself.

We'd built the fire in Belgrave Street where the Council were knocking all the houses down. There was tons of waste ground, so there was no danger, and we'd found two old sofas and three armchairs to throw on the fire.

Norbert dropped from the branch and landed in some dog dirt. Barry and me laughed because he got it on his hands. I told him it served him right for trying to break the branch.

'You're stupid, Norbert. You know the Park Ranger said we could only take the dead branches.'

Norbert was wiping his hands on the grass.

'I thought it *was* dead.'

I threw a stick at him.

'How could it be dead if it's still growing? You're crackers you are, Norbert.'

The stick caught him on his shoulder. It was only a twig.

'Don't you throw lumps of wood at me! How would you like it if I threw lumps of wood at you?'

'Don't be so soft, Norbert, it was only a twig.'

Norbert picked up a big piece of wood, and chucked it at me. Luckily it missed by miles.

'You're mad, Norbert. You want to be put away. You're a blooming maniac.'

'You started it. You shouldn't have chucked that stick at me.'

He went back to wiping his hands on the grass.

'Was it heckers like a stick. It was a little twig, and it's no good wiping your hands on the grass, you'll never get rid of that pong.'

Suddenly, Norbert ran at me, waving his hands towards my face. I got away as fast as I could but he kept following.

'If you touch me with those smelly hands . . .
I'm warning you, Norbert!'

I picked up a brick, and threatened him with it.

'I'm telling you, Norbert . . .'

Just then I heard a voice from behind me.

'Hey!'

It was the Park Ranger.

'You lads, stop acting the goat. You!'

He meant me.

'What do you think you're doing with that?'

'Nowt . . .'

I dropped the brick on the ground.

' . . . Just playing.'

'That's how accidents are caused. Now come
on, lads, you've got your bonfire wood. On your way
now.'

I gave Norbert another look, just to let him
know that I'd meant it. He sniffed his hands.

'They don't smell, anyway.'

Barry and me got hold of the bottom branches
and started dragging the pile, and Barry told Norbert
to follow on behind.

'Norbert, you pick up anything that falls off,
and chuck it back on. Come on, Tony and Trevor'll
be wondering where we are.'

Trevor Hutchinson and Tony were back at Belgrave
Street guarding the fire. You had to do that to stop
other lads from nicking all the wood you'd collected,
or from setting fire to it. Not that it mattered, because
if they did we'd just nick somebody else's.

Mind you, I wouldn't have been bothered if our fire *had* gone up in smoke, because it didn't look like my mum was going to let me go on Monday anyway. And even if she did, she certainly wouldn't let me have my own fireworks. I'd been on at her all morning about it while she'd been ironing.

'But why, Mum? All the other lads at school are having their own fireworks, all of 'em. Why can't I?'

Why was my mum so difficult? Why did she have to be so old fashioned?

'Go on, Mum . . .'

She just carried on with her ironing.

'It washes well, this shirt.'

It was that navy blue one my Auntie Doreen had given me for my birthday.

'I'd like to get you another one. I must ask your Auntie Doreen where she bought it.'

'Why can't I have my own fireworks, Mum? Why?'

She just wouldn't listen.

'I'm old enough, aren't I?'

'Will you remind me there's a button missing off this shirt?'

'Aren't I?'

'I don't know what you do with the buttons off your shirts. You must eat them.'

She was driving me mad.

'Mum, are you going to let me have my own fireworks this year or not?'

She slammed the iron down.

'Oh, stop mithering will you? You're driving me mad.'

'Well are you or aren't you?'

She put the shirt on a pile, and pulled a sheet out of the washing basket.

'No! You'll come with me and your Auntie Doreen to the firework display at the Children's Hospital like you do every year, and if you don't stop mithering you won't even be doing that. Now give me a hand with this.'

She gave me one end of the sheet and we shook it.

'It's not fair. Tony's having his own fireworks this year, and he's three weeks younger than me, and Trevor Hutchinson's mum and dad have got him a five-pound box.'

We folded the sheet twice to make it easier to iron.

'Then they've got more money than sense, that's all I can say.'

'I'll pay you back out of my spending money, honest.'

My mum gave me one of her looks.

'Oh yes? Like you did with your bike? One week you kept that up. I'm still waiting for the rest.'

That wasn't fair, it was ages ago.

'That's not fair, that was ages ago.'

I'd promised my mum that if she bought me a new bike, a drop handle-bar, I'd pay her some back every week out of my spending money. But she didn't give me enough. How could I pay her back?

'You don't give me enough spending money. I don't have enough to pay you back.'

'Why don't you save some? You don't have to spend it all, do you?'

Bloomin' hummer! What's the point of calling it spending money, if you don't spend it?

'Mum, it's called *spending* money, isn't it? That means it's for *spending*. If it was meant for saving, people would call it *saving* money. You're only trying to get out of it.'

I was fed up. My mum was only trying to get out of getting me fireworks. She came over.

'Don't you be so cheeky, young man. Who do you think you're talking to?'

I thought for a minute she was going to clout me one.

'Well, even if I had some money saved, you wouldn't let me buy fireworks, would you?'

She didn't say anything.

'Well would you . . . Eh?'

She told me not to say 'Eh' because it's rude. I don't think it's rude. It's just a word.

'Well, would you, Mum? If I had my own money, I bet you wouldn't let me buy fireworks with it.'

'Stop going on about it, for goodness' sake. You're not having any fireworks and that's final.'

It blooming well wasn't final. I wanted my own fireworks this year and *that* was final. Blimey, kids much younger than me have their own fireworks. Why shouldn't I?

'Apart from being a waste of money, they're dangerous.'

Dangerous. Honest, she's so old fashioned, my mum.

'Mum, there are instructions on every firework. As long as you light the blue touchpaper and retire, they're not dangerous.'

She started going on about how many people were taken to hospital every Bonfire Night, and how many children were injured, and how many limbs were lost, and if all fireworks were under supervised care like they are at the Children's Hospital, then there'd be far less accidents. She went on and on. I'd heard it all before.

'But I'll be careful, Mum, I promise. Please let me have my own fireworks.'

That's when she clouted me.

'Are you going deaf or summat?'

'What?'

It was Norbert shouting from behind.

'Y'what, Norbert?'

He picked up a branch that had fallen off, and threw it back on the pile.

'I've asked you twice. How many fireworks have you got? I've got over two pounds' worth, so far.'

Trust Norbert to start on about fireworks again. He knew I hadn't got any, because we'd talked about it the day before. Barry didn't help either.

'I've got about two pounds' worth an' all, and my dad says he might get me some more.'

It wasn't fair. I bet if I had a dad, I'd have plenty of fireworks. It wasn't fair.

'My mum hasn't got mine yet.'

Norbert snorted. He's always doing that.

'Huh, I bet she won't get you none either. She didn't last year. She wouldn't even let you come.'

'That was last year, wasn't it? She's getting me some this year.'

If only she was.

'Well, she'd better be quick, they're selling out. They've hardly got any left at Robinson's.'

Robinson's is the toy shop we all go to. Paul Robinson used to be in our class, but about two years back he was badly injured by a car. He doesn't go to our school any more. We see him sometimes in the holidays, but he doesn't seem to remember us.

'All right, all right, don't panic, she's getting them this morning, isn't she? She ordered them ages ago.'

I don't think Norbert believed me.

'Oh . . . How many is she getting you?'

He isn't half a pest, Norbert. He goes on and on.

'I don't know. I'll see when I get home at dinner time.'

When we got back to Belgrave Street, Tony was throwing stones up in the air, seeing how high he could get them, and Trevor was riding round on my bike. There were stones and bits of glass all over the place.

'Hey, Trevor, gerroff! You'll puncture it.'

I took my bike off him, and leaned it against a rusty oil drum. Tony started to load the wood on to the fire.

'You've been ages. What took you so long? It's nearly dinner time.'

Barry pointed at Norbert, who was throwing a branch on to the bonfire.

'Ask him, monkey-features. We spent twenty minutes trying to drag him off a tree!'

The branch rolled back and nearly hit Norbert in the face. He had another go, but it fell down again. While he was doing this, Trevor crept up behind him. He grinned at Tony, Barry and me and took a jumping jack out of his pocket. He lit it, threw it down by Norbert's feet and ran over to us. Norbert threw the branch up again and this time it stayed on top, and just as he was turning round with a cheer, the jumping jack went off and scared the living daylights out of him. We all laughed like anything, but Norbert didn't think it was funny.

'Who did that? I bet it was you.'

He ran towards me.

Trevor pulled another jumping jack out of his pocket and waved it at Norbert. Norbert went for him, but Trevor was too quick. Norbert chased after him and got him in a stranglehold. Somehow, Trevor got out of it.

'Blooming heck, Norbert, your hands don't half pong. What've you been up to?'

Barry and me laughed our heads off. So did Tony when we told him. Trevor didn't. He ran off home to have a wash. It was dinner time by now, so we all decided to go home. Except Norbert. He never goes home on a Saturday. His mum just gives him some money for his dinner, and he stays out all day. I wouldn't like it if my mum did that. I went over to get my bike.

'See you, Norbert.'

Norbert had gone back to throwing branches on to the fire.

'Yeah, maybe see you later.'

'Yeah, maybe.'

I started walking with Tony and Barry, pushing my bike, but then I decided to cycle on ahead.

'I'd better get going. My mum'll be getting fish and chips.'

We always have fish and chips on a Saturday. I pedalled off just as Barry called after me.

'We'll come round after, have a look at your fireworks.'

Oh blimey! I braked.

'Oh, I've just remembered, I've got to go to my Auntie Doreen's with my mum. My Auntie Doreen is doing her hair. I've just remembered.'

That wasn't a complete lie. My mum was going to my Auntie Doreen's to have her hair done, but I didn't have to go with her. Ooh, why had I opened my big mouth earlier on? They're bound to find out my mum hadn't bought me any fireworks, especially when I don't turn up for the bonfire on Monday. Why was I the only one not to have my own fireworks?

I took a short cut through the park. You're not

supposed to cycle in the park but it was a lot quicker. Anyway, there was hardly anybody about and the Park Ranger was most likely having his dinner. As I was going past the swings and slides, I saw this ginger-headed lad sitting on the kiddies' roundabout. It was going round very slowly, and he had a brown paper bag on his lap. Nobody else was about.

'Hey, you're not supposed to ride bikes in the park.'

He had a blooming cheek, because children over twelve aren't allowed on the swings and round-abouts, and this lad looked about fourteen.

'Well, you're not supposed to ride on the round-abouts if you're over twelve.'

He pushed himself round a bit faster with his foot.

'I know.'

He was a funny-looking kid. I didn't know him, but I'd seen him around a few times. He was always on his own. I think he went to St Matthew's. He held up the paper bag.

'Do you want to see summat?'

I wondered what he'd got in it.

'No, I'm late for my dinner.'

He stopped the roundabout with his foot.

'I've got some fireworks in this bag.'

I got off my bike, and wheeled it over. He did have fireworks in his bag. Tons of them. Bangers, volcanoes, silver cascades, dive-bombers, jumping jacks, flowerpots – everything. Every firework you'd ever seen.

'Where did you get them?'

He looked at me.

'From a shop. Do you want to buy 'em?'

'I haven't got any money.'

That's when I thought of it. I must've been mad. I *was* mad.

'I'll swap my bike for them.'

He got off the roundabout.

'All right.'

He held out the paper bag and I took it, and he took my bike and cycled off.

I must've been off my head. I ran home clutching my paper bag. I went in the back way, and hid my fireworks in the outhouse, behind the dustbin. I didn't enjoy my fish and chips at all. I kept thinking about my stupid swap. How could I have been so daft? I still had to go to the firework display at the Children's Hospital with my mum.

After dinner, my mum asked me if I wanted to go with her to my Auntie Doreen's.

'No, Mum, I said I might meet Tony and Barry.'

What I thought I'd do was go back to the park and try to find that lad and ask him to swap back. I mean, it wasn't a fair swap, was it?

'All right then, love, but if you go anywhere on your bikes, be careful.'

I felt sick.

After my mum had gone, I went outside and got the bag of fireworks. I was looking at them in the front room when the doorbell rang. It couldn't have been my mum because she's got a key, but I put the fireworks in a cupboard just in case and went to answer it. Norbert, Barry and Tony were standing there. Barry looked at the others, then looked at me with a kind of smile.

'We saw your mum going up Deardon Street. She said you were at home.'

I didn't say anything. I just looked at them. Norbert sniffed.

'Yeah. So we thought we'd come and look at your fireworks.'

Norbert grinned his stupid grin. I could've hit him, but I didn't have to.

'You don't believe I've got any fireworks, do you?'

Tony and Barry didn't say anything. Norbert did.

'No!'

'I'll show you.'

I took them into the front room, and got the bag of fireworks out of the cupboard. I put them on the carpet, and we all kneeled round to have a look. They were really impressed, especially Norbert.

'Blooming hummer, did your mum buy you all these?'

'Course. I told you.'

Norbert kept picking one up after the other.

'But there's everything. Look at these dive-bombers. And look at the size of these rockets!'

Tony picked up an electric storm.

'These are great. They go on for ages.'

The three of them kept going through all the

fireworks. They just couldn't believe it. I felt really chuffed.

'I'd better put them away now.'

Norbert had taken out a sparkler.

'I've never seen sparklers as big as these. Let's light one.'

'No, I'm putting them away now.'

I wanted to get rid of Barry, Tony and Norbert, and see if I could find that lad in the park. I'd proved I'd got my own fireworks now. I'd make up some excuse for not coming to the bonfire on Monday, but none of them could say I hadn't been given my own fireworks. None of them could say that, now.

'Go on, light a sparkler, just one. They're quite safe.'

Well, what harm could it do? Just one sparkler. I got the matches from the mantelpiece, and Norbert held it while I lit it. When it got going, I took hold of it, and we all sat round in a circle and watched it sparkle away. Suddenly, Tony screamed.

I looked down and saw lots of bright colours. For a split second I couldn't move. I was paralysed.

Suddenly, fireworks were flying everywhere. Bangers went off, rockets were flying. Sparks were shooting up to the ceiling. It was terrifying. Norbert hid behind the sofa, and Tony stood by the door, while Barry and me tried to put out the fireworks by stamping on them. I could hear Tony shouting, asking if he should fetch my mum.

'Yeah, get her, get her, she's at my Auntie Doreen's, get her!'

I don't know how long it took us, it could have been half an hour, it could have been five minutes, but somehow Barry and me managed to put all the fireworks out. The room was full of smoke, and we were coughing and choking like anything, and I couldn't stop myself from shaking, and even though I was sweating, I felt really cold.

As the smoke cleared, I saw my mum standing by the door, her hair wringing wet, and all I remember thinking was that I wouldn't need an excuse for not going to the bonfire on Monday.

# THE MILE

What a rotten report. It was the worst report I'd ever had. I'd dreaded bringing it home for my mum to read. We were sitting at the kitchen table having our tea, but neither of us had touched anything. It was gammon and chips as well, with a pineapple ring. My favourite. We have gammon every Friday, because my Auntie Doreen works on the bacon counter at the Co-op, and she drops it in on her way home. I don't think she pays for it.

My mum was reading the report for the third time. She put it down on the table and stared at me. I didn't say anything. I just stared at my gammon and chips and pineapple ring. What could I say? My mum looked so disappointed. I really felt sorry for her. She was determined for me to do well at school, and get my O Levels, then get my A Levels, then go to university, then get my degree, and then get a good job with good prospects . . .

'I'm sorry, Mum . . .'

She picked up the report again, and started reading it for the fourth time.

'It's no good reading it again, Mum. It's not going to get any better.'

She slammed the report back on to the table.

'Don't you make cheeky remarks to me. I'm not in the mood for it!'

I hadn't meant it to be cheeky, but I suppose it came out like that.

'I wouldn't say anything if I was you, after reading this report!'

I shrugged my shoulders.

'There's nothing much I *can* say, is there?'

'You can tell me what went wrong. You told me you worked hard this term!'

I *had* told her I'd worked hard, but I hadn't.

'I did work hard, Mum.'

'Not according to this.'

She waved the report under my nose.

'You're supposed to be taking your O Levels next year. What do you think is going to happen then?'

I shrugged my shoulders again, and stared at my gammon and chips.

'I don't know.'

She put the report back on the table. I knew I hadn't done well in my exams because of everything that had happened this term, but I didn't think for one moment I'd come bottom in nearly everything. Even Norbert Lightowler had done better than me.

'You've come bottom in nearly everything. Listen to this.'

She picked up the report again.

'Maths – "Inattentive and lazy".'

I knew what it said.

'I know what it says, Mum.'

She leaned across the table, and put her face close to mine.

'I know what it says too, and I don't like it.'

She didn't have to keep reading it.

'Well, stop reading it then.'

My mum just gave me a look.

'English Language – "He is capricious and dilettante." What does that mean?'

I turned the pineapple ring over with my fork. Oh heck, was she going to go through every rotten subject?

'Come on – English Language – Mr Melrose says you're "capricious and dilettante". What does he mean?'

'I don't know!'

I hate Melrose. He's really sarcastic. He loves making a fool of you in front of other people. Well, he could stick his 'capricious and dilettante', and his rotten English Language, and his set books, and his horrible breath that nearly knocks you out when he stands over you.

'I don't know what he means.'

'Well, you should know. That's why you study English Language, to understand words like that. It means you mess about, and don't frame yourself.'

My mum kept reading every part of the report over and over again. It was all so pointless. It wasn't as if reading it over and over again was going to change anything. Mind you, I kept my mouth shut. I just sat there staring at my tea. I knew her when she was in this mood.

'What I can't understand is how come you did so well at Religious Instruction? You got seventy-five per cent.'

I couldn't understand that either.

'I like Bible stories, Mum.' She wasn't sure if I was cheeking her or not. I wasn't.

'Bible stories? It's all I can do to get you to come to St Cuthbert's one Sunday a month with me and your Auntie Doreen.'

That was true, but what my mum didn't know was that the only reason I went was because my Auntie Doreen slips me a few bob!

'And the only reason you go then is because your Auntie Doreen gives you pocket money.'

'Aw, that's not true, Mum.'

Blimey! My mum's got eyes everywhere.

She put the report back into the envelope. Hurray! The Spanish Inquisition was over. She took it out again. Trust me to speak too soon.

'I mean, you didn't even do well at sport, did you? Sport – "He is not a natural athlete." Didn't you do *anything* right this term?'

I couldn't help smiling to myself. No, I'm not a natural athlete, but I'd done one thing right this term. I'd shown Arthur Boocock that he couldn't push me around any more. That's why everything else had gone wrong. That's why I was 'lazy and inattentive' at Maths, and 'capricious and dilettante' at English Language. That's why this last term had been so miserable, because of Arthur blooming Boocock.

He'd only come into our class this year because

he'd been kept down. I didn't like him. He's a right bully, but because he's a bit older and is good at sport and running and things, everybody does what he says.

That's how Smokers' Corner started.

Arthur used to pinch his dad's cigarettes and bring them to school, and we'd smoke them at playtime in the shelter under the woodwork classroom. We called it Smokers' Corner.

It was daft really. I didn't even like smoking, it gives me headaches. But I joined in because all the others did. Well, I didn't want Arthur Boocock picking on me.

We took it in turns to stand guard. I liked it when it was my turn, it meant I didn't have to join in the smoking.

Smokers' Corner was at the top end of the playground, opposite the girls' school. That's how I first saw Janis. It was one playtime. I was on guard, when I saw these three girls staring at me from an upstairs window. They kept laughing and giggling. I didn't take much notice, which was a good job because I saw Melrose coming across the playground with Mr Rushton, the deputy head. I ran into the shelter and warned the lads.

'Arthur, Tony – Melrose and Rushton are coming!'

There was no way we could've been caught. We knew we could get everything away before Melrose or Rushton or anybody could reach us, even if they ran across the playground as fast as they could. We had a plan you see.

First, everybody put their cigarettes out, but not on the ground, with your fingers. It didn't half hurt if you didn't wet them enough. Then Arthur would open a little iron door that was in the wall next to the boiler house. Norbert had found it ages ago. It must've been there for years. Tony reckoned it was some sort of oven. Anyway, we'd empty our pockets and put all the cigarettes inside. All the time we'd be waving our hands about to get rid of the smoke, and Arthur would squirt the fresh-air spray he'd nicked from home. Then we'd shut the iron door and start playing football or tig.

Melrose never let on why he used to come storming across the playground. He never said anything, but we knew he was trying to catch the Smokers, and he knew we knew. All he'd do was give us all a look in turn, and march off. But on that day, the day those girls had been staring and giggling at me, he did say something.

'Watch it! All of you. I know what you're up to. Just watch it. Specially you, Boocock.'

We knew why Melrose picked on Arthur Boocock.

'You're running for the school on Saturday, Boocock. You'd better win or I'll want to know the reason why.'

Mr Melrose is in charge of athletics, and Arthur holds the school record for the mile. Melrose reckons

104

he could run for Yorkshire one day if he trains hard enough.

I didn't like this smoking lark, it made me cough, gave me a headache, and I was sure we'd get caught one day.

'Hey, Arthur, we'd better pack it in. Melrose is going to catch us one of these days.'

Arthur wasn't bothered.

'Ah you! You're just scared, you're yeller!'

Yeah, I was blooming scared.

'I'm not. I just think he's going to catch us.'

Then Arthur did something that really shook me. He took his right hand out of his blazer pocket. For a minute I thought he was going to hit me, but he didn't. He put it to his mouth instead, and blew out some smoke. He's mad. He'd kept his cigarette in his hand in his pocket all the time. He's mad. I didn't say anything though. I was scared he'd thump me.

On my way home after school that day, I saw those girls. They were standing outside Wilkinson's sweetshop, and when they saw me they started giggling again. They're daft, girls. They're always giggling. One of them, the tallest, was ever so pretty though. The other two were all right, but not as pretty as the tall girl. It was the other two that were doing most of the giggling.

'Go on, Glenda, ask him.'

'No, you ask him.'

'No, you're the one who wants to know. You ask him.'

'Shurrup!'

The tall one looked as embarrassed as I felt. I could see her name written on her schoolbag: Janis Webster.

The other two were still laughing, and telling each other to ask me something. I could feel myself going red. I didn't like being stared at.

'Do you two want a photograph or summat?'

They giggled even more.

'No, thank you, we don't collect photos of monkeys, do we, Glenda?'

The one called Glenda stopped laughing and gave the other one a real dirty look.

'Don't be so rude, Christine.'

Then this Christine started teasing her friend Glenda.

'Ooh, just because you like him, Glenda Bradshaw, just because you fancy him.'

I started walking away. Blimey! If any of the lads came by and heard this going on, I'd never hear the end of it. The one called Christine started shouting after me.

'Hey, my friend Glenda thinks you're ever so nice. She wants to know if you want to go out with her.'

Blimey! Why did she have to shout so the whole street could hear? I looked round to make sure nobody like Arthur Boocock or Norbert or Tony were about. I didn't want them to hear these stupid lasses saying things like that. I mean, we didn't go out with girls, because . . . well . . . we just didn't.

I saw the pretty one, Janis, pulling Christine's arm. She was telling her to stop embarrassing me. She was nice, that Janis, much nicer than the other two. I mean, if I was forced to go out with a girl, you know if somebody said, 'You will die tomorrow if you don't go out with a girl', then I wouldn't have minded going out with Janis Webster.

She was really nice.

I often looked out for her after that, but when I saw her, she was always with the other two. The one time I did see her on her own, I was walking home with Tony and Norbert and I pretended I didn't know her, even though she smiled and said hello. Of course, I sometimes used to see her at playtime, when it was my turn to stand guard at Smokers' Corner. I liked being on guard twice as much now. As well as not having to smoke, it gave me a chance to see Janis. She was smashing. I couldn't get her out of my mind. I was always thinking about her, you know, having daydreams. I was forever 'rescuing' her.

One of my favourite rescues was where she was being bullied by about half a dozen lads, not hitting her or anything, just mucking about. And one of them was always Arthur Boocock. And I'd go up very quietly and say, 'Are these lads bothering you?' And before she had time to answer, a fight would start, and I'd take them all on. All six at once, and it would end up with them pleading for mercy. And then Janis would put her hand on my arm and ask me to let them off . . . and I would. That was my favourite rescue.

That's how the trouble with Arthur Boocock started.

I'd been on guard one playtime, and had gone into one of my 'rescues'. It was the swimming-bath rescue. Janis would be swimming in the deep end, and she'd get into trouble, and I'd dive in and rescue her. I'd bring her to the side, put a towel round her, and then walk off without saying a word. Bit daft really, because I can't swim. Not a stroke. Mind you, I don't suppose I could beat up six lads on my own either, especially if one of them was Arthur Boocock. Anyway, I was just pulling Janis out of the deep end when I heard Melrose shouting his head off.

'Straight to the Headmaster's study. Go on, all three of you!'

I looked round, and I couldn't believe it. Melrose was inside Smokers' Corner. He'd caught Arthur, Tony and Norbert. He was giving Arthur a right crack over the head. How had he caught them? I'd been there all the time ... standing guard ... thinking about Janis ... I just hadn't seen him coming ... oh heck ...

'I warned you, Boocock, all of you. Go and report to the Headmaster!'

As he was going past me, Arthur showed me his fist. I knew what that meant.

They all got the cane for smoking, and Melrose had it in for Arthur even though he was still doing well at his running. The more Melrose picked on Arthur, the worse it was for me, because Arthur kept beating me up.

That was the first thing he'd done after he'd got the cane – beaten me up. He reckoned I'd not warned them about Melrose on purpose.

'How come you didn't see him? He's blooming big enough.'

'I just didn't.'

I couldn't tell him that I'd been daydreaming about Janis Webster.

'He must've crept up behind me.'

Arthur hit me, right on my ear.

'How could he go behind you? You had your back to the wall. You did it on purpose, you yeller-belly!'

And he hit me again, on the same ear.

After that, Arthur hit me every time he saw me. Sometimes he'd hit me in the stomach, sometimes on the back of my neck. Sometimes he'd raise his fist and I'd think he was going to hit me, and he'd just walk away, laughing. Then he started taking my spending money. He'd say, 'Oh, you don't want that, do you?' and I'd say, 'No, you have it, Arthur.'

I was really scared of him. He made my life a misery. I dreaded going to school, and when I could, I'd stay at home by pretending to be poorly. I used to stick my fingers down my throat and make myself sick.

I suppose that's when I started to get behind with my school work, but anything was better than being bullied by that rotten Arthur Boocock. And when I did go to school, I'd try to stay in the class-room at playtime, or I'd make sure I was near the teacher who was on playground duty. Of course, Arthur thought it was all very funny, and he'd see if he could hit me without the teacher seeing, which he could.

Dinner time was the worst because we had an hour free before the bell went for school dinners, and no one was allowed to stay inside. It was a school rule. That was an hour for Arthur to bully me. I used to try and hide but he'd always find me.

By now it didn't seem to have anything to do with him being caught smoking and getting the cane. He just seemed to enjoy hitting me and tormenting me. So I stopped going to school dinners. I used to get some chips, or a Cornish pasty, and wander around. Sometimes I'd go into town and look at the shops, or else I'd go in the park and muck about. Anything to get away from school and Arthur Boocock.

That's how I met Archie.

There's a running track in the park, a proper one with white lines and everything, and one day I spent all dinner time watching this old bloke running round. That was Archie. I went back the next day and he was there again, running round and round, and I got talking to him.

'Hey, mister, how fast can you run a mile?'

I was holding a bag of crisps, and he came over and took one. He grinned at me.

'How fast can *you* run a mile?'

I'd never tried running a mile.

'I don't know, I've never tried.'

He grinned again.

'Well, now's your chance. Come on, get your jacket off.'

He was ever so fast and I found it hard to keep up with him, but he told me I'd done well. I used to run with Archie every day after that. He gave me an old tracksuit top, and I'd change into my shorts and trainers and chase round the track after him. Archie said I was getting better and better.

'You'll be running for Yorkshire one of these days.'

I laughed and told him to stop teasing me. He gave me half an orange. He always did after running.

'Listen, lad, I'm serious. It's all a matter of training. Anybody can be good if they train hard enough. See you tomorrow.'

That's when I got the idea.

I decided to go in for the mile in the school sports at the end of term. You had to be picked for everything else, but anybody could enter the mile.

There were three weeks to the end of term, and in that three weeks I ran everywhere. I ran to school. I ran with Archie every dinner time. I went back and ran on the track after school. Then I'd run home. If my mum wanted anything from the shops, I'd run there. I'd get up really early in the mornings and run before breakfast. I was always running. I got into tons of trouble at school for not doing my homework properly, but I didn't care. All I thought about was the mile.

I had daydreams about it. Always me and Arthur, neck and neck, and Janis would be cheering me on. Then I dropped Janis from my daydreams. She wasn't important any more. It was just me and Arthur against each other. I was sick of him and his bullying.

Arthur did well at sports day. He won the high jump and the long jump. He was picked for the half mile and the four-forty, and won them both. Then there was the announcement for the mile.

'Will all those competitors who wish to enter the open mile please report to Mr Melrose at the start.'

I hadn't let on to anybody that I was going to enter, so everybody was very surprised to see me when I went over in my shorts and trainers – especially Melrose. Arthur thought it was hilarious.

'Well, look who it is. Do you want me to give you half a mile start?'

I ignored him, and waited for Melrose to start the race. I surprised a lot of people that day, but nobody more than Arthur. I stuck to him like a shadow. When he went forward, I went forward. If he dropped back, I dropped back. This went on for about half the race. He kept giving me funny looks. He couldn't understand what was happening.

'You won't keep this up. Just watch.'

And he suddenly spurted forward. I followed him, and when he looked round to see how far ahead he was, he got a shock when he saw he wasn't.

It was just like my daydreams. Arthur and me, neck and neck, the whole school cheering us on, both of us heading for the last bend. I looked at Arthur and saw the tears rolling down his cheeks. He was crying his eyes out. I knew at that moment I'd beaten him. I don't mean I knew I'd won the race. I wasn't bothered about that. I knew I'd beaten *him*, Arthur. I knew he'd never hit me again.

That's when I walked off the track. I didn't see any point in running the last two hundred yards. I suppose that's because I'm not a natural athlete . . .

'Sport – "He is not a natural athlete." Didn't you do *anything* right this term?'

Blimey! My mum was still reading my report. I started to eat my gammon and chips. They'd gone cold.

# THE FOURSOME

I looked at myself in the long mirror. Fantastic! Yes, those new trousers were definitely it. Sixteen-inch bottoms and no turn-ups – boy, I couldn't wait for Barry to see them. Mind you, I'd wanted fifteen-inch bottoms, but there was no chance of that with my mum. She thinks anybody who wears drainpipes will end up in approved school.

'A teddy boy – that's how you'll end up. It'll be velvet collars and long jackets next. Then those thick crêpe shoes, I know.'

Blimey! Just because one of my mates had ended up in a teddy boy gang. I had teddy boys morning, noon and night. Just watch, any second now and she'll come out with her borstal line.

'You'll end up in borstal, that's what'll happen to you.'

Told you.

'Don't be daft, Mum!'

'Don't you talk to me like that. You're still not too old for a quick slap.'

So, that's how it was. Sixteen-inch bottoms was the best I could do. But I knew there'd be more trouble when I brought the trousers home, and there were no turn-ups. I was right.

'But they're not finished. Where are the turn-ups?'

'There are no turn-ups.'

'I can see that. Where are they?'

'Turn-ups are out. They're old fashioned. This is the new style.'

Seeing as I'd bought the trousers out of my own money that I'd saved from my newspaper round, there wasn't much my mum could do about it.

'Well, you big jessie.'

And that was all she said.

But still, they did look great. I tilted the mirror forward a bit more, so that I could see how the tapered bottoms rested on my shoes. Terrific!

I was beginning to feel a bit nervous. This was the first date I'd ever had. The first proper date. Well, actually, it was a foursome. Barry had arranged it. He'd been on a couple of dates before, so he was quite experienced. We'd met these two girls at our school intersocial, we had one every Christmas with the girls' school near by. It's the big event of the year, because it's the only time our school has anything to do with the girls' school. In fact, for a week before the intersocial, we had dancing lessons in the main hall every lunchtime. You should have seen us. All the boys trying to learn to dance – together! I partnered Barry. We took it in turns to be the girl. By the end of the week, I could do a slow waltz!

At the intersocial, Barry had danced most of the time with this girl called Kath and he asked her out for the following Saturday, but she'd already arranged to go out with her best friend Valerie, and that's how the foursome was arranged: Barry and Kath, and me and Valerie. I'd had one dance with Valerie, so we sort of knew each other. She wasn't bad looking at all. In fact, going by standards in the girls' school, she was quite pretty.

Now which tie should I put on – my Slim Jim, or that fancy Paisley one that I got from my Auntie Doreen for digging her garden? I think the Slim Jim – yeah, Jim's the him, I'll look great in that. As long as my mum doesn't see. To her, Slim Jim ties and bicycle chains go together. Now how do you do a Windsor? Across, under, across, under again – oh, I haven't enough tie left over, now. Across, under, under again, back across, and you get a big fat mess. Right, once more, and if I don't get it right this time I'm not going. Across, under, under again, back across and third time lucky – a perfect Windsor knot, and just enough left over to tuck in my trousers.

I liked looking in this mirror. My spots didn't look too bad. Who are you kidding? You look like the 'before' bloke in that acne advert. Oh, how is it you always look your worst when it matters the most? Ah well, Valerie knows what I look like.

My collar didn't look too bad, considering I'd had to use matchsticks instead of whale-bones. I'd been thinking about this date all week. In fact, I couldn't think about anything else. Now I kept wondering whether to go or not. Well, of course I wanted to go, I wouldn't miss it for anything. Mind you, I hadn't let on to Barry that I was keen. I made out I was doing him a favour when he asked me.

'Look, Kath'll only go out with me if you'll take her friend. Go on, take her out, she's not bad looking y'know.'

I didn't have to think twice. I liked her.

'I don't know, Barry, I'm not right keen.'

'Oh, well, if you're not I suppose I'll have to ask Norbert Lightowler.'

'All right, Barry, but only because you are my best friend.'

'You're a good lad. I'll fix it up then.'

And he arranged to meet them outside the Odeon at quarter to eight.

Now for a touch of after-shave – not that I had anything to shave. I'd only used this stuff once before when I went to our Maureen's birthday party. Maureen's my cousin. That was a waste of time and all. The oldest girl there was only thirteen and that was our Maureen. What a lousy party. A load of giggling schoolgirls all asking me what kind of perfume I used. At least Valerie would appreciate the exhilarating freshness, the new experience in after-shave. I slapped some on my face. Ooh, smashing stuff this. It certainly was a new experience. I looked in the mirror. What it did was make my pimples look healthy. After a few seconds, the stinging stopped, and I must say, it *was* quite an exhilarating freshness.

I just had my hair to do now, and I'd be ready. Barry had a great hairstyle, a Tony Curtis. They were all the rage. He could only have it like that at weekends though, because at our school they're banned by the Headmaster. Barry says that he's jealous because he's bald. He might be right, I don't know. It just seems to me that whenever you try to look smart or be a bit different, you're suddenly branded as a hooligan and everybody's telling you you're halfway to borstal. It seems daft to me.

I couldn't have a Tony Curtis anyway, my hair just won't go that way. Barry says it's because I've got a double crown. So I do it with a parting and a big quiff at the front. The trouble is, I keep getting a tuft of hair sticking up at the back. It's my double crown I suppose. Barry never has that trouble. He's invented a special hair lotion – sugar and water mixed. It makes his hair as stiff as a board.

Hey what time was it? I hadn't been watching the time at all. I went to the top of the stairs.

'Hey, Mum, what time is it?'

'Eh?'

'I said what time is it?'

'Come down here.'

I don't know! My old mum! She's getting deaf in her old age.

'What's wrong, are you going deaf?'

'Y'what!'

I knew why she couldn't hear. She was running the tap in the kitchen. It's always the same when you're in a hurry.

'Look, Mum, all I wanted was the time.'

'Oh . . . ten to seven.'

I could see that for myself now, from the kitchen

clock. What a fantastic clock as well. It's one of those like a frying pan that you hang on the wall, and it has a smiling face painted on it. It had hung above the fireplace for as long as I could remember. My mum was very fond of it. She says it's never been a minute out since she's had it.

'Yes, ten to seven. It's dead right, that is. It's never been out since I've had it.'

Ten to seven. I'd better get a move on, I was supposed to be meeting Barry at seven o'clock down in town. We'd arranged to meet early.

'Tarah, Mum, I've got to go.'

I thought I'd go out without my mum saying anything, but that would've been too much to hope for.

'Hey, just a minute.'

Oh dear, here we go.

'Er, what, Mum?'

I tried to make it sound as if I had no idea what she wanted.

'Er, what do you want?'

'Where do you think you're going dressed like that?'

Oh, if she started an argument now, I'd never get away.

'Dressed like what, Mum?'

'Don't act the innocent with me, you know what I mean.'

'No, I don't.'

I could see that if I wasn't careful, I was going to be here for ages.

120

'Those tight trousers and that bootlace round your neck.'

She meant my Slim Jim.

'That's my Slim Jim.'

'And why don't you get your hair cut?'

I knew it was best not to argue, but I couldn't stop myself.

'What's wrong with my hair?'

My mum was really getting into her stride now.

'Why don't you use your tie for a hair-ribbon? And what's that smell, have you been at my perfume?'

'Don't be daft. It's my after-shave.'

'Oh, I see. Well, when you're in court with all your other teddy boy friends, don't you come running to me.'

'Oh, I'm off.'

And I went before she could say anything, though I could hear her shouting after me.

'And be careful!'

I don't know, me and my mum, we always seemed to be squabbling these days.

I didn't know whether to wait for a bus, or start walking to the next stop – it's a penny cheaper from there. I decided to walk and, of course, when I was right between the stops, a bus went past, so I ended up walking all the way. I was about a quarter of an hour late when I got to town, and Barry was already waiting for me.

'Hey, where've you been? I've been standing here freezing for quarter of an hour.'

'Sorry, Barry. I had a bit of a doo-dah with my mum.'

I could see Barry looking at my new trousers.

'Hey, are those your new pants?'

'Yes. What do you think?'

'They're great, kiddo, great!'

Barry had some new trousers on as well. A sort of bronzy colour.

'Yours are new an' all, aren't they?'

'Yeah, first time on. What are your bottoms?'

'Sixteens. What's yours?'

'Fifteens.'

Huh, Barry was lucky! His mum and dad let him wear just what he wanted.

'I wanted fifteens, but Mum wouldn't let me.'

As we weren't meeting Kath and Valerie outside the Odeon till quarter to eight, we had about twenty minutes to kill, so we went for a coffee. It was a new coffee bar that had only been open a couple of weeks. I'd never been before, but Barry had.

It was quite full inside, so Barry told me to look for somewhere to sit while he got the coffees.

'What do you want?'

'Tea, please.'

I wasn't too fond of coffee.

'You can't have tea in a coffee bar.'

'Course you can.'

'Oh, all right.'

While I was looking around, I saw a couple of people I knew. One of them was a teacher at our school. Funny, you don't expect to find people like that in a coffee bar. I saw two seats on their own near the window. I signalled to Barry and he followed me over.

'Here's your tea.'

'Ta.'

It was the funniest cuppa I'd ever had.

'Hey, Barry, I asked for tea.'

'It is tea. It's lemon tea. That's what you drink in coffee bars.'

'Oh.'

We didn't take long over our drinks because it wasn't far off quarter to eight, and we were just going when Barry said he wanted to tell me something.

'Yeah, what is it?'

'Well, just one thing. Err . . . when we get inside the pictures . . . err . . . if I start kissing Kath, you'll have to start kissing Valerie.'

'Y'what?'

I thought he was kidding at first, but he looked very serious.

'Y'see it's like that on a foursome.'

'Well, what if she doesn't want to kiss me?'

'Of course she will. You just follow me, you'll be all right. Here, have a peppermint.'

I must say, Barry was very confident. I didn't like the sound of it at all. I mean, I hardly knew her. How would I know if she wanted to kiss me? Oh, heck.

The Town Hall clock was just striking quarter to as we got to the Odeon. I could see Kath waiting for us but I couldn't see Valerie.

'Hey, Barry. Mine hasn't turned up.'

'Of course she has. She's probably inside getting some sweets.'

Kath saw us coming and came to meet us. I left all the talking to Barry.

'Hi, Kath, where's Valerie? Inside?'

She gave me a funny sort of look, and I knew what was coming. She'd probably gone and got chickenpox, mumps, or something like that.

'She isn't here. It's her dad.'

Her dad? What's her dad got to do with it? This was too much for me.

'What's her dad got to do with it?'

'He won't let her come. He says she can't go out with *you* – because you're a teddy boy!'

# THE EXAM

I looked at the exam paper. 'Northern Universities Joint Matriculation Board. History: Advanced Level.' Bit like seeing an old friend, no, an old enemy, that'd be more like it. We'd been doing practice exam papers like these for eighteen months now, and I'd grown to hate them. Well, this time it was the real thing. The climax of seven years at grammar school. I had to finish this paper. It wasn't just a rehearsal for the big day. No excuses like:

'Well, sir, I thought this time I'd just concentrate on the Napoleonic Wars, sir,' which translated meant, 'What a lousy paper! There was only one question I could do, the Napoleonic Wars.'

I couldn't bring myself to read this real paper at first. I kept thinking about my mum. I kept thinking about what had happened the other day. Why should a little thing like that have made such a difference? But it did. Nothing seemed important any more.

I looked round the hall. The school had hired it specially, because there has to be a three-foot space between each desk. The school hall would have been big enough for a two-foot space, but not for three. This hall belonged to the Territorial Army, and every now and again we could hear what sounded like five

125

hundred men marching by. Usually, we sit our exams at the Mechanics Institute, but this year somebody had forgotten to book it up, and the Amateur Operatic and Dramatic Society had beaten us to it and were rehearsing *The Dancing Years* there.

Before the exam started, Mr Holdsworth, the invigilator (he's the woodwork master at our school, and he taught me about five years ago, but I don't think he knows me from Adam now), anyway, he told us all not to take any notice of the noises outside. He didn't tell us that half the army would be on the move. I think I'd have preferred *The Dancing Years*!

As I was looking round, I could see all the other lads engrossed in their work. I could see Norbert Lightowler picking his nose. I had to laugh to myself. For seven years I'd watched Norbert Lightowler pick his nose. He can't help it. He doesn't know he's doing it. It must help him concentrate, I suppose. I mean, some people bite their nails when they're concentrating, and some people chew gum. Well, Norbert, he picks his nose.

I remember when we first came to the school, one of the teachers shouted out, 'Wrong way home, Lightowler.' We didn't know what he meant, of course, but everybody soon realised, except Norbert. After a while nobody noticed any more. We just left him alone.

It's funny really. Out of our crowd there's only Norbert and me still here. Barry left even before O Levels. He should never have gone to a grammar school. His mum and dad weren't at all pleased when he passed his scholarship. Too much expense they said. Actually, they didn't believe him at first. They said it wasn't possible. You couldn't blame them, either. Nobody thought Barry'd get to grammar school. Anyway, he left before he was sixteen. He's working in a butcher's shop now. Doing all right, too. I saw him the other day. He's assistant manager. Reckons he'll be manager when they open a new branch.

'I'm telling you, kid, when I'm managing this branch I'll be knocking up forty or fifty quid a week basic, and then there's my commission.'

I told him about prospects and future and all that. You know, like my mum tells me. But I didn't convince him. I didn't even convince myself.

'What are you talking about, future and prospects? Nineteen and managing my own shop nearly. That isn't a bad future, is it?'

I had to agree with him.

'I mean what do you do at weekends? How much money do you have to spend?'

I told him about my grocery round.

'I do my grocery round at Atkinson's. I get a couple of quid for that.'

'A couple of quid!'

'Yes, and my mum gives me another couple.'

'Not much, is it – four quid?'

'It lasts me!'

Does it heckers like last me. By Thursday, I always have to cadge off my mum.

'Well, all I can say is that leaving school was the best thing that's happened to me.'

As I was reading the exam paper, I started thinking that leaving school would've been the best thing to happen to me, too. It's ridiculous, I'm nearly eighteen and still at school. Barry's right. It's OK to talk about the future and prospects, but what about the present? Life's just passing me by.

Norbert was still picking his nose, only twice as much now, because he was writing more quickly. Oh, I'd better get on with the exam, I suppose. I started reading through, and ticked the questions I thought I could answer.

But honest! I reckon one of the biggest mistakes of my life was passing the scholarship to grammar school. I would've been all right if I hadn't gone to the grammar. I'd've left school at fifteen, got a regular job, and by now, I'd have some cash in my pocket. No, I don't mean that, but it does all seem a waste of time. Same with these A Levels. I'm not bothered about going to university. But my mum talks to me about prospects and future, and how she's going to work hard so I can go on studying. I can't turn round and tell her she's wasting her time, because, well, she's my mum. She's always right. At least, I used to think so, anyway, until the other day.

I mean, if it hadn't been for my mum, I would've jacked this lot in ages ago, like Barry and Tony. Mind you, with Tony it was a bit different. He wanted to stay at school.

Tony was always cleverer than me. Even at

primary school, he was always top of the class. The brain of the school we used to call him. We were in the same class at the grammar, and he was always in the top three. He was good at sport as well. Not like Arthur Holdroyd who's good at exams, and that's all. It sounds rotten, but I can't think of anybody who likes Arthur Holdroyd, not even the teachers. He's very clever, but slimy with it. I can't even imagine his own family liking him. Or like Dennis Gower. Now he used to be brilliant at sports – cricket, soccer, running, jumping – absolutely terrific, but he was as thick as the custard we have for school dinner. Mind you, if I had the choice, I mean to be like Arthur Holdroyd or Dennis Gower, I'd rather be like Dennis any day.

Now Tony had the best of both worlds. He got seven O Levels in one go, but then he had to leave. His mum and dad couldn't afford to keep him on. I don't think they realised how clever he was. Anyway, there's all his brothers and sisters, three brothers and two sisters, all younger than him, so you can see why he had to leave school to bring a bit more money in. I remember, he left in July and we both went camping for a week in the Lake District. Then he started work the day after we got back. He went as an apprentice engineer to Bulmer's.

Bulmer's is a big engineering works near us. His dad works there as well, and his mum goes in part-time, cleaning. Quite a family affair really. I sometimes kid him on about it.

'Get a few more of your family at Bulmer's, and you might as well move in.'

'No need for that. There's talk of them transferring the works to our house.'

That's not far off the truth either. It's a right tip is their house. Thousands of kids running round with no clothes on, or perhaps just a vest or an odd sock. His mum shouting at everybody, mostly at his dad, who never takes any notice because he's too busy working out which horses are going to lose that day. Oh, it's a right blooming hole is that house. And Tony used to sit at the table amongst the bread and jam and condensed milk doing his homework. I used to wonder how he could do any work at all with that racket going on.

'How the hell you can do your homework in that blooming row, I don't know.'

'Oh, it doesn't bother me. I just get on with it.'

And every exam he'd come out in the top three. It's a shame he had to leave school, he'd have done really well. Mind you, he's doing all right now. He'll be finishing his apprenticeship soon, and then, like Barry, he'll be knocking up quite a good wage. He's engaged and all, but she's decided she wants to wait until he finishes his apprenticeship before they get married, and he's agreed.

'You see, once I'm qualified we'll be able to save about ten or fifteen pounds a week for a deposit on a house.'

'Yes, but don't you think you're a bit young to get married?'

'I'll be going on for twenty. That's not young these days.'

You see, it seems daft. I'm still at school, and there's Tony arranging to get married. I've agreed to be his best man.

Oh, dear! Hey, come on, I'd better get started on this paper. Question number one: 'Walpole was the first Prime Minister of this country. Comment!'

What a daft question! 'Walpole was the first Prime Minister of this country. Comment!' So what? Walpole *was* the first Prime Minister of this country! *Walpole* was the first Prime Minister of this country!

Good God! Norbert's actually using a handkerchief. I don't think I've ever seen that before.

Norbert Lightowler is actually using a handkerchief! Comment! Poor old Norbert. You know, his dad makes him do the pools every week, and if he doesn't win, he gets thumped. That's what makes me feel guilty. I'm really the only one who's got it easy. My mum's perfect.

At least, that's what I used to think. I mean, what she did the other day shouldn't make such a difference. It wasn't stealing, it was harmless really. It was nothing.

We'd been out shopping at Atkinson's, where I do my grocery round, and when we got outside, my mum looked all pleased with herself.

'Hey, Mr Atkinson gave me a pound too much in the change.'

And that was it. She just put it in her purse and

forgot about it. And all I could think was, if it had been me, she'd have sent me straight back. But she just dismissed it. I never said anything to her, but everything seemed different from then on.

Suddenly, Mr Holdsworth shouted something out.

'All right, boys, you can stop writing now.'

I didn't know what the hell was going on at first, and then it dawned on me – the exam was over! I looked at my watch. Blimey, I'd been daydreaming for three hours. Three hours! Mr Holdsworth came round, collecting up the papers. He nearly passed out when he saw mine.

'Well, I'll go to Sheffield!' And he just stood there looking at me.

I couldn't think of anything to say, so I mumbled something about it being a difficult paper, and that I'd been unlucky with the questions.

When my mum asked me that night how I'd got on, I just told her I didn't finish the paper.

That didn't bother her.

'Oh, you'll pass with flying colours, I know you will. You'll be at the university soon . . .'

I've been working at Bulmer's for three months now. My mum was very upset at first when I didn't get into university, but she was all right after a while. It's not too bad at Bulmer's; it's a change from school, anyway. I don't see much of Tony, though. You see, I'm in the office. I'm a white-collar worker. My mum's very proud of me.

# The Swap

*In memory of my dear parents*
*Edith and Freddie Layton*
*and*
*to the City of Bradford*
*that made them so welcome*

# Contents

# THE TREEHOUSE

The first time I ever saw Mr Bleasdale take the register, I couldn't take my eyes off him. That was because he didn't take his eye off me. Yes – his eye. His left eye.

It was on my first day at Grammar School and I'd never seen anything like it. I'd been put in 1B and Mr Bleasdale was our form master. He also taught Latin and he could look down with one eye to read, write or take the register and at the same time could keep his other eye on the class. And it never blinked. It just stared at us making sure nobody misbehaved while he was calling out our names.

'Barraclough . . .'

'Yes, sir!'

'Boocock . . .'

'Yes, sir.'

'Cawthra . . .'

'Sir . . .'

Everybody answered when they heard their name called out. Nobody dared to look round to see what the lad shouting out looked like.

We were all nervous anyway, it being our first day at the Grammar, but none of us had seen anything like this. We just sat staring straight ahead at Mr Bleasdale's eye.

'Edwards . . .'

'Yes, sir.'

'Emmott . . .'

'Sir . . .'

'Gower . . .'

'Sir . . .'

How did he do it? How could anyone look down with one eye and stare straight ahead with the other? It was impossible. I tried it. I looked down at my desk with my right eye, just like Mr Bleasdale, and tried to keep my left eye up. It was impossible.

But it wasn't. Mr Bleasdale could do it. Perhaps *all* Grammar School teachers could do it . . . Oh dear . . .

'Holdsworth . . .'

'Yes, sir.'

'Hopkinson . . .'

'Yes, sir . . .'

'Hopwood . . .'

'Sir.'

Oh dear. At High Moor Primary we used to get away with murder when the teacher wasn't looking. Especially in Miss Dixon's classes. Here we wouldn't be able to do anything – except work. Certainly with Mr Bleasdale 'cos he'd always be looking.

'Lightowler . . .'

'Yes, sir.'

Even Norbert Lightowler was behaving himself. And he was dressed smartly for once. Well, for him. He hadn't got a brand new blazer like everyone else – his mum couldn't afford it, but she'd managed to get hold of a second-hand one from somewhere. It was miles too big for him but Norbert didn't seem to mind. Norbert was the only other lad I knew in 1B. We'd been at High Moor together and everybody was surprised when he'd got into Grammar School – especially Norbert. His mum wasn't very pleased because it meant him staying on at school till he was sixteen. She'd have rather he left as soon as possible and get a job and bring some money in like the rest of his brothers and sisters. That's what my mum said anyway.

At Primary School I'd always found Norbert a bit of a nuisance, always telling me I was his best friend, forever hanging round trying to get into our gang. But today I was glad he was sitting next to me. At least I *knew* somebody, had somebody to talk to. Tony, my best friend, had come to the Grammar as well but he'd been put into 1 Alpha. I couldn't wait to ask him if *his* teacher could watch the class with one eye while he looked down with the other.

'McDougall . . .'

'Sir.'

'Mudd . . .'

'Sir.'

Mudd. Fancy having a name like that, Mudd. Everybody giggled and a few including me and Norbert looked round to see what he looked like. He was a big lad, probably the biggest in the class. I wouldn't be laughing at his name again.

'Thank you, gentlemen, you've got this next five years to get to know each other so I'd be grateful if I could have your undivided attention for the next few minutes.'

I turned back to the front as Mr Bleasdale carried on calling out our names, his right eye on the register, his left eye on us.

'Nunn . . .'

'Yes, sir.'

That was the *first* time I'd seen Mr Bleasdale. It was the last time our class would be so well behaved for him.

By the end of morning break on that first day I'd found out the truth. Or at least Norbert had. I was in the playground telling Tony about Mr Bleasdale's trick when Norbert came up to me. He'd already torn one of his blazer pockets.

'Hey, you'll never guess what I've just found out.'

'Shurrup a minute will you, I'm just telling Tony about Mr Bleasdale. Honest, Tony, he can look down and write with his one eye, and watch the class with his other. Both at the same time.'

I could tell Tony didn't believe me, the way he was looking.

'Honestly, it's true. It's a fantastic trick, isn't it, Norbert?'

Nobert wiped his nose with his sleeve and nodded.

'Yeah . . . It'd be even better if he could see out of the eye he's watching with.'

I looked at Norbert. He wiped his nose again, with his other sleeve this time.

'Y'what?'

'It's a glass eye. It's not real. It's made of glass . . .'

I sat at my desk staring at the glass eye. I still found it hard to believe he couldn't see me, even now, nine months later. It looked so real – except that it never blinked.

Norbert had no doubts – he was mucking about as usual and Bleasdale looked up just in time to see him flicking a paper pellet at David Holdsworth.

'I saw that, Lightowler. I'm not blind, you know. Get on with your revision. You got exams in three days.'

'Yes, sir.'

Norbert shoved his head into his Latin textbook and sniggered at the lads around him. When Bleasdale looked down – with his one eye – Norbert made a funny face at him, putting his fingers to his ears and waggling them, and sticking his tongue out. He's not bothered about school work and exams, Norbert. *I* had to do well or I'd be in big trouble with my mum. If I didn't do well – *very* well – not only would I be in big trouble but I wouldn't be allowed to go on the school trip to London to see the Festival of Britain.

Mr Bleasdale and Mr Melrose were organising it. It was a day trip and it was going to cost fifteen pounds. I was dead lucky to have my name down because when I'd asked my mum if I could go, she'd said no. In fact she'd said no, no, no!

'No, no, no! Where do you think I'm going to get fifteen pounds from? You must be living in cloud-cuckoo-land, young man.'

'We can pay in instalments, Mr Bleasdale says so.'

She gave me one of her looks.

'Oh, does he? Well you can tell Mr Bleasdale that I'm still paying for your school uniform in instalments, and your satchel, and your bike . . .'

That's when she saw the tear in my blazer.

'Just come here a minute.'

Oh no, it was that stupid Norbert's fault when he'd been trying to get ahead of me in the dinner queue. He'd got hold my pocket and swung me round. That's how it had ripped. Stupid idiot.

'Look at your new blazer. What on earth have you been up to?'

143

I don't know why she keeps calling it my 'new' blazer. I got it last September.

'That's a brand new blazer – look at your pocket. Take it off!'

I tried to tell her it was Norbert's fault but she wouldn't listen. She just yanked the blazer off my back and got her sewing machine out. She's paying for that in instalments too.

'You're lucky it's torn on the seam.'

I didn't say anything else about the school trip to London. I didn't dare.

'And don't you dare talk to me about school trips to London . . .'

I didn't have to. I was dead lucky. I got given the money. All fifteen pounds. In fact I had over fifteen pounds in my Post Office Saving Book. Sixteen pounds, four and fourpence to be exact. I'd put the one pound four and fourpence in last Saturday. One pound from my Auntie Doreen for clearing out her garden shed, and four and fourpence for the empty Guinness and Lucozade bottles I'd found in there. I'd taken them to the corner off-licence on my way to Youth Club. My mum had told me off for taking the one pound.

'It's far too much. Your Auntie Doreen can't afford that kind of money. How long did it take you to clean the shed out?'

'Nearly an hour! I was late for Youth Club.'

It hadn't really taken me that long. I was there for the best part of an hour but I'd spend a lot of the time looking at these old magazines. They were called 'National Geo-something' and they were ever so interesting. Pictures of natives with darts through their lips, that sort of thing. I'd asked my Auntie Doreen if I could have them but she wouldn't let me.

'No, they belonged to your Uncle Norman and it wouldn't be right to give them away. Put them back in the shed.'

So back they'd gone under the old deckchairs and watering-cans and paint pots. And fishing tackle! Ooh, I'd love to have had a go with that fishing tackle. I'd asked my Auntie Doreen even though I knew what she'd say.

'No, it wouldn't be right, it were your Uncle Norman's.'

I don't know how long ago my Uncle Norman had died – I mean I'd never even known him – but it seemed daft to me shoving all these good things to the back of the shed.

'Nearly an hour! A pound for less than an hour! That's more than I get from Mrs Jerome.'

My mum goes cleaning for Mrs Jerome three mornings a week. It's a great big house on the other side of the park. It's where the rich people live. They've got a treehouse in their garden and Mrs Jerome lets me play in it sometimes. She's ever so nice. It's thanks to her I'm going on the school trip because she gave me the money.

I'd been over there playing in the treehouse one Saturday morning while my mum was cleaning and Mrs Jerome had brought out some orange squash and some chocolate biscuits for me. Not just on one side. Chocolate on both sides. They were lovely. I think Mrs Jerome likes me coming to play in the treehouse because all her children are grown-up. Except one, he got killed in the war. Anyway she'd started asking me how I was enjoying Grammar School and I'd said all right and what did I want to be when I grew up and I'd said I didn't know and who was my favourite film star and so

145

on. And then she'd asked me what was happening in the school holidays, was I going anywhere? And I'd told her we'd probably be doing the same as usual, going on the odd day trip to Morecambe and Scarborough with my mum and my Auntie Doreen and she'd said she and Mr Jerome would be doing the same as usual, a cruise to the Canary Islands. She'd said that I could play in the treehouse while she was away.

'Actually, I'm ever so excited because Mr Jerome has arranged for us to stop off in London for a few days to visit the Festival of Britain.'

And I'd told her about the school trip to London to see the Festival of Britain too, and how it cost fifteen pounds and how I couldn't go because my mum couldn't afford it.

Well, the following Tuesday I'd come home from school and my mum was sitting at the kitchen table holding a small book. She'd looked as though she'd been crying.

'What's the matter, Mum? Are you all right?'

She hadn't said anything, she'd just given me the little book. It was a Post Office Savings Book. I'd opened it and it had my name written inside and there was fifteen pounds in the account.

I'd looked at my mum and I couldn't tell whether she was pleased or cross.

'You're not going to London if you do badly in your exams. If you don't do well – very well – that money's going straight back to Mrs Jerome!'

I stared at my Latin textbook.

'Amo, Amas, Amat . . .'

It was all Greek to me. The bell went for home-time and everybody started packing up.

Bleasdale was tapping on his desk to get our attention. Norbert was practically out of the door.

'One minute, gentlemen, and that includes you, Light-owler – homework!'

Everybody groaned. I had tons already. French revision, an English essay, Maths.

'I'm not setting any homework tonight . . .'

Everybody cheered.

'But I want you to do some extensive revision.'

Everybody groaned again.

'I shall be giving you a written vocabulary test tomorrow . . .'

More groans.

'It'll be your last test before the exams. Now go home, you horrible lot, and do some work!'

We piled out into the corridor and the headmaster hit Norbert on the side of his head and told him to stop running. He and a few others were off to play cricket in the schoolyard.

'Who's coming? It's Yorkshire against Lancashire. I'm Freddie Truman. And when I'm batting I'm Willie Watson.'

I didn't want to play cricket. I wanted to get on with my revision. I wanted to go to London. Anyway I never got a chance to bat. By the time it came to my turn we usually got kicked out by the caretaker.

I don't know why I went to play in the treehouse. It's not even on my way home. But I started walking with David Holdsworth and he goes that way through the park. Maybe

I wanted to show off to him, I don't know, but that's what I did. I pointed to it as we went up the hill past Mrs Jerome's.

'You see that treehouse. Up there. I'm allowed to play in it.'

He looked at it. It's about fifteen feet up in a big syca-more tree.

'I bet you wish you were.'

'I am. Honest.'

I couldn't stop myself from smiling and because I was smiling he thought I was lying. I soon showed him I wasn't. I led the way up the ladder.

After we'd been playing for about a quarter of an hour I decided it was time to go.

'I've got to go soon. I've got to get on with my revision.'

David was pretending to be a commando in Korea.

'Pow, pow! Oh, don't go yet. It's great up here. Pow, pow!'

I wish we had gone. We wouldn't have been there when Norbert came past. It was David who saw him first, running up the hill.

'Look, there's Norbert. He must've got kicked out by the caretaker. Pow, pow! You're dead, Norbert.'

He looked round to see where the voice had come from.

'What are you doing up there? I'm coming up.'

I tried to stop him. I wanted to get home. Besides, even though *I* was allowed to play in the treehouse I didn't think Mrs Jerome would like it if half the school turned up. It was a good job she was away.

'No, Norbert, we're going now.'

But he was halfway up the ladder.

'Oh in't it great. Don't tell any of the other lads, we'll keep it for ourselves.'

Keep it for ourselves. He had some cheek, did Norbert.

'*I'm* the only one allowed to play here. I know the owner. Now come on, get down!'

He didn't get down. He came in.

'Hey, you'll never guess what I've found . . .'

He started rummaging under his jumper.

'These were in the dustbin we used as a wicket – look!'

He held out some sheets of paper with purple writing on it but I couldn't tell what they said because the writing was backwards.

'It's rubbish this, all the writing's backwards.'

'It is not rubbish, they're our exam papers. These are the stencils that Mrs Smylie runs all the copies off . . .'

Mrs Smylie's the school secretary.

' . . . These are the questions we'll be getting. Look, 1B – Summer Term.'

Holdsworth grabbed one of the papers. We looked at it. Norbert was right. It was 1B Summer Term spelt backwards.

'Yeah, look – this is geography backwards.'

He knelt down and started going through the questions, working out what they said. Norbert knelt down opposite him.

'They're all here. English, Latin, French, Religious Instruction.'

They started reading the questions out loud . . . *I* didn't want to hear them. I didn't want to cheat. I wanted to do well in my exams. I wanted to go to The Festival of Britain but I didn't want to cheat.

'Stop. You mustn't, it's not right . . .'

I tried to get the papers before either of them could read any more. I was going to tear them up and throw them away but Norbert stopped me.

I don't think he meant to push me that hard. Fifteen feet doesn't sound very high, but it is when you're falling out of a treehouse.

I didn't do much that summer. There's not much you can do when you've broken both your legs. I didn't do the exams either. I couldn't with my right arm in plaster. My mum made me go to school though. She said there was no reason why I couldn't sit and read while the others did their exams. But I didn't do much reading. I spent most of the time staring at Bleasdale's glass eye . . . Thinking about the school trip I wouldn't be going on.

My mum used the fifteen pounds to mend the treehouse.

# THE SECOND PRIZE

I could hear my mum upstairs bustling about, getting herself ready, asking my Auntie Doreen which hat she should wear.

'What do you think, Doreen, the black velvet I wore to Matty's funeral or the royal blue with the cherries? Which looks most suitable?'

I heard my Auntie Doreen thinking. You could always hear her when she was thinking – she sucked in her breath and it made her false teeth rattle.

'It's not a funeral we're going to, is it? It's a prize-giving. I'd wear the royal blue.'

My mum couldn't make her mind up.

'I don't know . . . the black velvet's very stylish and it goes with my two-piece . . . mind you, so does the royal blue . . . I don't know. Maybe I shouldn't wear a hat. I don't want to be overdressed, do I? You're not wearing a hat.'

I could hear my Auntie Doreen sighing now. It's funny how her teeth didn't rattle when she breathed out, only when she breathed in.

'Well, whatever you do, you'd better do it fast or we're going to be late!'

I was sitting at the top of the stairs listening, my stomach churning. My stomach seemed to have been churning for the last two weeks, ever since I'd heard I'd won the second prize. I'd been ready for ages. I was wearing my best suit, the one my mum had got in the sale at Lewis' in Leeds, and this was only the second time I'd worn it. The first time was at my Uncle Matty's funeral and I'd got into trouble with my mum at the tea afterwards. It had been my Auntie Winnie's fault, Uncle Matty's wife. She hadn't seen me for years and she'd come rolling over towards me just as I was about to eat another cream horn. I'd been really careful eating the first one because my mum had warned me not to spill '*anything*' on my new suit. When I saw Auntie Winnie coming towards me I was more worried she was going to spill her glass of sherry over me and I started backing away.

'Eeh, is that our Freda's lad? I'd never have recognised you . . .' And the next thing I knew she was putting her arms round me and giving me a big hug and a kiss.

It was horrible. It wasn't just the smell of the sherry on her breath. She had a wart on her upper lip with long hairs growing out of it and I could feel it. I could feel something else too – the cream horn being squashed onto my chest. Onto my new suit. While she was hugging and kissing me and saying how proud Uncle Matty would have been to see me grow into such a fine young man she finished off the sherry and asked me to get her another one.

My mum had gone mad when she saw the state of my new suit. She'd taken me straight into the bathroom.

'Brand new, and you have to go and get cream all over it! I could cheerfully throttle you!'

'It wasn't my fault, Mum . . .' And I'd explained how Auntie Winnie had hugged me and squashed the cream horn.

She didn't say much. She just rubbed away with a flannel and muttered something about Winnie and her drinking and something about driving Matty to an early grave. My mum and Auntie Winnie didn't get on that well. That's why we hardly ever saw them.

Anyway it had come back from the dry-cleaners looking as good as new – well it was new, I'd only worn it the once – and I sat at the top of the stairs waiting to set off for the prize-giving, my stomach churning.

The doorbell rang and I heard my mum going into a panic.

'Ooh, that'll be the taxi and I'm nowhere ready. If that's the taxi, love, tell him I'll be a couple of minutes.'

I went downstairs to answer the door. I wouldn't have minded if she took another couple of hours, I was dreading the whole thing. It *was* the taxi.

'My mum's not ready yet, she'll be a few minutes.'

It was the same driver who'd taken us to the station when we'd gone to Uncle Matty's funeral.

'Well, she booked me for quarter-to, I'll have to charge waiting time. Can I use your lavatory?'

'Yeah, it's out the back.'

I showed him to the toilet and went back in to hurry my mum up. Not that I wanted to get there quickly – I wished we didn't have to go at all – but I didn't want my mum to get charged too much waiting time.

'It's only just quarter-to now, he was early. Are my seams straight, Doreen?'

Auntie Doreen checked my mum's stockings and my mum checked my Auntie Doreen's stockings, then my mum straightened my tie, brushed the dandruff off my jacket and off we went downstairs. They were both wearing hats – my mum had the royal blue on and Auntie Doreen was wearing

153

the black velvet. My mum slammed the front door shut and was looking in her handbag for her keys.

'Hey Doreen, I hope we're not overdressed.'

My Auntie Doreen was looking in her powder compact, dabbing her nose and making funny in and out movements with her lips.

'I don't think so. It's not every day one of the family is summoned to the Town Hall to be presented with a prize, is it?'

They both smiled at me and my Auntie Doreen kissed me on the cheek. I felt terrible. If they only knew the truth.

As she was double-locking the front door my mum started going on about keeping my best suit clean.

'And don't you spill *anything* on that suit. We don't want a repeat of last time.'

I was just about to tell her for the umpteenth time that it wasn't my fault but my Auntie Doreen did it for me.

'Leave him alone, Freda. You can't blame him. You know what our Winnie's like when she's had a drink. Now come on, let's not keep this taxi waiting any longer.'

And we set off down the path.

We'd just got into the car when my Auntie Doreen noticed that there was no driver.

'Hang on – where's the driver?'

I explained that he'd asked to use the toilet.

'He's probably still out there, Mum. You've locked him out the back!'

She sighed and got the keys back out of her handbag.

'And he wants to charge me waiting time. I'll charge him toilet time . . .!'

154

She scurried off up the path and my Auntie Doreen smiled at me.

'Are you excited?'

I looked at her. If only she knew how I really felt. Should I tell her the truth?

'Auntie Doreen . . .?'

'Yes, love?'

It'd be easier to tell her than my mum. She'd get rid of the taxi and we'd go back into the house. I'd go upstairs to my bedroom while she and my mum would go into the kitchen. My Auntie Doreen would make her a cup of tea and gently tell her the truth . . . And I'd sit at the top of the stairs trying to listen . . . No I wouldn't, I wouldn't *want* to listen, I wouldn't want to hear. I'd lie on my bed and wait . . . And after a while, after Auntie Doreen had gone home, my mum would come up and her eyes would be all red and I'd still be lying on the bed and she'd tell me not to lie on the bed in my best suit and I'd look at her . . . at her red eyes and her disappointed face . . . and I'd wish I'd never said anything.

'Yes, love?'

I saw the taxi driver coming down the path with my mum.

'It's the same driver who took us to the station when we went to Uncle Matty's funeral.'

It was all I could think of saying. I couldn't tell her the truth. Not with my mum all dressed up in her royal blue hat and everything, so proud of me and excited. How could I tell her that it shouldn't be me getting this prize? The driver was laughing to himself as he got in the car.

155

'I tell you, that's a first . . . Wait till I tell the wife. I hope you're not catching a train?'

My mum wasn't laughing. She put on her posh voice.

'No, we're going to the Town Hall. Main entrance.'

The driver started the engine. Oh, the way she said it in that stupid voice. 'We're going to the Town Hall. Main entrance.' And why did she have to waggle her head like that? And smile as if she had a piece of lemon in her mouth? Knowing that I shouldn't even be getting this prize made it even worse. If only she hadn't had to go away to Blackpool none of this would have happened.

My mum and my Auntie Doreen do voluntary work for the old folk. I don't know how old these old folk are because my mum and my Auntie Doreen aren't young. Anyway, not long after I'd started at the grammar school they took the old folk on an outing to Blackpool to see the illuminations which meant my mum staying away. So she arranged for me to sleep the night with Mr and Mrs Carpenter at number 23. I often went to their house if my mum was going to be late back from work or anything like that but this was the first time I'd gone to stay all night.

'You sure you don't mind? I can try and get someone else to go to Blackpool in my place.'

*I* didn't mind.

'No, I'll be all right.'

I liked going to Mr and Mrs Carpenter's. They're ever so kind. I think they like me coming because they don't have any children. They had a son once called David but he died when he was a baby. He came too early or something. Mr Carpenter has this fantastic collection of tin soldiers

156

and he lets me play with them. I think they're quite valuable.

'Well, it's only for one night. Are you sure you'll be OK?'

'Yes!'

Oh, my mum didn't half go on sometimes. I wouldn't have minded if she stayed away a bit longer, but I didn't say that in case it upset her.

'I'll be all right. Honest.'

I think my mum thought I was being brave because she spoke in the same sort of voice she put on when I had to have an injection at the doctor's.

'Well, I'll take your things round to Mrs Carpenter's in the morning before we set off for Blackpool and you go straight there after school. You'll be all right.'

I didn't go straight there after school because Mr Carpenter met me and took me into town for an ice cream and then we went to Dyson's toy shop and he said I could choose anything I wanted up to two pounds. I didn't like to at first because I thought my mum might be cross but he said it was his treat and nothing to do with anybody else and I should choose what I wanted.

'But no more than two pound, mind, and don't say anything to Mrs Carpenter about having an ice cream or you'll get me into trouble. We've got a big tea waiting at home.'

I chose a box of coloured pencils at first because I'd got art homework to do but Mr Carpenter told me to choose something else.

'I've got a load of crayons at home, I'll give you some. Treat yourself to something you really fancy.'

What I'd really wanted was this commando that had a string in its back and when you pulled it said different orders like 'Enemy at one o'clock' and 'Do you surrender?' and other things. It was great. It cost one pound nineteen and eleven and I put the penny change in the box for deaf children. We got back at about half past five and Mrs Carpenter must have known we'd be going into town because she wasn't surprised how late we were.

'Now – are you hungry?'

I looked at Mr Carpenter. I couldn't say, 'No, I've just had a big ice cream.' Luckily Mrs Carpenter carried on talking.

'Because we can either eat now or you can do your homework first.'

'I'd like to get my homework done, Mrs Carpenter.'

'Good idea. Now, we've got roast chicken for tea. Do you like chicken?'

I *loved* chicken. We only have it at Christmas and Easter.

'I *love* chicken.'

Mr Carpenter got a whole load of coloured pencils out of a drawer and gave them to me.

'Can I keep all these?'

'Aye, 'course you can. Now what's this art you have to do?

I told him the choice Mr Clegg the art teacher had given us.

'We have to draw either a street scene or a woodland scene. I'm going to do a street scene.'

So he cleared a space at the table for me and sat down to read his paper while Mrs Carpenter went into the kitchen to finish off her ironing.

I started my picture using the coloured pencils Mr Carpenter had given me. I drew a zebra crossing. Then I drew a car and a boy and a girl waiting to cross. I'm not very good at drawing – I never have been – and I suddenly realised Mr Carpenter was standing behind me, watching. I felt a bit embarrassed.

'It's not very good, is it?'

He smiled.

'Don't use your crayons straight off. Do it lightly in pencil to start, then you can rub it out and change it if you want. Look.'

He got himself a chair, sat down beside me and started drawing on a new piece of paper. He copied what I'd done, the zebra crossing, the car, the boy and girl, but in pencil like he said. He was a good drawer.

'Now, what else do you want, couple of shops? Someone on a bike maybe? I know, let's have a police car.'

Mrs Carpenter came in from the kitchen and when she realised what he was doing she told him off.

'Hey, he's supposed to be doing that homework, Denzil, not you.'

'I'm just giving the lad a bit of a hand, that's all. He's got the hard work to do, he's got to colour it all in.'

Mr Carpenter went back to his paper and I started colouring. It took me ages. There were lots of people in it now, a lady pushing a pram, a couple of the old folk going into a Post Office (that was my idea), and a boy on roller skates. And there was a Woolworth's and a dry-cleaner's, and a National Provincial Bank. When I'd finished, it was a really good picture. The best I'd ever done. Well I knew I hadn't done it but like Mr Carpenter said, I'd done the hard work, I'd done all the colouring. Anyway I didn't think it mattered. As long as Norbert Lightowler didn't see it. We'd been at High Moor Primary together before we'd gone to the grammar school and he knew I wasn't good at art. And it *wouldn't* have mattered if Mr Clegg hadn't shown it to the headmaster . . .

Art is the last lesson we have on a Thursday morning and when the dinner bell went Mr Clegg told us to leave our homework on his desk on the way out.

'And make sure you've put your name on the back, otherwise I'll not know which of these works of art belongs to which genius. Lightowler, name on the back, lad.'

Norbert came back and signed his picture. Mr Carpenter had rolled mine up and put a rubber band round it which was good because it meant nobody could see it. Norbert had wanted to have a look but I'd told him I couldn't be bothered to unroll it.

'I bet it's not as good as mine.'

Norbert took his out of a folder to show me and David Holdsworth.

'Look at that. A Woodland Scene by Norbert Lightowler. Good, innit?'

It was quite good. A bit messy but then Norbert's work always is. And he'd put in monkeys and tigers. Holdsworth started laughing.

'You don't get tigers and monkeys in a wood, that's more like a jungle scene.'

Norbert had just sniffed and wiped his nose on the back of his sleeve.

'Well, there are monkeys and tigers in *this* wood, so tough!' And he put it back in his folder.

As Norbert was writing his name I put my picture on Mr Clegg's desk. I'd signed it on the back the night before. We went off into the playground and I didn't think much more about it.

The next time we had art Mr Clegg picked out a few of the pictures and told us what was right and what was wrong.

'You see, look at Hopkinson's – this chap here is taller than the Belisha beacon.'

Everybody laughed and Hopkinson went all red. He's always going red.

'Now Lightowler's isn't bad at all . . .'

Everybody turned round and looked at Norbert. He licked his thumb and wiped it on his chest, all cocky.

'It's a bit messy,' – everybody laughed and Norbert screwed up his nose – 'but the perspective is good. Mind you, Lightowler, I did say a woodland scene, not a jungle scene.'

We all laughed again and that was it. We went on to something else. I was a bit annoyed. My picture was much better than Norbert's but Mr Clegg never mentioned it. Not then anyway. He did a few weeks later. Well, he didn't, the headmaster did.

We were in the middle of a Latin lesson with Mr Bleasdale when the headmaster and Mr Clegg came in. The headmaster whispered something to Bleasdale then all three looked at the class. I thought they were looking at me . . . They were! Bleasdale told me to stand up. I didn't know what was going on. The headmaster took a pace forward and the whole class was staring at me. I couldn't think what I'd done wrong.

'This boy has brought great honour to the school.'

I couldn't think what I'd done right.

'Some weeks ago you were set some work by Mr Clegg. You were asked to draw a street scene. One of these drawings was quite outstanding and Mr Clegg showed it to me . . .'

I could feel myself going red. My legs felt like jelly.

' . . . and I agreed with him. It was outstanding and I sent this drawing up to London to be considered in this year's National Road Safety Art Competition . . .'

My heart was pounding. I tried to swallow but my mouth had gone all dry.

'I am delighted to say that this drawing has won a Regional second prize in the under-12 category, which means that this lad has come second in the whole county.'

Mr Clegg started clapping and the headmaster joined in, then Bleasdale and then the whole class. I thought I was going to be sick. My stomach started to churn . . .

It was churning now in the back of the taxi.

I looked out of the window. We were on the main road heading for the city centre. The driver was tapping his fingers on the steering wheel, waiting for the lights to change.

'So, what's going on at the Town Hall today?'

My mum looked at me. She put on her posh voice again. She put it on every time she told someone.

'The National Road Safety Art Competition. Regional prize-giving. My son's won second prize in the under-12s. Second in the whole county!'

I was sitting in the middle, between my mum and my Auntie Doreen, and I could see the driver looking at me in his mirror. He smiled.

'Second in the whole county, eh? You must be a good artist.'

I just about managed to smile back.

'Not bad.'

'Not bad? You must be a lot better than "not bad" to come second in the whole county. He's too modest, your young lad.'

My mum put her arm through mine. We turned right into Delius Street. We were nearly at the Town Hall.

'Well, that's the funny thing. Art has never been his strong point, has it, love . . .?'

I shook my head.

'But he's just started at the grammar school and his new art teacher must have brought out hidden talents, eh love?'

I nodded. I felt sick. My mum carried on chatting to the driver.

'I haven't seen it yet, you know. Me and my sister were away in Blackpool when he did it. We'll be seeing it for the first time today. We're ever so proud of him, aren't we, Doreen?'

My Auntie Doreen took hold of my other arm and I sat between them as they held me close.

Yes, they were so proud of me. Everybody was so proud of me. Mr Clegg, the headmaster, my mum, my Auntie Doreen. That's why I hadn't said anything right at the start. I'd planned to go to the headmaster the day after he'd told me in class, explain to him what had happened, *how* it had happened, but he announced it in assembly. I'd even had to go up on the stage and shake his hand while the whole school applauded.

We pulled up outside the Town Hall. We were there. While my mum was paying him the driver asked me what the prize was.

'Fifteen pounds in National Savings stamps.'

He nodded and said very nice and told my mum he wouldn't be charging waiting time.

'I should think not, we were waiting for you.' And we went up the steps into the Town Hall.

There were lots of other prize-winners going in, girls as well as boys, and most had their mums and dads with them. Some had their grandparents. On the invitation it had said we were allowed 'four per family'. I never knew my grandma – she died when I was two – and my grandad died a couple of years ago. My mum had invited Mr and Mrs Carpenter but thank goodness they couldn't come, they'd had to go to a wedding in Doncaster. When my mum had told them about me coming second Mr Carpenter didn't ask me if it was for the picture I'd done at his house – and I didn't tell him. He must have known, though. He knew I wasn't good enough to win a prize.

We were walking through this big entrance hall with stone pillars and marble floors. Quite a few of the prize-winners were wearing their school uniforms but my mum had wanted me to wear my best suit. Norbert Lightowler had torn my blazer trying to get ahead of me in the dinner queue and even though my mum had mended it, it was still a bit scruffy.

Everybody was talking in whispers and our footsteps echoed everywhere. It reminded me of when we went into the church at Uncle Matty's funeral. At the far end a commissionaire was directing people.

'National Road Safety – main chamber at the top of the stairs. Main chamber at the top of the stairs for the National Road Safety prize-giving.'

My stomach churned even more when I heard him saying 'prize-giving'. Soon I was going to be presented with a prize that I had no right to. A prize for something I hadn't done. I felt sick. I had to go to the toilet. I whispered to my mum.

'All right, love, we'll ask at the top of the stairs.'

We went up this wide staircase and on the walls on either side were old-fashioned pictures of old men. This lad's mother was telling him that they were portraits of previous Lord Mayors and that maybe one day his portrait would be up there and they both laughed. She talked loudly so that everybody around could hear and she put on a posh voice like my mum, only I think she *was* posh because he called her 'mummy' not 'mum' and I heard her saying how bad the traffic had been coming from Harrogate and Harrogate's a very posh place.

Another commissionaire explained where the toilets were and my mum told me to wait for her and Auntie Doreen outside the ladies and I went into the gents. There was nobody in there, thank goodness. I just wanted to be on my own for a minute. I felt terrible. All the other winners were smiling and laughing and were so excited. I felt like a cheat. I was a cheat. *I* hadn't won the second prize, Mr Carpenter had. I didn't want this rotten prize but what could I do about it? I'd been awarded it and I'd have to accept it. Thank goodness I hadn't won *first* prize otherwise I would have had to go to London. All the top Regional winners had to go for the National prize-giving. At least after today it'd all be over with. I splashed some water on my face, had a drink and went to meet my mum. I had to use my hanky to dry myself because there was no towel.

165

To get into the main chamber we had to show our invitation to the commissionaire and my mum got into a panic because she thought she'd forgotten it. She couldn't find it in her handbag.

'Eh, Doreen, I think I left it on the hall table when I was looking for the camera . . .'

I was hoping she wouldn't find it. Auntie Doreen was helping her look.

'Freda, I said "Have you got the invitation?" Twice I reminded you.'

'I know, I know!'

My mum was getting into a right state and I felt sorry for her. But I felt more sorry for myself and I was praying like mad.

'Please God, don't let her find it, don't let her find it, then they won't let us in and we can go home and I won't get presented with the prize.'

My mum didn't find it. But we didn't go home.

'You're all right . . .' The commissionaire winked at me. 'He looks like an honest lad. We don't want him going home without his prize, do we?'

*No*, I wanted to shout, I'm not an honest lad, I didn't do the picture, Mr Carpenter did it and I *do* want to go home without my prize. But I just said thank you and we went into the main chamber.

The seats were in rows with a gangway down the middle. My mum wanted to be near the front so she could get a good photo of me receiving my prize so we sat in the third row. The main chamber was ever so big and around the room were more portraits of previous Lord Mayors. On the wall facing us, in gold lettering, were the names of every Lord Mayor since 1874 and there was a scroll of honour like we've got at school with a list of people who had been killed in both world wars. At the front was a stage with three pictures on easels marked first, second and third. There was a little lad in front of us getting all excited because one of them was his and his mum and dad told him to calm down. At the side on the floor were all the winning pictures stacked up. I sat between my mum and my Auntie Doreen reading the names of the Lord Mayors, wishing the whole thing was over.

I could hear the lady from Harrogate in the row behind.

'Yes, Jeremy's won first prize in the under-12s. Of course what he's most excited about is the trip to London.'

My mum smiled at me and squeezed my hand. I suppose she thought I was wishing I'd come first so that I'd be going to London. I smiled back and started reading the names of the people who'd been killed in the First World War.

'Albert Bartholomew ... Douglas Briggs ... Maurice Clarkson ...'

Then it started, the prize-giving.

One of the officials blew into a microphone and a man from London welcomed everybody and said the standard had been extremely high and that the judges had found it extremely difficult to decide on the three winners in each category and he was extremely pleased to introduce the editor of the *Yorkshire Post* to present the prizes. Then he asked for the under-10 winners to come up on the stage.

They stood in front of their own easel and as their name was called out and the editor presented the prizes everybody clapped. The little lad who'd got excited was Graham Duck-worth from Otley and he'd come third. The lady from

Harrogate tapped my mum on the shoulder and asked if she'd mind taking her hat off because people behind couldn't see. My mum went a bit red and looked quite cross but she and my Auntie Doreen took them off and put them under their seats. The under-10 pictures were taken away and the under-11s were called up. As they were going up on the stage their pictures were put on the easels. They were really good and everybody clapped again as each name was called out.

Then it was my turn.

'Can I have the winners from the under-12 category, please?'

My mum and my Auntie Doreen turned towards me with great big grins on their faces. I stood up and slowly squeezed past the other people sitting in our row. A man at the end patted me on the back and said 'Well done, lad.' Jeremy from Harrogate was already walking up the gangway and I followed him. We watched them take away the under-11 pictures and went on the stage and stood in front of our easels. The third winner was a tall lad with ginger hair and a birthmark on his cheek who did a thumbs-up to the audience. I stared ahead, trying not to look at my mum, but out of the corner of my eye I saw her taking a photo. There was a flash and when I looked at her she signalled at me to smile. I could hear them behind me putting our pictures on the easels but I didn't look round. I didn't want to see mine. I just kept on looking at the back of the room. I concentrated on this coat of arms above the door. I felt as if I was going to cry. How had I got myself into this mess? Why hadn't I told the truth right at the beginning? I could hear the man from London tapping the microphone.

'And now, ladies and gentlemen, boys and girls, we

come to the under-12 category. Once again the standard has been extremely high and third place is awarded to Trevor Hainsworth from Driffield.'

Everybody clapped him as he got his prize and he did another thumbs-up to the audience.

'And the second prize goes to . . .' And as I heard my name being called out I felt a pain in my stomach and to stop myself from bursting into tears I just made myself keep looking at the coat of arms at the back. It was a blue and red and gold shield and standing on their hind legs on either side of the shield were a golden stag and a silver ram and on top of the shield was a knight's helmet. That was in gold too. Then the editor was shaking my hand.

'Congratulations. Well done, young man.'

I think I said 'thank you', I can't remember now. I could hear my mum saying 'smile' and there was another flash but I didn't look at her. I couldn't.

'And the first prize in the under-12s goes to Jeremy Collins from Harrogate for this magnificent drawing . . .'

Underneath the coat of arms in gold lettering was written 'Honesty – Toil – Honour'.

'And of course Jeremy will go forward and represent this county at the National awards early next year.'

'Honesty – Toil – Honour.' I kept looking at the coat of arms as Jeremy got his prize from the editor. Twenty-five pounds in National Savings stamps. 'Honesty – Toil – Honour.'

Nobody heard me at first because of all the clapping and when it died down I said it again, quietly. The man from London wasn't sure if he'd heard me properly.

'What did you say?'

'It's not my picture. I didn't do it.'

I don't think most people in the audience knew what was going on because I said it so softly but they knew something was wrong because they started whispering to each other and all the officials on the stage were in a huddle. I could hear them saying that these were the winning pictures and that they were definitely in the right order. One of them took me on one side.

'What are you talking about, lad?'

'My picture – it's not mine. I didn't do it!'

And I turned round and pointed.

And it wasn't mine. I mean it wasn't the one Mr Carpenter did. It was a different picture altogether. It wasn't as good as Mr Carpenter's. I could see Jeremy staring at me. He looked strange, sort of frightened.

Then I saw why – Mr Carpenter's picture was on *his* easel. Mr Carpenter had won first prize, not Jeremy – but he hadn't said anything. The man from London was tapping the microphone again.

'I'm sorry, ladies and gentlemen, we seem to have a little confusion. If you could . . . er . . . bear with us for a moment we'd be most grateful. Thank you.'

Then he turned back to me.

'Are any of these drawings yours?'

The tall lad with ginger hair got quite cross.

'Well, he didn't do this one. It's mine!'

The audience was getting fidgety. I couldn't understand why Jeremy hadn't said anything yet but I suppose it was still dawning on him that he hadn't won the first prize after all. He looked stunned. I felt happier than I had done for weeks.

'No, I didn't do any of these.'

I knew that when it came round to Jeremy telling them that he hadn't done the picture on his easel either, they'd probably take the frame off to check and they'd see my name on the back. I didn't care. I'd tell them the truth. But they didn't check. Jeremy didn't say anything and they gave him first prize.

I don't know how he could accept a prize for something he hadn't done. I couldn't.

# THE PIGEON

## PART ONE

It was on the Thursday, during Latin with Mr Bleasdale, that
Arthur Boocock sent the note round. Three days after the
new boy had started. Latin's the last lesson before our dinner
break and we were doing translation while Bleasdale was
marking. We always muck about in his lessons 'cos you can
with his glass eye. You just have to make sure that his good
eye is looking down. Duggie Bashforth read the note, checked
that only the glass eye was looking, nodded at Arthur
Boocock, and passed it on. Kenny Spencer read it, nodded
at Arthur and gave it to Duncan Cawthra. Cawthra read it,
gave Arthur a nod and passed it to David Holdsworth. I
wondered what it said. Usually it was something to try and
make you laugh and get you into trouble. Or sometimes we
played 'the grot', when we passed anything round, somebody's cap or an exercise book, anything, and you had to
get rid of it before the bell went. Once it was a dead mouse
that Norbert had found down by the Mucky Beck. The
Mucky Beck is a small stream in Horton Woods. It's great
for frogspawn. Well it used to be. My mum doesn't let me
go there any more. Not since that lad from Galsworthy Road
Secondary Modern had got attacked. She'd read it in my
Auntie Doreen's paper.

'I don't want you playing down Horton Woods any

more, 'specially near the Mucky Beck. A lad from Galsworthy Road's been assaulted down there.'

She gave the paper to my Auntie Doreen and pointed to the bit she'd been reading.

'But I like playing down there. Mucky Beck's great for frogspawn.'

'You're not to go, I'm telling you. It's dangerous.'

What was my mum talking about? The Mucky Beck's only about six inches deep. My Auntie Doreen tutted to herself and gave the paper back to my mum.

'I don't know what the world's coming to, I really don't.'

'How can it be dangerous? Mucky Beck's only about six inches deep.'

'I don't want you going there, do you hear? A lad's been assaulted.'

I wasn't sure what she meant. What's 'a salted'? And why was it in the paper? I knew it was bad. My mum had her serious face on and whenever my Auntie Doreen reads something in the newspaper and says 'I don't know what the world is coming to', I know it's bad.

'What's a salted?'

My mum looked at my Auntie Doreen.

'He was attacked. A man attacked him. That's what it means.'

'Why?'

They looked at each other again, the way they look when they don't want to tell me something. They're always doing that. They weren't telling me the truth. They think I can't tell but I can.

'Why did he attack him? Was he a madman?'

He must have been mad to attack a Galsworthy Road

174

lad. Galsworthy Road Secondary Modern is where you go if you don't pass your scholarship to the Grammar and they're tough. I've heard some of them carry knives and things. I don't know if it's true but I wouldn't like to get into a fight with one of 'em. My Auntie Doreen got hold of my hand.

'Listen, love, this man was a bit sick in the head. There are people like that. That's why you must never go off with strangers. Do you understand?'

What was my Auntie Doreen talking about? I know all about strangers. My mum's always telling me. And we had a talk at school about it with Reverend Dutton, our scripture teacher. 'Course I wouldn't go off with a stranger. I'm not stupid. Anyway what's going off with strangers got to do with having a fight with someone? I bet the Galsworthy Road lad had cheeked him off or something – they're always getting into trouble.

''Course I wouldn't go off with a stranger. I didn't go with that bloke in the park who asked me if I wanted an ice cream, did I?'

It had happened in the Easter holidays. We'd all taken some bottles back to the shop, Tony, me and Norbert, and we'd gone to the park to spend our money at the fair. After I'd spent all mine, mostly on the slot machines and one go on the rifle range, I'd wandered around on my own for a bit while Tony and Norbert were on the dodgems.

I'd gone over to the waltzer and while I was watching and thinking that there was no way that *I'd* go on it – it goes at about a hundred miles an hour – this bloke had started talking to me.

'It's dead good, the waltzer. Best thing at fair.'

I'd told him it was too fast, that I wouldn't dare and that I hadn't got any money anyway.

'I'll pay for yer, young 'un, I've got tons o' money.'

I'd watched it whirling round and round. If it had been the dodgems I might have gone – I love the dodgems – but I didn't fancy the waltzer.

'No thanks.'

'Do you want an ice cream? I'll buy you one.'

That's when I'd realised he was a stranger. I'd remembered everything my mum had told me.

'No! And if you don't leave me alone I'm gonna tell a policeman.'

The man had just shrugged and sniffed and wandered off. Then I'd felt bad. Maybe he was just being friendly, nice. Norbert said I should have gone on.

'I would have. Free ride. And free ice cream. I'd have said yes.'

Yeah, Norbert would have. He's stupid. He doesn't realise about strangers. I don't think his mum and dad have told him properly. I don't think they're bothered. They never know where he goes and what he's up to. If he wants to go to the pictures and it's an 'A' he gets a stranger to take him in. He just goes up to any bloke who comes along and says 'Can you take us in, mister?' I'd never do that. It's dangerous. And he's always going down the Mucky Beck on his own. I never do that – I always go with the others.

'I never go down the Mucky Beck on my own, Mum. I'm not daft. I'm not like Norbert Lightowler.'

She'd leaned across the table and put her face really close to mine.

'You're not to go down there any more, do you understand?'

'Never?'

'Never!'

'Not even with the others?'

That's when she'd got her mad up.

'You don't go down there! Right? End of story!'

So that's why I don't go down the Mucky Beck any more. I'd like to but if my mum found out . . . Well, my life wouldn't be worth living . . .

The note was still going round the class. David Nunn was reading it. He nodded at Arthur and passed it on. What did it say? I was dying for it to come round to me. Geoff Gower had it now – he's only two desks away. He passed it to Normington who sits next to me and then just my luck, Bleasdale stopped marking.

'All right boys, stop writing. You should have finished by now. Who didn't complete that translation?'

Norbert put his hand up.

'What a surprise, Lightowler . . .'

He looked at his watch.

'Right, we're going to spend the last ten minutes before the bell goes going over those first conjugation verbs . . .'

He turned round and while he was rubbing the blackboard clean Norbert made a face at him.

'Not one of you got them all correct . . .'

Norbert stopped – just in time.

' . . . apart from McDougall.'

Bleasdale started writing on the board and we all jeered – quietly – and Norbert wrote 'SWOT' on a piece of paper and held it up. He always comes top in Latin does Alan McDougall.

'*Festino* – I hurry . . . *Ceno* – I dine . . . *Conor* – I try . . . Not hard enough some of you . . .'

While he had his back to us I held my hand out to Normington for Boocock's note and he gave it to me.

> *Meeting. Smokers corner. Dinner-time.*
> <u>*Don't tell the Pigeon.*</u> *Pass it on.*

'*Voco* – I call . . . *Celo* – I hide . . . *Postulo* – I demand . . . *Postulo* that you all learn these verbs at home tonight. There will be a test tomorrow . . .'

Everybody groaned. I looked at the note again. He'd underlined 'Don't tell the Pigeon'. That was the new lad. Why shouldn't we tell the new lad? What was Boocock going to do? He's a bully is Arthur Boocock. Everybody's scared of him. Except Gordon Barraclough. That's 'cos he's a bully too.

'*Pugno* – I fight . . .'

He'll hit you for anything will Arthur Boocock. He's got funny hair, tight little curls, and he hates it and once a lad from 3B called him 'Curly' and Boocock went mad. He smashed him. He was a lot bigger, this lad, and two years older but Arthur pulverised him. Another time when I was standing in the dinner queue talking to Keith Hopwood I'd tried on his glasses, just for fun and said everything looked a bit fuzzy. I'd had to shout 'cos it was noisy and Arthur Boocock had turned round and said 'Don't you call me fuzzy' and thumped me.

'*Oppugno* – I attack . . .'

178

He'd started on Monday, the new lad. I feel sorry for him. His mum had brought him on his first day. That's why I feel sorry for him. We have English first thing on a Monday with Melrose. I hate Mondays and I hate Melrose. We have Melrose for English then we have him for football straight after. When we went into the classroom he was standing talking to the new lad and his mum.

'Come along, boys, quick as you can, please, settle down . . .'

That's what I hate about Melrose. Any other time he'd be shouting and hitting us but whenever there's a parent there it's all 'Come along, boys, quick as you can, please, settle down.'

'We've got a new boy starting today. This is William Rothman. He's moved here from London. William, would you like to take that desk in the second row, next to Keith.'

If his mum hadn't been there it would have been 'Rothman, sit there, next to Hopwood.' Just as he'd been about to sit down, his mum had done something terrible. She'd kissed him – right in front of us all. Everybody'd started giggling, and trying to be quiet had made Norbert snort and that'd made us laugh even more. Melrose had looked at us and the vein under his eye had started to throb. That'd made us shut up. The new boy, his face all red, had sat down. I'd felt so sorry for him. If my mum ever kissed me in front of the class . . . well, I'd just want to die. I suppose that's how he felt. He hadn't looked at anybody, he'd just stared at his desk. I'd felt so sorry for him. And it had got worse. Just as she'd been about to go his mum had turned at the door.

'Sank you, boys, I'm sure Villiam vill be OK viz such nice boys as you . . .'

That's how she talks, sort of funny.

' . . . But you vill look after my little pigeon, von't you?'

Everybody'd tried their best not to laugh, even Melrose. The new lad had just kept looking down and as soon as his mum had gone we'd all burst out laughing. We couldn't help it.

'All right, all right, that's enough, calm down . . . You'll frighten the little pigeon.'

And that'd made us laugh even more. He's rotten is Melrose.

'*Voco* – I call . . . *Veto* – I forbid . . .'

I didn't nod at Boocock, I just passed the note to Keith Hopwood. He read it and I watched the Pigeon hold his hand out to take it. But of course Hopwood didn't give it him, he passed it to Douglas Hopkinson who sits in front of him in the front row. You could see the Pigeon wondering what was going on. I felt so sorry for him. Everybody called him the Pigeon now.

'*Ceno* – I dine . . . *Indico* – I judge . . .'

The bell went and we started putting our books away.

'Now think on, I want all those learning for tomorrow. I'm going to test you.'

Norbert started grumbling on the way out.

'It's not blooming fair. He shouldn't be giving us any homework. We have Geography and French on a Thursday, not Latin.'

'Are you complaining, Lightowler?'

'No sir . . .'

Smokers' Corner is at the top end of the playground in

the shelter under the woodwork classroom. It's where Boocock and Barraclough and all that lot go to smoke their cigarettes during break. I tried it once. It was horrible. It made me cough and I nearly threw up and they all laughed at me. And I got a sore throat. They all think they're so good, big men puffing away at their fags, blowing the smoke down their noses. They only do it to keep in with Boocock and his gang. I never go up to that end of the school yard, I just keep out of it. But I couldn't keep out of it now. I had to go. We all had to go. Boocock's orders. If you didn't you'd get thumped. I could see the others heading for the shelter. I wondered what it was all about. So did the Pigeon. He was watching them.

'Where are they all going?'

He didn't talk like us. He didn't talk funny like his mum, he talked sort of . . . well, sort of posh. If only he was a bit more like us maybe he wouldn't get teased so much.

'What's happening?'

I didn't know what to say to him.

'Y'what . . .?'

'Everybody seems to be going to the top end of the playground. Where are they all going?'

It would have to be me he was asking.

'Er . . .'

What was I supposed to say?

'Er . . .'

'That note you were all passing round. It was about me, wasn't it?'

'Er . . .'

'That's why they're all going up there, isn't it? It's something to do with me.'

'I don't know...'

It was true, I didn't know. Boocock's note had said 'Don't tell the Pigeon' but it didn't mean it was about him. Maybe he just didn't want him there 'cos he's new... I didn't know...

He wears these glasses with really thick lenses and black frames and he took them off and cleaned them with his hanky. He screwed up his eyes and looked towards the top of the playground.

'*I* know...'

He put his glasses back on and wandered off. I called after him.

'See you later, Pigeon – er, Rothman – William...'

He didn't turn round, he just carried on walking towards the cloakrooms.

I heard Norbert calling me.

'C'mon – we're all waiting!'

I watched the Pigeon going in then ran up to Smokers' Corner.

They were all puffing away at their cigarettes. Well, not all of them, Boocock and Barraclough of course, Geoff Gower, Kenny Spencer, Norbert, Holdsworth, Normington, Duggie Bashforth, Douglas Hopkinson and most of the others. Keith Hopwood looked sick. Alan McDougall wasn't smoking, he was on guard. That's why they never got caught – there was always somebody keeping watch. Boocock puffed on his fag. He took a deep breath, held the smoke inside for ages and then blew it out. He didn't cough. He never coughs.

'What were you talking to him about?'

Some spit shot out from the gap between his two top

teeth. They all do that when they're smoking. It just missed me.

'Nowt. He was just asking where everybody was going.'

'What did you say?'

'Nowt. He asked me if the note that was going round was about him.'

'What did you say?'

'Nowt.'

More spit. This time it was Barraclough and it didn't miss me, it just caught my shoe.

'Watch it, Barraclough.'

He just sneered at me and blew some smoke in my face while Boocock took another puff.

'Well I'll tell you all summat about the Pigeon . . . He's a Jerry!'

We all looked at him. Nobody knew what to say. Keith Hopwood took a drag on his cigarette and coughed and looked at Boocock. He went all red, not 'cos of the smoke, because he was embarrassed.

'It just w-w-went down the wr-wr-wrong w-way, Arthur. Sorry . . .'

Boocock didn't look at him. He just wet his fingers, put his cigarette out and dropped it into the top pocket of his blazer.

'A bloomin' Jerry. In our class.'

The others started putting theirs out. Norbert put his in his shoe.

'You mean a German, Arthur?'

''Course I mean a German. Don't you know what a Jerry is?'

Norbert grinned.

'Well my gran has a jerry under the bed in case she has to go in the night.'

Everybody laughed. I laughed even though I've got a jerry under my bed 'cos we've got an outside lav.

'I don't care about your soddin' granny, Lightowler. The new lad's a German. That's why his mum talks funny.'

Nobody said anything. We weren't sure what we were meant to say. Barraclough put his cigarette out.

'How do you know, Arthur?'

'My dad told me. She came into our shop. Ordered this German magazine.'

Arthur's mum and dad have got a newsagent's and tobacconist's just off Cranley Street. That's how he gets all his cigarettes. He nicks 'em.

'His dad talks funny an' all. They're all bloomin' Germans, whole family.'

I couldn't see what he was making such a fuss about. The Pigeon doesn't talk funny.

'Well, I don't think the new lad's a German. He talks just like us only a bit posher.'

Boocock screwed his face up and came towards me. I thought he was going to hit me for a minute.

''Course he's a bloody German. His mum and dad are German, that makes him a German and it's like my dad says, you fight the Nazis for six years and then they come and live next door to you. It's not right!'

They all started agreeing and mumbling to each other, saying it wasn't right, and Norbert crouched down and started moving about like a boxer.

'You mean he's a Nazzi? The Pigeon's a Nazzi?'

''Course he is. My dad says all Germans are Nazis, and

we shouldn't kid ourselves they're not. That's what my dad says.'

Boocock was talking rubbish. Not all Germans were Nazis, I don't care what his dad says. A lot of Germans ran away from the Nazis. I'd seen a picture at the Gaumont a couple of weeks back with my mum and my Auntie Doreen. It was all about this family escaping from Berlin. That's what it was called, *Escape from Berlin*. It was an 'A' film. It was great.

'I think you're wrong, Arthur. A lot of Germans ran away from the Nazis.'

Some of the others had seen *Escape from Berlin* and agreed with me. Norbert had seen it. He'd probably asked a stranger to take him in.

'He's right, Arthur. A lot of Germans had to escape from the Nazzies. You ought to go and see *Escape from Berlin*, it's great. It's an "A" though, you'll have to get someone to take you in.'

I don't know why Norbert calls them Nazzies when they're called Nazis. They weren't called Nazzies in *Escape from Berlin*. Boocock looked at us all and some more spit shot out from between his teeth.

'All right, the Pigeon might not be a Nazi but he's a German and we fought them in the war, didn't we? They're our enemy.'

What was Boocock talking about? The war's been over for nearly ten years. My mum says we've got to forgive and forget. He wouldn't be at our school if he was our enemy. His mum and dad wouldn't live in England, would they?

'And I'll tell you summat else . . .'

He stopped.

185

'Push off, Pigeon! This is private!'

We all turned round and saw him standing there, staring at us through his thick glasses. I wondered how long he'd been listening.

'Go on, push off, you little squirt! This is nowt to do with you.'

He didn't push off. He took a step closer. He went right up to Boocock.

'For your information, Boocock, my parents aren't German, they're from Austria. But I don't suppose you've heard of Austria, have you, Boocock? I could show it to you on a map if you like . . .'

We all stood there gawping. You don't talk to Arthur like that. Nobody talks to Arthur like that, not even Gordon Barraclough.

'And my father was in the British army as it happens. He fought against the Germans. And another thing, I was born in London. I'm English, Boocock, just like you.'

Boocock took a step in towards him. Oh no! If they have a fight Boocock'll pulverise him.

'You might be English, Pigeon, but you're not like me. You're not like any of us, are yer?'

We all looked at each other. What was he talking about? Norbert asked him.

'How do you mean he's not like any of us, Arthur? 'Cos he was born in London and talks different?'

Boocock looked at the Pigeon for a couple of seconds and sort of smiled. It was more of a sneer really.

'He knows what I mean . . .'

*I* didn't. What *did* he mean?

'It was his lot that killed Jesus . . .!'

What was he on about now? Who are 'his lot'?

'That's why he doesn't come to morning assembly. He's a Jew! And the Jews killed Jesus!'

We'd all wondered why every morning while we have assembly in the main hall, the Pigeon goes into a classroom at the back and always comes out after 'Our Father, who art in Heaven'. The first morning Reverend Dutton had taken him there David Holdsworth and me had heard him telling him when to come out.

'You sit in here, Rothman, and after the Lord's Prayer when you hear the Headmaster making the announcements, you can come out and join us . . .'

Boocock was still going on at him. I'd never seen a Jew before. He didn't look any different to me.

'That's why he brings his own dinner every day, in't it, Rothman? Our food's not good enough for you!'

The Pigeon's a lot smaller than Boocock and he was looking up at him through his thick glasses. He wasn't scared though. He didn't look it anyway. He just stood up to him, giving as good as he was getting.

'You're pathetic, Boocock.'

We were all waiting for Arthur to belt him one. But he didn't. I couldn't understand it. I don't think he was used to anybody standing up to him like that. He might have thumped him but he left it too late, the Pigeon just walked off. We all stood there, nobody knowing what to say . . . We could hear the bell going for dinner-time . . . Lads were starting to line up and I could hear Melrose telling them to stop talking . . . It was stupid, this, you couldn't blame the Pigeon for Jesus getting killed . . . It wasn't fair . . .

'Arthur, you can't blame the Pigeon for Jesus getting killed. It wasn't his fault, was it?'

The next thing Boocock had grabbed me by my shirt and had his face right close to mine. He nearly choked me.

'Listen you, you'd better make up your mind whose side you're on – the Jews or the Christians!'

He pushed me away and I grabbed this pillar to stop myself from falling. I grazed my hand and ended up on my bum with everybody looking down at me. They all followed Boocock to the dinner queue. Except Barraclough. He stood over me, a leg on either side.

'Yeah, you'd better make up your mind whose side you're on!'

And he kicked me.

From then on nobody spoke to the Pigeon. We all ignored him. Everybody. Me as well. He was always on his own. Every break. Every dinner-time. On the school bus to football. In the changing room. On the way to school. On the way home from school. Nobody talked to him. I knew it was wrong but I was a coward, I just did what all the others did. I was too scared of Boocock and Barraclough to do any different. I'd tried sticking up for him once and look what happened. It was all of us against him, the whole class. It must have been terrible for him. If it had been me I don't think I'd have gone to school. Or I'd have got my mum to talk to the headmaster or something. But the funny thing was, the Pigeon didn't seem that bothered. He didn't take any notice. He just carried on as if it wasn't happening. It was like *he* was ignoring *us*. And when anybody teased him he'd just smile. You'd have thought the teachers would have said something but they didn't seem to notice what was going on. Melrose made it worse. One Friday the Pigeon brought in a letter for him.

'Ah, for me, Rothman – it's not often I get a letter by pigeon post.'

Everybody laughed. I laughed even though I didn't understand the joke, and the Pigeon just took off his glasses, wiped them on his hanky and gave one of his little smiles. Boocock sits in the front row and while Melrose was looking at the letter he turned round and whispered, loud enough for the Pigeon to hear.

'I bet it's from his mum asking us to be a bit nicer to her little pigeon . . .'

We all sniggered. The Pigeon just carried on wiping his glasses, he didn't seem to notice. Melrose finished reading the letter.

'So, Jewish festival is it on Monday? You won't be here? It's all right for some, eh Rothman?'

He put the letter in the envelope and gave it back to him.

'All right, lad, but you'd better give this to Mr Bleasdale, he's your form master.'

So it wasn't about us. I wish it had been. I'd have been glad if we'd all been told to stop it. Picking on him, ignoring him, treating him the way we were. Even if we'd got into trouble. Boocock couldn't do anything to us then, could he? Not if we'd been told by Melrose or the headmaster. I couldn't understand why the Pigeon didn't get his mum and dad to write. I would have.

Next morning I did my grocery round. I do it every Saturday. Ronnie Knapton used to do it and when his dad got a job in Leeds and they'd had to move I'd asked Mr Killerby if I could do it.

'How old are you, lad?'

'Eleven.'

Mr Killerby had sucked in his breath and shaken his head.

'I'm nearly twelve – I'm older than Ronnie Knapton!'

'Aye, but he's a big lad for his age. Can you ride a two-wheeler?'

What did he think I was, a little kid? Did he think I still rode round on a tricycle? I was one of the first in our street to ride a two-wheeler.

''Course I can, I've got a Raleigh three-speed.'

'Aye lad, but can you ride one of them with a full load?'

He'd pointed to the delivery bike standing in the back of the shop. It was a big black thing with old-fashioned handlebars and a basket at the front where the box of groceries went. The space between the crossbar and the pedals was closed in and on it was written KILLERBY'S – GROCERIES & PROVISIONS – FREE DELIVERY. If Ronnie Knapton could ride it I blooming well could. He wasn't that much bigger than me.

''Course I can.'

'Have you got your mum's permission?'

''Course I have.'

I hadn't. I'd thought I'd see if I got the job first.

'All right then lad, start Saturday. Half past nine. You should be finished by about half one. And you get three and six.'

Ronnie Knapton had got four shillings.

'Ronnie got four shillings . . .'

'Aye, but he started on three and six. We'll see how you get on.'

I'd asked my mum as soon as I'd got back from seeing Mr Killerby and of course she'd said no.

'Absolutely not, you're far too young!'

'I'm older than Ronnie Knapton.'

'You might be, but he's bigger than you.'

Blimey, you'd think Ronnie Knapton was a giant the way people go on. If it hadn't been for my Auntie Doreen she wouldn't have changed her mind. My Auntie Doreen thought it was a good idea.

'I think it's very commendable, Freda. Let him earn a bit of pocket money. It's not as if he's delivering papers, wandering round in the dark like a lot of them do. He'll be riding a bike. That's what he does on a Saturday morning anyway . . .'

I've been doing it for about six weeks now. Whenever I ask Mr Killerby how I'm getting on he says all right but he still only gives me three and six. Some of the people I deliver to give me money though. There's one old lady, Miss Boothroyd, she always gives me threepence, every week. Even if she's not there and I have to leave the box on the back step there's always an envelope that says *Killerby's Delivery Boy* with a threepenny piece inside. She's nice. At another house they always give me a glass of orange squash. The worst delivery is to a house at the top of Thornton Hill – it's so steep – but it's great on the way back.

That Saturday, after I'd got back from Thornton Hill, I parked the bike and went through to the back of the shop to get my next box. When a delivery's ready to take, Mr Killerby writes the name on a scrap of paper and puts it on top of the groceries, so I started sorting through my boxes. That's when I saw it – *Rothman, 12 Oak Park Crescent*. He only puts the address when it's a new customer. I was looking at it when Mr Killerby came in from serving in the shop.

'No lad, leave that till last. They're a Jewish family. They have their Sabbath on a Saturday, so they've gone to church. They said they'll be back after one.'

I did the rest of my deliveries, got my threepence from Miss Boothroyd, and at ten past one I was turning into Oak Park Crescent and looking for number twelve. I was hoping there'd be nobody in and I could leave the stuff on the back doorstep. I didn't want to see the Pigeon. I wouldn't have known what to say to him.

It was a big house with its own drive. It's quite a posh road, Oak Park Crescent. All the houses are big but a lot of them have been turned into flats. On the front gate there was a sign, DR JULIUS ROTHMAN, with lots of letters after his name. Underneath it gave the surgery hours. I didn't know the Pigeon's dad was a doctor. But then I didn't know anything about the Pigeon. Nobody did. We never talked to him.

I pushed the bike up the drive past a sign that said SURGERY with an arrow underneath pointing to the back of the house. I went to the front door and rang the bell. Nothing. I rang again. Still nothing. There was nobody in. Thank goodness. I took the box of groceries round the back, left it on the step and just as I was getting on the bike they came walking up the drive. The Pigeon was talking to his dad and didn't see me at first. His mum smiled at me.

'Ah, are you bringing my sings from Mr Killerby, za grocer?'

192

I nodded.

'Yes, they're round the back. Mr Killerby told me to leave it there if you weren't in.'

'Zat's fine.'

She said something to the Pigeon's dad.

'Schatzi, gib den Kleinen ein paar Pennies.'

I couldn't understand what she was saying but his dad started searching in his pockets.

'Here you are, young man, a little somesing for your troubles.'

Boocock was right, his dad talked funny as well. He held out a shilling for me. A shilling!

'No, it's all right. Honestly.'

If it had been anybody else I'd have taken it like a shot but it wasn't right. We were all being horrible to the Pigeon at school and here was his dad wanting to give me a shilling. It wasn't right. But he kept on holding it out.

'I can't. P—'

I just stopped myself from calling him Pigeon.

'William, tell him.'

His mum looked at the Pigeon, then at me.

'You know each uzzer?'

The Pigeon smiled and told her my name.

'We go to the same school, mummy. We're in the same class.'

She asked me to come into the house and have something to eat with them.

'No, no thank you. I can't. I've got more deliveries to do . . .'

I couldn't stand it. They were being so nice to me. I just wanted to get away.

193

'I've got to go!'

I started to get on the bike but his mum came over and took hold of my hands.

'I vant to sank you. All of you. You have been so kind to my Villiam. He tells me every day vot good friends you are. It's not easy to join a new school and you have all made him feel so velcome . . .'

Then she smiled and squeezed my hands.

I felt sick. I wanted to throw up. I wanted to tell her the truth. We're horrible to your William. We don't talk to him 'cos Arthur Boocock says the Jews killed Jesus. 'Cos Arthur Boocock's a bully and we're all scared of him. 'Cos I'm a coward and I don't want them all not talking to me like they don't talk to him . . .

'I've got to go, Mrs Rothman.'

I started cycling away. I heard the Pigeon calling and running after me. I had to stop at the end of the drive 'cos of the road. He caught me up and pressed the shilling into my hand.

'Don't worry. I won't tell Boocock.'

We looked at each other for a minute and I hated him. How could he tell his mum how nice we all were, how friendly we all were, how welcome we all made him? I wanted him to tell her the truth.

'Why don't you tell her, Pigeon, why don't you tell her?'

He looked at me through his thick glasses.

'She worries about me.'

He went up the drive and when he got to the front door he smiled. It wasn't one of his little smiles. It was a sad smile. I watched him go in.

194

I got on the bike and pedalled off as fast as I could. I went up Heaton Hill and when I reached the top I stopped and threw the shilling into Lilycroft reservoir. I threw it as far as I could. Then I cycled back to Mr Killerby's. I couldn't stop crying all the way . . .

# THE PIGEON

## PART TWO

On the Sunday morning we went to church, my mum, me and my Auntie Doreen. We go every week. It's boring. Boring hymns, boring sermon. Standing up, sitting down, standing up, kneeling down, standing up, sitting down. I hate it. While I'm sitting, standing and kneeling I daydream. That's the only way I can get through. I think about all sorts of things. Nice things. Going to the pictures or the fair. School holidays. Anything to make the time go quick. Sometimes I think about my Sunday dinner. I can spend the whole time in church thinking about lovely roast beef or roast lamb or roast pork. I don't know what my mum or my Auntie Doreen would say if they knew that when the Vicar says 'Let us pray' and we all kneel on those cushion things and put our heads on our hands all I'm praying for is roast beef and Yorkshire pudding . . . with lovely crunchy potatoes, just the way my mum makes them.

But on that Sunday I didn't think about any of those things. All I could think about was the Pigeon. I couldn't stop thinking about him.

'Let us pray . . .'

Everybody knelt down and closed their eyes.

'Our Father, which art in heaven . . .'

I looked at my mum on one side and my Auntie Doreen on the other. They had their eyes closed.

'Hallowed be thy name . . .'

I closed my eyes. I didn't pray for roast beef and Yorkshire pudding this time, I prayed properly.

'Please God, make Arthur Boocock leave William alone. I know he's a Jew and the Jews killed Jesus, but it's not his fault. William had nothing to do with it . . .'

I didn't call him Pigeon – it didn't seem right, not when you're praying.

'Please make Boocock stop picking on him . . . Let him be like everybody else in our class even if he is a Jew.'

That's when I heard it, a little voice inside my head.

'You don't have to be like all the others. You don't have to ignore him . . .'

It was like God was talking back to me.

'Be his friend. Talk to him. There's nothing stopping you.'

No, there's nothing stopping me – except that I'm a coward. If only I wasn't such a coward.

'Please God, make me not be a coward so that I can be William's friend even if the others aren't . . .'

'Don't be such a big Jessie . . .!'

He sounded more like my mum now.

'Look at William. He goes home every night and tells his mum how friendly you all are and how welcome you've made him.'

I know, God, I know. You don't have to tell me.

'*You* wouldn't do that. You'd go home crying. And you'd stay off school, wouldn't you? You're soft, you are.'

I know, I know. I told you, I'm a coward. I am soft. I don't know how the Pigeon does it – sorry, William. He's a titch. Tons smaller than me but he's not scared of Boocock.

Look at the way he stood up to him the other day. What was it he said? 'You're pathetic, Boocock!' Yeah, that was it. 'You're pathetic, Boocock!' Just like that . . . And the way he'd looked at Arthur, stared at him, daring him to hit him. Boocock would have thumped me. He did thump me and all I'd said was you couldn't blame the Pigeon for Jesus getting killed. Why didn't he thump the Pigeon? Why did he just let him walk away . . .? 'Cos he can tell . . . He knows the Pigeon isn't scared of him. Not like me . . .

'Please God, make something happen to Arthur Boocock so that it all stops.'

I didn't mean anything bad like getting run over or getting ill or . . . well I wouldn't have minded – I hate Arthur Boocock – but if he got run over I wouldn't want it to happen 'cos I'd prayed for it. No, I just wanted someone to pick on him like he picks on everyone else. Let him be the one who gets bullied for a change, then he'd know what it's like.

'Please God, make Arthur Boocock get bullied. Let him have a taste of his own medicine for once – please . . .!'

I dreamt about the Pigeon that night. It was horrible. I was delivering a box of groceries on Mr Killerby's bike, pedalling as fast as I could. The whole class was chasing me and shouting and throwing stones. Arthur Boocock was leading them and I pedalled faster and faster. But it was like there was no chain on the bike. The pedals went round but I wasn't getting anywhere. I looked back and saw Boocock being run over by this big truck. Then Boocock's mum and dad were chasing me, and Melrose. And they were all shouting 'Traitor, traitor' and they came closer and closer. And I pedalled faster and faster. Suddenly I was at the top of a hill, I think it was Thornton Hill but it was twice as steep, no, much more than that, ten times as steep, it was a sheer drop and I started going down faster and faster. Then I saw, it wasn't groceries in the cardboard box – it was the Pigeon! He was tiny, about a foot high, sitting in the box at the front of the bike and he was smiling at me. We were going to crash and I was trying to scream but no sound came out and the Pigeon just kept on smiling. We were up in the air now, the bike was gone and the cardboard box and we were falling to the ground and the Pigeon was still smiling. He wasn't scared, not like me. He wasn't scared 'cos he had wings on his feet. He could fly. He flew off smiling while I was falling . . . falling . . . falling . . . Then I woke up. It was horrible. I didn't know where I was. I stared at the ceiling and at the wallpaper for what seemed like ages. Then I heard my mum calling me to get up and I realised that it was my wallpaper I was staring at.

'Come on, move yourself, it's ten to eight. If I have to come up there there'll be trouble.'

'Gower . . .'
    'Yes, sir.'
    'Hopkinson . . .'
    'Sir.'
    'Hopwood . . .'
    'Yes, sir.'
Monday morning. English with Melrose. Then football, with Melrose. I hate Mondays.
    'Illingworth . . .'
    'Yes, sir.'
    'Lightowler . . .'
    'Sir.'

'Stop slouching, Lightowler.'

'Yes, sir.'

I couldn't get the dream out of my head. It'd been so real. Boocock getting run over by that truck. It was like it had really happened. I looked over to his desk. I never thought I'd ever be pleased to see Arthur Boocock but I was today. He was messing about with a small mirror. Pollywashing. That's getting the sun in the mirror and shining it into someone's face. He was pollywashing Keith Hopwood, right in his eyes. Boocock kept shining the sun in his face, taunting him, and Hopwood was getting mad. He'd done the same thing to the Pigeon last week during history. He'd shone the sun into his eyes all during the lesson. But the Pigeon wasn't like Hopwood. He didn't go mad. He didn't do anything. He just carried on working as if it wasn't happening even though his left eye was watering like anything. He just didn't seem to notice.

'Rothman . . . Rothman.'

Melrose looked up and Boocock hid the mirror under his desk just in time.

'Rothman . . .?'

A few of them sang-song it together:

'Not here, sir.'

Melrose nodded and wrote in the register.

'Oh, that's right, Jewish holiday or some such nonsense. All right for some, eh lads?

'Yes, sir.'

'Spencer . . .'

'Sir.'

'Tattersall . . .'

'Yes, sir.'

All during English, whenever Melrose wasn't looking, Boocock carried on pollywashing Hopwood, making his eyes water even more. When the sun went behind a cloud he stopped and started flicking paper pellets instead. One got him right inside his ear. Later on, in the cloakroom, while we were getting our stuff for football Hopwood was grumbling and showing me his sore ear.

'I'll be glad when the P-Pigeon gets back and B-B-Boocock can start p-p-picking on him again.'

And I thought to myself, not just Boocock, we'll all be picking on him. You, me, everybody. 'Cos we're all scared of Boocock.

We don't have any playing fields at our school. We go on a special bus to Bankfield top, about two miles away. The bus was late and Melrose told us to wait inside the school gates.

'McDougall, fetch me when the bus comes. I'll be in the staff room. And *be quiet*! No messing about.'

Norbert made a face at Melrose behind his back.

'S'all right for him. We wait here and he goes off and has a nice cup of tea.'

Boocock was leaning against the wall, a stupid sneer on his face.

'Good. Gives me chance to have a fag.'

And he took a cigarette out of his top pocket. While he lit up the others looked around, nervous, in case anybody was at the classroom windows. Boocock wasn't bothered. Nothing ever scares him. Big 'ead! I watched him, leaning against the wall, showing off, holding his cigarette between his thumb and his big finger with the lit end tucked inside his hand so nobody could see it. And blowing smoke down his nose. He thinks he's so good, doesn't he? He thinks he's so tough. He is . . . Why doesn't he ever cough? I wish the smoke would catch in his throat and make him cough. I wish he'd choke. Norbert was up on the school gates looking out for the bus.

'Bloomin' hummer – look at the Pigeon!'

We all looked through the gates. He was coming down the road with his mum and dad and they were all dressed up. They must have been on their way to their Jewish church.

His mum was wearing a big hat with cherries on it and round her shoulders she had this fur thing and it had an animal's head at one end. It looked like a fox's head. And his dad was wearing a bowler hat and the Pigeon was wearing a hat too. It wasn't a bowler but it was the sort of hat grown-ups wear. He looked stupid. They got nearer and everybody started whistling and shouting. His mum waved at us.

'Look, Villiam, all your nice schoolfriends are vaving to you.'

The Pigeon was blushing like anything. He sort of nodded and walked on, trying to get his mum and dad past as quick as he could, but she came over to us. Oh no, I didn't want her to see me. I didn't want her saying hello to me in front of all the others. I worked my way to the back and hid behind Duggie Bashforth and David Nunn.

'Hello, boys. I vant to say sank you to you all . . .'

I knew what she was going to say. I peeped at the Pigeon. He was cringing. He knew what she was going to say as well.

'You have made Villiam feel so velcome in his new school. He tells me every day vot good friends you are. His farzer and I really appreciate your kindness . . .'

She smiled. Nobody said anything. They all looked at each other. Someone laughed, I think it was Norbert, and that set some of the others off. The bus came and McDougall went off to fetch Melrose. I kept myself hidden behind Bashforth, crouching down a bit, making sure the Pigeon's mum couldn't see me.

'Vell boys, ve must go. Have a good game of football. Come along, Villiam.'

She said something to the Pigeon's dad in German or whatever language they talk and walked off. The Pigeon didn't follow, he stood there looking at us all. Then I realised, it wasn't the others he was looking at – it was me. He knew why I'd been hiding behind Duggie Bashforth and he was looking right at me like . . . well, like I was a piece of muck. All right, Pigeon, I'm not like you, I'm a coward, I don't want your mum to see me. She might say hello and the others would know I've been talking to you. You know what would happen then, don't you? Nobody would talk to *me*. I want to be friends with you but I daren't . . . Stop looking at me like that . . . Bloody bus. If it hadn't been late none of this would have happened . . . Stop looking at me, it's not my fault.

'Villiam, come now, ve are late . . .'

Go on, go, your mum's calling you. It's not my fault you're a Jew! He stayed looking at me a bit longer, then he shook his head and followed his mum and dad.

The others all burst out laughing and Barraclough started taking off his mum.

'Sank you for looking after my Villiam. You have made him feel so velcome in his new school . . .!'

They all laughed and Norbert and a few others took her off as well.

'Come on, Villiam, ve are late . . .'

'Vell boys, have a good game of football . . .'

'I vant to say sank you, you have made Villiam feel so velcome . . .'

'*Shut up!*'

I couldn't help it. It was like it was someone else shouting, not me.

'*Shut up!*'

They were all looking at me. My stomach was churning. Why had I shouted like that? Why hadn't I kept quiet? Boocock was looking at me. He came over. He put his face close to mine.

'Who are you telling to shut up?'

I could smell the cigarette on his breath. I wish someone had seen him smoking. I wish he'd got taken to the headmaster. I wish he'd got the cane. I wish he'd get expelled. I wish he'd leave me alone. It's not fair. Oh God!

'Well, it's not fair, Arthur, she can't help talking like that, she's not English.'

'That's right . . .'

He starting punching me in the chest, pushing me backwards.

' . . . and I've told you before, you want to make up your mind whose side you're on, the Jews or the Christians.'

He got hold of my shirt and twisted his hand round, choking me. I could hear Barraclough and a few others laughing.

'Come on, whose side are you on, theirs or mine?'

It's stupid, this, Boocock. The Pigeon's all right. His mum and dad are all right. Why do we have to choose sides? Why are you such a bully? I wish you'd die, Boocock.

205

'Yours, Arthur . . .'

He let me go. I don't know if it was 'cos I'd said I was on his side or 'cos he'd seen Melrose coming.

'Right, on the bus – and keep the talking down! Light-owler, what've you got in your mouth?'

'Chewing gum, sir.'

'Get rid of it.'

He spat it out.

'Not there, lad – in the bin!'

Nobody sat next to me on the bus. We were on the top deck while Melrose sat downstairs reading his paper like he always does. They were all talking and laughing and taking off the Pigeon's mum again. Well, let them. I wasn't going to say anything this time. It was nothing to do with me. Why should I worry about the Pigeon?

'W-w-what I c-can't understand is w-w-why he told h-his mum w-w-we're all his f-f-friends?'

'Cos he's not soft like you, Keith Hopwood, or me, or any of you. He doesn't want his mum to worry so he hasn't told her that we don't talk to him 'cos the Jews killed Jesus. And he's not scared of Boocock neither. I'd love to have said it, but I didn't dare. I didn't want to end up like him with no friends, with nobody talking to me.

Nobody did talk to me for the next sixty minutes. They shouted at me. I was in goal. We lost.

On the way back though everything was all right. It all seemed forgotten. Boocock and Barraclough were busy teasing Hopwood. They'd pinched one of his football boots and were hanging it out of the window pretending to drop it. I sat at the back with Norbert and David Holdsworth playing I-Spy. Hopwood was going mad, he looked like he was going to cry.

'G-g-give it b-back, give it b-back or I'll tell. I'll r-report you . . .'

The more he shouted the more Boocock teased him. I heard Melrose coming up the stairs.

'Hey, Arthur – Melrose!'

He pulled the boot back through the window, gave it back to Keith and turned to the front. Melrose looked around for a few seconds, told us all to keep the noise down and went back downstairs. After he'd gone Boocock turned round and gave me the thumbs-up.

'Ta.'

I gave him the thumbs-up back and smiled.

'That's all right, Arthur.'

Yeah, everything was all right now. I was on Arthur's side and the Pigeon could look after himself. I wasn't going to stick up for him any more. I was going to keep my mouth shut. And I would have done if I hadn't met those Galsworthy Road lads on my way home from school.

Monday afternoons aren't so bad. Double woodwork, boring 'cos I'm no good at it, history which is my best subject – I got 48% in the test – and the last lesson is RI with Reverend Dutton. That's boring as well and we all mess about but he never seems to notice and we make fun of him 'cos he wears a wig. Even when he does get mad with any of us he always says sorry afterwards. He's not like a proper teacher, Reverend Dutton, he's too nice. When the bell goes everybody makes a mad rush for the cloakrooms even if he's in the middle of a sentence. You wouldn't dare do that with Melrose or Bleasdale or any of them.

'And so, boys, we read in St Luke 20 "that Jesus went into the Temple and began to cast out them that sold therein, and them that bought, saying unto them . . ." '

The bell went and we could hear Reverend Dutton still talking to us while we were running down the corridor.

'Thank you, boys, we'll pick up from there next time . . .'

I felt a smack on the back of my head.

'Where's the fire?'

It was Melrose.

'Nowhere, sir.'

'Then walk!'

He gave me another crack on the head and I walked the rest of the way. I could hear Hopwood shouting in the cloakroom.

'G-give it b-back, it's not f-fair, give it b-back.'

Boocock had pinched one of his boots again and him, Barraclough and Norbert were throwing it to each other.

'Come on L-Lightowler, g-give it 'ere.'

He tried to grab it but Norbert threw the boot to me. Oh, what was I supposed to do with it?

'Go on, g-give it to us. B-be a sp-sp-sport.'

I felt sorry for Hopwood but if I gave it to him they'd all have a go at me, wouldn't they? Same as sticking up for the Pigeon. All that happens is that *I* get picked on.

'Catch, Arthur!'

I lobbed it over his head. Stupid Hopwood tried to get it, fell over and caught his chin on one of the pegs.

'Aahh, bloody 'ell! Aahh!!'

He really hurt himself. He was rolling about on the floor screaming.

'My chin! My bloody chin! I'm gonna report you.'

The funny thing was he wasn't stammering. It was the first time I'd heard him talk without stammering.

'Aw my chin!'

'What's all the shouting about?'

Melrose! We looked at Hopwood. He was sitting on the floor still rubbing his chin.

'What are you doing down there, Hopwood? What's going on?'

'I f-f-fell, sir. I c-caught my ch-ch-chin o-o-on one of the pegs, sir . . .'

He looked at Boocock.

'It w-w-was an accident, sir.'

'Well get up and get off home. You shouldn't be mucking about in here. Come on, all of you, out!'

He went marching up the corridor shouting that if any of us were still there when he came back in three minutes we'd be there till six o'clock! Boocock kicked the football boot over to Keith.

'We was only havin' a bit of fun. You can't take a joke, you.'

Barraclough started taking him off.

'Yeah, we w-w-was only havin' a bit of f-f-fun.'

They went, laughing their heads off. I picked it up for him.

'Here you are, Keith.'

'S-s-sod off!'

My boots were tied together hanging on my peg, so I put them over my shoulder, got my bag and I went.

He asks for it, does Keith, screaming and shouting like that. He shouldn't take any notice of Boocock. He should just ignore him, he'd soon stop. Who am I to talk, mind? Why do I open my big mouth? So Arthur Boocock can thump me? Well not any more. I'll just go along with all the others. Keep out of trouble. Yes, once I'd made up my mind that I was on Boocock's side, that I was going to keep quiet, I felt much better. The Pigeon can fight his own battles, I'm gonna keep my mouth shut from now on.

I turned up St Paul's Terrace and that's when I saw them. These two lads sitting on a wall at the top of the road. They must have been about twelve or thirteen. They were bigger than me anyway. At first I thought they were feeding pigeons but when I got nearer I could see it wasn't bread they were throwing, it was gravel. They were looking at me so I crossed over.

'Grammar School ponce!'

I didn't look up. St Paul's Terrace goes into my road so I just kept walking. I wanted to get home as fast as I could.

'Yeah, Grammar School tart!'

Oh no, I bet they go to Galsworthy Road Secondary Modern. Please don't let them be Galsworthy Road lads.

'Not good enough for you, are we? Just 'cos we go to Galsworthy Road . . .'

Oh heck. They carry knives, Norbert had told me. And they hate Grammar School lads. I shouldn't have worn my blazer. I should have put it in my bag. I started walking a bit quicker. Not too quick, I didn't want them to see that I was scared. Oh no, they're crossing over. They're following me!

'You think you're good, don't yer, just 'cos you go to the Grammar School?'

They were behind me. I kept walking. I turned into my road. I could hear them following.

'Well you're not. We can lick you at anything. I could take you on one arm behind my back.'

The other one laughed.

'I could take him on both arms behind my back.'

It's a long road, ours, and we live right at the other end. All I had to do was reach home, then I'd run in and I'd be all right. I felt my trouser pocket to make sure I'd got my keys. Yeah, they were there. All I had to do was keep walking for a few minutes and I'd be all right.

'You're all soft, you Grammar School lot, you're all jessies.'

One of them kicked my heel and tried to trip me up. I didn't look round. I kept going. I just wanted to get home.

'Look, he daren't even look at us. He's soft.'

They caught me up and started shouldering me, one on each side, pushing me from one to the other. Why were they picking on me? 'Cos I'm at Grammar School? It's stupid. Same as picking on the Pigeon 'cos he's a Jew or picking on Reverend Dutton 'cos he wears a wig or Keith Hopwood 'cos he's got a stammer. It's stupid.

'Look at him, he's gonna cry. He's a big cry-baby . . .!'

'Yeah, big Grammar School cry-baby's gonna cry!'

They were right. I could feel the tears in my eyes. I was trying to stop myself but I couldn't. I was going to cry. Don't let me cry, please don't let me cry . . . Then I saw her. My mum! I couldn't believe it. She must have got off work early. She'd just turned into the road. I waved.

'Mum!'

She waved back. I was going to be all right.

'That's my mum. You'd better go if you don't want to get into trouble.'

211

They laughed. They weren't bothered.

'You think we're scared of your big fat mum?'

They waved – and she waved back at them and went inside. She went into the house. She left me with them.

'*Mum*!!'

They didn't thump me that hard. Just once in the stomach and they threw my bag and my boots over a wall into one of the gardens. Then they ran off.

'What are you crying for, love? What's happened?'

She sat me down in the kitchen and I told her all about it. I couldn't stop crying.

'Why did you go in? Why didn't you wait?'

It was stupid saying that, it wasn't her fault.

'I didn't know, love. I thought they were your friends.'

She was sitting next to me, her arm round my shoulder. The tears were running down my cheeks. But I wasn't crying about what had just happened. It was everything else. Everything that had been happening with the Pigeon. It wasn't right. I knew it wasn't right and I decided. I wasn't going to be on Boocock's side.

I got to school early next morning and looked for him. He was bottom end of the playground on his own as usual. He was sitting on his bag, reading. My heart was thumping.

'Hi, William.'

He looked up, surprised.

'Hello.'

I fished out the bag of sweets I'd bought.

'Do you want a Nuttall's Mintoe?'

'Thank you . . .'

He was just going to take one but stopped. I could see

him looking behind me. I turned round. Boocock, Barra-clough, Norbert and Hopwood and a few others were coming towards us. My heart started thumping even more. He didn't say anything. He just stood staring at me.

'I'm not gonna be on your side, Arthur. I think it's stupid. I don't think we should have sides.'

I was still holding the bag of sweets. Boocock looked at me.

'Traitor!'

He would have hit me but William stepped in front and thumped him right in the stomach – hard. Boocock couldn't believe it. None of us could. He couldn't speak. I think it was 'cos he was winded but it might have been 'cos he was surprised, I wasn't sure. He got his mad up then and went for William – and William hit him again. Harder. I looked at Boocock lying on the ground, holding his stomach and crying. God had answered my prayers at last. Boocock was getting a taste of his own medicine. And all I could think was that it was a good job I *hadn't* prayed for anything bad to happen to him, like getting run over or getting ill.

William went back and sat on his bag and started reading again. I followed him.

'You're a good fighter, William.'

He looked up and smiled.

'My father says we must only use violence as a last resort. I think that was a last resort, don't you?'

I didn't know what he was talking about. I held out the bag of sweets.

'Here, have a Nuttall's Mintoe . . .'

# THE PIGEON

## PART THREE

William doesn't go to our school any more. He goes to a boarding school where there's more Jews. I think his mum and dad thought it was better for him. I still see him in the holidays and I see his mum and dad every Saturday when I take their groceries. His dad always gives me a shilling. It's a shame he went to another school 'cos by the time he left everybody liked him – except Boocock.

# THE YO-YO CHAMPION

'Black suede crêpe-soles! For school? Do you hear that, Doreen?'

My Auntie Doreen hadn't heard 'cos she was reading my mum's *Woman's Weekly*. We'd just had our tea. Gammon and chips and a pineapple ring, my favourite. My Auntie Doreen always comes for tea on a Friday and she always brings the gammon. She works on the bacon counter at the Co-op. I think she gets it for free.

'What was that, Freda?'

My mum poured herself another cup of tea.

'We're going to Crabtree's tomorrow morning to get his Lordship some new school shoes and do you know what he wants? Black suede crêpe-soles. Like those teddy boys wear. Black suede crêpe! For school!'

They both laughed and my mum shook her head as if suede crêpe shoes were the daftest thing in the world. It wasn't fair. Arthur Boocock's mum and dad had let him get some, and Kenny Spencer's. So had Gordon Barraclough's. Tony had got some as well. And David Holdsworth. Even Keith Hopwood said he was getting some – but I don't believe him. He's soft, is Keith Hopwood. He was just saying it to keep up with all the others.

'But Mum, everybody's getting them. Tony's got a pair.

217

Even Keith Hopwood's getting some. Keith Hopwood! Everybody's getting them.'

'Well you're not. You'll have proper black leather lace-ups. Proper school shoes and I don't want you playing football in them neither.'

My Auntie Doreen didn't help. She said that black suede shoes were very vulgar and my mum gave her a funny sort of look and smiled.

'I know why *you* don't like black suede shoes . . .'

My Auntie Doreen gave her a funny look back.

'Yes, and he was very vulgar too, just like his shoes . . .'

And she smiled as well. They're always doing that, my mum and my Auntie Doreen, saying things to each other that I can't understand and then smiling their secret smiles.

'Who's vulgar just like his shoes?'

I don't know why I bothered asking. I knew they wouldn't tell me. They never tell me.

'Oh, just someone your Auntie Doreen knew a long time ago.'

Then they did it again. Smiled at each other. Did they think I didn't notice? Well I did notice. I always notice. But I can never understand what they're smiling about.

I didn't care. All I cared about was getting some black suede crêpes. Who said school shoes have to be black leather lace-ups anyway? It wasn't fair.

'Who says school shoes have to be black leather lace-ups anyway? What's wrong with black suede crêpes? Who says you can't wear black suede crêpes?'

As soon as I said it I knew I shouldn't have. My mum banged her fist on the table. She made me jump. She made my Auntie Doreen jump. And she spilt her tea.

218

'I do! I say you can't wear black suede crêpes. Now fetch me a cloth.'

I didn't say anything more about my new shoes 'cos the big red blotch had come up on her neck. She always gets it when she's upset or excited and I know that's when to shut up. I fetched the cloth from the kitchen and gave it to her.

'I'm sorry, Mum . . .'

She didn't say anything, she just mopped up where she'd spilt the tea. But the blotch was starting to fade. Thank goodness . . .

Crabtree's is the big posh department store in town and we always go there to buy my new school shoes. It takes ages. You have to take a ticket with a number on, then sit down and wait for your number to be called out. We took our ticket and sat down.

'Sixty . . . Ticket number sixty . . .?'

I liked coming to Crabtree's. Not with my mum, that's boring, but I sometimes go after school with Norbert and Tony and anybody else who wants to. The first time we went was to look at the 'moving staircases'. Norbert told me about them. I didn't believe him.

'Moving staircases! How can a staircase move?'

I laughed and Norbert got quite cross.

'I'm telling you, I was in Crabtree's on Saturday and they've got moving staircases now. I went on them.'

I was sure he was having me on. I'd been in Crabtree's lots of times. I'd been up and down in the lifts but I'd never seen a moving staircase.

'Well, how do they work then, these moving staircases?'

'You stand on the first step and you go to the top and then you get off.'

'How do you go down?'

Norbert looked at me as if I was stupid.

'They've got moving staircases that go down as well.'

I couldn't see it. I just couldn't imagine a staircase that moved. It was impossible.

'It's impossible. How can a staircase move?'

'We'll go down to Crabtree's after school and you can see for yourself.'

And we did. And Norbert was right, they did have moving staircases. I couldn't believe it. We went from the ground floor up to the fifth floor and then down again. We did it three times. Then we got thrown out 'cos Norbert started walking down one of the moving staircases that was going up.

We often go to Crabtree's after school. We go up and down in the lifts or on the moving staircases and look at all the toys and at Christmas they have a grotto and you can walk through for free. And sometimes they have a stand and give things away. One time there was a lady asking people to try bits of cheese. Norbert and me went back three times before she realised and told us to push off. I didn't like it – it tasted of soap – but it was free. Another time they were asking people to try Ribena and gave away miniature bottles. We got two each. The one thing I don't like about going with Norbert is that he pinches things. I don't know how he does it. They never see him. *I* never see him and I'm with him all the time. I don't even know *why* he does it. He steals things he doesn't even want. He throws them away. One time it was a reel of blue cotton. Another time it was a wooden spoon. The last time we'd come out of Crabtree's it was a ball of wool he'd taken.

'Why do you do it, Norbert? You're going to get caught one day.'

He grinned at me.

'That's why I do it – to see if they can catch me . . .'

Then he laughed and threw the ball of wool in a rubbish bin. He's mad. He just likes stealing. Mind you, his dad's in prison for thieving. Maybe it runs in the family.

'Sixty-one . . . Ticket sixty-one . . .?'

My mum was in quite a good mood so I'd decided I was going to give it one last go, see if I could persuade her to get me black suede crêpes. It was just a matter of choosing the right moment.

'Sixty-one . . . Number sixty-one . . .?'

A fat man with a red face and a long droopy moustache held up his hand.

'Sixty-one? Over 'ere, and about bloody time . . .'

My mum looked at him and tutted to herself. She doesn't like swearing.

'Twenty minutes I've been waiting. Over twenty bloody minutes. Bloody ridiculous!'

My mum wriggled in her chair and tutted again while this lady apologised to the fat man.

'I'm very sorry, sir, but Saturdays are our busy day. We're serving as fast as we can.'

'Aye, well you need more bloody staff then, don't you? Over twenty minutes to get from ticket bloody fifty-eight to sixty-bloody-one? Bloody ridiculous!'

That's when my mum got her mad up.

'Do you mind not using that kind of language? There's children present.'

My mum wriggled in her chair again and folded her arms. Everybody was looking at us and I could feel myself going red. Why did she have to interfere like that? It was none of our business. That's what the fat man thought as well.

'You mind your own bloody business, it's nowt to do with you . . .' and he mumbled something about 'bloody busy-bodies'.

'It is my business if you swear in front of my young lad. I'll thank you to keep your foul language to yourself.'

The fat man suddenly stood up. He came over and glared at my mum.

'I'm not shopping 'ere. I'll take my bloody money elsewhere . . .!'

And he stormed out. It all went quiet. My mum was shaking a bit and I could see the red blotch on her neck. That was it. I could forget about my suede crêpes now.

'Sixty-two . . . Ticket sixty-two . . .?'

The lady who'd been serving the fat man came over to us.

'I'm sorry about that, madam.'

My mum was still sitting up straight with her arms folded.

'There's no need for that kind of language. Not in Crab-tree's anyway.'

The lady had a badge on her jacket that said Assistant Manager.

'Especially not in Crabtree's, madam. We've had trouble with him before. I think he's a bit funny.'

'Ticket sixty-three . . . Sixty-three . . .?'

The assistant manager apologised again and went off to serve number sixty-three. It was a woman with a ginger-headed lad that I sort of knew. I've seen him around. He goes to St Bede's. I don't like him. I see him sometimes on my way home from school when I cut through the park. He and his mates are always hanging round the swings. They smoke. And they have spitting competitions. They go as high as they can on the swings and see who can spit the furthest. It's disgusting. He was staring at me so I stared back . . . Once on my way home from school I'd thought he was going to hit me. A few of them were sitting on the roundabout going round slowly. He'd jumped off and stood in front of me. I'd been scared stiff. He'd put his face right close to mine.

'Who are you for, Churchill or Attlee?'

I hadn't known what he was on about.

'Come on, who are you for, Churchill or Attlee?'

I didn't know what to say. I wasn't for either of them. He'd put his face even closer, our noses were nearly touching.

'I'm only asking you once more, kid. Churchill or Attlee, who are you for?'

'Churchill . . .'

He'd smiled.

'That's all right, then.'

And he'd gone back to the roundabout. I dread to think what would have happened if I'd said Attlee. I'd only said Churchill 'cos I knew he was the Prime Minister . . . While his mum was talking to the assistant manager Copper-nob and me carried on staring at each other . . . He won – I

223

looked away. When I looked back he was still staring at me and he put his tongue out at me. I looked away again.

'What's our number, mum?'

She showed me. Seventy-two.

'Seventy-two? It's going to take ages!'

She turned on me and put her face close to mine, like the ginger-headed lad did in the park that day.

'Don't you start. I've had enough with that nasty man!'

Copper-nob was staring at me again, sneering, watching me getting told off by my mum.

'Sixty-four . . . Ticket number sixty-four . . .'

The fat man was right. It was taking ages . . . Oh no, Copper-nob was trying on black suede crêpes! It wasn't fair.

'Mum . . .'

'Mm . . .?'

'I was just wondering . . .'

'What?'

'I was just wondering . . .'

The red blotch was still there.

' . . . if I could go and look at the toys? It's going to be a while before they get to seventy-two.'

She looked at her watch.

'Ten minutes. Back here by twenty past. No later.'

'Thanks, Mum.'

I ran out. Copper-nob was walking up and down trying on his new shoes and I could hear the assistant manager telling his mum how good suede crêpes were.

'They're very durable, madam. Last for ever. All the lads are wearing them.'

Yeah, all the lads except me.

I love the toy department in Crabtree's, there's so much

to look at. They've got the biggest display of lead soldiers anywhere. (That was another thing that Norbert pinched once, two lead soldiers and a cannon – he didn't throw them away.) On the ceiling there's all these wire tracks and hanging from them are little carriages. When you buy something the assistant puts your money into one of the carriages, pulls a handle and the carriage zooms across the ceiling to another assistant sitting in a cash desk behind a glass screen and she sends the carriage back with the change. It's fantastic watching all these carriages zooming all over the place.

Sometimes they have people doing special toy demonstrations. Like the spinning top that you could balance on the point of a pencil or the rim of a glass and it spun for ages. It cost half-a-crown, a special demonstration price. Once a lady was showing how you could make your own balloons. She squeezed this coloured stuff out of a tube, rolled it into a ball, stuck in a plastic straw and blew it into a balloon. That was half-a-crown as well. Everything they demonstrate always seems to cost half-a-crown.

'Just two and sixpence. A half-a-crown for the Lumar yo-yo . . .'

That's when I saw him. Well, I heard him first. I was looking at the lead soldiers, they'd had some new ones in. Irish guards. I turned round.

'The best yo-yo money can buy for only two shillings and sixpence. The price of a fish and chip supper . . .'

There he was, a yo-yo in each hand, doing these wonderful tricks.

'The Lumar yo-yo will last a lifetime . . .'

On his stand was a big poster, *Don Martell – Yo-yo Champion of Great Britain*, and there was a photo. It showed him doing his yo-yo tricks. He looked a lot younger and he was wearing a bow tie. A few people were watching and I went over.

'Come closer, don't be shy. I'm going to show you how the yo-yo can give you hours of pleasure. After just a few minutes' practice you too will be "walking the dog" . . .'

And he sent the yo-yo spinning down to the floor. When it reached the end of the string it spun round and round and then he walked towards us and the yo-yo rolled along the ground, just like a dog on a lead. He flicked his wrist and the yo-yo went flying up in the air. Another flick and it disappeared into his hand.

'Walking the dog, ladies and gentlemen, a yo-yo trick any one of you here today can master within minutes. You!'

He was pointing at me.

'Me?'

'Yes you, young man. Do I know you?'

Everybody turned round and looked.

'No.'

'We have never met?'

'No.'

'Please step forward.'

I felt myself going all red as I went towards him.

'Now, young man, which hand do you write with?'

I held out my right hand.

'This one.'

The Yo-yo Champion picked up a red yo-yo and fixed the string on my big finger.

'Just do what I do.'

He flicked the yo-yo out of the back of his hand towards the floor and it stayed spinning round at the end of the string like before. There was no way that I was going to do that. But I flicked it out of my hand just like he showed me and I couldn't believe it. It was spinning just like his.

'I don't believe it, ladies and gentlemen, look at that.'

There was my yo-yo at the end of the string spinning round and round. It looked like it could have gone on for ever.

'Let's see if he can "walk the dog".'

He turned sideways, let his yo-yo drop to the floor and started walking. With my yo-yo still spinning I copied him. I let it slowly drop down to the floor. It worked. The yo-yo rolled along the ground and I followed it. I was walking the dog just like Don Martell.

Everybody was clapping as he flicked his yo-yo up in the air and then flicked it back into his hand. He turned to watch me. I flicked my hand just like he'd done and the yo-yo flew up into the air. Another flick and it rolled up the string and I caught it in my hand.

'The lad's a natural. A future champion, which is very important because next Saturday, a week today, we will be holding a competition here in the store to find the Yo-yo Champion. First prize will be a grand silver cup inscribed with the champion's name and a Crabtree's gift token to the value of ten pounds.'

A silver cup and a ten pound token. I could go in for it . . . if I had a yo-yo.

'And I am selling the world-famous Lumar yo-yo at the special demonstration price of a half-a-crown. Two shillings and sixpence.'

Half a crown . . . Maybe my mum would get me one . . . My mum! I looked at the clock which was above the lady who took the money in the cash desk. Half past! She'd told me to be back by twenty past. Oh no! I started to run off.

'Oi! I'm not giving them away, young man. Half-a-crown.'

I still had the yo-yo in my hand. I'd forgotten. I ran back, took the string off my finger and gave it to him.

'Sorry – I'm late for my mum.'

I didn't know which would be quicker, the lift or the moving staircase. I looked up at the lights that tell you which floor the lift is on. The 'G' was lit up. It was on the ground floor. The lift would be quicker. Come on, lift, come on . . . The 'G' went out and a couple of seconds later the doors opened.

'Basement-*ah*. Toys-*ah*, Household Goods-*ah*, Electrical Goods-*ah* . . .'

He always talked like that, the man who worked the lift. It makes me and Norbert laugh.

'Basement-*ah*. Toys-*ah*, Household Goods-*ah*, Electrical Goods-*ah* . . .'

He only had one arm. His other arm was just an empty sleeve pinned across his chest. I went in the lift and who do you think was coming out in his brand new black suede crêpes? Lucky beggar. He looked at me and gave me one of his sneery lop-sided grins.

'Mind the doors-*ah*.'

We started going up. Shoes were on the second floor.

'Ground Floor-*ah*. Haberdashery-*ah*, Furnishing Fabrics-*ah*, Glassware-*ah* . . .'

Come on, come on! If we missed our turn my mum was going to go mad. We started moving again, thank goodness.

228

'First Floor-*ah*. Ladies' Fashions-*ah*, Knitwear-*ah*, Cafeteria . . .'

I suppose it was impossible to say 'Cafeteria-*ah*'. Come on! Why couldn't they all hurry up? I could see people going up the moving staircase. I ran out and started running up the moving stairs – it had to be quicker. It would have been if it hadn't been for these two women. They wouldn't let me go past.

I asked nicely.

'Excuse me.'

They just ignored me.

'Excuse me.'

One of them looked at me then turned away and they carried on talking. Grown-ups can be really rude sometimes.

We got to the top and I ran as fast as I could to the shoe department.

'Second Floor-*ah*. Menswear-*ah*, Shoes-*ah*, Gentlemen's Hairdressing-*ah* . . .'

I'd have been better off staying in the lift. Oh no! The clock in the shoe department said twenty-five to. Fifteen minutes late. What was my mum going to say?

'Hello, love, did you have a nice time?'

She wasn't cross.

'Yeah, great . . .'

I couldn't understand it.

'Seventy-one . . . Ticket number seventy-one . . .'

That was why. They hadn't reached us. I was so lucky.

'I've been watching the British Yo-yo Champion. He let me have a go.'

She was reading her *Woman's Weekly*.

'That's nice . . .'

229

'I was quite good at it.'

'Were you, love . . .?'

She wasn't really listening.

'Yeah. They've got a competition next Saturday to find the yo-yo champion. The winner'll get ten pounds and a cup . . .'

I was just about to tell her that they cost half-a-crown and ask if I could have one when I heard someone calling my name. It was Keith Hopwood. He was with his mum and dad. Keith's dad's ever so small, not much bigger than Keith, and his mum's huge. They looked a bit like Laurel and Hardy. Mrs Hopwood was carrying two big carrier bags and was puffing and blowing. She put her shopping down and sat next to my mum.

'Eeh, I could do without buying shoes this morning, I can tell you. Has your lad been nagging you as well?'

My mum wasn't sure what she was on about.

'How do you mean?'

Mrs Hopwood slipped off her shoes and wiggled her toes about.

'These blessed black suede crêpes they're all wearing.'

'Ticket number seventy-two . . .'

My mum looked at me. Mrs Hopwood was still rubbing her foot.

'Still, if they've all got them what can you do? You can't say no, can you . . .?'

They looked great. I walked up and down like the assistant manager told me.

'They're very durable, madam. Last for ever. We've sold masses of them.'

I didn't ask my mum to buy me a yo-yo. I'd got my black suede crêpes. That was enough.

On the Monday I wore them to school and I felt really good. Arthur Boocock was wearing his. So was Tony, and David Holdsworth and Kenny Spencer and Gordon Barraclough. Keith Hopwood wasn't. They'd sold out. I'd got the last pair. Even Norbert had got some. He'd got them from Crabtree's on the Friday night after school. We looked at him. He knew what we were all thinking.

'I didn't nick 'em, you know. My mam got 'em for me.'

He must have been telling the truth. Even Norbert couldn't pinch a pair of shoes . . . I don't think . . .

'I nicked this though.'

He put his hand in his pocket and pulled out a yo-yo. It was yellow, just like the one Don Martell had been using.

'This feller was demonstrating 'em. All different tricks. There's a competition on Saturday. I can't do it though, I'm useless.'

I could.

'I can. Let's have a go.'

Norbert gave me the yo-yo. I wound up the string and slipped it on my big finger. Everybody was watching. Flick! The yo-yo came out of the back of my hand, went down the string and spun nicely. I lowered it to the floor, nice and slow, and 'walked the dog'. Flick! The yo-yo went up in the air. Flick! It rolled up the string and I caught it. Everybody was really impressed and Norbert said I could keep it.

'I don't want it, I can't even make it go up and down. Anyway, I nicked something better.'

He rummaged about in his pocket again and this time

231

he brought out a grey crayon. He's so stupid, Norbert, he'd risk getting caught for a crummy crayon.

'It's not a crummy crayon. It's a good trick, this. I'll show you. Someone look out for Bleasdale.'

We had Latin next and Bleasdale was always late. Norbert got on a chair and started drawing on one of the windows. It was a good trick. When he'd finished it looked like the window had been smashed. It was brilliant, dead realistic. Bleasdale didn't notice it, he just told us to open our books at page forty-seven. Everybody started giggling and when he asked us what was the matter we all pointed at the 'broken' window.

'Dear oh dear. Does anybody know how this happened?'

Norbert put his hand up.

'Yes sir, it was me.'

Bleasdale looked surprised.

'Well, Lightowler, your honesty is most commendable but I'm afraid you'll have to go and see the headmaster, tell him what you've done. Off you go, lad.'

We all burst out laughing and Norbert got on the chair, spat on the window and started cleaning it with his mucky handkerchief. Even Mr Bleasdale laughed. He's a good sport.

When my mum got home from work that night I was playing with the yo-yo in the kitchen. I told her that Norbert had given it to me 'cos he didn't want it. Well it was true. I just didn't tell her that he'd pinched it from Crabtree's.

'I'm going to go in for that competition on Saturday.'

'What competition's that, love?'

'At Crabtree's. The yo-yo championship. First prize is a silver cup with your name on and a ten-pound gift token.'

'Oh, that's nice . . .'

I knew my mum hadn't been listening. I went into the front room to practise. I practised every night that week. You've got to practise if you want to be a yo-yo champion. Every day after school, I'd go down to Crabtree's and watch Don. Loop the Loop, Baby in the Cradle, Round the World, all sorts of tricks. Then I'd go home and try them out.

That's what I was doing when I broke the blue vase. I couldn't help it. It wasn't my fault. I was practising.

'It wasn't my fault, Mum, I was looping the loop. I can nearly do it now.'

She looked at me with one of her looks and I thought I'd better shut up quick. I knew why she was so mad. The vase had belonged to my grandma.

'That vase belonged to my grandmother – your *great*-grandmother. It's been in our family for years.'

My *great*-grandmother! I'd always thought it had been my grandma's.

'You always said it were my grandma's.'

'It was and your great-grandma's before her but it doesn't matter now, does it? It's broken.'

She started picking up the pieces.

'Maybe you could glue it together . . .'

She gave me another look.

'I'm sorry, Mum. I didn't mean to break it. It was an accident.'

'Just be careful with that yo-yo. I don't want any more accidents.'

I wouldn't have minded but I wanted to win the yo-yo competition for her, not for me. Well that's not really true. I wanted to be the Yo-yo Champion, 'course I did, but I'd decided that if I won I was going to use the ten-pound voucher to buy her a pearl necklace. She'd been looking at it in the jewellery department after we'd bought my shoes.

On the Friday I was in the kitchen practising Baby in the Cradle – that's when you have to get the string in your left hand and make a triangle shape and then rock the yo-yo to and fro inside the triangle. Don Martell makes it look dead easy but it's not, it's one of the hardest. Anyway, I was in the kitchen practising when the front doorbell rang. It turned out to be Norbert. He walked straight in. He never waits to be asked, doesn't Norbert.

'My mam's not back from work and I've lost my key.'

He usually kept it on a string round his neck.

'It must've come off when I had that fight with Barraclough.'

He's always fighting with Gordon Barraclough, they hate each other. He saw the yo-yo in my hand.

'Hey, do that walking the dog again.'

We went into the kitchen and I did Walking the Dog. Then I did the Loop the Loop and Round the World. And I showed him Baby in the Cradle. It was the best I'd ever done it. Norbert couldn't believe it.

'How come you're so good?'

'I've been practising.'

And I told him I was going in for the competition at Crabtree's.

'Well if you win you ought to give me half the prize money. It's my yo-yo.'

I told him to sod off and I went through all my tricks again. Norbert had a go but he'd been right, he was useless. Then he brought out his grey crayon.

'Hey, do you want to play a good trick on your mam?'

He looked around the kitchen.

'We'll do it on the mirror.'

We've got a mirror on the wall above the fireplace and Norbert stood on a chair.

'I did this on my mam and it didn't half fool her.'

He started drawing and when he'd finished it looked ever so realistic. It really looked like the mirror was broken.

'When does your mam get back from work?'

I put the chair back and looked at the mirror again. It was brilliant.

'About quarter past six.'

'You watch her face when she walks in. You'll have a real good laugh.'

I didn't see her face when she came in and I didn't have a real good laugh.

After I'd practised my yo-yo for a bit and lit the fire and peeled the potatoes for my mum, Norbert and me went out to play tip and run in the back alley. We only played for about ten minutes 'cos Norbert hit the ball into Mrs Chapman's and she wouldn't give it back.

'I'm sick of your balls coming over here. I've told you before. Now go away!'

She used to be nice, Mrs Chapman. She used to give us sweets and biscuits and let us go in her garden to fetch our ball. That was before Mr Chapman died. Now she's narky. Anyway Norbert went off home and I went in.

'Is that you?'

My mum was back. I couldn't wait to see her face. She came into the hall from the kitchen and I saw her face. It was like thunder.

'You and that bloody yo-yo . . .!'

I'd never heard her swear before. I was shocked.

'What's up?'

'What's up? . . . What's up! You've smashed my mirror, that's what's up!'

Oh no, she really thought it was broken. And she thought I'd done it with my yo-yo.

'Mum, it's all right, honest. I'll show you.'

I went past her into the kitchen. I'd wipe off the crayon, show it was a joke and we'd have a real good laugh . . . It wasn't there. The mirror had gone. All that was there was a mark on the wall where it had been hanging.

'Where is it? Where's the mirror?'

My mum was shaking she was so cross.

'Where do you think it is? In the dustbin. A cracked mirror's no good to me.'

In the dustbin! I couldn't believe it. Stupid Norbert and his stupid jokes.

'And don't go looking for that blessed yo-yo – that's on the fire.'

On the fire! My yo-yo! I looked and there it was, melting. My yellow yo-yo. I could just make out the 'LU' of 'LUMAR'. I felt sick. I ran out to the dustbin. Everything would be all right. I'd get the mirror, clean it up, tell my mum how Norbert had done it with his trick crayon and we'd have a real good laugh. And I was sure my mum would take me down to Crabtree's first thing in the morning and get me another yo-yo.

I looked in the dustbin and there it was – in pieces. Smashed to smithereens. My mum must have been in a hell of a temper when she threw it away.

We did go down to Crabtree's next morning, but not to

buy a yo-yo. A letter came for my mum in the post. She read it, said 'Wonderful' and handed it to me. It was from the headmaster.

*Dear Parents,*

*It has come to my notice that a number of boys have taken to coming to school wearing suede crêpe shoes similar to those favoured by so-called 'Teddy Boys'. I do not consider this to be appropriate footwear for school, nor outside school for that matter, and I am writing to ask you to ensure that your son wears regulation school shoes.*

*Any boy who persists in coming to school wearing suede crêpe shoes will be sent home.*

*I would request your co-operation in this matter.*

*Yours sincerely,*

*J. A. Ogden B.Sc.*
*Headmaster*

While we were waiting for our turn to buy some 'proper' school shoes I went down to the toy department. Copper-nob won the yo-yo championship. He wasn't half as good as me.

# THE BEST DAD

You always knew when Norbert's dad had come out of prison. Norbert would come to school covered in bruises. This time it was on his back. A big red mark that went from his shoulder right across to the bottom of his spine. It looked bad. I saw it when we were getting changed for gym. So did Mr Melrose.

'Turn round, Lightowler.'

Norbert turned round and Melrose frowned.

'Good God, lad. Who did that to you?'

Norbert put on his T-shirt.

'Nobody, sir. I fell off a wall.'

Norbert looked at me. He hadn't fallen off a wall. His dad had done it. He hadn't told me but I knew. His dad was always hitting him but Norbert would never tell.

'You fell off a wall?'

You could tell Melrose didn't believe him.

'Take your top off, lad.'

Norbert took his T-shirt off and Melrose had a closer look.

'It doesn't look like you fell off a wall to me. Looks more like someone's hit you with a belt.'

Norbert looked at me again. He didn't have to worry, I wouldn't say anything.

'Who hit you, lad? You can tell me, there's nothing to be frightened of.'

That's where he was wrong. There was one thing for Norbert to be frightened of – his dad. That's why he never told.

He had done once, years ago, at primary school when we were in Miss Taylor's class. He'd been late that morning but nobody had noticed till Miss Taylor was taking the register.

'Patricia Jackson?'

'Here, miss.'

'Trevor Jenkins?'

'Yes, miss.'

'Olwen Knowles?'

'Present, miss.'

I'd hated Olwen Knowles. She used to sit behind me and she was always whispering and giggling and making me turn round and then I'd always get into trouble.

'Stop turning round. Face the front while I'm taking the register. Jacqueline Lambert?'

'Yes, miss.'

I didn't like her either. Jacqueline Lambert! She used to eat with her mouth open and talk at the same time. It was disgusting. That was one of the good things about being at Grammar School. No girls.

'Dennis Leach?'

'Yes, miss.'

Dennis Leach. He'd left in the middle of the next term. He'd jumped off a bus while it was still moving and banged his head. After that he wasn't the same Dennis. He couldn't read any more and he talked funny and spit always used to dribble out of his mouth. He'd left and gone to a special school near Ilkley. He still lives there and his mum and dad and little brother go and visit him at weekends.

Even now when I'm going out on my bike or going to school my mum always says, 'Be careful. Remember what happened to Dennis Leach.' I once heard her telling my Auntie Doreen that he was a vegetable and when I'd asked her what she meant she just said he'd gone a bit simple. I knew that – that was why he'd gone to the special school – but I couldn't see what that had to do with vegetables.

'Mary Lewthwaite?'

'Yes, miss.'

'Norbert Lightowler? . . . Norbert Lightowler?'

He wasn't there.

'Norbert Lightowler?'

'Not here, miss.'

We all used to sort of sing-song it together.

'Not here, miss.'

Miss Taylor had tutted to herself and carried on.

'David Naismith.'

'Yes, miss.'

Just then the classroom door had opened and he'd walked in. We'd all stared at him. Olwen Knowles had giggled. She used to giggle at anything, did Olwen Knowles, but I don't think she'd meant to be nasty. It was seeing Norbert come in like that. He'd got a black eye and his lip was all swollen. He'd looked awful. The only one who hadn't noticed straight away had been Miss Taylor 'cos she was still doing the register.

'Jennifer Parkinson?'

'Here, miss.'

'Why are you laughing, Olwen?'

She'd gone red and pointed at Norbert.

'I'm sorry, miss. It's Norbert . . . Look at his face, miss . . .'

She'd looked.

'Norbert! Whatever's happened?'

Norbert hadn't said anything for a minute. He'd looked like he was going to cry. Then he'd blurted it out.

'My dad hit me, miss!'

Miss Taylor had taken him to the headmaster and his mum and dad had been called to the school.

That was the last time Norbert ever said that his dad had hit him.

His mum hadn't come, just his dad, and when he'd turned up Norbert told the headmaster and Miss Taylor that he'd been lying. He said he'd been playing in the park and that he'd fallen out of a tree and that's how he'd hurt his face and he'd blamed it on his dad 'cos he knew he'd have been in trouble for not going straight to school. It was all a lie. He hadn't fallen out of a tree, his dad *had* hit him. I know 'cos Norbert had told me that afternoon, on our way home from school.

'I wasn't gonna say he'd done it when he was standing there looking at me. So I made it up. Said I'd fallen out of a tree.'

He'd sworn me to secrecy. He tells me everything, does Norbert. He says I'm his best friend. I suppose I am really. He hasn't got any others. I just feel sorry for him. I always have, ever since that day when he'd stood there with this black eye going blue and his lip all swollen telling me what had happened in the headmaster's study.

'What did the headmaster say?'

Norbert had wiped his nose on his sleeve and shrugged.

'He made me apologise to my dad.'

That night his dad had hit him again – but not where it showed . . .

'Come on, Lightowler, there's nothing to be frightened of, lad. Who hit you?'

'Nobody, sir . . . Honest . . . I fell off a wall, sir.'

Melrose looked at him. Norbert looked worried. He knew that Melrose didn't believe him. That's why I said it.

'It's true sir, he fell off a wall. I was with him, sir.'

'When?'

'Yesterday, sir.'

What could I do? I hate lying but if Melrose didn't believe Norbert he might take him off to the headmaster like Miss Taylor had done in our old school. And his mum and dad might be called in. I didn't want him to get into trouble with his dad.

'He just slipped, sir. We was playing "dares", sir . . .'

Now I couldn't tell if Melrose believed *me*.

'*Were* playing dares. You *were* playing dares.'

'Yeah, we was, that's how he hurt his back, sir . . .'

I hate being Norbert's best friend. He's not *my* best friend, Tony's my best friend. But Norbert hasn't got anybody so I have to help him.

'I dared him to walk on Pickersgill's wall, sir.'

Norbert looked at me like I'd gone mad. It was sort of true. We had walked on Pickersgill's wall, but it was a few weeks back and it was me that had fallen, not Norbert. Pickersgill's is a big garage near our school. We go past it on our way home and there's a high wall with a sign saying

TRESPASSERS WILL BE PROSECUTED and all along the top there's bits of green glass to stop people climbing on it and we're always climbing on it. Norbert had dared Tony and me to walk on it. Tony hadn't 'cos he'd remembered his mum was taking him to the doctor for his athlete's foot and he'd gone straight home. So Norbert and me dared each other and that's when I'd fallen. I hadn't hurt myself too bad, just grazed my knee and my elbow. But I'd ripped my blazer and my mum had gone mad when I'd got home.

'I don't know what you get up to at school! Look at this!'

She'd spread the blazer out on the kitchen table trying to work out the best way to mend it.

'How did you do it?'

I hadn't said anything. I wasn't going to tell her that I'd done it climbing Pickersgill's wall. Then she'd looked up and pointed her finger at me.

'Have you been fighting?'

'No . . .!'

I'd been so pleased to be able to tell her something that wasn't a lie.

' . . . I haven't been fighting.'

'Are you sure? If you've been fighting, young man, I'd rather know.'

'Mum, I've not been fighting. Honest.'

Well, it was the truth. I hadn't done it fighting. If my mum'd said to me 'Did you do it climbing Pickersgill's wall?' I'd have said yes 'cos I don't like lying.

'How did you do it then?'

I still didn't say anything . . . I sort of shrugged – but I didn't say anything, I didn't lie. But I was lying now to

Melrose. I had to, to protect Norbert. He was looking at us. He turned to Norbert.

'Is this true, Lightowler?'

'Yes, sir. He dared me so I did it and I fell off. It looks worse than it is, sir.'

Norbert's good at lying. *I* believed him the way he said it.

'Bit of an idiotic thing to do, don't you think, climbing high walls that have got bits of glass embedded in them?'

We both nodded.

'Yes, sir.'

'Yes, sir.'

'Especially when the Head made an announcement about it in assembly last week . . .'

Had he? I hadn't known that. When?

'Only last Friday the headmaster told the whole school that he'd had complaints from Pickersgill's garage about boys climbing on their wall . . .'

Last Friday? I hadn't heard him make any announcement . . .

'And he made it quite clear what would happen if any boys were caught doing it again . . .'

Last Friday . . .? Last Friday . . .?

'They would be severely punished!'

I remembered now, I hadn't been in assembly last Friday. I'd been late for school 'cos we'd had a leak in the bathroom and my mum had told me to wait at home for Mr Cranley, the plumber.

'I can't take time off work – you'll have to be here to let him in.'

'But Mum, I'll be late for school. I'll get into trouble.'

'Don't worry, it's an emergency.'

And she'd given me a note for Mr Bleasdale explaining about the leak and everything.

'Now once Mr Cranley gets here you can go straight to school. All you have to do is let him in and show him where the leak is.'

I'd been quite pleased. We have maths first thing on a Friday and I didn't mind missing it. But Mr Cranley had turned up not long after my mum had gone so all I'd missed was blooming assembly. I'd got to school just as everybody was filing out and nobody'd blooming noticed. I hadn't even had to give the blooming note in. You can be sure any other time somebody would have noticed and I'd have been in trouble.

'So – you're both in big trouble, aren't you?'

We nodded.

'Yes, sir.'

'Yes, sir.'

He blew his whistle.

'Right, you lot, while I'm gone, three times round the playground . . .'

While he was gone? Where was he going? I was hoping it wasn't what I thought it was.

'I've got to go and see the headmaster for a few minutes.'

It was. He was going to tell the headmaster. It wasn't fair. I'd only been trying to help Norbert. David Holdsworth put his hand up.

'Sir, it's raining.'

'*Four* times round the playground . . .'

Everybody jeered and Kenny Spencer asked Holdsworth why he didn't keep his trap shut.

'Five times for you, Spencer!'

Everybody laughed and Melrose turned to me and Norbert.

'You two, follow me. Lightowler, put your top on.'

The gym is separate from the rest of the school and we followed Melrose across the playground to the main building. He was walking so fast that we had to run to keep up with him.

I couldn't believe it. We were being taken to the headmaster for something we hadn't done. We had climbed on Pickersgill's wall, yes, but that had been ages ago, nothing to do with the headmaster's announcement last Friday. Why hadn't I kept my mouth shut? Just 'cos I felt sorry for Norbert. Well, I felt sorry for myself now and I wasn't going to be his best friend any more.

The others were on their first lap. Arthur Boocock and Gordon Barraclough were leading – as usual. They're the best at sport and they're Melrose's favourites. Boocock's the best at running and Barraclough's the best at football and they're both blooming good at cricket.

'That's it, Arthur, Gordon. Show them how it's done, lads.'

That's it, Arthur, Gordon. Show them how it's done! Blooming Melrose. It was 'cos it was Melrose that I'd stuck up for Norbert. Melrose is always picking on him. Well, he'll have to stick up for himself from now on. And why was his dad always hitting him anyway? If he hadn't got such a horrible dad none of this would have happened. I'd hate to have a dad like Norbert's . . . If I *had* a dad. Arthur and Gordon were miles ahead now. Kenny Spencer was next, then Duncan Cawthra, but they were nowhere near. At the back Keith Hopwood was strolling along talking to Douglas Bashforth.

'Hopwood! Bashforth! Get moving! Put some effort into it!'

They both groaned and started running. Slowly. Arthur and Gordon would be lapping them in a couple of minutes. It's no wonder that they're so good at sport – their dads are good at it. Gordon's dad once had a trial for Manchester United and Arthur's does cross-country running. At Sports Day last year they came first and second in the fathers' race. Gordon says his dad's going to win this year 'cos he's been doing special training but Arthur says he hasn't got a chance.

'He might be good at football, your dad, but my dad's best at running. He won last year and he's gonna win this year.'

'No he won't, 'cos my dad's best.'

'I bet you half-a-crown.'

'You're on!'

So they've bet each other half-a-crown. Who cares? It doesn't mean much, the fathers' race, if you haven't got a dad.

We got to the main building and followed Melrose up the corridor to the headmaster's study. He knocked and a couple of seconds later a green light came on saying ENTER.

'You two wait here.'

As soon as he closed the door I turned to Norbert but before I could say anything he called me an idiot.

'Y'what?'

'Why did you have to go and tell him it was Pickersgill's wall I fell off? Idiot!'

'*I* didn't know, did I? I wasn't in assembly last Friday. I was only trying to help you. I wish I hadn't now!'

Norbert went quiet. 'I know. It's not your fault.'

'No, it's bloody well not, it's your rotten dad's fault! He shouldn't bloody hit you!'

That's when he thumped me. Well, he didn't thump me really, more sort of pushed me away. But it was what he said . . . I couldn't believe it.

'At least it's better than not having a dad!'

How could he say that? I wanted to say to him, how can you say that? Your dad hits you. He belts you. He's always belted you. And you daren't tell anybody 'cos he'd belt you even more. And you think that's better than not having a dad? How can you say that? But I couldn't speak. I just couldn't get the words out. And I didn't have to. It was as if he could tell what I was thinking.

'He's still my dad, in't he? He's still my dad . . .'

The door opened and Melrose came out.

'When you've seen the Head come straight back to the gym.'

'Yes, sir.'

'Yes, sir.'

Melrose went. Me and Norbert waited there. I didn't say anything. I didn't even look at him. I was mad with myself. I'd got myself into trouble for sticking up for him and here was Norbert sticking up for his dad. I couldn't understand it. It wasn't true. It can't be better than not having a dad. I was better off having no dad than a dad like his. I must be. I'd hate to have a dad like his.

The green ENTER light came on and we entered. The headmaster went mad with us.

'What were the two of you thinking of . . .?'

Neither of us said anything.

'Well . . .?'

'Don't know, sir . . .'

'Don't know, sir . . .'

'What did I say in assembly last Friday . . .? Eh . . .? What did I say? Anybody playing in the vicinity of Pickersgill's garage will be severely punished!'

'Yes, sir.'

'Yes, sir.'

I thought about telling him that I hadn't been in assembly last Friday but it wouldn't have made any difference. He'd have just said we shouldn't have been there in the first place . . . and I'd have probably got into more trouble for not giving the note in . . . Anyway Norbert had been in assembly so there was no excuse.

'Have either of you got anything to say before I punish you?'

'No, sir.'

'No, sir.'

He went to the cupboard. Oh no! I knew from other lads what he kept in there. He brought it out. The cane! We were going to get the cane. It wasn't fair. I hadn't done anything wrong and we were getting the cane . . .

I thought about it. For a split second I thought about it – 'Sir, he didn't fall off Pickersgill's wall. We were nowhere near Pickersgill's wall. His dad hit him. His dad's always hitting him . . .' I looked at Norbert. Maybe he'd tell him . . .

250

Tell him, Norbert, tell him . . .! But he didn't. He just stared straight ahead.

'Right, who's going first?'

I wanted to get it over with. *I* wanted to go first.

'Me, sir.'

But Norbert already had his hand up.

'Right, Lightowler. Bend over, lad.'

Oh no, I'd thought it was going to be on my hand. We'd only got our gym shorts on. It was going to hurt even more. This was the worst day of my life. Norbert bent down and the headmaster lifted the cane up in the air. I couldn't watch. I looked away and closed my eyes. It whooshed through the air and I felt sick as I heard it hit him. What was I going to feel like when it was my turn?

I took a deep breath. My teeth were clenched together like anything. I turned to take Norbert's place but he was still bent down and the cane was up in the air again. Whoosh! This time I saw it. He hit him as hard as he could. He's going to do this to me next, that's all I could think of, he's going to do it to me.

'Last one, Lightowler.'

Another one? Whoosh! Three times! I'm going to be caned three times! I couldn't believe it . . .

'Well done, lad.'

'Well done'? What did he mean, 'well done'? 'Cos he didn't cry? 'Cos he didn't shout out? Is that what he means by 'well done'? If I cry or scream does that mean I won't have done well? Does it mean I'll get an extra one for not 'doing well'? I felt sick.

'OK, lad. Bend over.'

I couldn't believe this was happening to me. It was like I

251

was in a dream. Whoosh . . .! It was the worst pain I'd ever felt.

Whoosh . . .! I thought I was going to throw up. All I'd tried to do was to stop Norbert getting hit by his dad and here I was getting hit by the headmaster.

Whoosh . . .! The last one. It was over. I think he said 'Well done, lad', I couldn't remember.

We didn't talk on the way back to the gym. But just as we were going in Norbert mumbled something.

'He only hits me when he's been drinking you know . . . my mam says he can't help it . . .'

I could only just make out what he said. I didn't care anyway.

'I don't care, it's nowt to do with me.'

'He's all right most of the time . . .'

'I said I don't care. And it's not true, Lightowler, I'd rather have no dad than one like yours, so you can sod off!'

Once we'd got back Norbert was his same old self, laughing and joking and mucking about. By breaktime it all seemed to be forgotten. Things like that don't bother him. He's used to being in trouble, I suppose. He's used to being hit as well. Me, it was all I could do to stop myself from crying all day. Well I wasn't going to stick up for him any more, I knew that, and he could stop thinking I was his best friend, and I didn't care what he said – I'd rather have no dad than one like his . . . But after a couple of days we were pals again and *I* forgot about it too. Until Sports Day.

Arthur's dad didn't win the fathers' race on Sports Day. Nor did Gordon's dad. Norbert's dad won it. Easily. I watched Norbert run up to him afterwards and give him a big hug.

'You're the best dad in the world, the best dad!'

And, for a moment, I thought maybe Norbert was right. Maybe it is better to have a dad like that than no dad at all . . . But I only thought it for a moment.

# THE SWAP

## PART ONE

I'd never seen Norbert cry before. Never. I've seen him *nearly* cry lots of times, like in the Easter holidays when we'd gone speedway riding up at Hockley quarry and he'd crashed into me on David Holdsworth's bike and he'd had to have five stitches in his leg. He didn't cry then. *I'd* cried and I was only bruised. And David Holdsworth had cried because the front wheel of his bike had got buckled. But Norbert hadn't cried. Norbert never cries. Not even when Melrose picks on him. Melrose is always making fun of Norbert, making him look a fool in front of everybody, and we all laugh as if it's all in good fun. I laugh as well but I don't like it. It makes my stomach churn because you can see that Melrose isn't doing it in fun. He does it 'cos he doesn't like Norbert. You can see it in his eyes. Well, I can. Like that time at Green Lane swimming baths. That's where we go once a fortnight for lessons. I hate it. It's always freezing cold and the water makes your eyes sting and I'm scared stiff of swimming because I can't swim. Anyway we were all getting into our trunks and Melrose was walking up and down, watching, like he always does, when suddenly his voice boomed out, echoing all round the swimming pool.

'You could grow potatoes in between those toes, lad!'

We all peeped out of our cubicles. I couldn't see who Melrose was talking to but I didn't need to.

255

'When did you last wash those feet, Lightowler? They're black bright. Come out here, lad, let everybody have a look. Gentlemen, come and look at Mr Lightowler's feet.'

Norbert came out of his cubicle and we all gathered round to look at his dirty feet. I felt ever so sorry for him, everybody staring while he stood there in his old-fashioned underpants. *They* didn't look too clean either. They were more grey than white. Melrose was looking at Norbert with a sort of sarcastic sneer on his face.

'Those underpants look like they could do with a wash as well.'

Melrose laughed and turned to us and we all laughed. I laughed but only because the others laughed. Norbert didn't, he just stared back at him.

'No, sir, clean on this morning. They're just old. They used to be my brother's.'

If it had been me I'd have been in tears by now, but not Norbert. He didn't even cry when Melrose made him have a shower with everybody watching. Norbert never cries. Never.

But he was crying now, sobbing his heart out. He was at the top end of the playground, in the shelter under the woodwork classroom. He didn't know I was watching him. I wouldn't have been if I hadn't left my anorak behind. We'd been using it as a goalpost when we'd played football after school and I'd already got home before I'd remembered that I'd left it behind. Well I didn't remember, my mum did. She'd bought it at the nearly-new shop for two pounds and she wanted my Auntie Doreen to see it.

'Wait till you see it, Doreen. Two pounds and it looks brand new. Go put it on, love.'

That's when I remembered where it was.

'Er . . . I left it at school.'

'Where?'

I didn't dare tell her where it really was, rolled up in a bundle at the top end of the playground . . . if it was still there. It could have been taken by now.

'I'm not sure . . .' My mum gave me one of her looks. 'I think it's in the cloakroom . . . on my peg . . . I think . . .'

I didn't like lying to my mum, that's why I kept saying 'I think'. It sort of makes it less of a lie. I think.

'It's all right, I'll go back and get it.'

My mum told me not to bother.

'If it's on your peg it'll be safe. It's got your name in.'

Oh sure, it'd be safe if it was on my peg. But it wasn't, was it.

'I've got to go back anyway, Mum, 'cos I've left my maths homework at school. I think . . .'

I ran back as fast as I could.

When I got to school it was deserted but I could see my anorak up at the far end of the playground where I'd left it.

Norbert and David Holdsworth had carried on playing after I'd gone. Trust them to leave it there like that. You'd think one of them could have looked after it for me, brought it in next day. Oh no, not them, they just go and leave it there in the middle of the playground. Any Tom, Dick or Harry could have stolen it. That's what my mum's always saying:

'Don't leave your bike out there. Any Tom, Dick or Harry could steal it.'

Or:

257

'Close the curtains, we don't want every Tom, Dick or Harry peeping in.'

When I was little I used to wonder who this Tom, Dick or Harry was. It used to worry me a bit because the man from the proo was called Tom. Why would he want to peep into our living room? Why would he want to steal my bike? And what was a proo? He used to come every Monday night and say, 'Tell your mam it's Tom from the proo.' And my mum would give him some money and he'd write in a little book. He doesn't come any more. It's Mr McCracken from the Prudential who calls and I know what the money's for now. You get it back when you're old or if you fall under a bus. My mum explained it all to me. I know what Tom, Dick or Harry means too. But it's funny how you don't understand these things when you're young.

I was putting my anorak on and thinking what a good job it was that Norbert and David had left it there even though it was a selfish thing to do when I heard this funny noise. It made me jump. It was coming from the shelter. At first I thought it was a dog or something. It sounded like a puppy whimpering. I went towards where the noise was coming from and saw him sitting on the ground in the shelter, all huddled up, and he was crying. He didn't see me. He had his head in his hands and was sobbing into his knees. He was mumbling something over and over but I couldn't make out what he was saying. I'd never seen Norbert cry and I didn't want him to see me watching him so I went back out into the playground. I leaned against the wall and listened. I didn't know what to do. I wanted to help him, ask him what the matter was, but then he'd know I'd seen him and he'd hate that. I couldn't just go home though, could I? I couldn't just leave him there, crying like that. He'd been all right when we'd been playing football and that was less than an hour ago. What had happened? Maybe he'd had a fight with Holdsworth? No, that wouldn't make Norbert cry. Norbert never cries . . . Well, he was crying now. Sobbing his heart out.

I was just about to go back into the shelter and ask him what had happened when I stopped and listened. I could make out what it was he'd been mumbling all this time.

'Bloody Melrose . . . Bloody Melrose . . . Bloody Melrose!'

What had Melrose done now? What had happened?

'Bloody Melrose . . . Bloody exchange – he can stick his rotten blooming exchange!'

I knew why he was crying now and there was nothing I could do. He was crying because he can't go on the school exchange. We're all going, all the boys in our year – except Norbert. Melrose arranged it. We'd all got a letter to take home to our parents. I'd given it to my mum as soon as she'd got back from work.

'What's this? You're not in trouble, are you?'

'No!'

Why does my mum always have to think I'm in trouble? Mind you, the last letter I'd brought home had been from Mr Bleasdale about me messing about in his Latin lesson. It hadn't even been my fault. We'd been playing the game where something gets passed round the class and if you've got it when the bell goes you're the loser. This time the grot was an old woolly hat that Norbert had found in the playground. I hadn't wanted to play but you've got no choice if you get landed with the grot and I got landed with it right at the end of the lesson. I knew the bell was going to go any second. I had to get rid of it. Everybody was sniggering and a few of them, mainly Norbert and Arthur Boocock and Barraclough, were doing the chant.

'Grot! Grot! Grot! Grot . . .!'

I threw the grot just as Bleasdale looked up with his good eye.

'Who's making that noise— Who threw that?'

And then the bell had gone and Keith Hopwood had ended up with the grot. I was sorry it had landed on his desk 'cos he's got a stammer. I'd got extra Latin, a letter to take home and a telling-off from my mum . . .

'It's from Mr Melrose. It's about going on a school exchange.'

She screwed up her eyes and held the letter a bit further away.

'Get my glasses would you, love? They're on the sideboard.'

I could see it was in purple stencil, like our exam papers – sometimes the writing's a bit smudged. I gave my mum her glasses and sat in the wicker chair while she read it through. Then she went 'hmm' and read the letter out loud.

*Dear Parents,*

*The boys in the first year have the opportunity to share an exchange for one week with St Augustine's Grammar School in Greenford, just outside London. At the moment the week suggested would be the first week in May and we are at the stage now where we need to know how many families would be interested.*

*Whilst there will be many exciting trips, visits to*
*Westminster Abbey and the Houses of Parliament,*
*the Tower of London . . .*

The Tower of London. It sounded great.

'The Tower of London? It sounds great. Can I go, Mum?'

'Hang on, love, let me finish reading it.'

*. . . Whilst there will be many exciting trips, visits to Westminster Abbey and the Houses of Parliament, the Tower of London* – She smiled at me. She was going to let me go, I could tell. She always smiles like that when she's being nice – *Madame Tussauds . . .*

'Madam Two Swords! That's a waxworks, Mum, it's famous!'

My mum told me to calm down and carried on.

*. . . the Tower of London, Madame Tussauds and possibly a tour round the Lyons Tea Factory (Mr Bleasdale is waiting to hear from his brother-in-law who works there), it will be very much a working holiday with set projects and field work, and each boy will be expected to keep a daily diary . . .*

She took her glasses off and gave me one of her looks.

'You see. It's not a fancy holiday you'll be going on. You're going to have to work. You'll be having set projects and field work and I'll want to see this diary when you get back. I'll want you to take it seriously.'

I didn't know what field work was but I didn't care. I just knew I wanted to go on this exchange. I wanted to see Westminster Abbey and the Tower of London and Madam Two Swords.

''Course I will.'

'Right. Well think on.'

She put her glasses back on and carried on reading.

... *The cost*—

'Mum, if it's a lot of money I'm not that bothered ...'

'Shut up and listen.'

*... I know that this is what will be uppermost in all your minds, especially in these stringent times. Apart from the fares to London (train or charabanc, still to be decided) and modest pocket money, the cost will be minimal because while our boys are down in London the boys from St Augustine's will stay with you, the parents. Your own day-to-day arrangements will be unaffected since your visitors will keep the same school hours as your sons and vice versa.*

*This will be an exchange in the true meaning of the word.*

*If you would like your son to be included in the St Augustine School exchange would you please let me know by Friday of this week together with a two pound deposit. (Non-returnable.)*

*Yours faithfully,*

*Brian T. Melrose Cert. Ed.*
*(Head of Sport)*

That's when it dawned on me.

I thought I'd be going to stay with a lad from this St

Augustine's school and then he'd come back and stay with me and my mum. But we were never going to see each other.

'So I'll never see the lad who stays here? We'll just swap for a week.'

My mum smiled.

'That's right – and with a bit of luck I'll get a nice young man who'll keep his room tidy and make his bed on a morning. That'd be a grand swap.'

I didn't go back and help Norbert, I set off for home. There was nothing I could do. Poor Norbert. But I couldn't understand it. When Melrose had told him that morning that he wouldn't be going on the exchange he hadn't seemed bothered.

'I don't care. I've been to Fountains Abbey. I bet Westminster Abbey in't half as good as that. And who wants to go round a boring tea factory with Bleasdale's boring brother-in-law? Melrose can stick his blooming exchange. I'm not bothered.'

It must have all been an act. He'd brought his non-returnable two pounds in along with everybody else. He'd wanted to go on the exchange. Everybody wanted to go. But then we'd got another letter to take home.

*Dear Parents,*

<u>*School Exchange – Sleeping Arrangements*</u>
*Please note it will be expected that each boy visiting from St Augustine's will have a bedroom to himself during his week's stay in your home. Likewise our lads will be shown the same courtesy whilst staying with the St Augustine families. This is a condition of the*

*exchange and is non-negotiable. I am aware that a number of our boys share with their siblings but I am sure that suitable arrangements can be made for one week in order to accommodate our guests.*

*If any parents have any questions or worries please do not hesitate to contact me at the school.*

*I would like to take this opportunity to remind all parents that the rest of the money must be handed in by next Monday.*

*Yours faithfully,*

*Brian T. Melrose Cert. Ed.*
*(Head of Sport)*

'What are siblings, Mum?'

'Brothers and sisters.'

'Oh.'

Well I was all right. I haven't got any brothers or sisters, I sleep in my own room. So does David Holdsworth. He's got an older brother but he's married and lives in Doncaster. Keith Hopwood shares with his little brother and his mum and dad are going to move him in with his sister while Keith is on the exchange. That's what most people are doing, just moving everybody around for the week. Except Norbert. He's got so many brothers and sisters that he doesn't just share a bedroom, he shares a bed. Norbert had told Melrose that his mum could arrange for the guest to have his own bed but he'd have to share the room with two of his brothers.

'And my mum says my little sister can go in with her for the week.'

Melrose had just sucked in his breath and shaken his head.

'I'm sorry, Lightowler, it's not on. I'll have to take your name off the list. I'm sorry, lad.'

I don't think he was sorry. Melrose doesn't like Norbert. I reckon he's glad Norbert's not going.

'Sir?'

'Yes, Lightowler?'

'My mum says can she have her two pound back?'

Melrose had said it was supposed to be non-returnable but muttered something about 'in the circumstances' and he got it back. And Norbert hadn't seemed bothered at all.

But he *was* bothered because there he was, sitting in the playground, crying his eyes out. Poor Norbert.

When I got home my mum made me stand in the middle of the living room while she and my Auntie Doreen admired my nearly new anorak.

'Now look at that, Doreen, two pounds. It looks brand new. It'll be ideal for this school trip.'

If my mum had known that half an hour before it had been lying in the playground being used as a goalpost, she wouldn't have been too pleased. I was still thinking about Norbert.

'Norbert's not going on the exchange now.'

She saw something on the sleeve and brushed it off with her hand.

'Oh, what's that, love?'

I took my anorak off and hung it in the hall. I didn't want my mum to look too closely in case there were any more dirty marks.

'Well, you know that letter we got from Melrose—'

265

'*Mr* Melrose!'

'Yeah, all right. Well, you know he said that everybody has to have their own bedroom? Well Norbert shares with two of his brothers. That's why he can't go.'

My mum looked at my Auntie Doreen.

'I'm sorry, I don't want to be uncharitable but I think it's a blessing in disguise. I wouldn't like to think of a son of mine spending a week in a house like that. And I wouldn't want someone like Norbert Lightowler spending a week in my house either. I'm sorry, I know it's not his fault, I feel sorry for the lad having a family like that, but . . . well, I think it's for the best. Do you fancy another cup, Doreen?'

They went into the kitchen and I could hear my mum telling my Auntie Doreen all about the Lightowlers. How mucky their house is, how the kids are always in trouble with the police, how *he's* in and out of prison. I suppose she meant Norbert's dad. My mum was right though. I mean it's not Norbert's fault but his house is horrible. You couldn't expect anybody coming on the exchange to stay there. I wouldn't . . .

*Dear Peter,*

*Thanks for your letter which I got yesterday. It was very nice to get your letter. I am looking forward to coming to stay at your house and meeting all your family. They all sound very nice. I hope you will enjoy staying at my house . . .*

We'd all got letters from the St Augustine boys and during one English lesson we had to write back. Melrose told us we had to write at least a page. He made Norbert write a letter even though he wasn't going just to give him something to do in the lesson. The lad I'm swapping with is called Peter Jarvis. He's got an older brother called Stephen and an older sister called Rosemary who's at teacher training college. His father works in insurance and his mother works for charity sometimes but doesn't get paid for it. He's in the school chess team and his favourite subject is chemistry. I think they must have done their letters at home not in class 'cos he didn't say much else. Just that he was looking forward to the trip and it was a shame we would never meet and that I could use his bicycle.

> . . . *I live with my mum and she is looking forward to meeting you. She has made me tidy my bedroom up so that it will be nice for you. I have got a wireless in my bedroom so you can listen in bed. It used to belong to my grandad but he died two years ago. The Home Service is a bit crackly but not bad. I love listening to the wireless in bed. My favourite is Have a Go with Wilfred Pickles and Up the Pole with Jimmy Jule and Ben Worris. I think they are very funny. I like listening to plays as well but usually I fall asleep before the end or my mum comes in and tells me to switch off and go to sleep. The other night I listened to a play called Night Must Fall and it was a murder play and I was scared stiff and I could not sleep. I had told my mum I had turned it off but I was so frightened I had to own up so I could go into her bed until I fell asleep. I am in 1 Beta and our form master is Mr Bleasdale. He teaches Latin and he has a glass*

*eye. My best friend is Tony Wainwright but he is in 1
Alpha. He is going on the exchange too. All the boys in
our year are going except one. My mum is going to
take you to Ilkley Moor to see the cow and calf. The
cow and calf are two rocks and one is bigger than the
other. The cow is the big one and the calf is the little
one. It is a very famous place and it is great for
climbing there. My mum is going to take you on some
other trips but I won't say where so it will be a
surprise . . .*

Melrose told us to finish 'cos the bell was about to go so I
just wrote that I hated chemistry and I was sorry that we
wouldn't meet and that he could use my bike as well. Then
Melrose collected all the letters to post to St Augustine's.
Except Norbert's. He threw his in the waste-paper basket.

*Dear Parents,*

*School Exchange – Travel Arrangements*
*Well, the big day approaches. Could you ensure that
your son is at the school on Saturday at 8.30 a.m. for
an 8.45 departure (prompt).*

*We will be going to Leeds by charabanc and there
we will pick up the 10.25 train to London (King's
Cross). The party will be led by myself, Mr Bleasdale
and Mrs Jolliffe. The St Augustine boys will be arriving
at our school at 5.15 p.m. (approx.) for you to pick
them up.*

*Attached to this letter is a list of clothes required,
etc. As your son will be representing the school, would*

*you please ensure that his blazer is in a presentable
state (buttons, torn pockets, etc). Also on the list is the
telephone number at St Augustine's. <u>Please telephone
only in a case of emergency.</u> Thank you for your co-
operation. Finally, would those who have not paid their
outstanding balance please do so by this coming
Wednesday as I shall be out of pocket.*

*Yours sincerely,*

*Brian T. Melrose Cert. Ed.
(Head of Sport)*

'Spencer . . .'
   'Sir.'
'Thompson . . .'
   'Yes, sir!'
'Tordoff . . .'
   'Sir!'
We were all on the coach waiting to go while Mr Bleas-
dale ticked off our names. Well, not all. Keith Hopwood
hadn't turned up, but he's always late for everything. I was
sitting next to Tony. Me and my mum had got there early so
the two of us could sit together and we were going to sit
next to each other on the train as well.
   'Wainwright . . .'
I nudged him and Tony put his hand up.
   'Present, sir!'
Everybody laughed and Mr Bleasdale smiled. He's quite
nice really.
   'Walsh . . .'

Everybody was so excited and talking to each other.

'Walsh . . .'

Brian Walsh was chatting away to Kenny Spencer and Duncan Cawthra. I leaned over and nudged him.

'Hey Walshie, he's called your name.'

I suppose it's hard for Mr Bleasdale to see properly when he's only got one eye.

'Is Brian Walsh here?'

Walshie stuck his hand up.

'Yes, sir!'

Mr Bleasdale ticked his name off.

'I know you're excited, lads, but keep the noise down and listen for your names. I'm not telling you again . . .'

He'd told us to pipe down about three times already. It was a good job it wasn't Melrose taking our names – he's not as nice as Mr Bleasdale.

All the parents were standing on the pavement waiting to wave us off. I could see my mum talking to Tony's mum and dad. Norbert had turned up as well. He was chewing bubble gum and he had his dog with him, a scrawny, scruffy-looking thing called Nell. He grinned at me and Tony and gave us a thumbs-up. I felt sorry for him.

'I feel sorry for Norbert.'

Tony looked at me.

'Why? He's not bothered. You know Norbert – he doesn't give a damn, does he?'

I knew different. I'd seen him in the playground. I didn't say anything. There was no point. And my mum was right, it was a blessing in disguise. You couldn't expect a stranger to stay at his house.

Suddenly a few of the lads started shouting.

'He's here, sir. Hopwood's here! Come on, Hopwood.' I could see him running towards the coach with his mum and dad and everybody cheered as they bundled him on. Mrs Hopwood was in a right state.

'I'm sorry, Mr Melrose, you know what the buses are like on a Saturday. We had to wait over half an hour . . .'

And the next thing we were on our way. Melrose and Mrs Jolliffe got on and the driver started revving up and everybody on the pavement started waving.

I looked out of the window and my mum gave me a little wave. I gave her a little wave back and she smiled. I smiled as well but I didn't feel like smiling. All of a sudden I felt frightened. I didn't want to go. All these weeks of looking forward to it and now I didn't want to go. I'd never been away from home for this long. She came over and said 'Are you all right?' through the window. Well, she didn't say it, she just moved her lips, but I could tell that's what she was asking. I nodded. But I wasn't all right. It was all I could do to stop myself from crying. It was going to be a week before I was going to see my mum again. I didn't think I could last that long. A whole week without seeing my mum. Norbert was waving as well and I started wishing I was Norbert, staying at home. Lucky Norbert, not having to go away for a week, not having to stay with a family he didn't know. I didn't want to go, I wanted to get off, go home with my mum, but the coach started moving off and everybody began cheering and I could feel the tears behind my eyes. Don't let me start crying, please don't let me start crying.

My mum started running alongside the coach. Why was she doing that? She looked funny. None of the other mums and dads were running alongside. Stop it, Mum, stop it.

I looked away. Please stop, Mum, you look silly, you're embarrassing me. I looked back and she was still there, running and waving and wiping her eyes with a hanky. Then thank goodness we started going faster and she slowed down. The coach stopped at some lights and I looked back. All the other mums and dads were walking off but she was still standing there, out of breath, waving and crying.

'Have a nice time, love!'

David Holdsworth and a few of the others went 'Have a nice time, love' and giggled.

'See you in a week, love!'

Why didn't my mum just go? Why didn't the lights change? Change lights, change!! They did change. But not in time. If they'd changed just a few seconds sooner nobody would have heard her.

'Keep an eye on him, Mr Bleasdale. He's all I've got . . .!'

Everybody started laughing, and what made it worse was they were all trying to hold it in. Couldn't she have shouted, 'Keep an eye on him, Mr Melrose' or 'Mrs Jolliffe'? No, she had to shout, 'Keep an eye on him, Mr Bleasdale.' Mr Bleasdale! The only teacher with one eye!

I turned away so nobody could see me crying. I wanted to blow my nose but I couldn't. My mum had packed my hankies in my suitcase.

# THE SWAP

## PART TWO

I could feel the tears in my eyes. I turned my head away and looked out of the window so that nobody could see. I think maybe Tony knew but he didn't say anything, he was talking to Kenny Spencer across the aisle.

I just kept looking out of the window and everything I saw made me feel worse. We went past Mrs Allsop's High Class Hairdressing Salon where my mum goes with my Auntie Doreen every Saturday afternoon. She'd be going there that afternoon and it made me feel more sad. We went past the end of our road and I could feel the tears running down my face. I wiped them away with my sleeve. If only I could blow my nose.

I was lucky. Nobody really noticed that I was crying. They would have done if it hadn't been for Keith Hopwood, but I was lucky. He threw up. It went everywhere, mostly over David Holdsworth's blazer. Everybody jumped back and started shouting.

'Sir, sir! Hopwood's been sick.'

'All over my blazer, sir. It's just been dry-cleaned, my mum'll go mad!'

Melrose told everybody to calm down and go back to their places. Holdsworth and Duncan Cawthra said they couldn't 'cos there was sick on their seats.

'Just sit down – *anywhere*! Use your common sense!'

Melrose was all red in the face and the vein under his eye was throbbing. When that vein throbs you know Melrose is really mad. Hopwood just kept saying he was sorry. He kept saying it over and over. And 'cos of his stutter he could hardly get his words out.

'I'm s-s-sorry, s-sir. I'm e-e-ever so s-s-sorry. Sorry, D-D-David . . .'

And he threw up again, mostly in the aisle, and everyone got out of the way again.

'S-s-sorry, s-sir, I c-couldn't help it . . .'

Mrs Jolliffe had a box of tissues and gave him some and Holdsworth took a few to wipe his blazer. Mr Bleasdale put his *Yorkshire Post* over Hopwood's sick while Mrs Jolliffe put her arm round him.

'Don't worry, Keith, it's not your fault. It's running for the coach, that's what's made you sick. Here, blow your nose.'

Then he started crying.

'No it's n-not. I've been f-feeling sick all n-night 'cos I was nervous about g-g-going. That's w-why I was late, 'cos I d-didn't want to g-go. I d-don't want to g-go now. I w-want to g-g-go home. I want to g-g-go *home* . . .!'

I leaned across and asked Mrs Jolliffe if I could have one of her tissues.

'Help yourself, dear.'

She didn't look round, she was busy looking after Keith. She probably thought I needed to wipe the seat or something so I took a few and blew my nose.

I felt better. Much better. Not 'cos I'd been able to blow my nose but 'cos I knew now that I wasn't the only one who was frightened about going away from home. I bet lots of us were scared but some are just better at hiding it than others.

'I want to g-go h-home, Mrs Jolliffe. P-please let me g-go home. I d-don't w-w-want to go London!'

And he started crying again.

Everybody was looking at him. If Keith hadn't been sick it would have been me everybody would have been looking at and me Mrs Jolliffe would have been comforting.

'Come on, dear, you come and sit with me and we'll have a little talk.'

As she went past I heard her whispering to Bleasdale and Melrose that he'd be all right and to leave it to her. The vein under Melrose's eye was throbbing like anything.

I looked out of the window again. I knew just how Keith was feeling. I'd never felt so sad in all my life. I didn't want to go to on this school exchange either. A whole week before I'd see my mum. And my Auntie Doreen. A whole week staying with strangers. I could feel the tears coming again. No! I wasn't going to cry. I wasn't. I wouldn't let myself. I didn't want everybody looking at me the way they'd all looked at Keith Hopwood. The way *I'd* looked at Keith Hopwood. Then I realised that Tony was looking at me. Looking at me the way *he'd* looked at Keith Hopwood.

'Are you cryin'?'

'No, 'course not.'

He didn't believe me, I could tell.

'Your eyes are all red.'

'I know . . .'

When my Auntie Doreen had come back from the doctor's last Thursday she'd told my mum she'd got an eye infection, con-something, and her eyes were all red.

'. . . I've got an eye infection. I got it off my Auntie Doreen.'

'You look like you've been cryin'.'

'I know. So did my Auntie Doreen.'

I turned away from him and looked out of the window again. We were just going past the GPO. The coach turned onto the Leeds road and headed out of town.

I kept thinking to myself, this time next week it'll all be over. That's how I stopped myself from crying. Whenever something horrible is going to happen to me, like having to have an injection, or having to go to the dentist, that's what I always think. In an hour, in a day, this time tomorrow, it'll all be over, forgotten. Well, it was the same with this blooming rotten school exchange. I just kept thinking to myself, this time next week it'll all be over – we'll be on our way home.

Hopwood was still crying when we'd got to Leeds station, but not as much. More sort of sniffing and he was sucking a barley sugar Mrs Jolliffe had given him. To calm his tummy down. Melrose got up and stood at the front next to the driver.

'We are now at Leeds station.'

We could see we were at Leeds station, there was a big sign that said so. Tony leaned over to me.

'Does he think we can't read?'

I giggled.

'What are you laughing at, lad?'

I could feel myself going red.

'Nothing, sir.'

''Cos if there's something that amuses you, lad, let's share it. Let's all have a bit of a laugh.'

I stared straight ahead at Melrose. Well, not at him, I sort of looked through him, behind him. It was the only way I could stop myself from crying. What was the matter with me? I could feel my bottom lip trembling. The driver winked at me and smiled. I suppose he was trying to cheer me up. I gave him a little smile back.

'Take that grin off your face, lad.'

I did. So did the driver. I don't know whose smile disappeared the fastest, his or mine. He turned round in his seat and started fiddling about with a cloth, wiping all the dials, and I looked down at my feet.

'I'm going to say something now and I shall only say it once. When I or Mr Bleasdale or Mrs Jolliffe is speaking, there will be absolute and total silence while you listen to our instructions. Is that understood?'

Nobody said anything.

'*Is that understood?*'

Everybody jumped, even the driver. He stood up and started polishing his windscreen.

'Yes, sir.'

'Good . . .'

The vein underneath Melrose's eye was throbbing again.

' . . . because only if you listen carefully and follow instructions will we avoid any mishaps and misunderstandings. Is that clear, gentlemen?'

'Yes, sir.'

'Excellent. Now when you get off the charabanc I want you all to line up in twos and I don't want to hear *any talking*. Hutchinson – lead off.'

We all followed each other off and started getting into

277

twos like Melrose had said. But a few of them started arguing. Illingworth wanted to be with Emmott, Emmott wanted to be with Duncan Cawthra, Cawthra was already with David Holdsworth and John Tordoff wanted to be with Tony 'cos they're in the same class and I was telling him that Tony was already with me and Tordoff said when they walked to swimming in twos they were always together and that they sat next to each other in class and I said that had nothing to do with it 'cos Tony was my best friend and we'd been best friends since Primary School . . .

'I said *no talking*! Into pairs – *now!!*'

We all turned and looked for our partners as fast as we could but I couldn't find Tony for a minute and the next thing I knew we were all in twos but Tony was with Tordoff and I'd ended up with Arthur Boocock. I can't stand Arthur Boocock. He's a bully and he's got bad breath. What makes it worse, he comes up right close when he talks to you. His face is always about an inch away. Melrose was standing on the steps of the coach.

'Better . . .'

And he steals, does Boocock. I'm positive he took my Ovaltiney pencil case. I should have put my name in it.

'Now that's what I want to see when I tell you all to line up in twos . . .'

It had disappeared one Friday afternoon and on the following Monday Arthur Boocock turns up with an Ovaltiney pencil case.

'Hey, look what I've got, an Ovaltiney pencil case an' all. It came on Saturday morning. I've scratched my initials inside so it doesn't get mixed up with yours. Look.'

It was mine. It had a dent where I'd dropped it on

my Auntie Doreen's kitchen floor. He'd scratched A.B. in my pencil case. But I couldn't prove it. If only I'd put my initials inside.

'I want you to take note of the person you are standing next to because this will be your partner for the week . . .'

Oh no! I didn't want to be with smelly Arthur Boocock every time we lined up . . . This was going to be the worst week of my life.

'Now you will all go with Mr Bleasdale to platform 4. I will follow with the luggage. Do *not* get on the train until you are told to. Mrs Jolliffe – will you take up the rear?'

Mrs Jolliffe was still holding Keith Hopwood's hand. I wondered if they'd be partners for the whole week. I reckoned they'd have to be 'cos there was no one else Hopwood could go with. I'd have rather been with Hopwood than Arthur Boocock. I'd have rather been with Mrs Jolliffe than Arthur Boocock. Spencer put his hand up.

'Sir?'

'Yes, Spencer.'

'What about us suitcases, sir?'

Everybody groaned and jeered and Arthur Boocock shouted, 'Wash your ears out.' He can talk – his ears are black bright. Spencer went all red.

'Do listen, lad. I just said I will bring all the luggage.'

Bleasdale stuck his hand up in the air, shouted 'Follow me' and we all followed. He kept his arm up all the way, shouting 'Left', 'Right', 'Straight on' and we started giggling. We went into the station just as a train was pulling out and the engine driver let out a great blast of steam making us all jump. We started laughing and talking and Mrs Jolliffe told us to be quiet and to keep our eyes on Mr Bleasdale. You

279

could hardly miss him with his hand stuck up in the air like that. He looked stupid. We got to platform 4 and he turned and held up his hand for us to stop. A whole carriage was reserved for our school. We could see Melrose and a porter coming down the platform pulling a trolley with all our cases on.

I felt a bit better. I like trains. I like the smell of the coal burning and the noise and the steam. I didn't like Arthur Boocock though.

'Hey Arthur, will you do us a favour? Will you swap with Tordoff so's I can be with Tony?'

Well, it was worth asking.

'What's wrong wi' me then?'

I don't like you 'cos you've got mucky ears and smelly breath and you're a bully and you stole my Ovaltiney pencil case. That's what I felt like saying.

'Nowt. Tony's my best friend, that's all.'

He smiled at me. Well, it was more of a sneer really.

'What'll you give us?'

He looked down at my blazer. He was staring at my Ovaltiney badge ... I thought about it but not for very long.

'I'll give you my Ovaltiney badge.'

'All right.'

He held his hand out and I gave it to him. He pinned it on his blazer. It was worth it. I could always send away for another one when I got home. All you need is four Ovaltine labels. When I got home ... Oh I didn't half wish I was home. He called over to Tordoff.

'Hey, Wing-nut!'

That's his nickname. Wing-nut. Melrose had started it

280

'cos of his sticky-out ears. Now we all call him Wing-nut.
He looked round.

'What?'

'Over 'ere – quick.'

Tordoff frowned.

'Quick!'

He came over, making sure Bleasdale and Mrs Jolliffe
didn't see.

'What do you want?'

Arthur was still pinning the badge onto his blazer.

'You're wi' me.'

Wing-nut didn't know what he was on about.

'Y'what?'

'You're wi' me, you're my partner.'

'I'm not.'

He started to walk back but Boocock got hold of his
arm and showed him his fist.

'Do you want thumping?'

You don't argue with Arthur Boocock. Wing-nut looked
at me and I shrugged as if I had nothing to do with it. Well,
as far as Wing-nut knew, I didn't. I turned to Boocock, all
innocent.

'Er . . . shall I go over there then, Arthur?'

He was still fiddling with my Ovaltiney badge.

'Yeah, push off.'

I shrugged again as if I didn't have a clue what was
going on and went over to Tony. I felt sorry for Wing-nut –
but not that sorry.

When we got on the train there were six of us to a
compartment. In ours we had me and Tony, Holdsworth and
Cawthra and Mrs Jolliffe and Keith who was a bit more

281

cheerful. She's all right, Mrs Jolliffe. She gave us all a barley sugar to settle our tummies and joined in when we played I-Spy. And after we'd had our sandwiches she gave us an apple each, to clean our teeth.

And when Keith started crying again she told him if he didn't stop she'd put him in the luggage rack. Not nasty. She said it in a kind voice and made him laugh.

'I'm sorry, miss, but I keep thinking about my mum and dad and it makes me cry. I can't help it. I even keep thinking about my little sister and I can't stand her.'

Everybody laughed but I wanted to say, I know what you mean, that's how I feel. And it must've been worse for Keith having a dad and a sister to miss as well. I've only got my mum. And my Auntie Doreen.

'Of course it's a bit frightening when you go away from home for the first time. Everybody's a bit nervous, Keith, but some don't show it as much as others.'

He nodded and took a bite of his apple. I put my hand up and Mrs Jolliffe laughed.

'You're not in class now. You don't have to put your hand up.'

I felt myself go red.

'I just wanted to say that I feel a bit like Keith does. I keep thinking about my mum all the time.'

Mrs Jolliffe smiled.

'You see, Keith. And I wouldn't mind betting that David and Duncan and Tony are feeling a little homesick. Aren't you, boys?'

I don't think they were at all homesick but Mrs Jolliffe gave them a little wink. She made sure Keith couldn't see. They looked at each other.

'Yeah . . .'

'A little bit . . .'

And Tony nodded.

'And do you think the boys from St Augustine's aren't feeling nervous? Of course they are. It's only natural. Now who'd like another barley sugar?'

We all put our hands up except Keith. He went to the lavatory. After he shut the sliding door Holdsworth told Mrs Jolliffe that he wasn't really feeling homesick and Cawthra said he wasn't either. So did Tony . . . So did I:

'No, me neither. I just felt sorry for Keith.'

Mrs Jolliffe leaned over and took hold of my hand.

'I know. It was very nice of you. Thank you.'

She squeezed my hand and smiled. I just about managed to smile back. I was such a liar. The others started playing I-Spy again. I didn't feel like it so I got my library book out. But I couldn't concentrate. All I could hear were the wheels on the track, talking to me:

*I want to go home . . . I want to go home . . . I want to go home . . . I want to go home . . .*

The coach was parked outside St Augustine's.

We were going home. The week was over. All the St Augustine parents were waiting to wave us off. I looked out of the window and I could see Mr and Mrs Jarvis and Stephen, the family I'd swapped with. Mrs Jarvis gave me a little smile and waved and Mr Jarvis took another photo. I smiled. I didn't feel like smiling though. I felt terrible. And so ashamed. I didn't want to go home. It had been the best week of my life . . .

*Dear Mum,*

*It is terrific here. I am having a great time. Mr and
Mrs Jarvis are really nice. They have got a Rover 90
car and have taken me to all sorts of places. They have
taken me on a picnic in the country and they have
taken me to posh restronts twice. They live in a posh
house, it is like a mansion and they have got two
bathrooms, one for me and Stephen, Peter's brother,
and another bathroom inside their bedroom for
themselves. There are three toilets in their house. I have
got bunk beds and I am sleeping in the top one. Tell
Peter. Peter's room is smashing. He has got his own
basin in his room and a lovely soft carpet everywhere
and his own desk built right across one wall. They
have got a lovely garden, it is massive and behind the
garden are fields and every night me and Stephen play
French cricket and when Mr Jarvis comes home from
work he joins in and so does Mrs Jarvis. She is very
nice and very pretty . . .*

I stopped writing and read the letter. Then I tore it up and
started again.

*Dear Mum,*

*We are having a great time. We went to the Tower of
London. It was great.*
    *And Westminster Abbey and the Houses of
Parliment. They were great. Yesterday we went to*

*Madam Two Swords except that it is not Two Swords
it is Tussords and it was great . . .*

It wasn't as long as the letter I'd torn up but it was longer
than the one Peter had sent to his mum and dad. Mr Jarvis
had read it out at breakfast.

*Dear Mummy, Daddy and Stephen,*

*I am having a good time. We went round a wool
factory. It was noisy. Looking forward to seeing you
soon.*

*Love,*

*Peter*

I wrote all about Keith Hopwood being homesick and about
Kenny Spencer and Douglas Goodall getting lost in the
underground station and how Melrose went mad and that I
hoped Peter was having a good time. And I put in another
letter for my Auntie Doreen. I didn't say anything about the
lovely house and the massive garden and Peter's smashing
bedroom and going to posh restaurants. I was worried it
might upset her.

The coach started moving off. We were going. Everybody was shouting and waving and Melrose was saying 'All
right, all right, calm down.'

I looked back and I could see Mr and Mrs Jarvis waving.
Stephen was running alongside trying to take a photo. I tried
my best to smile but I could feel the tears coming. I was

going home and I felt miserable. Why did I feel so miserable? Holdsworth and Cawthra started singing 'One green bottle' and a few others joined in. Keith Hopwood was one of them. It was the first time he'd looked happy all week.

We got off the bus at the end of our road and the conductor handed my mum my suitcase.

'I'll carry that, Mum.'

'You're all right, love.'

We walked towards our house. It felt strange being back. Everything looked different. So . . . dreary.

'Eeh, it'll be good to have you home. He was a nice enough lad, that Peter, but he was so quiet. He had nothing to say for himself, it was like being on my own.'

I walked along next to my mum. We got to our gate. Peter would be going home in the Rover 90 . . . to his lovely house . . . I thought about his bedroom and the bunk beds and the garden.

My mum opened the front door and we went in.

The hall looked so dark. I'd never noticed that before. And there was a funny smell that I'd never noticed before. A bit like cabbage. Old cabbage. And it felt so cold.

'Are you glad to be home?'

'Yeah, 'course I am.'

I felt like a real traitor. I wasn't glad to be home. I was glad to see my mum. 'Course I was. But I wasn't glad to be home. I kept thinking about Mr and Mrs Jarvis . . . I felt like a real traitor.

'Let's have a cup of tea and you can tell me all about your holiday.'

I put the kettle on while my mum unpacked my suitcase.

'What on earth have you got in here . . .'

She was going through all the pockets.

'Old sweet wrappers, empty crisp packets . . . Do you want these comics?'

I told her I'd read them so she bundled them all into a carrier bag and asked me to throw it away.

I went outside to put it in the dustbin. I stood in the backyard and looked around. It all looked so scruffy. Peter would probably be playing French cricket with his dad and Stephen in the garden now . . . I wished *I* was still there. I wished I had a dad and big brother and a big garden and a Rover 90 – and I wished I could stop wishing these thoughts – and a big posh house and a mum like Mrs Jarvis. No! No! I love my mum. Why was I thinking horrible things like this? Why was I feeling homesick for the wrong home? I went to the midden and threw the carrier bag into the dustbin. That's when I saw it. An envelope torn in half with the name 'Jarvis' written on it.

At first I thought it was from Mr and Mrs Jarvis to Peter but then I saw half the address and I realised it was the other way round. It was from Peter to his mum and dad. It was half of a letter. I scrabbled around in the dustbin and after a minute or two I found the other half. I put the two bits of paper together . . .

*Dear Mummy and Daddy,*

*I hate it here. I want to came home. I am missing you all the time. This house is horrible. It is dark and dirty and cold and it smells. Please come and fetch me, I don't want to stay here . . .*

And he wrote horrible things about my mum, that she was old and ugly, like an old witch and that he couldn't understand what she was saying and the toilet was outside . . .

> *And there's no garden and she's got a sister and they drink tea all the time and she makes me call her Auntie Doreen and I can't understand her either. Please PLEASE let me come home. There are no carpets here. Daddy can come in the car. Please.*
>
> *Love,*
>
> *Peter*
> *XXX*
>
> *Don't be upset when you get this letter.*

I screwed up his letter, threw it in the bin, wiped the tears away with my sleeve and went back in the house. My mum was pouring the water into the teapot.

'Come on, love, your Auntie Doreen'll be here in a minute. We'll all have a nice cup of tea.'

I got the cups and saucers out and put them on the table. My mum smiled at me.

'Are you pleased to be home?'

I put my arms round her and hugged her as hard as I could.

'Yes, Mum – it's lovely . . .'

# The Trick

*For Gordon Roddick,*
*with affection*

## Acknowledgements

'Happy Birthday' words and music by Patty S. Hill and Mildred Hill copyright © 1935 (renewed 1962), Summy-Birchard Music, a division of Summy-Birchard Inc., USA. Reproduced by kind permission of Keith Prowse Music Publishing Co. Ltd, London WC2H 0QY

'On the Good Ship Lollipop' words and music by Sidney Clare and Richard A. Whiting copyright © 1934, Movietone Music Corp./EMI April Music Inc., USA. Reproduced by permission of Sam Fox Publishing Co. (London) Ltd/EMI Music Publishing Ltd, London WC2H 0QY

'We'll Meet Again' words and music by Ross Parker and Hughie Charles copyright © 1939 Dash Music Company Ltd. Used by permission of Music Sales Ltd. All Rights Reserved. International Copyright Secured

Children are blind to sarcasm – they take it as truth

*– Overheard on a train*

# Contents

# Contents

# THE PROMISE

'This is the BBC Light Programme.'

'Come on, Doreen, it's on!'

It's the same every Thursday night. We have to get our tea finished, clear the table, get the pots washed and put away so we can all sit round the wireless and enjoy *ITMA* with Tommy Handley.

'Doreen! She does it every time, goes out to the lavatory just as it's starting.'

Except I don't enjoy it. I can't understand it. I don't know what they're talking about.

'Tell her to hurry up, will you, love?'

I went out the back to call my Auntie Doreen but she was already coming up the path pulling on her black skirt. She'd come straight from work.

'He's not on yet, is he?'

He was. I could hear the audience on the wireless cheering and clapping the man who'd just shouted, '*It's That Man Again!*'

'Just startin', I think.'

She ran past me into the house.

'Freda, why didn't you call me?'

'I did.'

I can't understand what they get so excited about. They all come out with these stupid things like, '*I don't mind if I do*,' '*Can I do you now, sir?*' '*Tee tee eff enn.*' What's funny about that? Don't mean a thing to me.

'What's funny about that, Mum? "*Tee tee eff enn*"? It doesn't even mean owt.

'*Ta Ta For Now!*'

'*Ta Ta For Now!*'

They both sang it at me, laughing like anything.

'It's a catchphrase. Now shush!'

What's a catchphrase? Why's it funny? Who is Tommy Handley anyway?

'What's a catchphrase, Mum? Why's it funny?'

'I'll tell you when it's finished.'

They waved at me to be quiet.

'Turn it up, Doreen.'

My Auntie Doreen twiddled with the knob on the wireless. Oh, there he goes again: '*I don't mind if I do*', and they both laughed even louder this time and my mum started taking him off.

'*I don't mind if I do . . . !*'

My Auntie Doreen had to take out her hanky to wipe away the tears that were rolling down her cheeks.

'Oh, stop it, Freda, you're makin' me wet myself . . .'

What's he on about now, this Tommy Handley bloke? '*Colonel Chinstrap, you're an absolute nitwit!*' and my mum and my Auntie Doreen fell about laughing.

Nitwit. That's what Reverend Dutton called me and Norbert the other day when we ran into him in the corridor. 'You are a pair of clumsy nitwits, you two.' Thank goodness his cup of tea wasn't too hot, it could have scalded him. If it'd been Melrose we'd run into it would have been more than nitwits, more like the cane from the headmaster . . . Oh no, the note! I'd forgotten all about it. I went out into the hall to get it from my coat pocket. We'd been given it at school for our parents. I was meant to give it to my mum when I got home. I went back into the kitchen. They were sitting there giggling away at Tommy Handley.

'Eeh, he's a tonic, isn't he, Doreen?'

The audience on the wireless were cheering and laughing.

'I've got nits.'

I handed my mum the note. She grabbed it. She wasn't giggling now.

'What do you mean, you've got nits? Who said?'

'Nit-nurse. She came to our school today.'

Next thing she was up on her feet and going through my hair.

'Oh my God, look at this, Doreen, he's riddled!'

'*Can I do you now, sir?*' the lady on the radio was asking Tommy Handley but my mum wasn't listening; she was halfway to the front door, putting on her coat.

'Get the kettle on, Doreen. I'm going down the chemist to get some stuff.'

'At this time of night? He'll be long closed.'

'Well, he'll have to open up then, won't he? It's an emergency. He can't go to bed with nits.'

She'd come back with two lots of 'stuff'. Special nit shampoo and special nit lotion.

'One and nine this lot cost! Come on, get that shirt off.'

She'd sat me at the kitchen sink while my Auntie Doreen had got the saucepans of hot water ready. Nit shampoo smells horrible, like carbolic soap only worse.

'Doreen, put another kettle on, will you? It says you have to do it twice.'

Another shampoo and then the special lotion. I'd had to sit there with it on for ages while my mum had kept going on about missing Tommy Handley.

'It's not his fault, Freda. He can't help getting nits.'

Then it had started to sting, the nit lotion.

'No, he's most likely caught them off that Norbert Lightowler. They're a grubby lot, that family.'

It had got worse, my head was burning.

'I don't like this, Mum. It's burning me.'

'Good, that means it's working . . .'

'Ow! Ooh! Mum, stop, please, you're hurting me . . .'

The nit lotion was bad but this was worse. She was pulling this little steel comb through my hair and it hurt like anything.

'Please, Mum, I don't like it . . . please . . .'

If I hadn't made her miss Tommy Handley I think she might have been a bit more gentle.

'You couldn't have given me that note as soon as you got back from school, could you? No, you had to wait till *ITMA* was on, didn't you?'

I don't know if it was the smelly nit shampoo or the stinging nit lotion or my mum dragging the metal comb through my hair, but I didn't feel very well.

'You know how much your Auntie Doreen and me look forward to it.'

I started to feel a bit dizzy.

'He's the bright spot in the week for me. I don't reckon we'd have got through the war without Tommy Handley, eh, Doreen? Him and Mr Churchill.'

'And Vera Lynn.'

'Oh yes, and Vera Lynn.'

It was getting worse. The room was going round now. Everything was spinning. What was happening? I don't feel well. I wish my mum would stop pulling that comb through my hair, she's hurting me. I feel funny. What are they doing now? They're singing. Why are they singing? Why are my mum and my Auntie Doreen singing?

*'We'll meet again, don't know whe-ere, don't know whe-en . . .'*
*'We'll meet again, don't know whe-ere, don't know whe-en . . .'*

Their voices seem miles away.

*'But I kno-oow we'll meet agai-in . . .'*
*'But I kno-oow we'll meet agai-in . . .'*

I'm fainting – that's what it is. I'm fainting. Now I know

what it feels like. When Keith Hopwood had fainted in the playground I'd asked him what it had felt like and he'd said he couldn't remember much except that everything had been going round and round and everybody's voices seemed to be a long way away. That's what's happening to me. Mum! Auntie Doreen! I can see them and they're going round and round. I'm fainting! I can hear them, they're singing and they're miles away. I'm fainting!

*'Some sunny . . .'*
*'Some sunny . . .'*

I was lying on the sofa and and my mum was dabbing my face with a damp tea towel, muttering to herself.

'Come on, Doreen, where've you got to? Hurry up, hurry up.'

My hair was still wet with the nit lotion but she'd stopped combing it, thank goodness.

'What happened? What's going on?'

'You passed out, love, you scared the life out of me. Your Auntie Doreen's gone to fetch Dr Jowett.'

The one good thing about fainting is that everybody makes a fuss of you. After Keith had passed out the caretaker had carried him to the staffroom and while they'd waited for the doctor Mrs Jolliffe had given him a cup of sweet tea and some chocolate digestives. With me it was a mug of Ovaltine and a Blue Riband on the sofa while we waited for Dr Jowett.

'Have you any more Blue Ribands, Mum?'

'I haven't, love. And I won't be getting any more till I get my new ration book.'

Why does all the good stuff have to be on rationing? I bet nit shampoo and nit lotion's not on rationing.

'Will I be going to school tomorrer?'

That'd be great if I could get off school, worth fainting for. Double maths on a Friday, I hate maths. And scripture with Reverend Dutton. Borin'.

'Let's wait and see what Dr Jowett says.'

And Latin with Bleasdale. Then we have English with Melrose. Worst day of the week, Friday. English with Melrose! Oh no! I haven't done his homework! I was going to do it after *ITMA*, wasn't I?

'I don't think I should, Mum. I might faint again. You never know.'

'We'll leave it to Dr Jowett, eh?'


'Breathe in. Out. In again.'

It wasn't Dr Jowett; it was a lady doctor who was standing in for him 'cos he was at a conference or something. I'd heard my Auntie Doreen tell me mum after she'd gone to get something from her car.

'Out. In. Cough.'

I breathed out and I breathed in and I coughed like she told me. The thing she was using to listen to my chest was freezing cold and it made me laugh.

'It's a relief to see him smiling, doctor. He looked as white as a sheet twenty minutes ago.'

The lady doctor wrote something on a brown card.

'Can I stay off school tomorrer?'

She carried on writing.

'I don't see why—'

Oh great. No maths, no Latin, no scripture, no Melrose . . .

'—you shouldn't go.'

What? No, no. 'I don't see why *not*.' That's what I thought you were going to say. That's what you're supposed to say.

'But I haven't done my English homework 'cos of all this.'

'I'll give your mother a note to give to your teacher.'

She smiled and gave me a friendly pat on my head. My hair was still sticky.

'I've got nits.'

My mum gave me one of her looks.

'Outbreak at school, doctor. You know what it's like.'

'Of course.'

'Maybe that's what made him faint. It's strong stuff, that lotion.'

She shone a light in my eyes.

'Unlikely.'

She looked down my throat and in my ears. After that she put a strap round my arm and pumped on this rubber thing. It didn't hurt, just felt a bit funny. She wrote on the brown card again.

'He's small for his age.'

'Always has been, doctor.'

'But he's particularly small. And he's anaemic. I'd say he's undernourished.'

I didn't know what she was talking about but my mum didn't like it. She sat up straight and folded her arms and the red blotch started coming up on her neck. She always gets it when she's upset.

'There's only so many coupons in a ration book, doctor. I do my best. It's weeks since this house has seen fresh fruit and vegetables. He gets his cod liver oil and his orange juice and his Virol. I do what I can. That nit lotion and shampoo cost one and nine. It's not easy on your own, you know.'

The doctor wrote on the brown card again.

'Excuse me, I'm just going to get something from the car.'

My mum watched her go. The blotch on her neck was getting redder.

'Who's she? Where's Dr Jowett?'

'She's standing in for him while he's at a conference. She's very nice. Came straight away.'

'Very nice? I don't think it's very nice to be told I'm neglecting my own son. I'll give her undernourished!'

'Give over, Freda, she said nothing of the sort. Don't be so bloody soft, we've just had a war. We're all undernourished with this bloody rationing!'

I don't know who was more shocked, me or my mum. You never hear my Auntie Doreen swear. You'd have thought it was my fault, the way my mum turned on me.

'And why did you have to tell her you've got nits? Showing me up like that.'

My Auntie Doreen was just about to have another go when we heard the lady doctor coming back.

'I was going to write a prescription for a course of iron tablets but I remembered I'd got some in the car.'

She gave my mum a brown bottle.

'I don't mind paying, doctor.'

The doctor didn't say anything, just smiled.

'Now, I'll tell you what he really needs – a couple of weeks by the sea.'

My mum looked at her, then burst out laughing.

'A couple of weeks by the sea! Yes, that's what we all need, eh, Doreen?'

The lady doctor put everything back in her black bag.

'It can be arranged. And it won't cost a penny. I'll talk to Dr Jowett.'

I looked at my mum and my Auntie Doreen.

'He'll probably have to take time off school, but it would do him the world of good.'

A couple of weeks by the sea! Free! Time off school! Sounded good to me.

DEAR MUM,
I HATE IT HERE. WHY DID DOCTOR JOWETT
AND THAT LADY DOCTOR SEND ME TO THIS
HORRABLE PLACE? I WANT TO COME HOME. YOU
PROMISED THAT IF I DID NOT LIKE IT HERE
YOU WOULD COME AND FETCH ME. I DON'T LIKE

IT SO FETCH ME WHEN YOU GET THIS LETTER.
MORCAMBE IS ONLY TWO HOURS AWAY. YOU
SAID SO YOURSELF . . .

Yeah, it sounded good 'cos I thought she'd meant all of us. Me, my mum and my Auntie Doreen. Nobody'd said I'd be going on my own. I wouldn't have gone, would I? My mum never told me. Dr Jowett never told me. He was in the kitchen talking to her when I got home from school on the Friday.

'Talk of the devil, here he is. Do you want to tell him the good news, Dr Jowett?'

He had a big smile on his face when he told me. I couldn't believe it. It turned out that because I'm small for me age and all that other stuff the lady doctor had talked to my mum about, we got to go to Morecambe for free. The council paid.

'And my mum doesn't have to pay anything?'

Dr Jowett pulled my bottom lids down and looked in my eyes, like the lady doctor did the night before.

'Not a penny. It's a special scheme paid for by the council to give young folk like yourself a bit of sea air. Build you up. You'll come back six inches taller. Now, do you want to go for two weeks or one?'

Why would I want to go for one week when we could go for two? I looked at my mum.

'It's up to you, love . . .'

If she'd have said, '*It's up to you, love, 'cos you're the one going, not me, I'm not comin', neither's your Auntie Doreen, it's just you on your own,'* I'd never have said it.

'It's up to you, love – do you want to go for two weeks?'

It'd be stupid not to go for two weeks when it's free. So I said it. Just like the man on the wireless.

'I don't mind if I do!'

We all laughed.

DEAR MUM,
PLEASE COME FOR ME. I CAN'T STAY HERE. I
HATE IT. YOU PROMISED YOU WOULD FETCH ME
IF I DIDN'T LIKE IT . . .

After Dr Jowett had gone we sat at the kitchen table and looked at the leaflet he'd left for us. It looked lovely. I listened while my mum read it out.

'"*Craig House – a home from home. Overlooking Morecambe Bay, Craig House gives poor children the opportunity to get away from the grime of the city to the fresh air of the seaside* . . ." Sounds lovely, doesn't it?'

'Yeah. What does that bit mean?'

'What bit?'

'That bit about poor children. Do you have to be poor to go there?'

She looked at me.

'Well, it is for people what can't afford it, like us. That's why we're getting it for free.'

'Oh . . .'

We both looked at the leaflet again.

'There's nothing wrong with it, love. It's our right. Dr Jowett says. I mean, it'd be daft to give free holidays to them that can pay for it.'

Yeah, that was true.

'I suppose so.'

MUM, WHY HAVEN'T YOU COLLECTED ME FROM HERE? YOU PROMISED. YOU SAID IF I WAS UNHAPY YOU WOULD TAKE ME HOME. PLEASE COME AS SOON AS YOU GET THIS. PLEASE . . .

It just never crossed my mind that I was going on my own. I had no idea. It wasn't till the Sunday night, when my mum was packing my suitcase, that I found out.

'Now, I've put you two swimming costumes in so when one's wet you can wear the other, and you've plenty of underpants and vests . . .'

Even then it didn't dawn on me. I'd felt good having my own suitcase, grown up. When we'd gone to Bridlington she packed all our things together but we'd only gone for two days. This time we were going for two weeks. I thought that's why she was giving me my own suitcase.

'. . . and I'm putting in a few sweets for you, some Nuttall's Mintoes, some fruit pastilles and a bar of chocolate. You can thank your Auntie Doreen for them, she saved up her coupons.'

I still didn't realise.

'Well, we can share them, can't we?'

311

'No, these are all for you.'

I thought she was just being nice, getting in the holiday mood.

'Now, this is important. I'm giving you these to take –' she held up some envelopes – 'they're all stamped and addressed so you can write to me every day if you like . . .'

You what? What are you talking about? What is she talking about?

'You don't have to write every day, I'm only joking, but I would like to get the occasional letter. They're here, under your pants.'

What was she talking about? When it all came out that I'd thought they were coming with me, she'd looked at me like I'd gone off my head.

'But why? What on earth made you think me and your Auntie Doreen were coming?'

''Cos you said.'

'I never. I never said we were all going.'

She was lying. She did.

'You did. When the lady doctor said I needed a holiday, you told her that's what we *all* needed, a couple of weeks by the sea. You ask Auntie Doreen.'

I'd cried and told her that I wasn't going to go and she said I had to, it'd all been arranged, I'd show her up in front of Dr Jowett if I didn't go. And it wouldn't be fair if I didn't go, it would be a wasted space that some other child could have used.

'It's not fair on me, 'cos if I'd known I wouldn't have said I'd go for two weeks. I wouldn't have gone for *one*

312

week. I'm not goin', I don't want to go. Please don't make me go . . .'

I cried, I begged, I shut myself in my bedroom. I wasn't going to go, I wasn't.

'I'm not goin'. You can't force me.'

She couldn't force me.

'Listen, love, if you don't like it, if you're really unhappy, I'll get straight on the train and bring you home.'

'Promise?'

'It's less than two hours away.'

'Promise?'

''Course.'

'Promise!'

'I promise.'

My mum let me sleep in her bed that night 'cos I couldn't stop crying.

'Come on, love, go to sleep, we've got to be at Great Albert Street at eight o'clock for your coach.'

'You promise to fetch me if I don't like it?'

'But you will like it and it'll do you good.'

'You promise, don't you?'

'As soon as I get your letter.'

And I fell asleep.

*Craig House holiday home*
*far far away,*
*Where us poor children go*
*for a holiday.*
*Oh, how we run like hell*

*when we hear the dinner bell,*
*far far away.*

DEAR MUM,
I HATE IT HERE. WHY DID DOCTOR JOWETT
AND THAT LADY DOCTOR SEND ME TO THIS
HORRABLE PLACE? I WANT TO COME HOME. YOU
PROMISED THAT IF I DID NOT LIKE IT HERE
YOU WOULD COME AND FETCH ME. I DON'T LIKE
IT SO FETCH ME WHEN YOU GET THIS LETTER.
MORCAMBE IS ONLY TWO HOURS AWAY. YOU
SAID SO YOURSELF . . .

That was the first letter.

DEAR MUM,
PLEASE COME FOR ME. I CAN'T STAY HERE. I
HATE IT. YOU PROMISED YOU WOULD FETCH ME
IF I DIDN'T LIKE IT . . .

That was the second letter.

MUM, WHY HAVEN'T YOU COME . . . ?

Why hadn't she come for me? She'd promised . . .

THIS IS THE THIRD TIME I'VE WRITTEN . . .

We'd been told we had to be outside the medical clinic in

314

Great Albert Street at eight o'clock for the coach. We were going to be weighed before we went and they'd weigh us when we got back to see how much we'd put on. My Auntie Doreen came with us, and even on the bus to town I made them both promise again. We turned into Great Albert Street at five to and I could see lots of kids waiting on the pavement with their mums and dads and grandmas and grandads. There was no coach. Good, maybe it had broken down and I wouldn't have to go. My mum carried my suitcase and we walked up the road towards them. A big cheer went up as the coach came round the corner at the top end of the street.

When we got closer I saw that some of the kids looked funny. One lad had no hair, another was bandy. There was a girl with these iron things on her legs. My mum gave me a sharp tap 'cos I was staring at the bald lad.

'What's wrong with him, Mum?'

'Alopecia, most likely.'

'What's that?'

'It's when your hair drops out. Poor lad.'

'Do you get it from nits?'

'Don't be daft.'

My Auntie Doreen told me it can be caused by stress or shock.

'Do you remember that teacher we had at primary, Freda, Mrs Theobold? She lost all her hair when her husband got knocked down by a tram.'

My mum shook her head.

'Oh, you do. She had to wear a wig.'

'I don't.'

We stood outside the medical clinic next to a woman with a ginger-headed lad. His face looked ever so sore, all flaky and red. My mum gave me another sharp tap. The woman got a packet of Woodbines out of her handbag.

'Oh, don't worry, missus, he's used to young 'uns staring, aren't you, Eric?'

Eric nodded while she lit a cigarette.

'Eczema. Not infectious, love. Had it all his life, haven't you, Eric?'

He nodded again. My Auntie Doreen smiled at him.

'Two weeks in Morecambe'll be just what he needs, eh?'

The woman coughed as she blew the smoke out.

'Don't know about him but it'll do me a power of good. I need a break, I can tell you.'

Just then a man came out of the clinic and shouted that we all had to go inside to be weighed.

'Parents, foster parents and guardians – wait out here while the luggage is put on the charabanc. The children will return as soon as they've been weighed and measured.'

Eric's mum took another puff on her cigarette.

'I don't know why they bother. Last year he came back weighing less than when he went, didn't you, Eric?'

Eric nodded again.

'And I swear he was half an inch shorter. Off you go then.'

I followed him into the clinic, where the man was telling everybody to go up the main stairs and turn left.

'Have you been before then, to Craig House?'

316

He'd been for the last two years.

'What's it like?'

'S'all right. Better than being at home.'

At the top of the stairs we followed the ones in front into a big room where we were told to take our clothes off. We had to strip down to our vests and pants and sit on a stool until we heard our name called out. There were four weighing scales, with a number above each one. I sat next to Eric. He didn't have a vest on and his pants had holes in them and whatever his mum had said he had, he had it all over, he looked horrible. I couldn't help staring. He didn't seem bothered though. He just sat there, scratching, staring at the floor.

'Eric Braithwaite, weighing scale three! Eric Braithwaite, weighing scale three!'

He didn't say anything, just wandered off to be weighed and measured. I sat waiting for my name to be called out. The girl with iron things on her legs was on the other side of the room. Her mum and dad had been allowed to come in and were taking the iron things off and helping her get undressed.

'Margaret Donoghue, weighing scale one! Margaret Donoghue, weighing scale one!'

That was her. Her dad had to carry her, she couldn't walk without her iron things. Eric came back, put his clothes back on and wandered off. He didn't speak, didn't say a word. They were going in alphabetical order so I had to wait quite a long time before I heard my name. When I did I had to go to weighing scale number four. A lady in a white coat told me to get on.

'There's nothing of you, is there? A couple of weeks at Craig House'll do you no harm.'

She wrote my weight down in a book.

'Now, let's see how small you are.'

Couple of weeks? I wasn't going to be there a couple of weeks. Not if I didn't like it. And I *wasn't* going to like it, I knew that much.

'Right, get dressed and go back to your mum and dad.'

'I haven't got a dad.'

'Ellis Roper! Weighing scale number four! Ellis Roper, weighing scale number four! You what, dear?'

'I haven't got a dad.'

'Well, go back to whoever brought you. Ellis Roper, please! Weighing scale number four!'

*Craig House holiday home*
*far far away,*
*Where us poor children go*
*for a holiday.*
*Oh, how we run like hell*
*when we hear the dinner bell,*
*far far away.*

We were on our way to Morecambe and those that had been before were singing this stupid song. I was in an aisle seat next to the bald lad. He was singing, so I knew it wasn't his first time. I'd wanted to get by the window so I could wave goodbye to my mum and my Auntie Doreen but by the time I'd been weighed and measured I was too late. Eric was next to me on the other side of the aisle. He wasn't singing, just sitting there staring into space. Behind me a girl was crying. She hadn't wanted to go. The driver and the man from the clinic had had to drag her away from her mum and force her on to the coach. Her mum had run off up the street crying, with her dad following. They didn't even wave her off. My mum had had to get her hanky out 'cos she had tears in her eyes.

'Don't forget to write – your envelopes are in your suit-case under your pants.'

'Course I wouldn't forget. I had it all planned. I was going to write as soon as I got there and post it straight away. My mum'd get the letter on the Tuesday morning, get on the train like she'd promised and I'd be home for Tuesday night. That's why I wasn't crying like the girl behind me. I was only going to be away for one day, wasn't I?

I was looking at the bald lad when he turned round. I made out I'd been looking out of the window but I reckon he knew I'd been staring at him.

'I've got alopecia.'

He smiled. He didn't have any eyebrows neither.

'Oh . . .' I didn't know what to say. 'How long have you had it?'

'A few years. I went to bed one night and when I woke up it was lyin' there on my pillow. My hair.'

I felt sick.

'It just fell out?'

'Yeah. It was after my gran got a telegram tellin' her that my dad had been killed at Dunkirk. I live with my gran. My mum died when I was two.'

I told him that I lived with my mum and that my auntie lived two streets away.

'Did *your* dad die in the war?'

'I don't know. Don't think so. I've never known him.'

He was all right, Paul, I quite liked him. He told me it wasn't too bad at Craig House. This was his third year running.

'It's not bad. They've got table tennis and football and they take you on the beach. And you get a cooked breakfast every mornin'. You get a stick of rock when you leave. It's all right.'

Maybe it wouldn't be as bad as I thought. Maybe I'd like it. Maybe I wouldn't want to go home.

MUM, WHY HAVEN'T YOU COME? THIS IS THE
THIRD TIME I'VE WRITTEN. I HATE IT HERE . . .

'Look – the sea!'

It was one of the big lads at the back shouting, the one who'd started the singing. Everybody leaned over to our side of the coach to get a look. Eric didn't; he just sat there, staring and scratching his face. For some of them, like the girl behind me, it was the first time they'd seen the sea. She was all right now, laughing and giggling and talking away

320

to the girl next to her. The man from the clinic stood up at the front and told us all to sit down.

'We'll be arriving at Craig House in five minutes. Do not leave this coach until I give the word. When you hear your name you will alight the charabanc, retrieve your luggage, which will be on the pavement, and proceed to the home.'

The coach pulled round a corner and there it was. There was a big sign by the entrance:

# CRAIG HOUSE

And underneath it said:

## Poor Children's Holiday Home

We all stood in the entrance hall holding our suitcases while our names were called out and we were told which dormitory we were in. There was this smell and it was horrible. Like school dinners and hospitals mixed together. It made me feel sick. There were four dormitories, two for the girls and two for the boys. I was in General Montgomery dormitory and I followed my group. We were going up the stairs when I saw it. A post box. I'd been worried that they wouldn't let me out to find a post box and there was one right here in the entrance hall. I could post my letter here in Craig House. It wasn't like a normal post box that you see in the street; it was made of cardboard and painted red and the hole where you put the letters was a smiling mouth.

I wasn't able to write it until late that afternoon.

When we'd been given our bed we were taken to the showers and scrubbed clean by these ladies and had our hair washed with nit shampoo. I tried to tell my lady that my mum had already done it but she didn't want to know.

'Best be safe than sorry, young man.'

Then we were given a Craig House uniform (they'd taken our clothes off to be washed). Shirt, short trousers, jumper. They even gave us pyjamas. And on everything was a ribbon that said 'Poor Children's Holiday Home'. You couldn't take it off, it was sewn on.

At last, after our tea, I'd been able to write my letter. I licked the envelope, made sure it was stuck down properly and ran down the main stairs.

'Walk, lad. Don't run. Nobody runs at Craig House.'

That was the warden. I walked across the entrance hall to the post box and put my letter into the smiling mouth. All I had to do now was wait for my mum to come and fetch me.

MUM, WHY HAVEN'T YOU COME? THIS IS THE
THIRD TIME I'VE WRITTEN. I HATE IT HERE.
THERE ARE TWO LADS THAT BULLY ME. THEY
HAVE TAKEN ALL MY SWEETS . . .

I hated it. I hated it. I couldn't see why Paul thought it was all right. Or Eric. Not that I saw much of them. They were in General Alanbrooke dormitory. I think I was the youngest in General Montgomery. I was the smallest any-way – they were all bigger than me. My bed was between the two who had started the singing at the back of the coach and at night after the matron had switched off the lights they said things to frighten me and they made these scary noises. I thought they might be nicer to me if I gave them each a Nuttall's Mintoe. When they saw all my other sweets in my suitcase they made me hand them all over. I hated them. I dreaded going to bed 'cos I was so scared. I was too scared to go to sleep. I was too scared to get up and go to the lavatory. Then in the morning I'd find I'd wet the bed and I'd get told off in front of everybody and have to stand out on the balcony as a punishment.

And I hated my mum. She'd broken her promise. You can never trust grown-ups.

DEAR MUM, YOU PROMISED. YOU SAID IF I WAS
UNHAPY YOU WOULD TAKE ME HOME. YOU
HAVEN'T COME. I AM SO UNHAPY. PLEASE FETCH
ME AS SOON AS YOU GET THIS . . .

I licked the envelope and stuck it down like I'd done with all the others. I walked downstairs to the entrance hall and went over to the post box. I was just about to put it in the smiling mouth when I heard Eric.

'What you doin'?'

'Sendin' a letter to my mum.'

Eric laughed. Well, it wasn't a laugh, more of a snort.

'It's not a proper post box. They don't post 'em.'

I looked at him.

'They say they post 'em but they don't. They don't want us pestering 'em at home.'

I still had the letter in my hand.

'I won't bother then.'

I tore it up and went back to the dormitory. The second week went quicker and I didn't wet the bed.


'You didn't send one letter, you little monkey.'

My mum wasn't really cross that I hadn't written.

'It shows he had a good time, doesn't it, Doreen? See, I told you you'd like it.'

She was annoyed at how much weight I'd lost.

# THE MAJOR

I should never have told my mum. I wish I'd never mentioned it. I felt stupid standing in my vest and underpants in the middle of the kitchen with a curly wig stuck on my head.

'Stand up straight while I fix your hair and keep still for goodness sake.'

You could hardly tell what she was saying 'cos she was holding these hairgrips in her mouth. She got hold of the wig and pulled the back of it.

'Doreen, just hold the front in place while I stick these bobby pins in, will you?'

Bobby pins, that's what they're called, not hairgrips, she had about six of them between her lips.

'Ow! That hurts!'

'Oh stop mithering, you'll thank me when you win, keep still.'

And she stuck another one in, right into my neck.

'Freda, you're going to swallow one of those if you keep talking, give them to me and I'll pass them to you as and when.'

My mum spat the bobby pins out into my Auntie Doreen's hand, took one and stuck it in the wig.

'Ow!'

'Stand still.'

'I don't want to go.'

'Don't start that again, not now, not after the effort me and your Auntie Doreen have put in.'

I wish I'd never mentioned it. I should never have told her about the fancy-dress competition.

*'Happy Birthday to you*
*Happy Birthday to you*
*Happy Birthday dear . . .'*

We all took a deep breath: '*David – Raymond – Christine . . .*'

The cinema manager held his hand over their heads and shouted their names into his microphone as he walked behind them on the stage. We all sang along, trying to keep up with him.

'Trevor – Margaret – and another David!'

'. . . *Trevor – Margaret – and Da-v-id . . .*'

Except Norbert sang '*and another Da-v-id*'.

'*Happy Birthday to you!*'

We tried to make the final 'you' last as long as we could, we do it every week, and Norbert went on longer than the rest of us and slid off his seat on to the floor, still singing and running out of breath. One of the usherettes pointed at him and pointed to the door.

'Any more and you're out. I've been watching you, lad.'

Uncle Derek, that's the cinema manager, gave them

their ABC Minors birthday cards and we all clapped while they went back to their seats. I'd gone up on the stage the week of my birthday and it's not just a birthday card you get, it's a pass that gets you in for free the next week with pictures of film stars on it, like Lassie and Laurel and Hardy and Roy Rogers and that girl in *The Wizard of Oz* – I didn't like that film, it gave me nightmares – and Mickey Mouse and Donald Duck, but best of all it says: 'PLEASE ADMIT BEARER AS MY GUEST' and it's signed by Uncle Derek.

The usherette was still watching Norbert. He got up off the floor and scrambled back into his seat.

'I haven't done nothin', missus. Honest. I were just singin'.'

'*And* messin' about. Don't think I don't remember you, lad, I do. I ejected you two weeks back for throwin' Butterkist.'

She went off to separate two lads near the front who were fighting. She got hold of them both by their collars and marched them up the aisle.

'If she chucks me out, you'll have to let me back in at the side door when the lights go down.'

'Me?'

I wasn't going to risk getting thrown out just to let him in again.

'I'll give you three sherbet lemons.'

I gave him the sort of look my mum gives me when I've said something stupid.

'Get lost, ask Keith.'

'He's gone to the lav.'

'Well, make sure he's back before you get chucked out.'

That's how he'd got in without paying earlier on. It's how he gets in every week, he never pays to go to the Saturday morning matinee, doesn't Norbert. He goes round the back of the picture house, up Shadwell Street, and gets Keith Hopwood to push down the bar on the inside of the side door. He gives Keith some of his sweets for doing it. Mind you, he never pays for them neither, he nicks them. We all do, every Saturday, me, Tony, Norbert and Keith Hopwood. But we're not going to any more, Keith, Tony and me anyway, we'd decided that morning.

'Now, boys and girls, we've got a wonderful selection of films for you today starting with the Bowery Boys . . .'

Everybody cheered and there were the usual boos.

'A Mighty Mouse cartoon . . .'

More cheers and boos.

'Shh, shush, listen to Uncle Derek now . . .'

We meet by the park gates every Saturday at around half past nine to get the bus into town, but we always go across the road to Major Creswell's first to buy our sweets. Well, to steal them. We pay for some, a few. But even if we had the money we couldn't buy more than a few, 'cos we never have enough coupons. Why do they have to have sweets on rationing anyway? It's not fair.

'And – the final episode of *Flash Gordon*!'

No boos this time. Cheering and shouting and whistling and everybody stamping their feet. It was deafening.

'And the big picture today, boys and girls . . .'

It's easy nicking sweets and stuff in the Major's shop, always has been, ever since he took it over from old Mrs Jesmond last year. Norbert always asks for something off the top shelf and while the Major's moving the ladder and going up it, Norbert just helps himself to whatever he wants. One time he even went round the counter and pretended to serve us.

'The big picture today, girls and boys . . . Shush, now listen, don't you want to know . . . ?'

'YES!'

Everybody shouted as loud as they could.

'Yes what?'

'YES, PLEASE!'

'The big picture is . . .'

I feel a bit sorry for the Major but I still do it with all the others. I never take as much as Norbert. The week before last he'd come out with a whole box of pear drops. I just take a few of the loose things that the Major has on the counter. A couple of Poor Bens or a Vimto bar or maybe a few sherbet lemons, hardly anything. You can't really call it stealing.

'The big picture is – *Tarzan*!'

Cheers, shouts, boos, stamping. We all went mad, specially Norbert. He stood on his seat and did Tarzan's jungle call. He was lucky the usherette didn't see him, she was too busy trying to catch these lads who were running up and down the aisle. I think they were from St Cuthbert's. They always go a bit mad, St Cuthbert's lads.

Anyway, I'm not going to do it any more, the stealing. None of us are – except Norbert. We'd decided to stop when the Major had asked us to look after the shop while he went upstairs to check on Mrs Creswell. He'd come down the ladder just as we'd put the stuff in our pockets. I was lucky he didn't catch me, I'd dropped a liquorice stick on the floor and got it away just in time.

'Listen, chaps, would you do me a favour? Would you keep an eye on things down here for a couple of minutes? I just want to pop upstairs and check on the little lady. The old girl's having one of her bad days, I'm afraid . . .'

The Major's wife is an invalid, she has to stay upstairs above the shop. We never see her, I think she's in bed most of the time. We don't even know what she looks like.

'I thought I'd make her a quick cup of tea. Have you got the time?'

Norbert's eyes lit up.

'Yeah, you're all right, Major Creswell, we'll watch the shop.'

'I don't want to make you late for your Saturday matinee.'

Norbert looked at us.

'No, it doesn't start till half past ten, Major, we've got tons of time, haven't we, lads?'

We all mumbled that we had plenty of time. We knew what he was going to do. And I knew what *I* was going to do.

'Thanks a lot, chaps, won't be long. Much appreciated.'

We watched him go into the back of the shop and heard him go upstairs.

'Are you all right, dear? Thought you might like a cup of tea, old thing. A bunch of my regular customers are very kindly looking after the shop . . .'

We looked at each other. Norbert had this stupid grin on his face.

'Bloomin' hummer, we can take what we like!'

Uncle Derek was 'shushing' into the microphone.

'Now, before we start the first film, I've got an important announcement to make . . .'

More boos. We all stamped our feet. Norbert looked round to check where the usherette was and stood on his seat to boo.

'No, no, listen, boys and girls, this is something very exciting, you'll like this, listen. Next week we're going to have, up here on the stage, a film-star fancy-dress competition . . . !'

Tons of boos.

'You have to dress up as your favourite film star and the first prize, courtesy of the Directors and Management of Associated British Cinemas – listen now, it's something special, quiet now – first prize will be a *year's* free pass to the ABC Saturday Morning Matinee . . .'

Stamping feet, cheering, whistling. I thought the roof was going to come down.

'Second prize, a free pass for six months and third prize,

331

a three-month pass. I told you it was special. Now remember, you do have to dress up as a film star . . .'

Norbert was shouting at me but I couldn't tell what he was saying with all the noise.

'Y'what?'

'Free pass for a year! Bloomin' hummer, I'm goin' in for that.'

I couldn't understand what he was so excited about, he gets in free anyway, every week.

'And now it's showtime!'

The lights started to go down and the curtain turned red, then deep red and went up slowly. The music started.

*'We are the boys and girls well known*
*As Minors of the ABC,*
*And every Saturday we line up*
*To see the films we like*
*And shout with glee . . .'*

Norbert went round to the back of the counter. He still had his stupid grin on his face.

'You lot listen out for him. What do you want? Liquorice cuttings? Oh look, sherbet lemons.'

I got hold of his jumper and pulled him back.

'No! He's asked us to look after the shop.'

Norbert pulled himself free and took a handful of the sherbet lemons.

'Sod off, I'm not missin' a chance like this.'

He put the sherbet lemons into one of his trouser pockets and grabbed another handful.

'Well, I'm not takin' anything. In fact, I'm putting my stuff back.'

I got the liquorice stick that I'd pinched out of my pocket and put it back in the box on the counter. Norbert was still taking stuff.

'Keith, listen out for him.'

'No, I'm p-p-putting mine b-back an' all.'

Keith emptied his pockets. So did Tony.

'So am I.'

Norbert stopped for a minute and looked at us.

'You're soft, you lot!'

He grabbed some dolly mixtures and ran out.

'I'll see you down there.'

He slammed the door shut. A second later it opened again and he came back in. I thought maybe he'd changed his mind and was going to put the sweets back, but he didn't. He went over to the lolly cabinet, took a Koola Fruta and ran out again. Every time he went in and out the shop doorbell rang. The Major thought it was customers, we heard him coming back down the stairs.

'Sounds like it's getting quite busy down there, dear, better go and relieve the troops. I'll pop up again later, old thing, when it quietens down.'

Tony, Keith and me waited for the Major to come back into the shop. He looked surprised.

'Oh! I thought I heard a couple of customers come in.'

I waited for the others to say something but they didn't.

'No, Major Creswell, it was Norbert . . . he was worried about bein' late so he went. He came back to . . . er . . . borrow some money for the bus.'

The Major went round the counter.

'Thanks for holding the fort, chaps. Here you are, a little something for keeping an eye on things down here.'

He held up three bars of Five Boys chocolate. We looked at each other, we didn't know what to do. We hadn't stolen any sweets now so I reckoned it was all right. I took one.

'Thanks, Major Creswell.'

Keith and Tony took theirs.

'Yes, th-thanks, M-Major.'

'Ta, Major.'

He held out another bar.

'And one for your chum.'

We stopped at the door. Nobody wanted to take it but I didn't have any choice, the Major threw it over and I was the one to catch it.

'Thank you, Major Creswell, we'll give it to him when we see him.'

As soon as we got to the bus stop we divided it into three and ate it on the way to the matinee.

*We love to laugh and have a sing-song,*
*Such a happy crowd are we.*
*We're all pals together,*
*The Minors of the ABC!'*

*

'And Mum, listen to this, first prize is a free pass for a year!'

As soon as I'd got home from the pictures, I'd told her about the fancy-dress competition.

'You have to dress as a film star, what shall I go as?'

'Ow!'

'Stand still.'

'I don't want to go.'

'Don't start that again, not now, not after the effort me and your Auntie Doreen have put in.'

I wish I'd never mentioned it. I should never have told her about the fancy-dress competition.

'What do you think, Mum? Charlie Chaplin?'

She was laying the table.

'We'll ask your Auntie Doreen when she gets here, she'll have some ideas.'

I love Saturdays. Matinee in the morning, then usually we have fish and chips for dinner, my Auntie Doreen gets them fresh from Pearson's on her way over.

'What do you think I should go as, Auntie Doreen?'

I shook some more vinegar over my fish and chips. My mum snatched the bottle out of my hand.

'Don't drown them like that, you'll spoil your dinner. What do you think, Doreen, Charlie Chaplin?'

My Auntie Doreen put some more vinegar on her fish and chips. She's like me, she has tons of it. My mum doesn't tell her she's spoiling her dinner.

'No, they'll be ten a penny, Charlie Chaplins. They'll all be going as Charlie Chaplin or Roy Rogers. We'll have to think of something different if he wants to win.'

She did.

'Shirley Temple? She's a girl, Auntie Doreen!'

We were on our way home from church on the Sunday and my Auntie Doreen was telling my mum her idea about me entering the fancy-dress competition as Shirley Temple. She had this big smile on her face.

'It just came to me, Freda, right in the middle of the vicar's sermon . . .'

'Auntie Doreen, I don't want to go as a girl!'

She wasn't listening. Neither of them were.

'You know when he was talking about us all being just ships that pass in the night, that song Shirley Temple sings came into my head you know, out of the blue . . .'

She started singing:

*'On the good ship Lollipop,*
*It's a sweet trip to a candy shop . . .'*

Then my mum joined in.

*'Where the bon-bons pla-ay,*
*On the sunny beach of Peppermint Ba-ay . . .'*

They both fell about laughing.

336

'It's a good idea, Doreen, there won't be any other lads going as Shirley Temple.'

I didn't want to go as a girl.

'Mum, I don't think I want to go as a girl.'

'Exactly, Freda, he's bound to win.'

*I didn't want to go as a girl.*

'But I don't want to go as a girl.'

They didn't hear me, they were too busy talking about what I was going to wear. My mum said she'd get me a curly blonde wig and my Auntie Doreen said she'd make me a dress with bows on.

'I've got some lovely gingham material, it'll be perfect . . .'

'I don't think I want to go as Shirley Temple, Mum . . .'

'And I'll make him a couple of gingham bows to go in his hair.'

They started singing again and skipping down the street:

*'On the good ship Lollipop,*
*It's a night trip, into bed you hop.*
*And dream awa-ay,*
*On the good ship—'*

'I'm not goin' as a bloody girl!'

'And you don't come out until I say so! I will not have you shouting and swearing at your Auntie Doreen in the middle of the street like that! Specially when she's trying to help you.'

She slammed my bedroom door shut. I'd said I was sorry. Twice.

'But I've apologised, haven't I? I've said I'm sorry!'

I could hear her stamping down the stairs.

'Twice!'

I opened the door a little bit.

'All right, I'll go as Shirley Temple if you want!'

I heard her coming back. I shut it quick.

'It makes no difference to us, you can go as Chu Chin Chow for all I care! And put your dinner plate outside the door when you've finished.'

I didn't know what she was talking about. I'd never heard of Choochinchow or whoever she was talking about. She was probably a girl too.

I didn't put my plate outside the door like my mum had told me. After I'd finished my dinner I sat on my bed for a while then I took it downstairs myself.

'Sorry, Auntie Doreen, I didn't mean to shout. Thank you for your help. I'd like to go as Shirley Temple.'

'Come here.'

I went over and she gave me a big hug.

'You go as you like, love, it was just an idea, something different.'

I looked at my mum. I didn't want to go as a girl but I didn't want to get into more trouble.

'No, I'd like to, I think it's a *good* idea.'

My mum smiled. My Auntie Doreen gave me another hug.

'Come on, Freda, get your tape measure out, I want to make a start on his dress when I get home tonight.'

I had to stand on a chair while my Auntie Doreen got all my measurements and they sang that stupid song again.

'On the good ship Lollipop,
It's a sweet trip to a candy shop . . .'

At least I wasn't in trouble any more.

'Stand still.'

'I don't want to go.'

'Don't start that again, not now, not after the effort me and your Auntie Doreen have put in.'

I wish I'd never mentioned it. I should never have told her about the fancy-dress competition.

'Now, let's get that dress on him, Doreen, see how it looks.'

Later on, after my Auntie Doreen had gone home, my mum asked me to run round to the off-licence in Mansfield Street to get her a bag of sugar.

'Here's the ration book, don't lose it, and here's the correct money. Straight there and straight back, it'll be getting dark soon.'

'Right, Mum.'

I was pleased to be helping her, I hate it when she's cross with me.

'Hang on, love.'

She opened her purse again.

'Get yourself something from the sweet shop, there's enough coupons.'

That would have been nice but the Major's is closed on a Sunday afternoon.

'He'll be closed.'

She told me to keep the money anyway, in case I saw something in the off-licence.

'Thanks, Mum.'

It was all right this. Worth going as Shirley Temple. Maybe it *was* a good idea, maybe I'd win. Even if it were only third prize I'd get a free cinema pass for three months.

I got the bag of sugar and a Wagon Wheel for myself and I started eating it on my way home.

When I went past Major Creswell's I stopped to look in the window to see what I would have bought if he'd been open. Probably some liquorice torpedoes. Or maybe sherbet lemons – if Norbert had left any, he'd taken tons. I was pressing my face against the door, looking at the sweets inside, when it opened. I couldn't believe it. The lights were all out and the closed sign was on the door but it just swung open. It hadn't been locked properly on the inside. The bell was ringing and I was standing inside the shop. I didn't know what to do. I reckoned the Major would have heard the shop bell so I waited for him to come down.

'Major Creswell? Major Creswell?'

Nobody came. I closed the door to make the bell ring again. He still didn't come down. All I could think was that it'd been a good job it was me and not Norbert who'd been leaning against the door, he'd have nicked everything by now.

'Major . . . Major Creswell?'

Still nothing. I went to the back of the shop and called up the stairs.

'Major Creswell? Are you there? The shop door wasn't locked properly . . .'

There was a light at the top of the stairs and I could hear music playing. I didn't know what to do. It was getting dark now, I had to get home for my mum. But I had to tell the Major. I couldn't just go. I went up a few of the stairs.

'Major? Major Creswell? Mrs Creswell . . . ?'

The music was quite loud, that was probably why he hadn't heard the bell. I went up a few more stairs and called a bit louder.

'Hello? Major Creswell . . . Mrs Creswell . . . Hello?'

When I got to the top of the stairs there was a landing, and the light and the music were coming from a room at the end of a corridor. The door was only half open. I walked towards it, tapped and peeped in. Mrs Creswell was sitting in a chair with her eyes closed, listening to the music.

'Mrs Creswell?'

I thought it was funny she was smoking a pipe but it was only when she spoke that I realised.

'Oh my God, old boy, you gave me the fright of my life.'

It wasn't Mrs Creswell, it was the Major.

'How on earth did you get in, old chap?'

He was dressed up as a woman.

'Sorry . . . your shop door . . . it was open . . . you hadn't locked it properly . . . Didn't you hear me shouting?'

He got up and went over to the radiogram. He was in high heels and nylon stockings like my mum wears, a red dress and he had long hair. He took off the record he was playing.

'Ah, I was in the world of Beethoven, old chum. Didn't hear a thing. Erm . . .'

He looked at me staring. He was wearing lipstick as well. And a pearl necklace.

'Are you going in for a fancy-dress competition, Major Creswell?'

It was all I could think of. Why else would he be wearing a dress?

'Er . . . no, no, this is – was – Mrs Creswell's. One of her favourites, actually. Listen, old boy, I haven't exactly been honest with you. I'm afraid Mrs Creswell . . . died some time ago.'

What was he talking about? She was here yesterday. He'd made her a cup of tea while we looked after the shop.

'I miss her so much, I sometimes pretend she's still here, pretend to make her cups of tea, that sort of thing. I know it sounds strange but it makes me feel better. That's why I wear her favourite dress sometimes too. Makes me feel closer to her.'

It was getting late. My mum'd be worried about me.

342

'I've got to go, Major, my mum'll be wonderin' where I am.'

He thanked me for letting him know about the door and told me to help myself to anything in the shop on my way out.

'No, it's all right, Major . . .'

He didn't know we'd been helping ourselves to stuff every Saturday for the last few months, ever since he'd taken the shop over.

'I'll just get going.'

He stopped me at the top of the stairs.

'Listen, old thing, I'd rather you didn't tell anybody about this, they might not understand. They might think I'm a bit silly, you know, laugh at me behind my back. Perhaps it could be – our little secret? Eh?'

I promised that I wouldn't tell anybody. And I didn't. Not even my mum.


'Where've you been? It doesn't take that long to go to the off-licence. I was beginning to get worried.'

I told her what had happened, that the shop door had opened when I'd been looking in, that I'd had to go inside and tell the Major that he hadn't locked up properly and that he was upstairs listening to music. I told her every-thing – except that he was wearing Mrs Creswell's dress. I kept that secret, like I'd promised.

*'We are the boys and girls well known*
*As Minors of the ABC,*

*And every Saturday we line up*
*To see the films we like*
*And shout with glee . . .'*

Uncle Derek was telling everybody who was entering the competition to line up by the steps on the left-hand side of the stage.

'Now, when I give the word, I want you to come up the steps, one by one, and walk slowly across the stage holding up your number. When you get to the middle, face the front so the Deputy Lord Mayor and the other judges can have a good look at you, then walk to the other side of the stage and go back to your seat. Music maestro, please!'

The ones at the front started going up the steps. Norbert, Keith and Tony hadn't bothered to enter and I could see them in their seats pointing and laughing at me in my Shirley Temple dress and wig.

Norbert was stuffing his face with sweets. I wondered where he'd stolen them from now Major Creswell's was closed. I couldn't believe the Major's shop had closed down. Norbert wasn't bothered. *I* couldn't stop thinking about it.

'Ow!'

'Stand still.'

'I don't want to go.'

'Don't start that again, not now, not after the effort me and your Auntie Doreen have put in.'

'Norbert's goin' to laugh his head off when he sees me.'

I was standing in the kitchen on a stool with my mum and my Auntie Doreen admiring me in the gingham dress. I was dreading Norbert and that lot seeing me. I'd told them that I was going as Shirley Temple, I'd thought it best, but now I was in the curly wig and the dress . . . oh hell, I was dreading it.

'He won't be laughing when you're going in for free every week.'

I didn't tell her that Norbert gets in for free every week anyway, I couldn't be bothered.

'I should have gone as Charlie Chaplin.'

My mum fiddled with my wig a bit more.

'You won't be saying that when you win. And your Auntie Doreen's right, there'll be Charlie Chaplins queuing right round the picture house.'

She picked up a carrier bag.

'Now, we'll take you down on the bus and here's your clothes for you to change into after the competition. Come on, let's get going, I'll buy you some sweets from Major Creswell's on the way.'

My Auntie Doreen got hold of her arm.

'Oh, I didn't tell you, did I? He's closed down, I went past this morning. There were police all over the place. He's been arrested.'

We both stopped at the door. He'd been arrested? The Major?

'Why Auntie Doreen? Why's he been arrested?'

She gave my mum that funny look they always do when they don't want me to hear something.

'Go and put your coat on.'

'But, Mum . . .'

'Go on, love, we'll be out in a sec.'

I went out and she shut the door. But I could still hear them whispering.

'What happened, Doreen?'

'Police caught him in town – dressed up as a woman.'

'Dressed up as a woman? That's disgusting. What's the matter with the man?'

'Seems he's done it before, lots of times. I was talking to a policeman outside the shop. They reckon he'll be going to prison.'

Going to prison? For wearing a dress? Why? I couldn't understand it.

'And I'll tell you something else – there's no Mrs Creswell. He lives there on his own.'

'Cos she died, didn't she. A long time ago. That's why he wears her dress, he misses her. That's why he pretends to make her cups of tea. But I couldn't tell them. I couldn't say anything, could I? I'd get into trouble for not saying anything last Sunday.

'Now, boys and girls, remember what Uncle Derek said – when you get to the middle, turn and face the front.'

I was standing on the steps, waiting to walk across the stage, thinking about everything that had happened. I just couldn't stop thinking about Major Creswell.

'Go on, it's your turn.'

It was the lad behind, pushing me on to the stage. He'd come as Charlie Chaplin. My Auntie Doreen had been right, Charlie Chaplins *were* ten a penny. So were Shirley Temples, there were tons of them. Uncle Derek was talking into his microphone.

'And now, boys and girls, another Shirley Temple – but a Shirley Temple with a difference. Don't forget to turn to the front and face the judges when you get to the middle.'

I started walking and there was a bit of clapping. I could hear Norbert shouting out but I couldn't tell what he was saying. I was still thinking about the Major. Why did he go into town wearing the dress? I couldn't understand.

'This Shirley Temple, boys and girls, is – and you'll never believe it – this Shirley Temple is a lad!'

Everybody cheered and whistled – and I won third prize.

When the Deputy Lord Mayor presented it to me he said, 'Here you are, young lady,' and everybody laughed. I think I laughed as well, I'm not sure. I was thinking about the Major. It wasn't fair. Here I was getting a prize for wearing a dress and he was going to prison for wearing one. It didn't seem right to me.

# THE AIR-RAID SHELTER

I couldn't stop crying and I was shaking. I couldn't stop myself from shaking.

'It was Mr Churchill's fault. Him and that Mr Attlee. If it hadn't been for them, none of it would have happened. We wouldn't have had the day off. I'd have been at school . . .'

I'd never even heard of Mr Attlee before that ginger-headed lad who goes to St Bede's had stopped me in the park one afternoon on my way home from school. He and his mates are always hanging round the swings. They smoke and they have spitting competitions. They go as high as they can on the swings and see who can spit the furthest. It's disgusting. A few of them were sitting on the roundabout going round slowly. He'd jumped off and stood in front of me. I'd been scared stiff. He'd put his face right close to mine.

'Who are you for, Churchill or Attlee?'

I hadn't known what he was on about.

'C'mon, who are you for, Churchill or Attlee?'

I hadn't known what to say. I wasn't for either of them. He'd put his face even closer, our noses were nearly touching.

'I'm only askin' you once more, kid. Churchill or Attlee, who are you for?'

'Churchill . . .'

He'd smiled.

'That's all right, then.'

And he'd gone back to the roundabout.

I dread to think what would have happened if I'd said Attlee. I'd only said Churchill 'cos he was the Prime Minister. Then, when I got home I found out he wasn't.

'Who's Attlee, Mum?'

'Lay a place for your Auntie Doreen, she's coming round to set my hair.'

I got another plate from the cupboard and a knife and fork out of the drawer.

'How many times do I have to tell you, fork on the left, knife on the right.'

'Sorry.'

She changed them all round, I'm always getting them wrong.

'This lad asked me who I was for, Churchill or Attlee? I didn't know what he was talking about. I've never heard of Attlee, who is he?'

She looked at me.

'You've never heard of Mr Attlee?'

I shook my head.

'Mr Clement Attlee, you've never heard of him?'

I shook my head again.

'No. Who is he?'

Now it was my mum's turn to shake her head.

'Well, I'll go to Sheffield! I don't know what they teach you at that school?'

'Who is he?'

I heard the key in the front door and then my Auntie Doreen coming down the hall.

'Sorry I'm late, stocktaking at work. Couldn't get away.'

My mum took one of the forks off the table and went over to the cooker.

'You're all right, Doreen, these potatoes need a couple more minutes. Hey, you'll never believe this. Ask his lordship here who the Prime Minister is.'

I knew that.

'He knows who the Prime Minister is, don't you, love?'

She bent down and gave me a kiss and ruffled my hair.

''Course I do. Mr Churchill.'

They looked at each other and my Auntie Doreen started laughing.

'No, love, Mr Attlee's Prime Minister, he has been for the last six years, since 1945.'

My mum wasn't laughing.

'It's not funny, Doreen. It makes you wonder what they're teaching them at school when they don't even know the name of the Prime Minister.'

I couldn't understand it. I'd always thought it was Mr Churchill. My mum was always going on about him, what a great Prime Minister he was.

'But, Mum, you're always saying what a good Prime Minister he was and how we wouldn't have got through the war if it hadn't been for him. Him and that Tommy Handley off the wireless.'

She started laughing as well. She gave me a hug.

'He was – during the war. He was wonderful, wasn't he, Doreen?'

My Auntie Doreen was hanging her coat up and tutting to herself.

'Wonderful. Inspiring. And how did we show our appreciation after the war? After he'd saved us from that madman Hitler? We kicked him out and voted Attlee and his lot in. Disgusting.'

My mum took the pan of potatoes over to the kitchen sink and poured the water out.

'He's not done a bad job, Mr Attlee, he's a good peace-time leader.'

'I don't want to talk about it! Makes my blood boil!'

I'd never seen her so cross. She sat down at the table but she'd forgotten to take her hat off.

'You've still got your hat on, Auntie Doreen.'

She didn't say anything, just sat there tapping her middle finger on the table.

'Wait till next Thursday, we'll see who's Prime Minister then. And it won't be your precious Clement Attlee, you mark my words.'

I wondered what was happening next Thursday. My mum put the potatoes into a dish and brought them over to the table.

'He's not my "precious Clement Attlee". I'm just saying he's done a good job. I think he's honest and honourable.'

I didn't like my mum and my Auntie Doreen arguing like this.

'What's happening next Thursday, Auntie Doreen?'

She wasn't listening to me.

'Well, you voted for him, didn't you? You're just like our dad, Labour through and through.'

My mum slammed the saucepan down on the table.

'Who I vote for is my own private business. It's nothing to do with you.'

I didn't like this. I wished I'd never asked who Attlee was now.

'What's happening next Thursday, Mum?'

She wasn't listening either, she was still going on at my Auntie Doreen.

'And what was it our mother always used to say, Doreen? Never discuss politics or religion at the dinner table!'

They both went quiet and we ate our tea. Sausage, potato and mashed-up turnip. I mashed my potato up as well and mixed it in with the turnip and some margarine. It was lovely. But nobody was talking. I didn't like it.

'What's happening next Thursday?'

Neither of them said anything, they just carried on with their tea. Then my Auntie Doreen got up and put her arm round my mum.

'I'm sorry, Freda, you're right, I spoke out of turn and I apologise. I just get very emotional when we talk about Winston Churchill.'

My mum gave her a hug.

'I know. I'm sorry I snapped at you. Go on, sit down and enjoy your tea.'

And my mum gave her a kiss. I was glad. I didn't like them arguing. Mind you, I couldn't understand what it was all about. What does it matter who the Prime Minister is? What was 'labour through and through' and what did it have to do with my grandad? And what was happening next Thursday? I didn't say anything though. I just asked my mum for some more sausage, potatoes and turnip.

I found out what my Auntie Doreen had been talking about next morning when I got to school. Norbert and Keith Hopwood and a few of the others were in the playground talking to Albert, the school caretaker, and they let out this big cheer. I went over. Norbert was jumping up and down.

'We're gettin' the day off next Thursday, we don't have to come to school.'

'Why?'

'General election.'

'What's that?'

'Don't know, but we're gettin' the day off, that's all I'm bothered about.'

It turned out that the next Thursday was voting day and the general election is when people over twenty-one have to choose who should be the next Prime Minister. Albert told us all about it.

'So they'll be using our school as a polling station and

you lot'll be having the day off, you lucky tykes. You'll all be getting a letter to take home.'

My mum wasn't pleased when she saw it. The letter.

'Well, it's all right them saying there's no school next Thursday but what are we supposed to do, us working mothers? Leave you at home on your own all day?'

She put it on the kitchen table and folded her arms.

'What's it say?'

'It says there's no school next Thursday.'

She picked it up again and read it out loud.

'"Dear Parents,

"This is to inform you that next Thursday, 25th October, the school will be one of the nominated polling stations for the forthcoming general election. As a result the school will be closed to pupils and I am writing to ask you to make alternative arrangements for your children . . ."'

She screwed it up and threw it on the fire.

'That's nice, isn't it? "Alternative arrangements"? What am I supposed to do? Take a day off work to look after you?'

'It's all right, Mum, you don't have to look after me, some of us are gettin' together. It's all arranged.'

She looked at me.

'What's arranged?'

'We're going to play.'

'Where? Not in the street.'

'No, 'course not, we'll go to the park.'

355

She frowned at me.

'And what happens if it rains?'

It wouldn't bother us if it rained, we'd be all right.

'We'll be all right, we'll go into Arkwright Hall till it stops.'

Arkwright Hall's great. It's a museum and you can get in for free. A lot of it's boring, just pictures and statues and stuff. But there's one room with machines in that show you how the steam engine and electricity and the telephone work and you can go on them. We often go in there. We usually get thrown out though, specially when you go with Norbert, he's always messing about.

'Arkwright Hall? And what happens when you get thrown out?'

'We won't.'

'You usually do.'

'We don't. Anyway, Keith Hopwood says we can go to his house, his gran lives with them. And we thought we could go to the pictures in the afternoon, those who get the money. *Canyon Raiders* is on at the Essoldo. It's a U, we can go in on our own.'

'And what about your dinner? Have you thought about that?'

We had.

'Fish and chips from Pearson's.'

She didn't say anything. Just looked at me.

'Who's "we" anyway? Who's in this little gang who've decided what they're going to do on election day?'

I told her. Me, Tony, Keith Hopwood, David

Holdsworth, Alan McDougall maybe, if his mum let him. I didn't tell her that Norbert would be with us, she doesn't like him.

'Well, as long as it doesn't include that Norbert Lightowler, you always get into trouble when he's around.'

I shrugged my shoulders.

'Not sure what he's doin'.'

'W-w-what shall we d-d-do then?'

It must've been about the third or fourth time Keith had asked and every time one of us had said the same thing back: 'Don't know, what do you want to do?' This time it was David Holdsworth.

'Don't know, what do you want to do?'

We were sitting on the wall in Keith's back garden. Me, Keith, David Holdsworth and Norbert. Alan McDougall's mum hadn't let him come and Tony had gone with his big sister to his gran's in Wakefield. I couldn't see what was wrong with going to the park like we'd said we were going to, but none of the others wanted to, specially Norbert.

'Park's borin', we're always goin' t'park, let's do summat different.'

All the others agreed but nobody could think of anything – except Norbert.

'Hang on, I've got an idea . . .'

I'd told my mum we were going to the park.

'I've got a great idea . . .'

I'd told her that I didn't know what Norbert would be doing.

'What about this . . . ?'

She'd said I always get into trouble when he's around.

'Let's go and play on the bombsite!'

They all thought it was a great idea. No! I wanted to go to the park like I'd told my mum. Go to Arkwright Hall if it rained. Have fish 'n' chips from Pearson's. Go and see *Canyon Raiders* in the afternoon. That's what I'd told my mum we were going to do. All of us. I'd got the money in my pocket.

'No, I think we should go to the park. We can go into Arkwright Hall if it rains.'

Norbert said Arkwright Hall was boring as well.

'It's all statues and old paintings. Anyway, I'm banned from there, I broke that machine that shows you how electricity works. I wor only playin' on it.'

David Holdsworth said the bombsite was better than the park.

'Yeah, we'll play there till dinner-time then go to Pearson's for us fish and chips, then go and see *Canyon Raiders*. It starts at quarter past one.'

I didn't want to go to the bombsite, my mum'd go mad. She was always telling me to keep away from there.

'You've got a lovely park you can go and play in and what do you lot do? Go and hang around that horrible bombsite. Why do you have to play there?'

'It's fun.'

She didn't understand, the bombsite's great. It's where a doodlebug landed in the war, Miss Taylor had told us all about it at school. There's all these bombed-out houses, nobody lives there any more and we run in and out playing commandos.

'Fun? It's dangerous. I don't want you playing around that bombsite any more, will you promise me . . . ? Promise!'

If it hadn't been for Mr Churchill and Mr Attlee I wouldn't have broken my promise. We'd have been at school and I wouldn't have gone to the bombsite. And I wouldn't have gone into the air-raid shelter.

No, that's daft, it was my own fault. I shouldn't have listened to Norbert. I shouldn't have gone with the others.

'You d-d-don't have to c-c-come with us. We'll see you at P-Pearson's.'

I watched them all going off. I didn't want to be on my own. What was I going to do all morning?

'Hang on, I'm coming with you.'

Norbert was right, it *was* better than the park. We were playing World War Two and me and Keith were against Norbert and David, we were the English and they were the Germans. Norbert always wants to be the German side. They were in the upstairs of this bombed-out house shooting down at us. He was wearing this old gas mask he'd found. He's mad, Norbert, it was probably full of germs but he still put it on, he wasn't bothered.

'S'all right, it's a good gas mask this, might be worth some money, I'm goin' to show it to my dad.'

359

I threw a pretend hand grenade that would have killed them but they carried on shooting.

'Norbert, you're dead, I threw a hand grenade.'

He shouted something but you couldn't tell what he was saying 'cos of his gas mask.

'Y'what? I can't tell what you're saying.'

He pulled it off.

'My gas mask protected me.'

'A gas mask can't protect you against a hand grenade. Anyway it's your turn, we died last time, didn't we, Keith?'

'Yeah, w-we died last t-t-time.'

David put his hand up.

'Truce. We're comin' down.'

We stopped playing World War Two and sat on this old sofa. There were tons of sofas and beds and armchairs around. And old stoves and kiddies' cots. And wardrobes and cupboards and old baths. All sorts of stuff. I can't remember the war, I was only a baby. I'm glad a doodlebug didn't fall on our house.

David had a bar of Five Boys chocolate. He gave us a piece each and he had two. It was his chocolate so it was only fair. It was nice of him to give us any, I wouldn't have.

'My mum said I had to.'

It was still nice of him, he didn't have to do what his mum told him. My mum had told me not to play on the bombsite. She'd made me promise. But I was here, wasn't I?

'If I hadn't given you any she'd have found out, she'd have asked me. She can always tell when I'm lying.'

So can *my* mum. I wish I hadn't come.

'I'm bored here now, let's go somewhere else.'

They all agreed. I couldn't believe it. Mind you, we'd been there for more than an hour and we'd had enough of World War Two. David said he fancied going to the park for a bit before we went for us fish and chips.

'We can have a go on the boating lake if it's open.'

Norbert said he couldn't, he wouldn't be allowed on.

'I'm banned. Ever since I turned that canoe upside down. Hey, I'll wear my gas mask, he won't recognise me, come on!'

We set off across the bombsite. I was so glad, I wouldn't have to lie to my mum now, I could tell her that we'd been in the park, got fish and chips from Pearson's like we said we would and gone to see *Canyon Raiders*. I just wouldn't tell her we'd played on the bombsite. Yes, I felt much better. Everything was all right now.

And it would have been if we hadn't bumped into Arthur Boocock. He was hanging around by the entrance to the air-raid shelter.

'Where you lot off to?'

'Park.'

We all said it together. David told him we were going on the boating lake. I wanted him to shut up, I didn't want Boocock coming with us, I hate him.

'I thought you were banned, Lightowler, for capsizing that boat.'

'I didn't capsize it, I turned it over and it wor a canoe

361

not a boat and I'm goin' to wear this, he won't recognise me.'

Norbert put the gas mask on. Boocock snorted.

'You look stupid. Anyway, t'boating lake's closed, it's only open on Saturdays and Sundays this time of year.'

Trust Boocock to muck everything up, I bet none of them would go now. We had to go to the park so I wouldn't have to lie to my mum.

'Me and Gordon were down there earlier on. S'all closed up.'

Him and Gordon Barraclough. I hate them. Norbert took the gas mask off.

'Where is Barraclough?'

Norbert hates Barraclough as much as I do. More. They're always fighting.

'In there.'

He pointed towards the air-raid shelter. He couldn't mean in there. Nobody goes in there. It's horrible. It's where all the people ran to when the doodlebug came down.

'I've bet him that I can stay in there longer than he can.'

I'd peeped through the door once. It's pitch black, you can't see a thing.

'He's m-m-mad, I w-wouldn't go in there.'

Just then there was a scream, the door opened and Barraclough came running out. He looked scared stiff.

'There's someone in there, I heard something.'

We all gathered round him asking what he'd heard.

'I don't know, a noise, it were like a cough and I heard footsteps. I didn't like it.'

It was good seeing Barraclough scared like this. We were the ones usually scared of things, not him. Everybody laughed at him.

'You can't see a thing and I'm tellin' you, I heard summat, there wor a cough.'

Norbert started teasing him.

'Maybe there's a ghost in there, maybe that's what you heard, a ghost with a cough.'

He started waving his arms around and making ghost sounds and Barraclough went for him. Me and Keith had to pull them apart.

'I bet none of you lot'd go in there. Come on, I dare yer, any of yer!'

Arthur said he had a better idea.

'Look, there's six of us 'ere, we'll all put sixpence in and the one who stays in the longest keeps the money. C'mon, a tanner each, that'll be three shillings for the winner.'

Norbert put his hand in his pocket.

'Here y'are, Arthur. Come on, Barraclough, put your money in.'

Barraclough didn't look too keen but he couldn't back down in front of Boocock and Norbert and he handed over his sixpence. Boocock turned to me, Keith and David.

'What about you three?'

I looked at the others. I didn't want to waste my money, Boocock was bound to stay in the longest. Then David took his money out.

363

'Might as well. You never know, I might win.'

I looked at him. How could he think he could beat Boocock? None of us would beat him, he wins at everything.

Well, me and Keith weren't going to waste our money.

'Come on, Keith, we'll go to the park.'

But he had his hand in his pocket.

'Keith, you said Barraclough was mad goin' in the air-raid shelter, you said you'd never go in there.'

He got his sixpence out.

'Yeah, b-but this is for m-m-money. Here y'are, Arthur, here's my t-tanner.'

They were all looking at me now. What was I supposed to do, be the only one not to do the dare? I'd never live it down, specially with Keith doing it. He's softer than me. I held out my sixpence. Norbert took it, gave it to Boocock and asked him how were we going to time it.

'How are we goin' to know who stays in the longest?'

'As soon as the first person goes through the door, all of us outside'll count.'

'And who's goin' to go first?'

'We'll do "One potato, Two potato" to decide the order.'

We all got in a circle round Boocock.

'One potato, two potato, three potato, four, five potato, six potato, seven potato, more – you're first, Keith.'

Norbert was second, then Barraclough. David was after Barraclough, then Boocock and I was last. Boocock pushed Keith towards the door.

'W-why do I have to g-go f-first?'

''Cos you were first to go out in "One potato, Two", now go on.'

Keith looked at us all, went in and we shut the door behind him.

'1–2–3–4 . . .'

We only got as far as 9 before the door opened and he came running out.

'It's horrible in th-there, you c-c-can't see anything.'

Everybody laughed 'cos he'd only got as far as 9. I was hoping I'd last *that* long. Next it was Barraclough's go. He went to the door and turned back.

'Keith, did you hear anything?'

Boocock laughed.

'He didn't stay in there long enough!'

'W-wait till you lot g-go in, you w-w-won't be laughing then.'

'1–2–3–4 . . .'

We all counted out loud.

'10–11–12 . . .'

He was beating Keith.

'15–16–17 . . .'

I didn't want Barraclough to win.

'28–29–30 . . .'

He came running out.

'I heard it again. The cough. There's someone in there, I'm tellin' yer.'

David went in and came out again straight away.

'It's too dark, I don't like it.'

Norbert went in.

'1–2–3–4 . . .'

He was inside for ages, we counted up to 53. He looked white when he came out but he had this big smile on his face.

'Beat that, Boocock!'

Then he threw up. Arthur Boocock went in.

'1–2–3–4 . . .'

I didn't want him to win the money.

'19–20–21 . . .'

I just prayed he wasn't going to beat Norbert.

'41–42–43 . . .'

Oh no, he was going to win, wasn't he?

'49–50–51–52 . . .'

Blooming Boocock!

'53–54–55 . . .'

The door opened and he came running out, holding up his arms like he was the champion.

'Shall I take the money now?'

Norbert pointed at me.

'Get lost, he's got his go yet.'

Boocock laughed at me. He was right, he might as well have taken the money. There was no way I was going to stay in there as long as him. I probably wouldn't stay in as long as David or Keith. I went to the entrance. Boocock was still laughing.

'Go on, we're not goin' to start counting till you're inside.'

They closed the door. It went black.

'1 . . .'

I could hear them counting outside.

'2 . . .'

It was horrible. I couldn't see a thing.

'3 . . .'

Three? Why are they counting slower for me?

'4 . . .'

I've nearly stayed as long as David . . . nearly. At least I won't be the worst.

'5 . . .'

Only 5? I've been in here for ages, how can I only be on 5? I'm going. I'm getting out.

'6–7 . . .'

I'll stay long enough to beat Keith then I'm going, just another couple of seconds.

'8 . . .'

Nearly there. At least I've beaten Keith and David. Right, I'm off, Boocock can have the blooming money, I'm not staying here any longer.

'10–11 . . .'

I'm in double figures. How long did Barraclough stay? Thirty? No, I can't stay that long, that's twice as long again.

'13–14 . . .'

'14? That's nearly 15 – halfway to Barraclough's score.

Maybe . . . maybe . . . I closed my eyes. I don't know why, it made no difference in the dark.

'15 . . .'

No, I can't stay any longer, I'm off. I've had enough. I opened my eyes again – and that's when I saw it – the light shining in my face. There was a man standing there, shining a torch in my face.

'16 . . .'

I tried to scream but I couldn't. Nothing would come out. My heart was pounding inside my chest.

'17 . . .'

I tried to run. I couldn't move. I was paralysed. Help! Help! No sound came out. I wanted to shout help but no sound would come out. Help!

'18 . . .'

He started coming towards me. Help! Help! Why won't any sound come out? He was horrible, he had these scabs all over his face and he was all whiskery.

'19–20–21 . . .'

'Don't vorry, zere iss nossink to be frightened of.'

I *was* frightened. He spoke funny, in this foreign accent.

'22 . . .'

Suddenly he grabbed hold of me by the shoulders. I was terrified. He's going to kill me. Help! Nothing's coming out. Why did I break my promise? Why did I come to the bombsite? Help! Please don't kill me. Then he smiled.

'I can help you. You can beat ze bully boy. Stay here for a few more secondz and you vill vin your competition.'

'27–28–29 . . .'

'You see, you are almost half of za vay zere.'

He smiled again and started coughing.

'Excuse me, I haff a bad chest, it makes me cough.'

Barraclough had been right, he had heard someone cough.

'Please, don't tell ze uzzer boys zat I live here.'

I couldn't believe it. He lived in the air-raid shelter?

'Zat's vy I have zis cough, it's very damp in here.'

Why would he want to live in the air-raid shelter?

'32–33–34 . . .'

'Why do you live here? It's horrible.'

He smiled again. His eyes were watering a bit.

'My dear boy, I am lucky to haff zis. I came from Germany viz nuzzink.'

He held out his hand.

'My name is Rudi.'

I shook it and told him my name.

'Where do you sleep?'

He shone the torch over to another part of the air-raid shelter and started walking.

'49–50–51 . . .'

I followed him.

'52–53 . . .'

There was a walled-off bit, like a separate room, and he pointed his torch into the corner. There was a mattress on the ground, an old sofa, a chair and a small cupboard. He must have found them all on the bombsite. And there were lots of empty tin cans. The smell was horrible. How could he live here? It was disgusting. Where did he go to the lavatory?

'56–57–58 . . .'

'You are ze vinner. Go! But please, don't tell anybody zat I am here. Ziss is our secret. *Ja?*'

I nodded and he shone his torch so that I could see my

way to the door. When I turned back to say thank you, it was all black again, he'd gone.

'Thanks, Rudi!'

'62–63–64 . . .'

I opened the door and the daylight made me blink for a couple of seconds. I could hear Norbert, Keith and David cheering, then I saw Norbert jumping up and down.

'Go on, hand it over, Boocock, he's the winner.'

Boocock and Barraclough couldn't believe that I'd stayed in the longest. None of them could. *I* couldn't believe it.

I was sitting in the kitchen watching my mum unload the shopping.

'Well, did you have a nice day, love? Did you go to the park like you said you would?'

She had her back to me. She didn't see me blushing.

'Yes.'

I wasn't lying. We had gone to the park, me, Norbert, Keith and David, but only after I'd said I'd buy them an ice-cream out of my winnings.

'And we went to see *Canyon Raiders*, it was good. And we got fish and chips from Pearson's like we said we would.'

'So, you had a good day, then?'

'Yeah.'

I wanted to tell her about Rudi, the German man, living in the air-raid shelter. How he lived there in the dark, sleeping on an old mattress, eating stuff out of tins. But I couldn't, could I? I'd have to tell her that I'd been down to the bombsite. That I'd broken my promise. *Twice.*

I'd gone back to the air-raid shelter after the pictures.

'Rudi? . . . Rudi? I've brought you something to eat . . . I thought you might be hungry . . . Hello . . . Rudi?'

I saw the light from his torch and then I heard him coming towards me. He called out my name.

'I've brought you some fish and chips, Rudi.'

I'd bought them from Pearson's out of my winnings. I didn't want the money anyway, I felt guilty.

He couldn't believe it. He took hold of them.

'Zey are varm. Sank you, sank you. You are a goot boy.'

His eyes filled with tears, I felt sorry for him. He was quite small, not much bigger than me, and he looked so old.

'I've got to go, Rudi. Sorry. My mum'll be home soon.'

He came over and gave me a hug. He smelt horrible. It made me feel sick. I pushed him away.

'You're squashing your fish and chips.'

My mum was putting her coat back on.

'Now listen, love, me and your Auntie Doreen have got to go and vote, I'm just popping round to fetch her. We won't be long.'

She picked up her handbag and went towards the back door.

'Mum – I've got something to tell you.'

'Oh, yes?'

She turned round.

'What, love?'

I looked at her.

'Norbert Lightowler came with us today, but we didn't get into any trouble.'

She smiled and came over.

'You've told me now, that's all that matters. As long as you tell me the truth.'

She gave me a kiss.

'You're a good lad.'

I felt sick.

'Rudi . . . Are you there . . . ? It's me . . .'

After school on the Friday I spent my last sixpence on a Cornish pastie and took it to the air-raid shelter for him.

'I've got you some food.'

He came shuffling round the corner shining his torch.

'Oh, you are a kind boy, haff you brought me fish and chips again? Zey vere most delicious.'

'No, sorry. I only had sixpence left. I've got you a Cornish pastie.'

I held out the paper bag.

'It's cold though. Sorry.'

'You are a goot boy.'

'Will you be all right?'

He smiled and ruffled my hair.

'Don't vorry, I vill manage. I am a survivor. Now go home or your muzzer vill vorry about you.'

*

'This is the BBC Home Service. Here is the six o'clock news and this is Alvar Liddell reading it. Mr Winston Churchill is back in 10 Downing Street. At seventy-seven he is tonight forming his first peacetime government after the Conservative Party's narrow general-election victory. Mr Churchill says he savours the challenge of a new beginning . . .'

'Is that good, Mum? Mr Churchill winning?'

She nodded at my Auntie Doreen who was reading the evening paper.

'Your Auntie Doreen obviously thinks so. Look at her. It's all right you smiling, Doreen, he only just got in.'

My Auntie Doreen put her paper down.

'Winnie's back, that's what matters. The country has spoken.'

My mum got up.

'Yes, well, Alvar Liddell's spoken. You've had your moment of glory.'

She went over to the wireless and switched it off. My Auntie Doreen went back to her paper.

'Actually, Freda, there's a very interesting article here. It's about Rudolf Hess. You know he made that secret flight to Britain? Well, according to this, he lived here for a while, in this road.'

My mum didn't say anything for a minute, just looked at her.

'Rudolf Hess lived in this road? Rubbish!'

My Auntie Doreen held out the paper.

'Well, according to this . . .'

373

My mum took it and started reading. I wondered what they were talking about.

'Who's Rudolf Hess?'

They weren't listening. My mum was still reading the paper.

'I don't like to think of that Rudolf Hess living round here, makes my stomach turn.'

'Who is he? Who's Rudolf Hess?'

My mum gave the paper back to my Auntie Doreen.

'Don't they teach you anything at that school? He was a German. A Nazi. He was Adolf Hitler's deputy. He came here during the war, secretly.'

She picked up the paper again.

'I can't believe he came here. They said he landed in Scotland. Why would he come here?'

No! Oh no! That's why he's hiding in the air-raid shelter. That's who he is! My stomach churned. He's a Nazi. Rudi's a Nazi. He's Adolf Hitler's deputy. He's Rudolph Hess and I've been giving him fish and chips and Cornish pasties. No! I'm a traitor. I'm a traitor!

'What's the matter, love, what's wrong?'

I couldn't stop crying and I was shaking. I couldn't stop myself from shaking.

'It was Mr Churchill's fault. Him and that Mr Attlee. If it hadn't been for them none of it would have happened. We wouldn't have had the day off. I'd have been at school.'

'What's wrong with him, Doreen?'

'I'm a traitor, Mum, I'm a traitor. I know where Rudolf

Hess is. I've been giving him fish and chips and Cornish pasties.'

My mum held me tight.

'You'd better fetch the doctor, Doreen, I think he's having a fit. He's talking gibberish.'

My Auntie Doreen started to go but I got hold of her arm.

'No, Mum. I broke my promise, I'm sorry. I went down to the bombsite. I know where Rudolf Hess is. He's living in the air-raid shelter. I'm sorry, Mum, I'm sorry.'

The tears were rolling down my face. I couldn't stop crying.

'I'm a traitor, I'm a traitor.'

'I don't know who you've been talking to, love, but it's not Rudolf Hess. He's in prison in Germany. They sent him back in 1945.'

Me mum got hold of me.

'Now you've told me you been down on the bombsite, I won't be cross with you, I just want you to tell me what happened. Who have you been talking to?'

They were looking at me, my mum and my Auntie Doreen, and my mum was wiping my face with a damp towel.

'You promise you won't be cross?'

'I promise, I give you my word. Now, just start at the beginning. Tell me what happened.'

And I did. I told her everything.

My mum was right, he wasn't Rudolf Hess. She told the police all about it and they went round to the air-raid shelter. They took him away and found him somewhere nicer to live. It turned out he *was* from Germany but he'd escaped *from* the Nazis. His name was Rudi Klein and he'd lost all his family in the war. They'd been killed by Hitler in a camp or something. I didn't understand and my mum said she'd explain it to me when I got older.

She broke her promise though. She did get cross with me.

'Just think if you'd gone into that air-raid shelter and it hadn't been that nice old man in there. If it had been . . . somebody . . . somebody . . .'

She was trying to think of the right word.

'The real Rudolf Hess?'

She looked at me.

'No, love, what I'm trying to tell you is that there are some really evil, wicked people in this world and it could have been someone . . . someone . . .'

Tears started coming into her eyes. She took hold of me by the shoulders. She held me really tight. It made me think of when Rudi got hold of me like that.

'You mean I could have been killed?'

That's when she started crying. She put her arms round me. I thought she was never going to let go.

# THE BACK BEDROOM

I'd just got back from school and was hanging up my coat when my mum came down the stairs.

'Your Auntie Doreen's coming round in a minute, we're popping in to see Mrs Bastow.'

'Ooh, can I go with you?'

My mum goes to do her hair for her sometimes 'cos it's hard for Mrs Bastow to get out with her gammy leg. She gets paid for it but my mum doesn't like taking her money. I've heard her telling my Auntie Doreen.

'I don't like to, Doreen. I mean they're both pensioners. I'd rather she kept her money but she won't hear of it.'

'She'd pay a lot more if she went to the hairdresser's, and you're helping her out. She's not embarrassed to ask you if she's giving you money.'

'Mm, I suppose so . . .'

I'm glad my mum helps her out. I love going there with her. Mrs Bastow brings out the biscuit barrel and tells me to help myself and Mr Bastow lets me play on his model railway. He's always in charge but he lets me control the speed of the trains and switch switches and things. It's in the back bedroom upstairs and it takes up the whole room. You can hardly open the door. You have to squeeze in and crawl under this table and you stand in a space in the middle and watch all these model trains zooming round the tracks. It's great. Mr Bastow says it's his pride and joy. His sanctuary he calls it. I'm not sure Mrs Bastow likes it.

'He's obsessed, he's like a big kid with that railway. If he goes before me, God knows what I'm going to do with it. Takes up the whole back bedroom, y'know.'

I'd asked my mum what *would* happen to the model railway if Mr Bastow went before Mrs Bastow.

'Oh, I don't know, she doesn't mean it. Anyway, nobody's going anywhere.'

That was only a couple of weeks back.

'Ooh, can I go with you? Mr Bastow might let me play on the trains.'

We heard my Auntie Doreen letting herself in. She called down the hall.

'Sorry to take so long, Freda, I didn't want to go round there in my work clothes. I went home to change first.'

She came into the kitchen and that's when it dawned on me. My mum had changed out of her work clothes as well.

'I'm not going round there to do her hair, love. We're going to pay our respects. Mr Bastow passed away this morning.'

'Passed away?'

My Auntie Doreen took hold of my hands.

'He's died, love, this morning.'

378

I'd thought that's what she'd meant.

'Mrs Bastow found him in the front room in his favourite chair.'

'Dead?'

'I'm afraid so. That's why your mum and I are going round. To pay our respects.'

I wondered what was going to happen to the model railway.

'How is she, Freda? Have you heard?'

My mum shrugged and told her that from what Mrs Priestley was saying, when she saw her in the butcher's, Mrs Bastow was bearing up. I was still thinking about the railway.

'I'll come with you, Mum.'

She looked at me.

'I'd like to pay my respects as well.'

My Auntie Doreen smiled and put her arm round me.

'I think that'd be lovely, Freda. She'd really appreciate it. You liked Mr Bastow, didn't you, love?'

'Yeah . . .'

My mum didn't say anything, just carried on looking. I knew what she was thinking and she was right.

'Yes, and he liked playing on his model railway. Don't you think you're going to be playing on that railway today, young man.'

''Course not. I just want to pay my respects, don't I?'

'Do you?'

'Yeah.'

379

My Auntie Doreen said she thought she was being a bit hard on me. She wasn't.

On the way we stopped off to get some flowers for Mrs Bastow. We went to Middleton's in Cranley Road but my mum didn't like the look of them.

'They'll not last more than a day or two, they won't.'

My Auntie Doreen agreed.

'And they're expensive. There's that florist the other end of St Barnabas Street. It's a bit out of the way but I think they're very reasonable and good quality.'

In one of the houses in St Barnabas Street we passed an old man sitting in a wheelchair, staring out of the front-room window into the street. I wouldn't have even noticed him if my mum hadn't stopped to talk. Well, she didn't talk exactly, she mouthed at him through the window. 'How are you, Mr Shackleton . . . ? All right . . . ? Lovely . . .' The old man didn't seem to see her, he just carried on staring as if we weren't there. There was a bit of spit dribbling out of his mouth. My mum waved and mouthed again, 'Bye-bye then, Mr Shackleton' and then said 'Shame' to my Auntie Doreen as they carried on walking. I looked at the old man. The bit of spit was down to his chin and his eyes were watering, but they never blinked. He was just staring straight ahead like he couldn't see me. I felt sorry for him. I gave him my own little wave and I was just about to go when I saw his hand move. I wasn't sure, it was so slow, but . . . yes, it was definitely moving.

'C'mon, love, the florist'll be closing soon!'

'Comin', Mum!'

I looked back and his hand was up a bit higher. He looked like he was trying to wave back. He moved his fingers. Just a bit. He *was*, he was waving back. I waved again, moving my fingers slowly like he was doing. He still didn't blink. He stared like he couldn't see me, like he was looking through me, and the dribble of spit was hanging from his chin now. Then his mouth moved. He was smiling at me, I'm sure he was. My mum was shouting for me to hurry up. I waved again and ran down the street and caught up with them.

'Who's that old man, Mum?'

'Eric Shackleton and I don't think he's that old. What is he, Doreen, forty-five? Fifty?'

My Auntie Doreen reckoned he was about fifty. That seemed old to me. She told me that he used to be a roofer, he mended roofs and about four or five years back he'd fallen off this house.

'He broke his back. He's been in a wheelchair ever since. He was a lovely man, wasn't he, Freda? Do anything for anybody he would.'

'Yes, and so handsome. Must've been over six foot tall. Breaks my heart to see him like that, sitting there, staring out that window. That's all he does all day.'

They both said 'Shame' again and we went into the florist's.

They took ages deciding which flowers to get for Mrs Bastow. The lady in the shop pointed to some blue ones.

'Irises are always acceptable whatever the occasion.'

My mum wasn't sure.

'It's not an occasion, I'm afraid, it's a bereavement. The lady lost her husband this morning.'

'You can't go wrong with irises, love.'

While the flower lady wrapped them up my mum chose a card that said 'With Sympathy' and wrote on the back.

'What are you puttin', Mum?'

She showed me. It said, 'Sorry for your sad loss, with love from Freda and Doreen'.

'Go on, you write something.'

'What shall I put?'

'It's up to you, you're big enough.'

I wrote, 'I'll miss you, Mr Bastow', signed my name and showed it to my mum.

'Aw . . . Look at that, Doreen.'

What I really meant was, I'll miss playing on the model railway with you, Mr Bastow.

'Aw, that's lovely. Very nice.'

'Thanks, Auntie Doreen . . .'

It was when we turned into her street that I said it.

'She must be worried about the model railway, y'know.'

They looked at me.

'He's gone before her, hasn't he?'

'What on earth are you talking about?'

That's the trouble with my mum, she never remembers anything anybody says.

'That's what Mrs Bastow said. If he goes before me, what am I going to do with it? Don't you remember?'

I thought she was going to clout me.

'For goodness sake, she's just lost her husband. The last thing she'll be thinking about will be model railways!'

'It takes up the whole back bedroom . . .'

She just caught my ear. Didn't hurt.

When we got to the house the curtains were closed. My Auntie Doreen said that's what you do when someone dies.

'Even when it's light outside?'

'It's custom, love, when someone dies, you draw the curtains. It's a mark of respect.'

'Oh . . .'

We were sitting round the kitchen table drinking tea. Mrs Bastow was sniffing into her hanky. She was holding a photo of Mr Bastow. I was wondering if I could take another fig roll from the biscuit barrel. She'd told me to help myself but I'd already had two. No, I'd better not.

'I can't believe it. I can't believe he's gone.'

She wiped her eyes.

'He was just beginning to enjoy his retirement.'

My mum held out the box of tissues for her and squeezed her hand.

'I know.'

'I can't believe it. I just can't believe it. Have another biscuit, love.'

I looked at my mum. Mrs Bastow pushed the biscuit barrel to my side of the table.

'Never mind looking at her, you help yourself, they're there to be eaten.'

My mum gave me a nod and I took another fig roll, then changed my mind and took a digestive instead.

'Don't touch them and then put them back!'

Mrs Bastow wasn't bothered.

'Take as many as you like, love, I'll not want them, I've got no appetite.'

My Auntie Doreen told her she had to eat.

'You've got to keep your strength up, Mrs Bastow.'

'I know, I know . . .'

She nodded and sighed. My mum and my Auntie Doreen sighed and it all went quiet. I finished the biscuit and went to get another, but my mum stopped me with one of her looks.

'She said I could!'

'Who's "she"?'

'Mrs Bastow. She said I could.'

Mrs Bastow nodded.

'He's all right. And that was lovely what you wrote on that card, love, I really appreciate it. And those flowers. Lovely. Thank you.'

And she started crying again. My mum put her arm round her.

'When's the funeral, Mrs Bastow?'

I tried to eat the biscuit as quietly as I could. It was a garibaldi. It were lovely.

'I'm not sure. The undertaker's sorting it all out. Do you want to have a look at him?'

I nearly choked on the garibaldi. What did she mean, 'Have a look at him'? I thought he was dead.

'He's in the front room. He looks ever so peaceful in death.'

That's where she'd found him, in the front room, sitting in his favourite chair. And he's still there? And she wants us to have a look at him? Why's he in the house when he's dead? I thought they got taken away. My mum stood up.

'That'd be very nice, Mrs Bastow, we'd like to pay our respects.'

I thought we'd come to pay our respects to *Mrs* Bastow, I didn't know you had to go and look at a dead body to pay your respects, I wouldn't have come. Then my Auntie Doreen stood up. So I did. Oh, I didn't fancy this at all. I didn't want to look at him dead in his favourite chair. My mum put her hand on my shoulder.

'You wait here, love, we won't be long.'

Oh, thanks, Mum, thanks. I don't have to go and pay my respects. Thanks. While they were in the front room looking at Mr Bastow I finished the garibaldi and then had another fig roll.

''Course he wasn't sitting in the chair, he was in a coffin! Wait till I tell your Auntie Doreen. Oh, I shouldn't laugh.'

We were back at home having our tea. I could hardly eat mine, I'd filled myself up on Mrs Bastow's biscuits. But I didn't let my mum see. I forced it down.

'Well, I didn't know, did I? She just said, did we want to have a look at him in the front room. I thought that was why she'd closed the curtains.'

She started clearing the table.

'That's nothing to do with it. Your Auntie Doreen told you, you always draw the curtains when somebody dies. Even if the coffin's upstairs. It's a custom, it lets people know there's been a bereavement. Come on, you're never going to finish, you've eaten that many biscuits. Anyway, that was a nice thing you did, offering to help Mrs Bastow like that.'

I put the lid back on the biscuit barrel. I'd better not have any more or I wouldn't be able to eat my tea . . . They seemed to have been in there a long time. I thought about Mr Bastow sitting in there. In his favourite chair. Dead . . . This was boring, waiting here when I could have been up in the back bedroom playing on the model railway. I bet Mr Bastow wouldn't have minded. I knew how to do it, all the switches and stuff. I bet he'd have been pleased. He was dead anyway, what did it matter? It was such a waste it not being used . . . I heard them coming down the hall. My mum sat Mrs Bastow down at the kitchen table.

'What you need, dear, is a nice cup of tea. Put the kettle on, Doreen.'

Oh no, not more tea. I wish I'd never come. So boring.

'I'm going to have to sort all his stuff out, y'know. I don't know where I'm going to start.'

What 'stuff' is she going to have to sort out?

'There's no hurry. You just get this funeral out of the way, then you can start thinking about things like that.'

Maybe she meant the railway. What was she going to do with it?

386

'I'll help you, Mrs Bastow.'

She came over and gave me a hug. She held on for ages. Her cardigan smelt funny. Sort of cabbage smell.

'He's special, this lad of yours. He does you credit.'

I set off for Mrs Bastow's. It was the Saturday after the funeral and I was going to help her sort the stuff out like I'd promised.

'And if she offers you any money you're not to take it, right?'

''Course not, Mum.'

I hadn't even thought about that, I was just hoping she might let me have a go on the railway.

'Come on in, love. This is ever so kind of you to give up your Saturday afternoon like this. You are a good lad. Now, what I want to do is make a start on that shed. You won't believe the stuff in there. He was a right hoarder was Mr Bastow, God bless him.'

I followed her into the hall, through the kitchen, out to the backyard.

'I've filled up the biscuit barrel. You've got a sweet tooth, haven't you? Nearly ate me out of house and home last time you were here, didn't you?'

She was laughing, I don't think she minded that I'd eaten so many biscuits. Anyway, she'd told me to help myself, hadn't she?

'Now, where did he keep that key?'

There was a big padlock on the shed door.

'I know, back in a minute. Do you want a glass of squash?'

She didn't ask if I wanted a biscuit.

'Please.'

While I was waiting I looked in through the window. There was lots of stuff. Tins of paint, a lawnmower and a rake and shovel and things. And all these magazines. But they were all on shelves in neat piles. Mrs Bastow came back with the key and some orange squash.

'It all looks quite tidy in there, Mrs Bastow.'

She took the padlock off and opened the door.

'Oh, it's tidy enough. He was always a tidy man was Mr Bastow, but there's a lot of junk in there. See all those paint pots? There'll only be a dribble in most of them, you mark my words. He couldn't throw anything away. And them magazines, they can all go.'

There were tons of them.

'What are they?'

'Oh, train magazines mostly.'

'He liked trains, didn't he.'

She sort of smiled.

'Oh, he was train mad, love. Used to drive me up the wall sometimes.'

She went quiet and shook her head. I was thinking that this'd be a good time to ask her. I was sure she wouldn't mind.

'Mrs Bastow . . . ?'

'Mm?'

'When I've finished, can I go and have a look at the model railway?'

I didn't ask her if I could play on it. I reckoned that if she let me have a look at it she'd be sure to say do you want to have a go. I mean, it wasn't as if I didn't know how it all worked.

'Y'what, love?'

'Can I go and have a look at the model railway when I've finished all the clearing out?'

She didn't say anything for a couple of seconds, just looked at me as if she didn't know what I was talking about.

'It's gone, love. It's not there . . .'

Now it was me looking at her. What was she talking about, gone?

'Mr Bastow got rid of it. About a week before he died.'

Got rid of it? Why would he get rid of it? He loved that railway.

'It took up the whole of that back bedroom, you couldn't clean in there. Mind you, when you look at what's happened it's a good job he did get rid of it, bless him. How would I have managed on my own?'

I couldn't believe it. He loved that model railway. Why would he get rid of it? You didn't have to clean in there. There was nothing to clean. It was all railway, wasn't it? There was no need to clean in there! I couldn't understand it.

'Shall we get started, love? Throw everything into these rubbish bags. I've got somebody coming round later to take 'em away. Only keep the paint pots that are heavy – there won't be more than a couple – otherwise get rid. Oh, and if you want to keep any of those train magazines for yourself, take as many as you like. I'll be glad to see the back of them.'

She went back into the house humming to herself. I started throwing the magazines into the rubbish bags. I didn't keep any for myself. I didn't want them. They were Mr Bastow's.

# THE WHITE ROSE

## *Part One*

A hundred and seventeen. A hundred and eighteen. I wish I'd never offered to clear out the shed for Mrs Bastow. A hundred and nineteen. I'd only done it 'cos I was hoping I might get a go on the model railway. A hundred and twenty, the last one! A hundred and twenty train magazines. I don't know why I counted them, I just did. And now they were all in the rubbish bags. Gone. Like the model railway. Mrs Bastow was surprised that I didn't keep any for myself. She didn't want them, so why should I? She didn't even care about the model railway. If Mr Bastow had said to me, 'Take as many as you like,' I would have. I'd have taken as many as I could have carried. But now I knew that before he'd died he'd got rid of the model railway – I don't know, I just thought, well, that's what Mr Bastow would have wanted me to do. Get rid of the magazines as well.

I went back into the shed and started clearing out all the old tins of paint. She was right, most of them were empty, there was hardly anything in any of them. One tin was heavier than the rest; it felt full so I put it on one side with the lawnmower and tools and other things that were going back in the shed. It looked like it had never been opened.

'Are you sure it's worth keeping, love? I don't want it if it's empty.'

She was coming down the garden with more rubbish bags.

'It's full, Mrs Bastow, I don't think it's even been opened.'

'Oh.'

I handed her the tin of paint. She screwed up her eyes.

'I can't read without my glasses. Does it say the colour? Read it out to me, love.'

'"Parkinson's Quality Paint".'

'No, the colour, love. I know it's Parkinson's, Mr Bastow always got his paint from there, they used to give him a good discount. What colour is it?'

'Er . . .'

I looked.

'Er . . . "Emulsion".'

'No, that's not the colour. What does it say on the label?'

I couldn't see a label.

'Er . . .'

Oh yes I could.

'"Lilac Heaven".'

She took it off me.

'Oh, I like lilac. That'll look good in the back bedroom.'

The model railway looked good in the back bedroom. Why did she make Mr Bastow get rid of it? That's what I wanted to say. But I didn't. I carried on clearing out the shed and she went back into the house with the tin of paint. It took me ages. I filled six bags with rubbish, empty paint tins mostly and a lot of old newspapers and broken plant pots. Then I started putting things back, the lawnmower and tools, a watering can and other stuff.

'Hang on, love, I just want you to give it a sweep. You can use that broom there.'

She came up the garden.

'You don't mind, do you, love?'

'No, 'course not, Mrs Bastow.'

'Course I minded. I wanted to go home, I'd had enough. It wasn't as if I was going to get a look at the railway now, never mind have a go on it.

'What about that cupboard? Did you clear it out?'

Opposite the shelves that the train magazines had been stacked on, there was a rickety old wooden cupboard with double doors. I hadn't even looked in it. I didn't know I was supposed to.

'No, Mrs Bastow, I didn't know I was—'

'It'll want clearing out, love, I'll bet you a pound to a penny.'

She opened the doors and it was full of rusty tins and smaller paint pots and old jam jars, some with paintbrushes in.

'This lot can go, it's all rubbish. Look, most of these brushes are brick hard, they're not worth keeping. Chuck the lot, then give the shed a good sweeping, there's a good lad. I'll go and get the dustpan and brush.'

I got another rubbish bag and started chucking

everything in. I just wanted to get home now. She hadn't even given me a biscuit. I didn't like Mrs Bastow any more.

I thought some of the stuff was worth keeping, jars full of screws and rubber bands. But she'd told me to get rid of it all, so I did. There was another pile of magazines. I thought they were more train magazines and I was just about to throw them into the rubbish when I saw the one on the top was called *The Wrestler*. It had a photo of this wrestler on the front. He was holding this big belt up in the air and it said:

*The White Rose*
*Yorkshire's Own Champion*

That's when I saw it.

### *Exclusive Interview with Eric Shackleton*

Eric Shackleton? Eric Shackleton! That was the old man my mum and my Auntie Doreen had stopped to say hello to the day we went to pay our respects to Mrs Bastow. The day Mr Bastow had died. The old man in the wheelchair, sitting in his front room, staring out of the window. I'm sure my mum had said his name was Eric Shackleton. But she'd said he was a roof mender. I opened the magazine and inside there were more pictures spread across two pages. In one photo he had his arm round this other wrestler's head, he looked like he was yanking it off. In another he had him pinned on the floor. The biggest photo showed him holding his arms up in the air, with a big grin on his face, wearing the big belt. Underneath it said:

*The White Rose Wins Fight of the Century*
*Shackleton Is New Yorkshire Champion*

I looked at the photograph. Maybe this was another Eric Shackleton. It must be. Maybe she'd said *Eddie* Shackleton. Yeah, that was it, she'd said Eddie Shackleton not Eric Shackleton. I mean, why would my mum say he mended roofs when he was a champion wrestler? Anyway, I still asked Mrs Bastow if I could keep the magazines.

'Well, you do surprise me, young man, I'd have thought it'd be the train magazines you'd want, not these. Do you like wrestling then?'

'Yeah –' I didn't tell her why I wanted them in case it wasn't the man in the wheelchair. 'I love it.'

'Oh.'

She asked me if I wanted a carrier bag to take them home in.

'Yes, please, Mrs Bastow.'

I didn't go straight home, I went through the park and stopped off in the playground. It was deserted. I sat on one of the swings and got the magazines out of the carrier bag. *The Wrestler* was the only one with anything about Eric Shackleton in it, the others were old gardening magazines and there was one *Woman's Weekly*. I put *The Wrestler* back in the carrier bag and threw the rest into the bin. I still didn't go home, I wanted to see if 'The White Rose' was the man in the wheelchair, so I went round to St Barnabas Street.

I didn't know what number house it was, all I remembered was that it was about halfway up on the right. It turned out to be forty-seven and there he was in his wheelchair staring out of the window. I smiled and gave him a little wave. He didn't seem to see me, he was just staring ahead like before. I opened the carrier bag, peeped inside at the photograph on the front of *The Wrestler* and looked back at him. He was lifting his hand and waving at me like last time, moving his fingers really slowly. And I'm sure he was smiling. It could be him. He could be 'The White Rose'. I hoped it was.

'Mum, you know that man in the wheelchair that you said hello to the other day?'

She was getting our tea ready, cauliflower cheese. I don't know why we're always having cauliflower cheese, my mum knows I don't like it.

'Y'what, love?'

'That man in the wheelchair you said hello to the other day, what was his name?'

'What man's that? Be a love and get the knives and forks out.'

I started setting the table.

'That man in the wheelchair in St Barnabas Street, Mr Shackleton. You said hello to him when we went to pay our respects to Mrs Bastow. What was his first name?'

She told me. Eric. Eric Shackleton. I wondered if he really was 'The White Rose'.

'Why on earth do you want to know?'

I got *The Wrestler* out of the carrier bag and showed it to her. She looked at it for a minute. I waited for her to say something. It wasn't him, was it? 'Course it wasn't.

'Where did you get this?'

I told her I'd found it in Mrs Bastow's shed.

'You didn't just take it, did you? I hope you asked her.'

''Course I did. She was throwin' it out anyway. We threw out tons of stuff. Is that him, Mum, is that the same Eric Shackleton?'

It wasn't going to be him, I knew it. How could it be? An old man in a wheelchair like that, how could he be a champion wrestler?

'Do you know, I'd forgotten he was a wrestler.'

It *was* him. He was 'The White Rose' and he lived two streets away. How could she forget?

'He wasn't just a wrestler, Mum, he was the Yorkshire champion. He was 'The White Rose'. Yorkshire's own champion. Look!'

I pointed at the front of the magazine.

'You said he was a roofer. You said he mended roofs. How could you forget?'

She explained to me that he was a wrestler in his spare time, mending roofs was what he did for a living.

'He was semi-professional, love, he got paid a bit but not enough to live on.'

'But he was the champion, wasn't he? "The White Rose". It says so, look!'

I pointed at the photo of him holding up the belt. She didn't say anything for ages.

'He was. That was the name he used to fight under, "The White Rose". Do you know, I'd quite forgotten.'

She carried on staring at his picture.

'"The White Rose". 'Course he was. It must have been not long after that that he fell off that roof and broke his back. Yes, look.'

She read out the date on the top.

'October 1947. There you are, just before Christmas 1947, I remember now. The snow was terrible and he slipped. It was all in the papers.'

And then it happened. I'd been hoping like anything that the Mr Shackleton in St Barnabas Street would be the Eric Shackleton on the front of the magazine. And now my mum had told me it was, I wished it wasn't. I didn't want 'The White Rose' to be an old man in a wheelchair. I wanted him to be like he was in the photograph.

'He must've been a good wrestler, Mum.'

She nodded and held out the magazine for me to take back.

'He was . . . he was a good roofer too.'

I took *The Wrestler* and ran up to my bedroom.

'Don't be hanging round up there, your tea'll be ready in a minute and wash your hands!'

I wasn't bothered about him being a good roofer. I was wishing he'd never been a roofer. If he hadn't been a roofer he might still be the champion. I sat on my bed and looked at his picture and I started to cry.

On the Sunday we were getting ready to go to church, my mum, my Auntie Doreen and me. While we were in the hall getting our coats on my mum told her about the magazine I'd got from Mrs Bastow. My Auntie Doreen remembered him.

'Yes, he did a bit of wrestling, I think he was quite good.'

Did a bit of wrestling? Quite good? Didn't she remember he was the Yorkshire champion? I didn't say anything, I didn't want to talk about it.

'He wrestled under another name, what was it now? White Fang, White Flash. I know it was something funny.'

'He was "The White Rose", Auntie Doreen, what's funny about that? He was the Yorkshire champion!'

I didn't mean to shout, it just came out. I wanted them to stop talking about him like that. My mum turned on me.

'Who do you think you're talking to?'

'Sorry . . .'

'How dare you shout at your Auntie Doreen like that?'

'He's all right, Freda—'

'No he's not!'

And she made me take my windcheater off.

'I won't have you talking to your Auntie Doreen like that. You'll stay here till we get back.'

'He's all right, Freda.'

'I'll not have him shouting at you like that. Come on, Doreen.'

'Sorry, Auntie Doreen—'

SLAM! They'd gone.

I could hear my Auntie Doreen telling my mum that I wasn't a bad lad, that I didn't mean anything by it, but I knew my mum wouldn't come back for me. Not when she's in a mood like that.

I wasn't bothered. Church is boring anyway. And I hadn't meant to shout at her. I was just fed up with nobody remembering who he really was. I couldn't understand it. You'd have thought that day we saw him, the day we went to pay our respects to Mrs Bastow, you'd have thought my mum would have said, 'You see that man there, he was the Yorkshire wrestling champion. "The White Rose" they called him, he was famous.' No, all she remembered was that he was a roofer. And my Auntie Doreen, she wasn't much better. 'Did a bit of wrestling.' He was only the champion of bloody Yorkshire! And what did she call him? White Fang. What the bloody hell is White Fang? He was 'The White Rose'.

'The White bloody Rose – that was his bloody name!'

I kicked the front door and ran up to my bedroom. I knew it was wrong to swear, even to myself, specially on a Sunday, but I couldn't help it. I wished now I'd never found the blooming magazine. If I hadn't found it he'd have just been an old man in a wheelchair, wouldn't he? I don't suppose I'd have thought about him again. But now I knew he was 'The White Rose' I couldn't stop thinking about him.

I sat on my bed holding *The Wrestler*. I felt like tearing the thing up. Tearing it up and throwing it the dustbin.

'I'm sorry I shouted, Auntie Doreen.'

'I know you are, love, you didn't mean it.'

I looked at my mum.

'I didn't mean it, Mum.'

'I know, let's forget about it. Eat your dinner.'

We were having our Sunday roast. Pork with lots of crackling and crunchy potatoes. It were lovely. I felt better now.

'Can I have some more gravy, Mum?'

Yeah, much better.

'Over my potatoes, please, Mum.'

'Yes sir, three bags full sir.'

We were laughing now. It was all forgotten.

'When you've finished your dinner, go and get that magazine. I want your Auntie Doreen to see how handsome Eric Shackleton was before he had his accident.'

I sat on my bed holding *The Wrestler*. I felt like tearing the thing up. Tearing it up and throwing it in the dustbin. So I did. I went downstairs, out into the backyard and threw it away. But I didn't tear it up. As I was looking at it in the bin, staring at the picture of 'The White Rose' holding up his belt, I thought of poor Mr Shackleton sitting in his wheelchair staring out of his front window and I was glad I hadn't torn it up.

I could hear the church bells ringing as I ran down St

Barnabas Street. I got to his house and there he was sitting in his wheelchair staring out of the window. I smiled and gave my little wave. This time he smiled back quicker, I think he recognised me. I went closer and held up *The Wrestler* magazine and pointed to his picture. He looked at it for ages, smiled again and slowly lifted up his hand. Then I realised it was his thumb he was holding up. He was giving me a thumbs-up sign. I pointed to his picture again and gave him a thumbs-up back.

A door opened behind him and a woman came in carrying a mug of tea or something with a straw in it. He had this sort of table across his wheelchair and the woman put the mug down on it and held the straw to Mr Shackleton's mouth. He pulled away and pointed at the window. At me. The woman turned round and started shouting.

'I've told you lads before, now go away before I call the police!'

'No!'

I held *The Wrestler* up for her to see and pointed to the picture on the front. She mouthed, 'Wait there,' and went out of the room. A couple of seconds later the front door opened.

'I'm sorry, love, there's a gang of lads sometimes tease my dad and make faces at him through the window, I thought you were one of 'em.'

I held out the magazine.

'No, I found this and I thought he might want to see it.'

She took hold of it and stared at the cover for a couple of seconds.

'There's more photos inside. Page four, look.'

She looked and smiled at me.

'He is "The White Rose", in't he?'

'He was, before he had his accident.'

What was she talking about? He *is* 'The White Rose'. Just because he's in a wheelchair, it doesn't stop him still being 'The White Rose'. If he *was* 'The White Rose' he still is. She gave the magazine back to me.

'No, it's for him. I want him to have it . . .'

I poured some more gravy over my potatoes.

'Wait till you see it, Doreen, you forget what a handsome man he was.'

They were still going on about the magazine.

'Run upstairs and fetch it, love, while I get the apple crumble.'

I love my mum's apple crumble.

'I haven't got it, I gave it to him.'

'Y'what? Who? What are you talking about?'

'Mr Shackleton – "The White Rose".'

And I told her how I'd gone round to his house while she and my Auntie Doreen had been at church.

'I thought it might cheer him up.'

My Auntie Doreen put her arm round me and gave me a big hug.

'What a lovely thing to do. You see what a thoughtful lad he is, Freda.'

She kissed me. I could smell roast pork.

'I bet he was pleased. What did he say?'

My mum tutted and sort of laughed as she was getting the apple crumble out of the oven.

'Doreen, the poor man can't talk, he hasn't said a word for years.'

She gave me some apple crumble.

'Custard?'

I love custard but only if it hasn't got lumps in it. My mum's is never lumpy, not like school custard.

'Yes, please.'

'I'm sorry, love, but that magazine won't have meant a thing to him, you know. It was a nice thought but you wasted your time.'

What was wrong with them all? It *had* meant something to him. He'd been really pleased. I burned my tongue on the custard.

'Careful, love, it's hot.'

'It's lovely, Mum.'

That's what the woman had said as well, that it wouldn't mean anything to him.

'No, it's for him. I want him to have it.'

The woman looked at the front cover again and shook her head.

'It's very nice of you, dear, but you might as well keep it for yourself. It won't mean a thing to him. He doesn't remember anything about those days.'

But I knew it *did* mean something to him. When I'd shown him the picture through the window he'd given me a thumbs-up sign, hadn't he? It must have meant something to him. I'm sure he remembered.

'I'd like you to give it to him, please.'

She sighed and shrugged her shoulders.

'Well, you might as well come in and give it to him yourself.'

'No, er, I've got to go home—'

She didn't hear me, I don't think she did anyway. She'd gone back down the hall so I followed her into the house and into the front room.

'Dad, there's a young lad come to see you. He's got something for you.'

She talked to him like he was a little baby, really slow and loud, like he was stupid.

'Do you remember when you used to wrestle, Dad? Do you remember? What did they used to call you? The – White – Rose.'

I couldn't understand why she was shouting. He wasn't deaf. He'd heard me when I'd tapped on the window and I'd only tapped quietly.

'The – White – Rose. Do you remember, Dad?'

He just looked at her. His eyes were watery. She turned to me.

'You can give it to him if you like but it'll not mean anything, he doesn't remember. Give us a shout when you've done, I'll be in the kitchen.'

She went. I took *The Wrestler* over to him.

'Mr Shackleton – I found this magazine and I thought you might want it 'cos you're on the front. Look.'

I held it up and showed him the photo of him holding up the champion's belt. I didn't shout like she'd done, I knew he wasn't deaf.

'That's you, in't it, Mr Shackleton? You're "The White Rose", aren't you?'

He looked at it and after a couple of seconds he looked at me and smiled. Then he did it again – the thumbs-up sign. He gave me the thumbs-up sign. See – he did remember.

'Can I have some more apple crumble, Mum?'

She gave me one of her looks.

'Please?'

'That's better. Doreen?'

'No thanks, love, I've had to loosen my skirt as it is. It was all lovely.'

I sat and ate my second helping of apple crumble and custard and thought about Mr Shackleton. I was so glad I hadn't thrown *The Wrestler* away.

# THE WHITE ROSE

## *Part Two*

I tap quietly on his front room window. His eyes are closed.
He doesn't open them. I tap again, a bit louder. He still
doesn't open them. So I tap even louder and he doesn't
move, he looks like he's dead. Hell fire, maybe he *is* dead.
My stomach churns and I knock on the window, really
loud this time. He opens his eyes. I made him jump.

'Hello, Mr Shackleton, sorry if I made you jump. I'm
on my way to school. I thought I'd surprise you.'

I've got used to it now, him sometimes being asleep when
I go round to see him, but that first time, that Monday
morning on my way to school, the morning Tony was off
with scarlet fever, it'd really frightened me. I'd really
thought he was dead. I hadn't shouted, I'd mouthed at him
like my mum does when she sees somebody who can't hear
her. She'd done it last Saturday afternoon when we'd passed
the hairdresser's and seen Tony's mum under the dryer.
She'd mouthed at her through the window.

'How is he? Is he getting any better? Is he still under the
doctor?'

Tony'd been off school with scarlet fever all week. Mrs

407

Wainright had mouthed back. I couldn't tell what she was saying but my mum could.

'What did she say, Mum?'

'He'll be back at school next week, he'll be coming round the usual time.'

Tony's my best friend. He lives two streets away and we always go to school together and he's always on time. But last Monday I'd still been waiting for him at twenty-five to nine when my mum had given me my dinner money.

'You'd better go without him, love, you don't want to make yourself late as well.'

I put my dinner money in my pocket and while I was putting on my coat there was a knock on the front door.

'Talk of the devil, here he is. Come on, love, get your school-bag, it's nearly twenty to nine.'

'It might be Norbert, Mum.'

Norbert Lightowler sometimes tags along as well but he's always late so we never wait for him. It'd turned out to be neither of them, it was Mrs Wainright. She was out of breath.

'I hope I haven't made your lad late, Freda, but our Tony's not well, looks like scarlet fever. I'm going to have to fetch the doctor. Will you tell your teacher when you get to school, love?'

I said I would and I got going. I'd had an idea.

I always try and see Mr Shackleton on my way back from school but when I'm with Tony and Norbert and some of the others I go home first and then I go and see him. I wouldn't want to go round there with any of the other lads, he might think it was that gang that tease him and make faces at him, especially Norbert 'cos that's just what he would do. He's stupid is Norbert.

Mr Shackleton's got used to me coming round on an evening, I think he looks forward to it. But last Monday, when Tony was poorly with scarlet fever and I'd been on my own, I thought I'd go and see him on my way *to* school. You know, surprise him.

I tapped quietly on his front-room window. His eyes were closed. He didn't open them. I tapped again, a bit louder. He still didn't open them. So I tapped even louder and he didn't move, he looked like he was dead. Hell fire, maybe he *was* dead. My stomach churned and I knocked on the window, really loud this time. He opened his eyes. I made him jump.

'Hello, Mr Shackleton, sorry if I made you jump. I'm on my way to school. I thought I'd surprise you.'

I think he could tell what I was saying. Even if he couldn't it didn't matter, he was just pleased to see me. He smiled. His eyes were watering and I waved to him. It's always the same, that's all we do. I wave to him, he smiles, gives me his thumbs-up sign, I give a thumbs-up back, then I go. But it had frightened me thinking he was dead like that.

'What's it like then, scarlet fever?'

'Bloomin' horrible—'

409

Another Monday. On our way to school. Tony was better.

'Temperature. Sore throat, you can hardly swallow and my cheeks were all red and your tongue goes red an' all.'

'Everybody's tongue's red.'

I stuck mine out and showed him.

'No, redder than that, really red. Strawberry red, my mum said it were.'

I was glad he was back, Tony's my best friend. But the week he'd been off poorly I'd gone past Mr Shackleton's every morning on my way to school and now I was worried that he'd be looking out for me. I didn't want him to think I'd forgotten about him.

'Oh no – I've left my dinner money on the hall table. You go on, I'll see you there.'

It was the first thing that came into my head. I ran off as if I was going back home, cut through Skinner Lane, ran up Beamsley Lane, turned left by the library, right into St Barnabas Street and then walked the rest of the way to Mr Shackleton's. I'd be all right, I wouldn't be late. Tony and me always give ourselves plenty of time. I just wanted to let him know not to look out for me in the mornings any more.

He wasn't there. There was no one in the front room. It was empty. I'd got so used to seeing him, sitting there at the window, it gave me a bit of a shock.

'What are you up to? No good, I should think, if you're like any of those other tykes that are always hanging round here.'

It was the lady next door. I hadn't seen her come out, she made me jump.

'Go on, get off to school before I call the police.'

'No, I'm lookin' for Mr Shackleton, I always wave to him when I go past, he knows me.'

She looked at me.

'Are you the lad that brought that magazine for him a few weeks back? The one with him on the front?'

I nodded.

'Yeah, *The Wrestler*. He was Yorkshire champion. "The White Rose", they called him.'

She smiled at me.

'That was a right nice thing to do, Brenda told me all about it. Gave her dad a whole new lease of life, she says.'

'Oh . . .'

I wasn't sure what she was talking about, but it sounded all right. She was still smiling anyway.

'You've just missed him, love. He was unwell in the night, Brenda's taken him to the doctor's.'

'Oh.'

'Bit of a temperature, nothing serious.'

I hoped it wasn't scarlet fever.

'Hey, it's nearly quarter to nine, you'd best get off to school, lad.'

'Yeah.'

She picked up the pint of milk that was on the doorstep.

'My friend had scarlet fever, he says it's horrible.'

I don't think she heard me, she'd gone back in the house.

*

411

'Fletcher . . .'

'Here, sir.'

'Garside . . .'

'Sir.'

'Gower . . .'

'Yes, sir.'

While Mr Parry was taking the register most of us were messing about like we always do, he never seems to notice. He never seems that bothered anyway. Sometimes when we have him on an afternoon we can do what we like 'cos he falls asleep. He has this bottle of medicine in his jacket pocket that he has to take and I think that's what makes him sleepy. When I have to take medicine my mum always measures it out on a spoon. Mr Parry drinks his straight from the bottle.

Barraclough was stuffing bits of paper down the back of David Holdsworth's neck, Kevin Knowles and Colin Lambert were playing Cat's Cradle under their desks, Geoff Gower and Norbert were firing paper pellets at each other and Arthur Boocock was giving Keith Hopwood a Chinese burn. Nearly everybody seemed to be mucking around.

'Keep it down while I take the register. Hardcastle . . .'

'Here, sir.'

'Holdsworth . . .'

'Sir.'

I was thinking about Mr Shackleton going to the doctor. I was hoping he was all right. I took some paper out of the middle of my geography exercise book and started drawing a picture of him. I was trying to do the one of him lifting up the belt when he became Yorkshire champion. I thought I'd give it to him on my way home from school but I'm useless at drawing. It looked stupid. It was rubbish. I put a moustache and a beard on him, screwed the paper up into a ball and threw it at Norbert but it missed by a mile so he didn't even notice. That's when I heard my name being called out.

'Yes sir, here, sir, sorry sir.'

'Three times I called your name out, lad, why don't you speak up? I'll tell you why, because you're mucking about like the rest of them. Now keep the noise down while I finish this register. All of you!'

'Yes, sir.'

We all sang it together.

'Yes, sir.'

'That's better. McDougall . . .'

The bell went. Home time at last. I hate Mondays, they're boring. I hate school, every day's boring. I ran as quick as I could to the cloakroom. I wanted to get away before Norbert and Tony and any of the others so I could go straight to Mr Shackleton's on my way home. I needn't have bothered, they were all staying on to play football in the schoolyard. I told them I had to get home. Norbert tried to persuade me to play, they were one short.

'You can stay on for a bit, can't yer?'

I could have done but I wanted to see Mr Shackleton.

'No, my mum's taking me to the chiropodist, I've got an in-growing toenail.'

I couldn't think of anything else. It was the first thing that came into my head, just like in the morning when I'd told Tony I'd left my dinner money at home. I didn't even know what an in-growing toenail was but my Auntie Doreen had been to the chiropodist with hers about two weeks back and it was all I could think of.

'I'd better get going, she'll be waiting for me.'

I couldn't believe it. She'd said he'd had a bit of a temperature, the woman next door. Nothing serious, that's what she'd said. Just a bit unwell in the night. And now he was dead. I couldn't believe it. As soon as I got there I knew. The front-room curtains were closed and I knew. I remembered what my Auntie Doreen had told me the day Mr Bastow had died.

'That's what you do when someone dies, love, you close the curtains.'

'Even when it's light outside?'

'It's custom, love. When someone dies, you draw the curtains. It's a mark of respect.'

I stared at the closed curtains. He was dead. Mr Shackleton. 'The White Rose'. The Yorkshire champion. Dead. And I started crying.

'What's up, love? Has that Boocock lad been hitting you again? I'll swing for him if he has. I will.'

I blew my nose and shook my head.

'No, it's Mr Shackleton, Mum – he's died.'

She didn't say anything for a second, she looked shocked.

'Are you sure? How do you know?'

'I went to wave to him on my way home from school, you know like I do, and his curtains are closed. He wasn't there this mornin' neither, he was poorly, he'd had to go to the doctor's, the woman next door told me. They never close his curtains, Mum, not even when it's getting dark. He likes to look out of the window as long as he can.'

I started crying again and my mum put her arm round me.

'Can we go and pay our respects, Mum, like we did with Mrs Bastow?'

''Course we can.'

'And take some flowers?'

''Course.'

The front-room curtains were still closed. I held the flowers while my mum rang the bell. After a couple of minutes the door opened.

'Hello, Brenda, I've just heard about your dad, I'm very sorry.'

My mum nodded at me to give the flowers. I held them out but she didn't take them.

'Sorry, Freda, heard what?'

My mum looked at me then at her.

'That he's . . . er . . . not well.'

'Well, he's got a bit of a cold and he had a slight temperature this morning. Why, had you heard different?'

My mum looked at me again.

'It's not my fault, Mum.'

I looked up at Brenda or whatever her name was.

'Why did you close the curtains?'

'Y'what?'

'You closed the curtains and my Auntie Doreen told me that's what you do to let people know when someone's died. I thought he'd died!'

If she hadn't laughed I think I would have started crying again. She laughed her head off, she couldn't stop laughing. Neither could my Auntie Doreen when my mum was telling her all about it later on.

'. . . and it turns out, Doreen, they've had some compensation money from the insurance, after all this time, and that's what they've spent it on. A television receiver! That's why the curtains were closed, they were watching it!'

My Auntie Doreen was laughing so much there were tears running down her cheeks.

'Honest, Doreen, I didn't know where to put myself. I could have cheerfully brained him.'

'It wasn't my fault, how was I supposed to know?'

My Auntie Doreen wiped her eyes and took hold of my hand.

'I've got to tell you, Freda, I'd have thought the same. If I'd gone past at four o'clock in the afternoon, and the

416

curtains were pulled to, I'd have assumed there'd been a bereavement. I would.'

She ruffled my hair and gave me a hug and my mum started laughing. So did I.

'Well, it's funny now, Doreen, but I can tell you it wasn't funny half an hour ago.'

I didn't see so much of Mr Shackleton after that. Most days when I went past after school the curtains were closed 'cos he was watching his television receiver. One Saturday afternoon when they were open I saw Brenda giving him a drink. She saw me and mouthed, 'Wait there,' went out of the room and a couple of seconds later the front door opened.

'Do you want to come in and watch the television with my dad? There's a programme just starting, he loves it.'

I went in and Brenda closed the curtains and it was like being at the pictures. I'd never seen television before, not properly. I've looked at all the flickering screens in the television shop in town while I've been waiting for the bus but you can't hear anything, you have to guess what they were saying.

We watched this programme called *Whirligig*, with a funny man with black hair and a puppet called Mr Turnip. It was good. When it finished a voice said, 'BBC Television is now closing down,' and Brenda switched it off and we watched this white spot getting smaller and smaller until it disappeared. I didn't know anybody with a television receiver except Mr Shackleton. It was like a magic box.

'Hey, wouldn't it be good, Mr Shackleton, if you could switch it over to another programme like on the wireless?'

Brenda wheeled him over to the window and opened the curtains. The light made me blink.

'Switch it over! That'll be the day. It's a miracle as it is, looking at someone talking to you in your own front room. The wonders of modern science!'

She went into the kitchen to put the kettle on and I sat with Mr Shackleton for a few minutes. He still had *The Wrestler* magazine on the table across his wheelchair. He pointed at the front cover, gave me the thumbs-up and smiled.

Brenda had said I could go round there and watch the television whenever I liked and I would have done if it hadn't been for my mum. She didn't want me to make a nuisance of myself so I didn't go. I'd wave to Mr Shackleton if the curtains were open when I went past but most times they were drawn to and I stopped going that way, especially after we broke up for Christmas.

'Oh, that's very nice, look at this, Doreen.'

My mum showed her a Christmas card that had been dropped through the letterbox.

'It's from Brenda Shackleton, she's invited us round on Christmas Night to watch *Television's Christmas Party* with Jimmy Jewell and Ben Warriss, isn't that nice of her?'

Jimmy Jewell and Ben Warriss! They're my favourites, I

love Jimmy Jewell and Ben Warriss, I always listen to them on the wireless.

'Am I invited? I love Jimmy Jewell and Ben Warriss.'

''Course you are, look what she wrote on the card.'

My Auntie Doreen passed it over and I read it.

'What *is* a new lease of life?'

I knew it was something good 'cos my Auntie Doreen smiled at me, same as the next-door neighbour had.

'It means when you gave him that wrestling magazine you made him very happy.'

She took the Christmas card back and read it again.

'Hey, Freda, I thought her name was Brenda Jackson?'

'It was, but after her husband left, she went back to Shackleton. He left about a year after the accident . . .'

My mum mouthed the next bit – but I could tell what she was saying:

'. . . told her he couldn't live with a cripple in a wheel-chair.'


It was really funny, *Television's Christmas Party*. It started at half past seven and finished at nine o'clock. Then we had some Christmas cake and we all had something called sweet sherry but I only had a bit. It tasted like medicine. Mr Shackleton liked it, I held his straw for him and Brenda started crying.

'I'll tell you something, Freda, he is good, that lad of yours. Given my dad a new lease of life he has.'

It was a good Christmas.

*

Holidays over. Back at school. Everybody talking about what they'd got for Christmas. Norbert asked me what my main present was.

'I got tons of stuff.'

'So did I, but what was your main present? I got a two-wheeler.'

Yeah, his dad had probably nicked it, he's always in trouble for thieving. So's Norbert.

'It's a Raleigh three-speed. What did *you* get?'

I'd wanted a Meccano set but my mum couldn't afford it. She'd got me a tin of Quality Street, a jumper from the Co-op, some socks, a *Beezer* annual and I'd got a shirt from my Auntie Doreen.

'Come on, you must've got a main present.'

'Meccano set. Big one.'

That shut him up.

'Don't like Meccano.'

And he went off, asking other people what they'd got for Christmas.

About three weeks after we'd gone back it was my turn to be ill. I didn't get scarlet fever like Tony but on the Sunday night I felt awful. I was hot and cold both at the same time and I could hardly swallow, my throat was so sore. Next morning it was worse and my mum had to stay off work to wait for Dr Jowett to come.

He took the thermometer out of my mouth.

'A hundred and three, open wide, say aah . . . again . . . once more . . . Laryngitis.'

He told my mum I had to stay in bed for a few days.

'I don't have to go to that Craig House home again do I, the one you sent me to in Morecambe?'

I didn't want to go there again, Craig House, I hated it.

'No, no. Plenty of fluids, couple of aspirin every four hours and you'll probably be back at school by the end of the week. He's got a mild dose of laryngitis.'

Mild dose! I felt terrible. That first day anyway. On the Tuesday I didn't feel so bad so my mum was able to go back to work and by the Wednesday I was enjoying myself. I was in my mum's bed – I always go in her bed when I'm poorly – I had no temperature and my throat hardly hurt at all. I had my comics, my *Beezer* annual, some grapes and a banana, a bag of pear drops from my Auntie Doreen and a big jug of Robinson's lemon barley on the bedside table.

'Now, I'll be back same time as yesterday to give you your dinner, around half past twelve, all right?'

Yeah, I was all right. Better than school, this. And I had the wireless. I love listening to the wireless when I'm poorly. Specially when I'm feeling better.

'You've got your lemon barley, and your comics and you can listen to the wireless so you won't get bored and Mrs Carpenter from number twenty-three might pop in, just to check on you, all right?'

My mum plumped up my pillows, kissed me on my forehead and filled my beaker with lemon barley.

'You've got no temperature, that's a blessing.'

'My throat's still a bit sore, though.'

I didn't want her sending me back to school too soon.

421

Mind you, even if I'd gone, I wasn't to know that I'd have been back home by dinnertime. Everybody was sent home early that Wednesday, the whole school.

'Do you want the wireless on?'

'Please.'

She switched it on, kissed me again and went downstairs.

'Bye!'

'Bye, Mum. See you later!'

I heard the front door slam as the wireless warmed up.

'. . . and now at ten to eight it's time for *Lift Up Your Hearts*.' I'd heard that yesterday. Boring. But I couldn't be bothered twiddling with the knob. Anyway, there'd be a story later on. I went through my comics. This looked good. *The Ox-Bow Incident*. A cowboy. Yeah, I'd start with that one, then I'd go on to *Radio Fun* then *Film Fun* and then my favourite, *Captain Marvel*. I always like to leave my favourite till last . . .

I didn't know where I was for a minute. My *Captain Marvel* was open on the eiderdown. I must have fallen asleep. What time was it? I hoped I hadn't missed the story on the wireless. There was just music playing. It wasn't the usual music like they play on *Music While You Work*, it was slow and boring. I wondered how long I'd been asleep? I leaned over to look at my mum's clock. Nearly quarter past eleven. Aw, I had missed the story, it comes on at eleven. I was thirsty. While I was having a drink of my lemon barley the music on the wireless stopped.

'This is London. It is with great sorrow that we make the following announcement.'

It went all quiet for a second.

'It was announced from Sandringham at 10.45 today, February 6th 1952, that the King, who retired to rest last night in his usual health, passed peacefully away in his sleep early this morning . . .'

The King was dead. King George had died. I stopped drinking my lemon barley and put the beaker back on the bedside table.

'. . . The BBC offers profound sympathy to Her Majesty the Queen and the royal family . . .'

I'd only just learned the words to *God Save the King*. We had to sing it every day at school. What were we going to sing now?

'. . . The BBC is now closing down for the rest of the day . . .'

Closing down? No wireless?

'. . . except for the advertised news bulletins and summaries, shipping forecasts and gale warnings . . .'

Shipping forecasts and gale warnings! I wished I hadn't read all my comics.

'. . . Further announcements will be made at 11.45, 12 o'clock and 12.15 p.m.'

Then this dreary music came back on. I didn't know what to do . . . I lay back and stared out of the window . . . It was quite a nice day . . . No it wasn't, the King had died . . . I didn't know what to do . . . Yes I did. 'Course I knew what to do. I got out of bed, went downstairs and pulled the curtains to in the front room. Then I came back upstairs, closed the curtains in my mum's room, got back into bed and lay there listening to the dreary music.

'Why are all the curtains drawn?'

My mum was back, I could hear her coming up the stairs.

'In here as well! What's going on? Why are all the curtains closed?'

She went over to the window and opened one of them.

'The King's died.'

'Y'what?'

'King George. He's died.'

'Oh, don't start all that again!'

And she opened the other curtain.

'It was on the wireless, Mum . . .'

His funeral was on a Friday and we all had the day off school to listen to it on the wireless. We were lucky though, my mum, me and my Auntie Doreen, we watched it on the television. Brenda invited us round with a few other people. She closed the curtains and I sat next to Mr Shackleton.

It was boring but it was better than being at school, I suppose. After we'd been watching for a while, I was holding the straw for Mr Shackleton while he was having a drink, when he pushed the cup away and I thought he'd had enough. He took hold of *The Wrestler* and held it out for me. He probably knew I was bored but it was too dark to read so I whispered to him that it was all right. I thought I was being really quiet but a few people turned round and my mum gave me a dirty look. Mr Shackleton kept pushing the magazine into my hand so I took it. Then he put his mouth towards the straw and I held the cup while he had another drink.

I thought the King's funeral was never going to finish, I could hardly keep my eyes open. At last it was over and Brenda switched it off while my mum and my Auntie Doreen and the others thanked her and said how wonderful it was and things like that. I watched the white spot disappearing.

'Thank you, Brenda, that was a wonderful experience . . .'

'I've never seen anything like it, Brenda, just think, you're in your front room and you're there at the same time . . .'

'I can't get over it, Brenda, wonderful. And that Richard Dimbleby, hasn't he got a beautiful voice? He brings it all to life, doesn't he?'

I couldn't understand what they were all going on about, it wasn't as good as *Whirligig*, I'd been bored as anything. So had Mr Shackleton, I think, 'cos he'd fallen asleep. Brenda opened the curtains.

'Now, who'd like a nice cup of tea? I'll put the kettle on.'

'I'll give you a hand, Brenda.'

'Me too.'

'Let me do it.'

His head was lolling on one side and some spit was

425

dribbling out of his mouth but it was when I saw that his eyes were open that I realised and ran into the kitchen and whispered to my mum.

My Auntie Doreen took me home while the others stayed to be with Brenda. We were walking up St Barnabas Street and I looked back. Brenda was closing the front-room curtains.

It wasn't till I got home that I realised I was still holding *The Wrestler*.

# THE BIRTHDAY PARTY

Reverend Dutton looked at his watch.

'Ah, half past three!'

He looked over at Keith Hopwood and smiled.

'I think this is the moment the birthday boy has been waiting for. Am I right, Mr Hopwood?'

Keith blushed and nodded.

'W-well, it's not my b-b-birthday till M-M-Monday but m-my dad's on n-n-nights next w-week so I'm having my p-party today.'

Reverend Dutton nodded, smiled again and looked round the class.

'Right then, all those of you who are lucky enough to be going to Keith Hopwood's birthday party, please leave now – quietly.'

That's what happens when you're having your party on a school day, you can take in a note from your mum to ask if those who are invited can leave early. The school never says no and it's great if you're one of the ones going. You feel really good leaving early, specially on a Friday afternoon when it's boring scripture with Reverend Dutton. You don't feel so good when you're one of the ones left behind.

'Come on, boys, quick as you can, please, the lesson's not over for the rest of us.'

And today I wasn't feeling so good. I couldn't believe it when Keith had told me I wasn't invited.

'But Keith, I'm one of your best friends, you're always comin' round to my house, why can't I come to your party?'

He just shrugged and said his mum had told him he could ask no more than five.

'Who have you got coming?'

He told me. Boocock and Barraclough? Norbert? Tony? David Holdsworth? I couldn't believe it. Well, I could believe David Holdsworth, he's Keith's best friend, he lives in the same street, just two doors away. And Tony, who's *my* best friend, is always invited to birthday parties, everybody likes him. But why Norbert? And why Boocock and Barraclough? They're always picking on Keith 'cos of his stutter.

'Boocock and Barraclough! Why are you askin' them? You don't even like 'em. They're always pickin' on you.'

He hadn't said anything.

'You're scared of them, aren't you? You just want to keep in with 'em.'

He went a bit red.

'B-B-Boocock s-s-said he'd th-thump me if I didn't invite them. You know w-what he's like.'

I do. It's hard to stand up to Arthur Boocock.

'Well, you could have invited me instead of Norbert.'

'I w-w-would have d-done, honest, but he g-gave me ha-ha-half a crown.'

Where would Norbert have got half a crown from? He'd probably nicked it.

'Where did he get half a crown from?'

Keith just shrugged again.

'Probably n-n-nicked it. Anyway, I've n-n-never b-been to one of *your* b-b-birthday parties.'

'That's 'cos I don't have one. You know I don't, my mum can't afford it.'

My mum's always asking if I'd like a little party at home but I want one like the others have, when you go out somewhere. Tony went to the zoo for his party. Duggie Bashforth had his at the transport museum and we all had tea there, that was one of the best. Geoff Gower's birthday was in the Easter holidays and his mum and dad took a load of us to the fair. Mind you, they've got tons of money, Gower's dad's got a greengrocer's. I never like to ask my mum for something like that though 'cos I know it would cost her too much money.

'If I did have a party I wouldn't invite you!'

Keith just sniffed and shrugged and walked off. It's all right for him, his mum and dad both work, they've got more money coming in.

'Come along, boys, hurry yourselves, I'm sure Mrs Hopwood is waiting for you with lots of jellies and fairy cakes.'

429

Everybody laughed and Reverend Dutton looked round the class.

'That's what birthday parties used to consist of when I was a lad. Potted-meat sandwiches, fairy cakes and jelly. Then we'd all play Pass the Parcel and Musical Chairs . . .'

He looked a bit sad. I wasn't sure but I think he had tears in his eyes.

'And sometimes we'd play Blind Man's Buff or Pin the Tail on the Donkey. Oh, happy times, we had such fun.'

Boocock snorted and we all started giggling. Keith told him that his party was going to be nothing like that.

'No, w-we're havin' f-f-fish 'n' chips for tea, Reverend D-Dutton, and then w-we're going to the p-p-pictures.'

'Oh, lovely. Well, off you go, have a nice time.'

He picked up his Bible and turned to the class.

'We have to get back to David and Goliath, don't we, boys?'

Everybody groaned.

'Now, where were we? Ah yes, Goliath yelled, "Choose a man from among you to come and fight me. If he can kill me the Philistines will be your servants. If I kill him all of you will become servants of the Philistines . . ."'

Who cared about David and Goliath and the Philistines when you could be having fish and chips and then going to the pictures? I watched them all following Keith out into the corridor. Boocock turned at the door, grinned and gave us all a thumbs-up. Why hadn't Keith invited me? I could understand him being scared of Boocock and Barraclough, but Norbert! Just 'cos he'd given him half a crown? I'm more his friend than Norbert is. Keith's always coming round to my house for tea and stuff. And I'm always sticking up for him, specially when he's being teased 'cos of his stutter. I never tease him like the others do. Like Norbert does. Norbert's always taking him off, pretending to stammer like he does. And then Keith goes and invites him to his birthday party instead of me just 'cos he'd given him half a crown. I wouldn't do that to him. I'd invite him to my birthday party. If I had one.

Reverend Dutton was still going on about David and Goliath.

'Now, boys, Goliath was this thundering giant of a man. He was over nine feet tall and everyone was terrified of him . . .'

Yeah, like Arthur Boocock, we're all terrified of him. Oh, roll on four o'clock . . .

On my way home I had to collect the washing from the launderette. It's in the block of shops near school and I have to take it there every Friday. It's called a service wash, the woman there does it all. I drop it off in the morning on my way to school and then pick it up on my way home. It wasn't so bad when it was just our stuff, I could manage to carry it, but now I have to take my Auntie Doreen's as well. It was my mum's idea after she'd been to that bring and buy sale at St Barnabas Church hall last year.


'Look at that, Doreen, it only cost me a pound at the bring and buy sale. A pound!'

There it was, standing in the middle of the kitchen.

My Auntie Doreen and me looked at it and then at each other and we burst out laughing.

'Well, it may have been cheap, Freda, but I'd say that's a pound wasted. What on earth possessed you to buy a pram?'

'You're not having a baby are you, Mum?'

She gave me one of her looks but I couldn't stop laughing. I wouldn't have been laughing so much if I'd known why she'd bought it.

'This is for you, young man.'

Me? What was she talking about? What would I be doing with a pram?

'And for you, Doreen. There's method in my madness. You'll both thank me.'

I didn't know what she was on about. Neither did my Auntie Doreen.

'Freda, what are you blathering on about? Why would either of us be interested in a pram?'

My mum sat back in her chair and folded her arms. She nodded at me with this big smile on her face.

'Every Friday he struggles to the launderette with our dirty washing, don't you, love?'

Oh no, I knew what was coming.

'And every week, Doreen, you struggle to the launderette with your two bags of washing.'

'Yes, on a Thursday, and it's a real pain I can tell you.'

'Not any more, it won't be, Doreen.'

She pointed to the pram.

'No, Mum, I'm not wheeling a pram to school, it's embarrassing.'

My Auntie Doreen was telling her what a good idea it was.

'I'm not doin' it, Mum. I'm not wheeling the washing in a pram.'

'Freda, that's a wonderful idea. Why didn't we think of something like that before?'

'I'm not doin' it, Mum, they'll all laugh at me . . .'

And they do. Every week. Boocock and Barraclough are the worst of course.

'Have you changed its nappy?'

'Is it a boy or a girl?'

'What's its name?'

Once, when I first started taking the pram, they'd picked up one of the bundles and started throwing it to each other and the dirty washing had ended up all over the pavement. Pants, vests. My mum's undies. All over the place. This lady had to help me collect it all up. It was awful.

Norbert and Keith sometimes tease me as well.

'Aw, l-l-look, Norbert, in't it b-b-bonny . . .'

'When are you havin' another one? You don't want an only baby, y'know, that's what my mam always says . . .'

Even Tony joined in once. He'd found this baby's bottle in the street and put it on my desk when he'd got to school. He did say sorry afterwards.

At the beginning I started leaving home late so that I wouldn't bump into any of them. I'd run like mad, pushing the blooming pram all over the pavement, running round people, and sometimes I'd end up being late for assembly and get into trouble, so now I don't care. If they see me and start saying things I just push the pram and ignore them. And most of the time they don't bother. They've all got used to it. Just shows, if you make out to people that you're not bothered by the things they say, they get bored and leave you alone.

Thank goodness I don't have to take the pram all the way to school, the woman at the launderette lets me leave it with her.

When I got there on my way home from school the washing was all folded up ready for ironing and the woman had put it in the pram.

'There you are, love, I've kept it all separate for you. That's your mum's stuff and that's your auntie's. See you next Friday, love.'

She held the door open for me.

'Ta.'

I wheeled the pram out and started walking up the road. If I've got the money I usually get twopenceworth of chips from Pearson's and eat them on my way home. I stopped, put the brake on the pram and started going through my pockets. Great, I found a couple of halfpennies, all I needed was one more penny. I was feeling in my inside blazer pocket when I saw them in the sit-down bit at the back of the shop. Boocock and Barraclough, Norbert, Tony and David Holdsworth. Keith was sitting between his mum and dad and Mr Hopwood was opening a big bottle of dandelion and burdock. I love dandelion and burdock. They were all laughing and eating lovely fish and chips. I wondered what they were going to see at the pictures. I found a penny in my inside pocket but I didn't buy any chips, I set off for home. I hate Keith Hopwood.

'Mum, you know it's my birthday next Friday?'

She was darning my socks. She looked up at me and smiled.

'Yes, I do know that, I don't think I'm likely to forget your birthday, love.'

She ruffled my hair.

'I can't believe what a big lad you're getting.'

She gave me a hug and kissed me on my forehead.

'I didn't mean that, Mum, what I meant was, can I have a party?'

She looked at me, surprised.

'I asked you if you wanted a party, you said you weren't bothered.'

I wasn't bothered then.

'I've changed my mind.'

I wasn't really that bothered now. I just wanted to have a birthday party so I could tell Keith Hopwood he wasn't invited. And not the kind of party I knew my mum would be thinking about. Mine was going to be different. Thanks to the lady in the fur coat I'd seen on my way home.

I was pushing the pram along Skinner Lane when this big car went over a puddle as it was pulling up. I got water all over my socks and shoes. I was soaked.

'Daddy, Daddy! It was the best birthday party ever, wasn't it, Mummy?'

I looked up and saw these girls coming out of the Rolarena. There were four of them and they were carrying roller skates and one of them was holding a balloon saying 'Happy 7th Birthday'. The girl's dad got out of the car, took the roller skates and opened the back door for them. They all got in, laughing and giggling, saying it was the best party ever. He opened the passenger door for the girl's mum, then went round to the back of the car and put the roller skates in the boot. The lady was wearing a fur coat and she stood on the pavement to take it off before she got in.

'The roller-skating was a huge success, Bernard, and the tea they laid on for the girls was first class, you couldn't fault it.'

As she was getting into the car I saw something drop out of one of the pockets of the coat. It was a piece of white paper. The man closed the boot and walked round the front to get in. Then I realised what it was she'd dropped.

'S'cuse me, mister, this fell out of her coat.'

I held it out for him. He came round, took it and tapped on the passenger-door window. The lady wound it down.

'Darling, look what you dropped in the street – a five-pound note! This young man found it.'

She looked ever so surprised and put her hand on her mouth. The girls in the back were singing happy birthday and laughing. The man had got his wallet out and was putting the five-pound note away.

'It fell out of your coat pocket, missus, when you were getting in the car.'

'Thank you, thank you so much.'

'S'all right.'

I went back to the pram and started wheeling it off.

'Hang on a second.'

It was the man calling me back. He still had his wallet in his hand.

'This is for you. A little reward.'

I went back. *Little!* It was a ten-shilling note. He was giving me a ten-shilling note.

'Thank you. Thank you very much, mister.'

He smiled.

'My pleasure. Buy something for yourself and the baby.'

I didn't like to tell him it wasn't a baby, just my mum and my Auntie Doreen's washing.

'I'll get your Auntie Doreen to do you a cake, she's a better baker than me. I'll do potted-meat sandwiches, they always go down well.'

No. I knew what I wanted to do for my birthday. And I couldn't wait to see Keith Hopwood's face when he found out what he'd be missing.

'No, Mum, I want to have it at the Rolarena.'

'What?'

'You can hire roller skates and they do a first-class tea.'

She looked at me like I was mad.

'The Rolarena?'

'Just a few of us. Me, Tony, Norbert and David Holdsworth, that's all.'

'I'm sorry, love, I can't afford anything like that.'

I couldn't stop myself from smiling.

'I can.'

And I showed her the ten-shilling note. She could hardly believe it when I told her how I'd got it.

Next day we went to the Saturday-morning matinee, me, Norbert, Keith and Tony. Keith was excited 'cos he'd be going up on the stage and getting his ABC Minors birthday card from Uncle Derek.

They were going on about Keith's party, the lovely tea and what a good time they'd had at the pictures and how Mr Hopwood had bought them ice lollies and Butterkist. They'd been to see *Ivanhoe* with Robert Taylor. I love Robert Taylor, he's one of my favourites, I was dying to see it. If Keith had invited me he'd have been coming to my roller-skating party. But not now.

'It's my birthday next week. I'm having a roller-skating party. At the Rolarena. And we'll be havin' our tea there.'

Norbert looked like the lady in the fur coat did when she'd been told she'd dropped the five-pound note.

'Roller-skating party! Oh, I'm comin' to that. I hope. Am I? Can I come?'

''Course you can. There's four of us goin'. You, Tony, me . . .'

I looked at Keith.

'And David Holdsworth . . . Sorry, Keith, my mum says I can ask no more than three.'

I couldn't stop myself from smiling.


When I got home from the Saturday-morning matinee I couldn't believe it. My mum was going on about the ten-shilling note. I couldn't understand what she was talking about.

'I know where you got it from, young man, you were never given it, you took it from my apron pocket, didn't you?'

'What?'

What was she talking about?

'I had a ten-shilling note in my apron pocket and it's gone and you come home with some cock and bull story about being given ten shillings by a man outside the Rolarena. I know where you got it, you took it out of my apron.'

This wasn't fair.

'I didn't, Mum, honest! I was given it.'

I had once taken a threepenny bit out of her apron, ages ago, when I was about nine, and I'd owned up afterwards. But I'd never take ten shillings.

'I didn't take it, Mum, honest.'

She looked at me. I could feel myself going red.

'Why are you going red?'

I didn't know why I was going red. I do that at school when we're asked to own up about something. I go red even when I haven't done it.

'I don't know, I can't help it, but I didn't take your ten shillings, honest.'

'I don't believe you, it's all too convenient this story about a man giving you ten shillings and then suddenly there's a ten-shilling note missing from my apron. You can forget about this roller-skating party now, that is not going to happen.'

I couldn't believe this. It just wasn't fair.

'But, Mum, I've already invited them.'

She started putting on her coat.

'Well, you'll just have to un-invite them, won't you? And don't bother taking your windcheater off, you're coming with me, you can carry my shopping.'

I was holding two heavy carrier bags, waiting for her to come out of Gower's greengrocer's. It's next to Pearson's fish and chip shop and I saw two lads from my school coming out. I turned away, I didn't want them to see that I'd been crying. She just wouldn't believe that I hadn't taken her money, even when I'd said cross my heart and hope to die. I was going to have to tell the others that I wasn't having a roller-skating party now. And wouldn't Keith Hopwood have a good laugh?

My mum came out of the shop and started walking up the road.

'I've just got to pick up a couple of things from the dry-cleaner's and that's it.'

I followed her. I didn't say anything more about the money, there was no point, she was never going to believe

440

me. Then, after we'd gone past the launderette we heard someone calling out to my mum. It was the lady who does the service wash.

'Ee, I'm glad I spotted you, love, I meant to give this to your lad yesterday . . .'

She held out a ten-shilling note.

'I'm not sure if it's yours or your sister's, it was in that pink blouse, in the breast pocket.'

My mum looked at me.

'Oh, love, I don't know what to say, I'm ever so . . .'

I felt sorry for her.

'I was sure I'd put it in my apron pocket, I could have sworn I did. Oh, love, I do apologise.'

She knelt down and put her arms round me.

'We'll go and book it now, we'll go straight to the Rolarena . . .'


Reverend Dutton looked at his watch.

'Ah, half past three!'

He looked over at me and smiled. I'd given him it the day before, the note from my mum asking if the ones going to my roller-skating party could leave half an hour early.

'I think this is the moment the birthday boy has been waiting for, am I right?'

I nodded.

'Yes, sir.'

'Roller-skating party, eh?'

'Yes, sir.'

I looked round the class.

'My goodness, that's very original.'

Keith Hopwood was glowering at me.

'In my day we used to have a little tea party then play games, Blind Man's Buff, Musical Chairs . . .'

We could hardly hear him 'cos of these fire engines outside, racing up the road, clanging their bells.

'Sometimes we'd play Pass the Parcel. That was my favourite, I used to love Pass the Parcel . . .'

More fire engines. Norbert and a few others got up to look out of the window.

'Then there was Pass the Parcel with forfeits. Do any of you still play that? Pass the Parcel with forfeits? It's the same as Pass the Parcel but every layer of paper contains a forfeit, you know, you had to sing a song or eat a teaspoon of mustard, those sort of forfeits. It was huge fun . . .'

Suddenly Geoff Gower shouted out and pointed.

'Sir, look at that!'

Everybody looked. The sky was full of black smoke. We all rushed to the window. There were more fire engines now and bells clanging like anything. We couldn't see any fire though.

'All right, boys, sit down, it's only a fire, back to your desks, please.'

Norbert was standing on the pipes to get a better look.

'Looks like a big one, sir, look at the sky.'

Reverend Dutton made him get down.

'It'll probably be one of the mills. The fire brigade are on their way, that's the main thing. Right, all those going to the roller-skating party can leave. Quick as you can, please.'

442

Now it was my turn. I went to the front of the class and Tony, Norbert and David followed me. I turned at the door and took one last look at Keith. He looked fed-up. Serve him right!

My mum had said she'd meet us by the school gates around twenty to four. She'd asked if she could leave work early and I was hoping she wouldn't be late. She'd booked the party for four o'clock and we were going to meet my Auntie Doreen there. We were standing by the gates, waiting for her, watching more fire engines racing up the road. There were police cars as well. The sky was getting blacker and blacker. It was quite exciting. This workman was walking past and Norbert asked if he knew what was going on.

'Oh, it's massive, lad, huge fire, must be nine or ten fire engines.'

We asked him if it was one of the mills.

'No, thank goodness. It's the Rolarena – went up like a tinder box. All wood, y'see. It's gone. Burned to the ground. There's nowt left.'

That's when I heard my mum. She was running up the road.

'I'm here, love! Sorry I'm late. There's been a big fire. No buses. I had to walk. Anyway, we'll be all right, we'll get there by four.'

We went to Pearson's for fish and chips and then to the pictures. *Prisoner of Zenda*. It was all right. But not as good as roller-skating.

# THE TRICK

'Where are *you* then, love? I can't find you.'

We were looking at the school photo. We had it spread out on the kitchen table, it was about three feet long. I was holding one end and my mum was holding the other.

'Over there somewhere, Mum, at your end.'

'I can't find you.'

'I think I was next to Keith Hopwood.'

'That's a big help, where's he?'

'I can't remember, it was ages ago when they took it.'

I leaned across to look where I was on the photo. I took my hand off my end and it rolled back up into a scroll.

We'd got them that afternoon. Mrs Garside, the school secretary, had brought them in during scripture and Reverend Dutton had handed them out at the end of the lesson.

'Now, boys, you'll be pleased to know that in this box, kindly delivered to us by Mrs Garside, is at long last the eagerly awaited school photograph.'

'About time, we paid for 'em ages ago!'

'Thank you, Boocock, we know we've been waiting a

while for these, and stop leaning back in your chair like that, take your feet off the desk.'

Boocock stared at Reverend Dutton and slowly did as he was told. As soon as he was sitting up straight Barraclough did the same thing, leaned back in his chair on two legs and put his feet up on his desk. Reverend Dutton looked at him, you could tell he didn't know what to do. He turned round, picked up the box of photos, then looked back at him. Barraclough still had his feet on the desk. So did Boocock.

'Stay behind afterwards, the two of you, we're going to have a little talk.'

They both laughed. They wouldn't stay behind, they just do what they like in scripture, we all do. You can get away with anything in Reverend Dutton's class.

He started coming round handing out the photos. They were all rolled up and held together with a rubber band.

'Now, don't open these here, boys, wait till you get home. They're very long, you'll get into a terrible mess.'

'Course everybody ignored him and started looking for themselves and laughing.

'Holdsworth, you've got your eyes closed . . .'

'Look at Gower, he's doin' a V-sign . . .'

'You'll get done for that, Gower . . .'

'Look at Jackie Parry – he's fast asleep . . .'

'Who's that idiot? You can't tell who it is, he moved . . .'

The photographer from London had told us we had to keep dead still while the photograph was being taken.

*

'This is not like a normal camera, it's a special camera to take panoramic photographs. It'll move from one side to the other, so you have to keep dead still . . .'

We were all in rows right across the playground. There were about six rows of older lads at the back standing on different-size tables – it must have taken the caretaker ages to set it all up. Then there was a row of chairs for all the staff and sixth-formers.

'We use this special camera at schools all round the country. It'll start taking the picture on *my left* and move all the way across to *my right* and you must keep *dead still* . . .'

First and second years were right at the front. Second years had been told to kneel and we were sitting on our bums. I was between Keith Hopwood and Duggie Bashforth.

'You mustn't move a muscle and that includes the teachers . . .'

Everybody laughed, well, those who'd been listening. That's when Ogden, the headmaster, got up.

'Quiet!'

We shut up quick.

'This gentleman has come all the way from London to take our school photograph. It is important you listen to instructions. Carry on.'

He went back to his chair that was right in the middle and the photographer from London carried on.

'Thank you, Mr Ogden. As your headmaster has just said, it's very important to listen to my instructions. The camera will move from left to right. When I start the

447

exposure it will take about forty-five seconds. Do you think you can keep still for forty-five seconds?'

'It's you, Cawthra, you moved, you couldn't even keep still for forty-five seconds!'

'It isn't me, I'm over there next to Emmott!'

'Oh. Who is it then? You can't tell . . .'

Reverend Dutton was still going round handing out the photos. I didn't unroll mine, I wanted to wait till I got home.

'One for you, Lightowler, the last one.'

Norbert hadn't been at school that day. You'd had to wear a school tie and a school blazer to be in the photo. He didn't have either.

'Not mine, sir, I'm not gettin' one. I'm not on it. I was off sick.'

'Oh, that's a shame, Lightowler.'

'Yes, sir, it is, sir.'

Reverend Dutton held up the last photograph.

'Have I missed anybody out?'

'No, sir . . .'

'Well, there's one left over, it must belong to someone.'

It went quiet. We all looked at each other. It was McDougall who put his hand up.

'It'll be Manningham's, sir . . .'

Reverend Dutton didn't know what to say for a minute. He went a bit red.

'Oh yes . . . yes, of course . . . Er, yes . . . I'll, er . . . yes . . .'

That was the last day Manningham had come to school, the day of the photo.

'Who's that, love, holding two fingers up to the camera? That's not a nice thing to do on a school photograph, is it?'

I was looking for Manningham. I couldn't find him.

'Geoff Gower. He said he was copying Mr Churchill.'

My mum looked at me.

'I don't think so. Anyway, it's *Sir* Winston Churchill now.'

'Oh . . .'

Where was Manningham? I was finding it hard to remember what he looked like.

'Ooh, my Lord, who's this? Look at his hair!'

'Who?'

'One of the teachers. I've never seen hair like it.'

She was looking at Reverend Dutton.

'Scripture teacher. He wears a wig.'

I carried on looking. Where was he? My mum was still going on about Reverend Dutton's wig.

'Poor man, someone should tell him, it looks ridiculous.'

There he is! There was Manningham, right at the end of the row – smiling.

'Take a card, any card . . .'

Norbert was watching out for Melrose while our class stood round in a group, watching Manningham doing another of his amazing tricks.

'Any card you like . . .'

Boocock pushed everybody out of the way.

'I'll choose it!'

He's always the chooser is Arthur Boocock, we never get a look-in.

Manningham turned away from us towards the black-board, covering his eyes.

'Don't show it to me, Mr Boocock, but remember the card.'

He calls everybody mister when he's doing his tricks. When he'd first come into our class I didn't know what to make of him. I'd thought he was a bit barmy, off his head. I didn't like him. He was a show-off.

'Memorise that card, Mr Boocock, make sure everybody sees it.'

He's not a show-off, though, he's just different. Different from anybody else in our school.

Boocock held up the card. It was the eight of Diamonds.

'Does everybody know what the card is?'

We all shouted 'Yes' except for Norbert.

'I don't, I'm over here looking out for Melrose, what is it?'

Manningham still had his back to us. 'Don't shout it out, Mr Boocock! Would you please show Mr Lightowler the card?'

Boocock held it up.

'Has Mr Lightowler seen the card?'

'Yes!'

We all said it together again.

'Then please replace the card into the pack that is sitting on the table. Anywhere in the pack, please.'

Boocock picked up the cards and pushed the eight of Diamonds into the middle.

'Now get on with it, Manningham, before Melrose comes.'

Manningham turned round, opened his eyes and looked at Boocock.

'You can't hurry magic, Mr Boocock.'

He took the cards and started to shuffle them.

I wish I could be like Peter Manningham. He's not scared of Boocock and Barraclough like the rest of us. He's not scared of the teachers. He's not even scared of Melrose. You could tell that from the very first day he'd come into our class.

'Leedale?'

'Here, sir.'

'Lightowler?'

'Sir.'

'Manningham?'

We'd all turned round to have a look at the lad who had been kept down. He should have been in the year above.

'Oh dear, Manningham. Relegated, were we?'

'I'm afraid so, sir, one of those things.'

And he'd just smiled at Melrose.

'Well, go on at this rate, lad, and you'll be in your twenties before you leave school.'

Melrose had looked round the class with his lip curling like it does and we'd all laughed. Not 'cos we'd thought it was funny – 'cos we knew Melrose expected us to. Manningham had just smiled again.

'You're dead right, sir. But don't you agree, there's always two sides to everything, sir? Advantages and disadvantages. Hopefully when I do leave, Mr Melrose, I'll be better educated, won't I?'

That's how he talked to teachers. If it'd been me or Norbert or any of the others, we'd have got clouted or kept in after school, but not Peter Manningham. He seemed to get away with anything. With everything.

'Not if you get expelled, you won't, and that's what'll happen if you don't sort yourself out, lad!'

Manningham had just smiled that smile of his.


'I'm now going to lay these cards on the table, face down. I will turn each card over until I come to the card that Mr Boocock chose.'

We all stood round the table, watching as he started picking them up. King of Clubs, six of Hearts, nine of Spades. How would he know that it was the eight of Diamonds Boocock had chosen? It was impossible. We all leaned in closer. Jack of Diamonds, five of Spades, two of Clubs . . .

'*What* may I ask is going on here?'

Stupid Norbert! Instead of looking out for Melrose like he was supposed to, he'd come over from the door and was watching with the rest of us. Everybody ran to their desks. Everybody except Manningham, he just carried on turning over the cards. Norbert looked at Boocock. He knew what was going to happen to him at break.

'Manningham! Collect those up and get to your desk!'

He didn't even look up. He just kept turning the cards over, showing each one to the class before he put it into the other pile. Eight of Spades, queen of Diamonds, four of Diamonds. He wasn't even hurrying.

'Just give me a couple of seconds, sir. We are coming to the climax of an amazing bit of magic.'

That's what I mean. You don't talk to teachers like that, especially not Melrose. You wouldn't even talk to Reverend Dutton like that. But Manningham did and he got away with it.

King of Diamonds, ace of Hearts, five of Clubs. He stopped turning over the cards and looked up at Melrose for the first time.

'Just a little bit of your time, sir, that's all I need. I think you'll be very impressed with this.'

He didn't even wait for Melrose to reply. He just smiled his smile and carried on picking up the cards, showing them to us and putting them aside.

Seven of Spades, nine of Clubs, king of Hearts. Still no eight of Diamonds. Melrose didn't say anything, he just stood there watching like the rest of us. That's when it dawned on me. That's how he got away with it. It was the way he always smiled at people after he'd said something. It was like magic. It was the same that day when he hadn't done his homework for Bleasdale.

*

453

'Frankly, young man, I'm not surprised that you've had to stay down a year, this is quite intolerable.'

Manningham had nodded.

'You're dead right, sir, but if you remember the weather was lovely last night, really mild and it was either doing my Latin homework or taking my granny out for a walk – she's in a wheelchair, sir, and she doesn't get out much and I thought, no, I'll take her for walk and honestly, sir, it did her the world of good . . .'

And there it was, the smile. And he wasn't putting it on, you could tell, it's just the way he is. Bleasdale wasn't sure what to say.

'Yes, well . . . er, that's very commendable, Manningham, it is important to look after your grand-mother, but listen, lad, I do want you to do that work for me, perhaps you could do it tonight.'

Manningham hadn't said anything for a couple of seconds, it was like he was thinking about it.

'I'll try, sir. I'll do my best.'

I'll try? I'll do my best? If any of us had said that we'd have been crucified, but not Peter Manningham. People just like him.

'Good lad, you can only do your best.'

Good lad? You can only do your best? God, I wish I could be like Peter Manningham . . .

He was still picking up the cards. Four of Hearts, ace of Clubs, ten of Clubs . . . there weren't many left.

'Well, gentlemen, we are coming to the end of the pack and I haven't yet found Mr Boocock's card.'

Boocock snorted.

'Well, I put it in there. Everybody saw me.'

Manningham carried on turning the cards over, showing us each one before he put it into the other pile. Seven of Hearts, three of Diamonds, eight of Clubs.

'Then, Mr Boocock, your card must be here.'

King of Spades, three of Clubs, five of Diamonds. Ten of Hearts, nine of Hearts, seven of Clubs . . . No eight of Diamonds.

'Gentlemen – there is only one card left. This, then, must be Mr Boocock's card!'

What a fantastic trick! How did he know which card Boocock had picked? And how did he make it the last card? How could he make sure it was at the bottom of the pile after he'd shuffled them? It was magic. He put his hand on it.

'So, gentlemen, this is the card chosen by Mr Boocock!'

He picked it up slowly and showed it to us . . . jack of Clubs! Jack of Clubs? It was the wrong card, he'd mucked it up.

'That wasn't my card, mine wor the eight of Diamonds.'

Everybody agreed with Boocock. Manningham was frowning, he couldn't understand it. I felt sorry for him.

'But that was the only card left. It can't have been.'

Boocock sneered.

'You're useless, Manningham!'

Barraclough, Hopwood, Norbert and some of the

others started jeering. They soon shut up when they saw Melrose looking at them.

Manningham was going through the pack of cards. Melrose put his hand on his shoulder.

'Come on, lad, let's get this lot cleared away, we've wasted enough time.'

Manningham was still looking at all the playing cards.

'You see, there is no eight of Diamonds here, but I believe Mr Boocock when he says that is the card he put back into the pack.'

Melrose started pushing Manningham over to his desk.

'Yes, well, I wouldn't believe everything "Mr" Boocock tells you, now come on, lad, let's get on with the lesson.'

Manningham held up his hands. 'The thing is, gentlemen, if Mr Boocock's card *was* the eight of Diamonds, where has it gone?'

Everybody groaned. The vein under Melrose's eye started to throb. If Manningham wasn't careful he was going to get a clout. I felt so sorry for him.

'Look, Manningham, you just need to practise a bit more. Now go and sit down before I lose my temper.'

'Mr Melrose! Would you please do me the honour of looking in the right-hand pocket of your jacket?'

Everybody stopped talking. Melrose looked at Manningham. We all looked at Melrose. No, it was impossible. The eight of Diamonds couldn't be in his pocket, we all saw Boocock put it in the middle of the pack. Oh no, Manningham was making a right fool of himself.

'Mr Melrose, would you please place your hand in the right pocket of your jacket and tell me what you find there?'

It was dead quiet. I looked around. Everybody was staring at Melrose. How could it be in his pocket? There was no way . . .

'I hope you're not wasting my time, lad.'

He was. He must be. There was no way . . . Melrose felt in his pocket and the vein under his eye started to throb again and he looked at Manningham. He pulled his hand out of his pocket and, yes, he was holding a playing card. Melrose looked at it, then showed it to us. The eight of Diamonds. It was magic.

For a second you could have heard a pin drop, then everybody started cheering and Melrose was slapping Manningham on the back.

And there it was again, that smile . . .

'Well, I still can't find you, love.'

I was looking at Manningham in the photo, wishing he was still in our class. I missed him.

'Look at this teacher, *he* looks like he's fast asleep.'

I didn't have to look. I knew who that was. History teacher. Jackie Parry. He wouldn't have even been in the photo if it hadn't been for Peter Manningham . . .

We were all watching him, trying not to laugh. His head kept dropping forward on to his chest, then he'd suddenly sit up straight and look at us like he didn't know where he was for a minute, then start falling asleep again. Once

Jackie Parry was asleep we could do what we liked, till then we had to make out we were reading whatever he'd told us to.

'Time for my medicine, boys. You know it tends to make me a bit sleepy, so while I close my eyes for a few minutes I'd like you to read the chapter on Martin Luther and the Reformation. Page seventy-one. Answer as many of the set questions as you can, boys.'

I used to think it really was medicine he had to take. I used to feel sorry for him, I hate taking medicine.

It's always the same when we have him in the afternoon, specially on a Friday when it's the first lesson after our dinner-break. When we have history on a Tuesday morning we really have to work, he never falls asleep then.

His head started dropping again and some spit was dribbling down his chin. Norbert couldn't help laughing and Boocock thumped him on the back of his neck and showed him his fist. I'm glad I don't sit in front of Boocock.

It was Norbert who'd told me what it was Jackie Parry was really drinking.

'Y'what?'

'It's whisky, like what my dad drinks.'

'What's that?'

'It's like beer, only stronger. He's an alkie is Jackie Parry.'

I hadn't known what he was talking about.

'What's an alkie?'

'Someone who likes drinkin'. My dad's an alkie.'

He'd said it like it was something good. Norbert had

told me all about his dad, how he hits him when he's been drinking. I hadn't known that's what they were called. Alkies.

'My mum says it's like they're poorly, that alkies can't help it, they have to drink.'

'They don't have to hit you. Jackie Parry doesn't hit anybody.'

Norbert had looked at me.

'No, he just falls asleep. There's different sorts of alkies . . .'

Jackie Parry was snoring now. Boocock went up to him and waved his hand in front of his face . . . then he tapped him on the shoulder . . . then he gave him a little push . . . he was fast asleep. Great, we could do what we liked.

'Hey, Ma-Ma-Manningham, d-do another of your tr-tr-tricks.'

Manningham smiled.

'Not tricks, Mr Hopwood, it's magic.'

We all started chanting.

'Manningham! Manningham! Manningham!'

We chanted quietly. Not 'cos we were worried about Parry waking up – we weren't bothered about that, but we didn't want to get him into trouble. It'd turned out that the headmaster knew Jackie Parry was an alkie and that Parry could lose his job 'cos of it. Me and Norbert had overheard the head talking to Melrose in the corridor outside the cloakroom one night after school. I'd had to go back for my windcheater. I'd got all the way home when I realised I'd left it on my peg. Norbert had come with me 'cos he'd had nothing better to do.

'He's an excellent teacher, I agree. First rate. But let's face it, Jack Parry's got a drink problem, he's an alcoholic.'

We heard Melrose telling the headmaster that it had only got worse since his wife had died.

'And he's fine in the mornings, Headmaster. Perhaps we could re-schedule his lessons.'

'I can't organise the school timetable around Jack Parry's drink problem, Brian. If he doesn't do something about it, he's going to have to go!'

Norbert and me had to stop ourselves from laughing, we didn't know Melrose's name was Brian.

'Manningham! Manningham! Manningham!'

I sat at the kitchen table looking at his smiling face in the school photo, thinking about that afternoon when he'd saved Jackie Parry from getting the sack.

'Manningham! Manningham! Manningham!'

Manningham stood up, went to the front of the classroom and held his hands out. We all went quiet. Without saying a word he took a piece of string from his pocket and held it up to show us.

'A simple piece of string, gentlemen.'

He tied a knot in it and wrapped it round the back of

his hands like he was going to do Cat's Cradle. That's what Boocock thought he *was* going to do.

'Cat's Cradle? Oh, brilliant trick, this, I don't think!'

Manningham took no notice. He wound the string round again so it was double.

'And now, gentlemen, I would like a volunteer.'

We all shouted at once.

'Me! Me! Me!'

'Mr Lightowler – would you please step forward?'

Norbert went up to the front with a big grin on his face. Manningham was holding the string with both hands.

'Mr Lightowler, would you take those scissors on Mr Parry's table and cut the string in two between my hands.'

'S'all right. I'll use my penknife.'

He's a fool, Norbert, we're not supposed to bring knives to school. He cut the string and Manningham told him to sit down again.

'So you see, gentlemen, I am now holding separate pieces of string.'

He held them up in his left hand and the loose ends dangled down.

'I am now going to tie these lengths of string together using only – my teeth!'

His teeth! How could he tie two pieces of string together with his teeth? It was impossible!

Using both hands he put the ends of the string in his mouth. We all sat watching. After about a minute he slowly started pulling one end of the string back out of his mouth. He kept pulling and when he'd pulled it right out, there it was – the string all in one piece, like when he'd started. It was magic, just like the eight of Diamonds.

Nobody could believe what he'd just done for a minute. Then we all clapped and shouted and those that could, whistled.

I think it was Holdsworth who must've seen him first 'cos he sits right by the door. All I know is I was still clapping and cheering when I heard someone shout, 'Ogden!' It went dead quiet. Nobody knew where to look. All you could hear was Jackie Parry snoring . . .

'And as you see, gentlemen, Mr Parry is now hypnotised!'

We all sat there gawping. Manningham was still at the front of the classroom, and he was pointing towards Jackie Parry. Melrose had come in as well now and was standing next to the headmaster. I could see Mrs Garside out in the corridor behind them.

'I will now bring Mr Parry out of his deep sleep. He will not remember anything.'

He went over to Jackie Parry's chair and started to wake him up gently.

'Three, two, one. Wake up, Mr Parry. Three – two – one! Wake up, Mr Parry!'

Jackie Parry opened his eyes and he looked like he didn't know where he was for a minute. We all just sat there. Manningham turned round to the headmaster.

'I shouldn't say this, Mr Ogden, magicians aren't supposed to give away their secrets, but just in case you're worried, I didn't really hypnotise Mr Parry. It's a trick. Isn't it, Mr Parry?'

And he smiled . . .

'Fancy falling asleep like that on a school photograph. You wouldn't credit it, would you?'

'It's Mr Parry, Mum. History teacher. He was ill. He's left now.'

I don't think he got the sack. He went off one Friday dinner time a few weeks ago and never came back. Melrose told us he'd decided to give up teaching. Bit like Manningham, he went home after the school photo and we never saw him again.

'Ah, I've found you, love, there you are! Oh, you do look handsome. Very smart. We'll have to get this framed.'

I looked all right, nothing special. Me and Keith had these stupid grins on our faces.

'Mum – that's Peter Manningham, there.'

I pointed him out.

'What a grand-looking lad.'

I could feel a tear running down my cheek. I couldn't help it. I missed him. My mum put her arm round me.

'I miss him, Mum. Why did he have to die?'

She squeezed me tight.

'I know, love, it's horrible. He had a hole in the heart, love. He was born with it. There's nothing anybody could have done. It could have happened at any time.'

'It's not like Mr Bastow or Mr Shackleton, Mum, they

were old. Peter was only young, he was only a year older than me.'

She gave me another squeeze.

'I know, love . . .'

I didn't say it but I thought it. Why did it have to be him? Why couldn't it be Boocock or Barraclough? Why couldn't they have had a bloomin' hole in the heart?

'He could do magic, Mum. Real magic.'

She smiled and gave me her hanky.

'I'll get your tea ready.'

I blew my nose and looked at the photo again. Poor Jackie Parry . . . Stupid Gower doing a V-sign, I bet he'll get the cane for that . . . Why was Illingworth wearing his school cap? Nobody else was wearing a cap . . . I looked at me and Keith again . . . That's when I saw it. His last bit of magic. I couldn't believe what I was seeing.

I unrolled the photo and looked back at Peter. There he was at the beginning of the row, smiling. I looked at the end of the row – and there he was again, kneeling with the second years. Smiling. Grinning. He was on the photo twice! He must have run round the back.

'Mum! Do you want to see some real magic?'

I wish I could be like Peter Manningham.